I0788206

PRESUMPTION OF SANITY

Richard Jan Hoekstra

ISBN
Hardback: 978-1-964289-72-4
Paperback: 978-1-964289-71-7

Presumption of Sanity, is the title of the fourth book in a series titled **Dying to Succeed**.

To date, twelve books make up this series, written first and foremost for your entertainment. In the future, God willing, additional books will be added.

The books in this series include:
Book 1, Winds of Success
Book 2, Living with Death
Book 3, Pretending to be Alive
Book 5, Running from Regret
Book 6, Longing to Go Home
Book 7, Afraid to Hope
Book 8, Waiting in Infinity
Book 9, Chasing after Time
Book 10, Casualties of Words
Book 11, Traveling into Chaos
Book 12, Snows of Fear

This book, like all the books in this series, is a continuation of the story of John Van Laan. Characters and locations in this book are better understood after reading the preceding books.

My books do not have chapters. They have episodes like journal entries, which are identified by place, date, and time. Most episodes are spoken in the voice of the main character, John Van Laan. However, at some point, I discovered that including the voices of supporting characters would be helpful. And therefore, the speaker is also identified at the beginning of each episode. Where only the time has changed from a previous episode, the date and place may not be repeated, but the speaker is always known.

Please forgive me if this is initially confusing. I am confident it will become easier to understand once you have read a few of the episodes. Should you have comments or questions, please feel free to email me at rhoekstra@sbcglobal.net

Richard Jan

"Greater is one day of tranquility than a year of striving after wind."

Contents

ACKNOWLEDGMENT

It is only fair that I acknowledge the help and encouragement that I received from New York Book Publishers. I went to them initially looking for guidance in editing, cover design, marketing, and distribution. They promised me that they could fulfill my needs. I accepted their proposal and began working with them virtually while living in the Midwest with their company's resources located in New York City. Our journey together has been an adventure; all in itself, one not taken lightly but traveled with some trepidation and concerns.

Special thanks go to Victor Hughes, who guaranteed me they would not let me down. And thanks to my daily contact, Serena Hoffman, for understanding my concerns and assuring me that everything was progressing as it should. And to Jim Bannister who took the time to talk to me when I needed a conversation. And to the many editors and artists who have contributed greatly to the final product. Thanks to them all for helping me achieve what I had hoped for when I first contacted New York Book Publishers.

AUTHOR'S NOTE

Although I am familiar with the colored gemstone industry as I worked in it for ten years, I don't pretend to be an expert on any level. My knowledge can best be described as that of a man traveling through a city without ever stopping for an extended period of time to experience the living conditions up close. And yet, as I contemplated my journey after it came to an end, I thought it was interesting and perhaps worthy of being a wonderful subject for a book.

But what I discovered as I wrote was that the real story was not the gemstone industry but how the cast of characters reacted to the challenges they faced - challenges similar to what we endure daily. And it is my hope that knowledge gained from existing for a time in their shoes as you read this book; may encourage you to live a fuller, more purposeful life.

Richard Jan

Page Left Blank Intentionally

PACIFIC OCEAN, SUNDAY, SEPTEMBER 14, 1998, NIGHT,

JOHN

Nue had handed me a gun.

He was acting calm at the time like his gesture was little more than a negotiating tool, similar to a paragraph in a legal contract written in an obscure language filled with hidden meanings, concepts not easily understood unless you were experienced in such matters. I was. I knew where to look for fool's traps. I knew because I had negotiated hundreds of contracts. I had learned to recognize the look of deceit on the faces of those who were trying to take advantage of me. I had learned because I had to, because I was rich and I was the CEO of a very successful company. People were always trying to take advantage of me.

But what I did not know was what to do about Nue's gun.

It felt heavy in my hand after he gave it to me: heavy, polished metal, an instrument of lethal destiny. I held it gently, afraid of its power. When the gun began to slip from my hand. I tightened my grip, afraid that if it fell on the floor, it would accidentally discharge.

Nue's giving me his gun had changed everything.

He knew it would.

After I told him I wished he was dead, he gave it to me and said I could use the gun to kill him without retribution. He promised me I would be allowed to walk away a free man. His men, his bodyguards, were given explicit instructions. No one was to harm me; hold me responsible for his murder. The decision to kill him was mine alone.

I believed him.

His word was absolute.

He came from another world, from Thailand, a country where he held great power, power over life and death. His word was law in his world. He could do as he wished.

He gave me the gun because he said it was time to move on, to bury the past. Either kill him now or call a truce. Kill him or negotiate a settlement; one or the other. This was the choice he gave me.

Death made this a hard decision. Too many deaths beginning with the death of my lover... along with the deaths of friends. Deaths caused by this man, by Nue, this man from Thailand who sat across from me negotiating with me like this was an ordinary business transaction. But what he desired was not ordinary, and I did not want to negotiate with him. But I also was not willing to kill him. I was not a killer. I was many things, but I was not a killer. Although... I thought about it. Thought maybe I could, thought about it for one brief second, but I didn't.

Ilana knew.

She knew I could not kill this man. 'Give me the gun,' Ilana had said to me. My beautiful, wonderful Ilana. She smiled and took control while I stood stupefied, unable to act. She told me to give her the gun. I did what she asked and it felt good to give her the gun, to feel the weight of the deadly instrument lifted from my hand. I gave her the gun, and we walked away. We packed our luggage at our hotel and took a taxi to the airport for the first available flight; no longer interested in staying in Hong Kong.

When we were finally seated comfortably in a 747, flying high above the Pacific Ocean traveling to San Francisco. I began to relax. From San Francisco, our schedule had us traveling to Washington D.C. and from there on to Charlottesville, where I live and work. But even though I felt more relaxed, I couldn't sleep. I tried, but it just wasn't happening. Mostly because I couldn't stop thinking about that man, about Nue, about what happened, about how easy it would have been to kill him.

Ben, one of our CIA bodyguards, had inspected Nue's gun in our hotel room after we returned from our meeting with him. Ben told me the gun was real and the bullets were real, no blanks. I could have killed Nue. All I needed to do was pull the trigger.

I did not find this news remarkable. I believed Nue when he said the gun was real. And I believed him when he said I would be allowed to walk away unharmed after killing him. Maybe I was wrong. But it was how he said it. He acted as if he had the authority to demand what he asked of his men. He had placed his life in my hands. Or perhaps he was simply a good judge of character. Perhaps he knew all along I wouldn't kill him. He took a calculated risk, assuming the probability of a deadly outcome was extremely low. He decided it was worth the risk. And if this was true, then his gesture had worked perfectly. It changed everything, changed how I thought about him. He was a smart man.

Before leaving Hong Kong, Guo, who was Nue's partner in crime, called me. He asked if he could come to my hotel room and give me an envelope from Mr. Nue. I told him to bring it but to be quick. We were leaving soon.

The envelope now resided in my briefcase, unopened. I wasn't ready to look at it.

Ilana turned to look at me with her big brown eyes. A blanket covered her body as she reclined on a seat in the first-class cabin of the plane. I saw her in a completely different light since my meeting with Nue. The way she acted at my meeting with Nue had been remarkable. I never expected her to be so strong, so understanding.

'Can you not sleep?' she asked.

'No, but don't worry about me. Get some rest.'

She smiled, 'I have slept. I think I will be awake now.' She sat up and stretched.

'You can go back to sleep,' I said. 'I will be alright.'

'No, I am not tired.' She leaned over her seat and gave me a kiss.

'Thanks, I needed that.'

'You are wondering about Mr. Nue, aren't you?'

'I suppose.'

'What did Charlie say?'

I had called Charlie and David while we were waiting for our plane at the airport and explained to both of them what happened. I tried not to leave anything out. I wanted their honest opinion.

Charlie is an agent with the CIA and a friend. He has been helping me ever since I got into a dispute with Nue. Actually, it was more than a simple dispute. People have been killed as a result of our conflict. The death that has affected me more than any other is the death of my former girlfriend, Monica. Her death was devastating. It took me a long time to get over it. And I had almost been killed as well, several times, in fact, all because Nue wanted me eliminated so he could take control of my company. He had made this very clear on more than one occasion. He thought my business rightfully belonged to him and his people in Thailand.

Charlie was helping me because my problems with Nue had international consequences; citizens of the United States had died as a result. The CIA was interested. His first reaction to my phone call was to jump all over me for getting into the mess in the first place. By all logic, he said I should be fish food in a Hong Kong harbor. And he berated me for taking Ilana with me. Said that was foolish.

I wondered if his reaction had something to do with Monica's death. The circumstances of the first meeting with Nue, the one where Monica was killed, and this last meeting were eerily similar. I couldn't argue with his logic. I could easily have been killed. But I wasn't.

'So, what are we going to do now?' I asked Charlie.

'Nothing different,' he said. 'You certainly can't trust this Nue guy, can you? Not after everything that has happened. He is lying to you, John. Setting you up for another fall,' Charlie then paused before suggested that we needed to go forward with his sting operation?

I should have known this was how Charlie would react. Still, I wanted to hear it from him. And concerning his sting operation, this was something Charlie had concocted to catch Nue in a lie. I told Charlie I needed some time to think first. I said I would call him after I returned to Charlottesville.

Charlie did say that he was glad I did not shoot Nue. Because surely I would now be fish food in the Hong Kong harbor. He reassured me I had made the right decision.

What I didn't tell Charlie was I couldn't kill Nue because it wasn't in me. My decision had nothing to do with trying to stay alive.

My call to David was different.

David and I had been friends since grade school. He is also my personal lawyer. He listened attentively to my story without comment. He then asked if I had looked at the contents of Mr. Nue's envelope. I told him I had not. I planned to look at it when

I returned to my office.

I asked him what he thought I should do.

He said he would like to see the contents of the envelope first. He added that Nue's behavior was interesting but probably explainable. However, it certainly was a remarkable story, and he was glad I hadn't been killed.

I thanked him for that.

We talked some more, mostly about nothing exceptional, friendly talk. He told me about his latest case. He knew I needed to think about something else, anything to take my mind off what happened in Hong Kong. He said he was at my cottage with his kids. The weather was beautiful. Maybe I should take a few days off, come to Grand Haven, Michigan and visit so we could talk in private. I think he heard some confusion in my voice and assumed I needed a break. I assured him I would call after returning to Charlottesville.

'Do you still hate this Mr. Nue?' Ilana asked quietly in the humming semi-dark atmosphere of the plane. Most of the other passengers were sleeping. A few were watching TV with headsets so they wouldn't disturb others.

'Interesting question,' I whispered.

'I think you should not hate this man anymore,' she volunteered as if it was the easiest thing in the world to do.

'Perhaps you are right.'

'But you don't know what to think about him, do you?' she correctly remarked.

'I don't. But then I don't know what to think about you sometimes.'

'Why, I am easy. You only have to love me. Am I not easy to love?'

'You are easy to love, but sometimes I wonder who you are.'

'Why do you say that?' she sounded surprised.

'Well, remember when you told Nue your name was Ilana something Emula.'

'Ilana Maria Rodriguez Emula,' she corrected me.

'Yes, well, you never told me your full name.'

'You never asked.'

'Okay, I'm asking now.'

'Okay, I will tell you now. My great-great-great grandfather was a very wealthy landowner in Belize when it was first colonized. He was born in Spain. Along with many British families, he logged the beautiful natural mahogany trees in the mountains and sent the wood to his native country on ships to build furniture, as did his British neighbors who sent wood to their native England. But when Spain tried to take control of Belize as they were doing in all of Central and South America, the British settlers drove them off. You perhaps know the story. The Spanish Navy was lured into the water behind the barrier reef, where they were attacked by British land guns and driven off. This is why my country is the only Central American country which speaks English as its native language.'

I listened without comment.

'But not everyone wins when something like this happens,' she continued. 'The British settlers knew my family was from Spain. They hated the Spaniards so much that they took my grandfather's land and all his money. He was penniless. He did not return to Spain because he was ashamed. Instead, he moved his family to my island and became a simple fisherman, where he lived the rest of his life in quiet disgrace. My brother and I are the last remaining relatives. We live a simple life just as our fathers taught us. But it was not always so.'

'So, this is how you got your name?'

'Yes, our name is all that remains of our heritage. I have been told that some land somewhere in Spain rightfully belongs to my family. But long ago it was taken by someone else.'

'Maybe we should travel to Spain and reclaim your land.'

'No, I am from Belize now. I do not want to be from anywhere else. Belize is my home, John.'

CHARLOTTESVILLE, VIRGINIA, MONDAY, SEPTEMBER 14, 6:30 P.M.

JOHN

The drapes across the tall floor-to-ceiling windows slid open when I pulled the cord and the late afternoon sun flowed into my office, casting shadows across the oriental carpets covering the wood floor.

I knew Charlie wouldn't approve. He had warned me to keep the drapes closed. Told me not to trust Nue. He was worried about a sniper's bullet coming through the glass and killing me, something which had almost happened in the past. But I had Nue's word I would not be harmed and I believed him. Stupid, maybe, but I did. Besides, I didn't think Nue would live behind closed drapes. His approach to life would be different. I could hear him say he would rather accept death than live in constant fear behind closed drapes.

When it is time to die, we die. Nothing can change that. So why not live until we die?

We didn't stop traveling until we arrived in Charlottesville — just kept going. I didn't want to be anywhere else but here... home, where, hopefully, I could finally get some rest.

Nue's unopened envelope was still in my briefcase. I was too exhausted to read it. Maybe tomorrow. I needed a day to let recent events sort through my weary subconscious before making any decisions.

The briefcase also held Nue's gun and unused bullets, untouched since my tense encounter with him. Turning over the briefcase, I emptied its contents on my desk, watching in lazy fascination as the metal projectiles rolled across the glass top and onto the floor. I picked up the gun and slid the empty magazine into it with a click while thinking about where to store the weapon. Out of sight was my first impulse, but this seemed wrong somehow. A small open space in a bookcase behind my desk appeared to be a better location, in between some books, hidden in the shadows, somewhere where I could see it. Because Nue was right. It was important. Maybe someday I would know how important. But for now. Now I only wanted it where I could see it and think about it. After collecting the fallen bullets, I placed them in a desk drawer.

Ilana came into my office as I was closing the drawer. Unless you knew where the gun was, it was difficult to find in the half light of the afternoon. Good, because for some reason I didn't want her to know where it was.

'I am lonely in your apartment, John,' she remarked with a sly smile.

'What are you talking about? We have been together most of the time for over a week. Aren't you getting a little tired of me?' I laughed.

'No, I am missing you. You have been gone from me too long.'

I got up from my desk and picked her up in my arms. 'How can you say you are lonely?' I asked after dropping her gently on a couch. 'We have been home for only about half an hour.'

'But your apartment, it is so big and you know... Ben and Steve have gone to their apartment... And I was all alone.' She said while looking up at me.

It was true. While staying at the Lodge at Pebble Beach and the hotel in Hong Kong, Ben and Steve had been our constant companions because Charlie insisted. I didn't mind. It was nice to have the guys watching over us. But it meant Ilana had almost no time to be alone.

And Ilana, well... she had become a different lady in my eyes since the meeting with Nue. I saw a side to her I had not seen before. Sure, I always knew she was a strong woman. It was one of the reasons I was attracted to her. But she had grown in my eyes during our trip, and I liked what I saw. She had great courage.

I knelt down beside her and kissed her cheek.

'And what do you think you are doing Mr. John?' she addressed me innocently as she had so many times in Belize.

I ignored her question while slowly unbuttoning her blouse.

Nue's gun on my bookshelf and Nue's unopened envelope lay on my desk. They both cried for my attention, but I didn't want to think about them. I only wanted to think about her. Tomorrow was another day. I could think about them tomorrow. Tonight, I wanted to spend time with her. Besides, tomorrow might never come.

She rose on one elbow and looked me in the eye. 'Are you sure this is what you want?'

Without comment, I kissed her bare breasts.

She lifted my head and asked. 'Do you want me?'

'I want you.'

'No one else?'

'No one but you.'

'Then you should have me.'

She took off her blouse and began to unzip her pants.

'No, let me,' I said in a sleep-deprived haze.

I was so tired from the trip that only the sight of her beautiful body kept me from falling into a deep coma-like sleep. My body ached for rest, but more than sleep, it ached for her. I slowly removed her clothes. She was naturally darker skinned than I, and I loved to see her smooth brown body. She smiled and let me kiss her from the soft curve of her neck to the taunt nipples of her full round breasts. From the soft, wet place between her thighs to the tips of her wiggling toes as she giggled when I tickled her feet with my tongue. When she could take it no more, she sat up and helped me undress. Evening shadows in shades of gray slowly covered my office as we lay on the couch in the dimming light of a tender embrace.

The walls around us began to fade quietly to dark, and the gun on the bookshelf was no longer visible after the sun receded through the trees to a place somewhere behind mountains in the distance.

TUESDAY, SEPTEMBER 15, 8:45 A.M
JOHN

The sky was bright in the morning outside the windows in my office when I finally woke.

But it was Nue's gun, his powerful negotiating tool, the object he had used to change my will, which first drew my attention. The gun lay heavy on my mind like a harbinger of bad tidings.

I had no memory of being covered with a blanket or falling asleep. But now a blanket covered me and my clothes were neatly folded over a chair. I assumed Ilana was responsible for caring for me. She was gone, probably in my apartment. I rolled over to get up, stretching slowly while attempting to think instead about her, about Ilana instead of the gun. I felt pretty good, like I had slept for days, slept deeply for the first time in a long time.

As I dressed, Nue's envelope on my desk caught my attention. I opened the envelope and removed the contents.

Dear Mr. Van Laan,

I hope this letter finds you in good health. It is my wish our meeting in Hong Kong put an end to our hostilities. We cannot change the past, Mr. Van Laan, but we can change the future. Please consider my proposal carefully. I will contact you in a few days for your reply.

Sincerely,

Nue

The smell of fresh coffee drifted into my office through the open door to my apartment. With plenty of time to deal with Mr. Nue later, I decided to check on Ilana first. After placing Nue's letter back on top of the contents of the envelope, I went into my apartment where I found her sitting at a table in the dinette doing a crossword puzzle from the morning paper when I entered the kitchen. I kissed her on the cheek. A big white terrycloth bathrobe that she must have found in my closet covered her body. She had wrapped the robe around her like a blanket. Only one beautiful bare ankle escaped its warming protection.

'May I make you some breakfast?' she asked.

'No,' I replied. 'I can get my own.'

She smiled and returned her attention to her crossword puzzle while I rummaged through the refrigerator for milk to add to my cereal. The contents of the envelope intrigued me the more I thought about it. I decided to return to my office with my bowl of cereal and peruse Nue's proposal as I ate.

When my cereal bowl was empty, I leaned against the back of my desk chair and thought about what I had read. In many ways, it was a remarkable document. It was clear Nue had given it considerable thought. On the surface, it appeared to be an honest effort to mediate a difficult situation. However, some aspects of his proposal were unacceptable. And from one major perspective, my perspective, his proposal made me angry. It assumed all the violence that had occurred in the past. All the deaths could be reduced simply to a matter of mediation: jobs and money. I wasn't sure this was possible. Monica and my friend Arny were dead in their graves because of the contents of this proposal. And two other partners, Vidu and Arthur, had also been killed. Mr. Nue's proposal assumed we could put aside these deaths as if they never happened and move on.

Although... it was obvious that he was attempting to make peace, and certainly, I wanted peace, but I wondered if I could do what he asked: completely forget about the past.

He had decided he could do that, but he had not lost what I lost. It was not the same for him. No one he knew or loved had died. But then... perhaps this was not exactly true. He had lost Lin, his associate in Hong Kong. Lin had died the same night as Monica. I assumed Lin was his friend, but I didn't really know.

Regardless, I had to ask myself if I could accept his deal. Or did I want something more from him, like some sacrificial lamb to even the score? I wondered what it would take for me to meet him on his terms. Did I require him to offer his first-born son, I mused, thinking of the story in the Bible about Abraham and his son?

The late summer sun rose in a blue sky as I looked outside. It was forecast to be a hot day in Charlottesville. Already, the worrisome noise of an air conditioning droned obnoxiously in the background. The trees outside were a dark green with the look of fall. A slight breeze blew away the morning mist. I couldn't decide how to respond to his proposal or whether it was even possible for me to respond. I needed an objective opinion and immediately thought of David.

Opening my laptop, I sent an e-mail to David, giving him an outline of the proposal and asking him to give me a call after reading it.

WEDNESDAY, SEPTEMBER 23, 11:55 A.M.
JOHN

Helen buzzed me through my intercom.

'A Mr. Nue is on the phone,' she said.

It was comical in a way, seeing Helen sitting outside my office in her workspace, alone in a room that was previously filled with people. It would have been far more efficient to bring her desk into my big office. I had plenty of space.

The truth was that only a few employees now worked in Charlottesville. Most of the company's staff was still in New York under Bob's supervision. This was fine with me. I had more pressing problems.

I had been home for over a week, and Nue's proposal was still unresolved. David and Charlie had been asked for their advice. And as I expected, each had a different take. David wanted me to see the good in it. Productive was the word I think he used. Charlie, on the other hand, said it was all a lie. He told me not to trust Nue. Nue had some evil plan in mind and I would not like the long-term consequences.

Unfortunately, after all their suggestions and conflicting perspectives, including my late-night ruminations, I wasn't any closer to a decision than when I began. I was not ready to talk to Nue. But I would probably never be ready, so now was as good a time as any.

'This is John Van Laan.'

Speaking with a clipped Oriental accent, Nue's command of the English language was excellent. 'Mr. Van Laan. Thank you for receiving my call. I hope you are well.'

'I am.'

'Do you have time to talk?' he asked politely.

'I do.'

'I assume you have read the contents of my proposal.'

'I have,' I replied simply.

'And is the proposal acceptable?'

He surprised me by immediately asking for my answer, but then he always surprised me on some level.

'It is a difficult proposal,' I replied.

'I see. Perhaps we can discuss it.'

'Okay.'

He remained silent, I suppose expecting me to begin. When I did not, he asked, 'Can you explain to me what you find difficult? I hope you understand I tried to give you terms which would be acceptable to you.'

'I do understand, but I don't think you understand how much suffering you have caused me. Your proposal suggests I make you an equal partner. Can you understand how difficult this might be for me?'

He waited a moment before replying. 'We cannot change the past. But we can decide to act differently in the future.'

'I understand, but do you understand how your actions in the past make that very difficult? When you attempted to kill me and destroy my company, you effectively closed a door to the possibility of our working together in the future.'

'That may be true for most men, Mr. Van Laan. But it does not need to be true for you.'

'I may not be the man you think I am.'

'Maybe not, but I am offering you the opportunity to be that man.'

'Do you understand what you are asking?' I heard my voice rising in frustration.

'I do.'

'Do you... Do you really think I can simply ignore the death of my lover as if it never happened?

In effect, the provisions of his proposal asked me to partner with him. He had offered some concessions, but in return, he wanted to join my company as if he were one of my original partners like Bob. I found his request revolting. I hoped my last statement might, at a minimum, slow him down and give him something to think about. Maybe even force him forget about his proposal and go away. But he didn't hesitate. It was like he knew what I would say before I said it. He had an answer for everything.

'Yes, you can,' he said calmly as if he were asking me to join him for lunch. 'There are times when we need to consider the effect our actions have on our world rather than only the small consequences they impose on our simple life. We all live crowded together on a very small planet, Mr. Van Laan. We have certain responsibilities to ourselves. But we have a greater responsibility to our world. This may be one of those times.'

I turned my desk chair so I could look outside. Trees were swaying in the wind as a thousand thoughts raged through my over strained brain. The man was making sense, but I did not know if I could accept his logic.

'Perhaps we should meet again in person.' I suggested, thinking perhaps I could set up the meeting that Charlie wanted: a sting operation where Nue would be recorded admitting to murder.

'No,' he reacted calmly, perhaps reading my mind. 'Nothing will be different tomorrow or the next day. It is time we decide.'

He infuriated me with his directness and his demands. It felt like before when he had three bodyguards standing at attention, blocking my escape. I was caged in. Now, that wasn't completely true, not this time. I could simply escape by hanging up my phone, but that would only delay what was inevitable.

'Okay, let's decide,' I said in frustration.

'What is your decision?' he asked as if it were the easiest question in the world.

'Are you asking for a yes or no answer?'

'I am.'

'It's not that simple. Let's go over your proposal point by point.'

'As you desire,' he said easily.

'Point one,' I began. 'Your proposal has Guo continuing as

the head of the Hong Kong office. That's a no... I won't allow it. I must have someone I trust in each of my Distribution Houses, men who are loyal to me only. When I give an order, I don't want to wonder if your guy will ask your permission before doing what I tell him. If this is to work, then I must have someone loyal to me in Hong Kong.'

I waited, assuming this was a deal breaker.

'I will remove Guo. You may appoint a replacement immediately,' he replied, much to my surprise.

I raised my next point, demanding his agents stop buying sapphire on the open market. Again, I assumed he would say no, but surprisingly, he agreed without hesitation.

I never dreamed I would get this far into the proposal. By now, I thought we would have come to a dead end. But it quickly became obvious that Nue had anticipated my objections and was prepared. I began to wonder if I was being manipulated, but I proceeded anyway, assuming finally I would suggest a roadblock which would put an end our negotiations.

Phillip was next on my list. I wanted Phillip out. Again, Nue easily agreed, much to my surprise.

I conceded Arthur and Lin's stock belonged to him since he had paid for it. I demanded he become involved in my board. If he wanted to be a stockholder, then he had to act like one.

He agreed.

We next discussed the building I owned in Hong Kong. He wanted it and I agreed to sell it to him, but only if he vacated it. He said he would and in return I conceded to him the profits from the Hong Kong Distribution House. In addition, I agreed to have a significant portion of our gemstones cut and polished in Thailand, providing much needed employment for his country.

Our negotiations continued, long and tedious. I kept thinking we couldn't possibly come to an agreement, but that wasn't happening. Finally, I paused before raising what I assumed would be the most controversial issue, an issue I thought would never be settled.

'Your proposal mentions nothing about my stock or the money you paid for it. For your information, this money is where you deposited it, and I assume you want it back.'

'I do not know what you are talking about,' he replied. 'I hope you understand.'

'Are you saying I can keep the money?' I asked.

'I know nothing about this money,' he replied.

'And my stock,' I asked.

'It is my understanding this stock belongs to you.'

I was completely confused. Millions of dollars were in a Swiss bank account, a bank account with my name on it. Apparently, he was willing to walk away from this money.

'I find your gesture magnanimous on the one hand and a little like paying me with blood money on the other.' I waited, thinking he might change his mind, but he said nothing.

'Okay, I have covered your proposal from my end. Do you have any questions?' I asked.

'I have no questions. I believe we have made a good agreement today. But please understand the decision to accept your terms is not mine alone. I must first present your proposal to my family. However, I feel confident they will be pleased with our progress. This should take only a few days. I will contact you when I have their answer. Until then, please accept my gratitude for your willingness to work with me.'

I had one more point I still needed to make clear to him.

'Okay, I understand. But there is still one thing I need you to understand... I really would rather not work with you, not now, not ever... But having said that, it is also true, as you have pointed out, that we all have times when it would be better to look beyond our short-sighted personal desires for the greater good, and this may be one of those times. And you were right when you said we should have talked years ago. For this, I take full responsibility. And for this reason alone, I agree to work with you now. I hope you understand what I'm telling you.'

'I think I do. Thank you, Mr. Van Laan. It has been good to talk to you. I will call as soon as I have a decision.'

His phone clicked off.

I sat very still, listening to silence... wondering what just happened.

SATURDAY, SEPTEMBER 26, 12:45 P.M.
JOHN

Ilana and I stopped by the country club where I was a member for lunch after a drive through the hills.

My office had begun to feel claustrophobic, too many long days working. I needed some time outside to enjoy the early fall scenery. Leaves were beginning to change color.

Our drive through the country was great, but stopping at the club was not a good idea. Ilana was not comfortable. She felt everyone was staring at her, and she was probably right. The snobby country-clubbers must have been captivated by this dark-haired beauty, wondering who she was. And to make matters worse, the beautiful woman spoke with a foreign accent. Establishment types don't like foreigners.

I had not bothered to warn Ilana about my reputation at the club. Apparently, local gossip mongers found my bachelor love life to be a particularly tantalizing subject for their twittering tongues. My golfing buddies had warned me on more than one occasion that the club fathers were not too happy with my behavior. Constantly showing up with a different girlfriend was not considered a good form for the family-orientated socialites.

And now, after an absence of over a year, I was once again sporting yet one more gorgeous woman, this time a beautiful dark-skinned foreigner. Their capricious tongues were surely wagging. I didn't care. I joined the club to play golf, not socialize. I told Ilana to ignore them. Don't let them spoil your lunch.

The last few days had been great. It felt like a weight had been lifted off my chest. Charlie's guys were still with us for our protection, but I wasn't sure we needed them. Not like before when I was constantly looking over my shoulder. It was different now. I trusted Nue to keep his word when he said he would not harm me. I felt I could finally relax and get out of the office without worrying.

Charlie's guys, on the other hand, became very uptight due to my newfound freedom. And I couldn't blame them because I had explained nothing to them. In fact, no one knew about my recent conversation with Nue except me. I decided to wait before telling anyone, including Charlie. Because if Nue called and said the deal was off, then my telling Charlie would have been a waste of time and effort. I knew he would object, and I didn't want to deal with him if it wasn't necessary. I could hear Charlie telling me in no uncertain terms: Nue's deal is a setup to get me to let down my guard. Beware, a sniper is waiting outside to take a shot. You are a dead man. You just don't know it. That's what Charlie would say.

Personally, I wanted to forget about the whole mess for a few days. Once Nue gave me his answer, and he agreed as I expected he would, I had some explaining to do. Not only would I have to explain it to Charlie, I would be obligated to take the proposal to my board. Preparation of that presentation would take time and effort. Although I was fairly confident I could get it approved. I assumed only one board member would be opposed. Vidu's brother in Sri Lanka had the most to lose. A portion of our cutting business would go from Sri Lanka to Thailand. But almost everyone else on the board would simply continue doing business as they had in the past. And my company would once again have its partial monopoly in the world of sapphire distribution, which would quickly return it to profitability and make our shareholders happy. In addition, prices of rough sapphire would increase, making the board members who were miners happy. So, I didn't anticipate too many problems.

Approval should be easy. In fact, it all seemed easy... too easy.

Our waiter came to refill our coffee cups.

'You seem far away today,' Ilana commented as she nibbled her sandwich.

'Sorry... Don't you like your sandwich?'

'You are not interested in my sandwich. Are you?'

'No, I guess not.'

'So, where are you, John? Because I don't think you are here with me.'

She was right. I had been ignoring her lately, and this wasn't fair because I was her only companion in the States, except for Helen. I decided to tell her about the agreement because it seemed good to tell someone. Besides, she was the one person who would understand it without a long explanation. She had been with me when I met with Nue.

'I agreed to Nue's proposal the other day,' I said simply.

She looked surprised. 'Is this why you look like a man who is lost?'

'Yes, I have told no one.'

'I will keep your secrets, John.'

'I know you will.'

I gave her the short version, the main issues as we ate our sandwiches. She was smart. She knew all the players. She understood. The country club crowd buzzed in the background as we talked. I kept my voice down. Steve and Ben were eating at the bar. They were not close enough to hear what I said. Still, I was careful. She listened without comment. When I was done, she sipped her coffee in silence. Half of my sandwich was still on my plate, now cold because I had been talking. I finished eating it while wondering how she would react.

She didn't take long. 'I think you are a good man, John Van Laan. And this Mr. Nue... not many men would have given you a gun as he did. I think he is a difficult man to understand, but for now, you have done right. It is our chance to have peace again. And the people of Thailand, they also need jobs. This is good for them. But you must be careful.'

'Why do I need to be careful?' I asked, mystified by her last sentence.

'This man is different. He is a hard man to understand. I am not sure I like this man.'

Just like a woman. She reduced the complete agreement and all its complex parts to a simple judgment on one man's character.

AMBERGRIS ISLAND, BELIZE, MONDAY, DECEMBER 7, 3:20 P.M.

JOHN

The single-engine turboprop commuter plane bobbed, slipped, and dipped while approaching the island airport; each jolt, a stomach-revolting, exhaling, bone-jarring pass over ethereal moguls in a clear blue sky.

Ilana was sitting beside me, belted tightly into her seat with her fingers digging into my arm. We were flying from the international airport in Belize City to Ilana's home on Ambergris Island in the north. She was very happy to be going home, except now when she was looking anything but happy.

I found a brown throw-up bag in a seat pocket in front of her. She took it from me without a comment. Here was a woman who never got seasick on a boat, but apparently, airplanes were a different matter.

'You okay?' I asked her.

'I will be fine,' she replied with obvious determination.

The green sea below our plane was dotted with whitecaps driven by a passing stormfront out of the north. The weather front had moved through the area earlier in the day. The pilot told us we would be flying in clear, sunny skies, but our trip might get a little bumpy. That was an understatement.

The airport was just ahead. I was sitting immediately behind the pilot, where I could look through the cockpit windows of our commuter plane. We were losing altitude fast. The pilot was power-driving towards a short runway, which appeared to be little more than a driveway between a few palm trees. The plane was fighting a severe side wind, flying at an angle to the airport runway, which was the only available landing strip on the island.

An old red baseball hat covered most of the pilot's curly, gray hair. A faded denim shirt, jeans, and cool aviator sunglasses passed for his aviator uniform. The wrinkled skin on the back of his neck was testimony to too much sun and cigarettes. I hoped he knew what he was doing. I probably shouldn't have been worried. He probably had more flying time than a 747 captain in a pressed blue suit.

I tightened my seat belt as the plane dropped suddenly, sliding sideways towards the runway before hitting hard on the concrete, bouncing once, jumping back into the air briefly, before finally settling down, rubber wheels squealing, snapping into alignment with the runway. The pilot hit reverse, and the engine roared in response. For one brief moment, I had an odd sensation that we were going to tip over on our nose before the runway ended. But the plane slowed quickly and taxied calmly to the end of the runway.

I was trying to remember the last time I landed at this airport. It wasn't much of a memory, actually. I was only vaguely aware of my surroundings at the time. My head was still in a hotel room in New York City. It was only weeks after Monica's death. All I wanted at the time was a bed and a bottle for the night. This time was completely different. I was actually looking forward to the trip. Winter had descended on Charlottesville with days and nights of cold. Ilana's mood had soured along with the depressing weather, matching the gray clouds and rain. She was trying to be cheerful, but it wasn't really in her. She badly needed some sunshine and warm waters to lift her spirits. I did, too. Too many long, hard days and nights of work in the last few months had left me weary. The rush of getting gemstones shipped to satisfy the commercial Christmas season had been taxing. As the holidays approached, business slowed. It was a good time to get away.

Our plane came to a standstill. Time to disembark. I reached over to help Ilana to her feet. She took my hand, walking shakily up the aisle.

'I will be okay now, John,' she said once her feet touched solid ground. 'I hope we don't have to do that again.'

'Just once more when we leave,' I said, reminding her this was a short visit, only a few weeks. We had come directly from London after a quarterly board meeting.

'Do we have to leave, John?'

'Yes, but let's not think about it now.'

A two-wide building, which looked better suited to a trailer park, served as the airport terminal in the town of San Pedro on Ambergris Island. Next to the building was a bench made from welded green metal bars sitting outside in the open air. Years of luggage scraping its painted surfaces had left the metal scratched and rusted in places.

We didn't have much in the way of luggage. Shorts, t-shirts, a couple of swimsuits, and a sweater for the evenings, along with the other usual necessities. We only needed two carry-on bags. The clothes we wore in London at the board meeting had been shipped back to Charlottesville. As we waited for our luggage to be removed from the plane and placed on the metal bench, a rather scraggly brown and white dog crept shyly around the corner of the dirty, tan, aluminum-sided building, looking sadly lost and hungry.

Travel brochures paint a different picture of Belize: warm sunshine, blue skies, and gentle ocean waves. All this is true, but it has its darker side. The starving dog was clear evidence of this other side. Windswept dusty streets and old wooden houses ignored for years were additional testaments to the dark side along with random piles of trash that no one seems too inclined to clean them up any time soon.

I remembered one house which was almost comical. It was a small square wood house built on stilts. I assumed the stilts were to make it hurricane-proof. They also provided a secondary service to the owner, which was less appreciated. A trap door installed in the floor of the house served a garbage release. The smelly stuff was conveniently dropped through the trap door daily, where it lay on the ground below the house in a stinking heap, rotting and smelling like a miniature garbage dump. I wondered how the owner could abide the smell, not to mention the mess. Did constant island breezes relieve the odor? And was he waiting for the next hurricane to sweep the trash away so he wouldn't have to clean it up himself?

'John,' Ilana interrupted my daydreaming, having regained her sense of balance and color to her face. 'I would like to visit my bother. Is this okay with you?' she asked.

'Yes, of course. When do you want to go?'

'Now?'

'Why now?'

'Because I have just now been thinking about him.'

'You don't want to wait until we have settled into our condo?'

'No. It has been a long time since I saw him. I think I need to go talk to him, and I want to do it now.'

'Do you want me to come with you?'

'No, I need to go alone,' she pleaded with her big brown eyes.

'Okay, I'll take care of getting our luggage to the condo. You go to your brother.'

'You sure?'

'Yes. Go.'

She turned and happily walked away, skipping down a dirt road that led into the town, puffs of dust rising from her feet.

I collected our bags from the rusty luggage rack and awkwardly threw them over my shoulder. Heading down a rocky walkway towards a gravel road behind the airport, I hoped to find a taxi cab to take me to our condo.

If I couldn't get a taxi, it would be a long, hard walk.

GRAND HAVEN, MICHIGAN, 2:45 P.M.

PHILLIP

Lake effect snow showers frequently envelop the resort town of Grand Haven, Michigan, in early winter.

It can snow off and on monotonously for days. Appearances of the sun can be a welcome relief from otherwise constant cold, dark gray clouds. These rare examples of glorious sunshine over virgin snow are usually all too brief. Prevailing chilly westerly winds constantly whip across the warm waters of Lake Michigan, gathering moisture into the air. Heavy, dense air rises into the sky, forming billowing dark gray clouds that obliterate the sun, cooling over frozen ground, and dumping thick white blankets of snow on the land.

Phillip labored through one of these frequent snow blizzards, mostly trying to ignore the conditions. No boots for him. He was wearing the same flat-bottomed black leather shoes he always wore, summer or winter. Slipping on the icy parking lot surface, he cursed, almost falling, catching his balance at the last moment by burying his bare hand into cold, icy slush, scraping the skin on his knuckles. No one heard him swear. The wind was blowing too hard, covering the noise of his curse. He was only a short distance from the back door of his office building. Pulling his thin trench coat around his body for warmth, he bent against the wind, gray ponytail blowing over his shoulders, hawk-like nose creating a convenient wind break.

Once inside the building, he took off his coat and shook it, shedding snowflakes into the air before they could melt into the fabric. After climbing the back stairs to his second-floor office, he presented a grim smile to Martha, his middle-aged employee, even though he didn't feel all that cheery.

Martha didn't look up when he entered, too preoccupied with her typing to be bothered by her gruffly boss.

A Federal Express package lay on his desk. 'Care Packages'

was what he called them, like something sent to needy people in Africa. This one came from Singapore. Others had arrived from different addresses in an effort to disguise their point of origin. He knew where they originated, the same place in the Far East, traveling to his office on different routes. And, of course, he also knew who sent them, his friends in Thailand.

In his mind, it should have been so different. He should have been in a new office, hiring employees, selling millions of dollars of gemstones every day. This was what he thought would happen. It didn't. Nue changed the terms of their agreement at the last minute, removing Phillip from John's board, demoting Phillip to a mere salesman, and sending him small allotments of stones to sell every month. Never as many gemstones as he requested, just these puny 'Care Packages.' Nothing approaching what he had been promised.

Martha came into his office with a cup of hot coffee. 'See the package?' she quipped.

'Yeah, I see it.' Phillip groused.

Martha said nothing. She knew he would react this way. She knew his dreams. He told her everything. His dreams had been put on hold. That made him angry. She could hear his long-distance telephone calls from her desk. He had argued long and hard with everyone he could think of calling. It had done him no good.

'Do you want to see the gems?' Phillip asked her, trying to be cheerful.

'Nah,' she turned to go back to the reception area where her desk was located because her phone was ringing. 'Want to take a call?' she yelled as she retreated.

'Not now,' Phillip replied.

After removing the protective plastic bubble wrap from around a bag of gemstones in the package, he spilled the bag of sparkling blue oval-cut sapphires on his desk. The gems were less than a carat in size, but in a pile under overhead fluorescent lights, their polished surfaces sparkled magnificently. He returned them to their bag and examined some other bags, noting the size, cut, and color of the gemstones in each of them.

The only good news was that his costs of these gems were very low, only slightly more than the approximate cost of shipping the stones to him. This was the one concession they made to him. He could make a tremendous percentage of profit from each sale. Still it was not what he had been promised, nothing like millions of dollars of gemstones which should have been flowing through his office.

He shoved his discontent aside for the moment. It was time to enter the stones from the new shipment into a special ledger which he kept in his office vault. Then, he would review the requests he had on his desk, match the gems from the shipment to the needs of his customers, repackage, invoice, and ship.

After the ledger from his vault was retrieved, the arduous task of hand-logging the new gemstones began. The stones would then be reentered a second time into the office computer. This work was accomplished by Martha, who could do it much faster. Only one aspect of this information was different from his personal ledger. Inflated costs were assigned to the gems. After office expenses and his salary were deducted, his accountant used these numbers to determine company profit and pay taxes.

The dollar difference between the cost figures he gave to his accountant and the actual cost of the gemstones was sent to a special overseas account, an off-shore bank account that only he could access. This off-shore money was rarely used, only occasionally when Phillip traveled overseas when it could not be traced to him, thus avoiding the prospect of being indicted for income tax evasion.

He was doing okay, saving money for his future. He was fine financially, but he knew he should be making so much more, millions more. If everything had gone as he had been promised, he would be super rich.

It wasn't the money that really bothered him. It was their betrayal. His Thai friends had promised him so much more. They made him angry. But what really made him mad was the reason for their change. John Van Laan. He was the reason. John had somehow convinced them to change his deal. And for this, his hatred of John had intensified.

Someday, he would get his revenge.

AMBERGRIS ISLAND, BELIZE, 7:05 P.M.

JOHN

A bright red bougainvillea overflowed the railing of the second-floor bedroom balcony, climbing the walls with an exuberant plethora of blossoms.

Six condos occupied the building, two per floor, three floors, side by side. All the units had a view of the sea. Our second-story unit contained one bedroom and bathroom, along with a comfortable living room and an efficient kitchen. It was okay. I would have preferred staying in the house I had previously rented on the beach, but that house had burned to the ground. The land where it stood had been purchased by me with the help of a lawyer in Belize City. Tomorrow, I plan to visit the site. I was told the house had not been touched since the night it was destroyed. And unfortunately, no one had been charged with the crime.

After unpacking my bags, I decided to enjoy the view from the balcony. Several months of clouds and cold had dulled my senses. It felt good to luxuriate in the sunshine and flowers, feel the warm breeze, and smell fresh sea air.

A couple of six-packs of Belican Beer and a few other groceries were cooling in the refrigerator. The taxi driver from the airport didn't mind waiting at the store. Ilana's favorite beer, coffee, chips, milk, cereal and some fruit had been purchased. I hoped she would approve.

The sun dropped in the west behind the condo as I twisted off the cap of a beer. Drinking a cold one while sitting on the balcony seemed a good plan while waiting for Ilana. I really wasn't interested in eating alone.

A gentle breeze drove the rolling blue-green sea as I relaxed on the balcony of the condo, watching waves lap rhythmically on shore, drowning out an uncomfortable silence. A few pelicans and frigate birds floated in the late afternoon sky, breaking the visual stillness. It seemed good to be back in Belize. In a way, I never felt completely at home in Charlottesville, not since returning. This place by the warm sea waters agreed with me more. I felt like I could rest here.

Weeks of hard work had made me very aware I was no longer the same man who had built a company from scratch eight years before. It wasn't my total passion anymore. A small part of my mind was always wandering outside the confinement of my office. Even when I was hard at work, I kept wondering why I was holed up in this place. It didn't seem to matter if I was on the phone or looking over some lengthy reports. A feeling of being away from home seemed to linger in my subconscious. Not because the work wasn't rewarding – it was. The last four months since I made the agreement with Nue had gone extremely well. My company had regained its place of dominance in the sapphire markets. As Nue promised, he had withdrawn his buyers from the rough gemstones markets. Miners now sold their stones exclusively to my company. In turn, I raised the prices I paid to them, which was good for them. My company was once more very profitable, and the Distribution Houses were making money. Everyone was happy.

A dock into the sea sat in front of the building. Tied up to the dock was my sailboat. I hadn't visited her yet. I wanted to wait for Ilana, wanted to renew our friendship with the sea together. The boat had been abandoned for months, docked in Cancun. Expensive marina fees had to be paid before it could be released. A professional captain was hired to sail her to Belize. Her deep blue hull now shined in the evening sun, the tall mast rising into a clear blue sky.

It began to get dark as I waited. Ilana must have had a lot of catching up to do with her brother. I expected her at the condo by now. However, I had not asked her how long she would be gone. I wished I had. I guess I just assumed she would be here in time for dinner.

Another beer and some nuts temporarily satisfied a growing hunger. If she returned soon, we could still walk into town for a late dinner.

In a way, it felt strange to be alone. For the last few months, she had been my constant companion. We were never apart for more than a few hours at a time. We didn't discuss it, but our time together had been great. The only thing which made our life less than idyllic was my work. Long days in my office were required to rebuild my company. And this time, I had to do it alone. Three of my original partners, Vidu, Arthur, and Lin, were dead. Their absence made the job more difficult.

Jason was also missing from my office staff. My former young assistant, whiz kid, the numbers guy, had taken the job in Hong Kong. He was now the CEO of our Hong Kong Distribution House. He had asked for the assignment. Jason knew I needed someone I could trust. He convinced me that all the work he had done as my right-hand man had prepared him for the job. Jason said he wanted to see the world. This was his opportunity. I told him the assignment might be dangerous. He wanted the job anyway. Said he was a single man without a family. He was willing to take the risk.

At first, I had been reluctant, but it turned out to be a good decision. Jason was doing a great job. From time to time, he called to ask a question. I didn't mind. I enjoyed our long-distance telephone calls. It was like he was still in his office down the hall.

A three-beer lethargy began to settle into my dull brain as I continued to wait for Ilana. It had been a long day of travel. I was tired and hungry. But not hungry enough to want to eat alone. Plus, I was becoming slightly concerned for her safety. I told myself not to worry. She was on her home turf. She had lived on this island all her life and never had a problem before. Why would she be in trouble now?

But that didn't stop me from worrying.

Charlie's guys weren't with us anymore. He had been my biggest problem when it came time to explain my agreement with the Thai group. I knew he would, and he was. He had been downright angry even after I had invited him to Charlottesville to tell him in person. Life goes on, I explained. All injustices in the world cannot be put right every time. This was one of those times.

He had wanted to yell at me. I could see it in his eyes. But he knew it would do no good. Instead, he stormed out of my office after telling me in a few choice words he thought I was crazy. His guys packed their belongings immediately and said goodbye. I have not seen or heard from him since. Now, I wished one of his guys was with us. He could have escorted Ilana, so I wouldn't have to worry.

In all other respects, my work had gone exceptionally well. The company was on a steep growth curve. To make matters even better, with Nue's help, we began to penetrate the world of emeralds. I could not have accomplished this on my own. And certainly not in so short a time. We currently control about twenty-five percent of international sales in emeralds. In a year we hoped to up this figure to sixty-five percent. Most of our success was tied to an agreement we had with a company in Columbia. Nue had been instrumental in helping us successfully negotiate that agreement. I had to admit that Nue had become a valuable partner in many ways.

Cash reserves had been replenished in the process. An annual dividend would be announced at the next quarterly board meeting. It seemed strange to be sending some of the money to Nue in Thailand. He had been my enemy only a short time before. Now, he was scheduled to receive a dividend. But it was as it should be. He owned stock in the company. He could not be denied. He would get a dividend like the other shareholders. And the Hong Kong Distribution House was making money for him. Its ownership had been settled in the last few months. It seems my former partner Lin had been a puppet of the Nue's Thai dynasty. The profits from Hong Kong had been going to the Thai from the beginning. I just never knew it. So, in that respect, nothing had changed.

In addition, several million carats of rough sapphire flowed each month to cutting factories in Bangkok. Nue had been pressuring me to visit his factories. I had put him off. Maybe in the future, I said. I was extremely busy.

And Ilana, well, Ilana continued to surprise me. She had become Helen's assistant. Without my knowledge, Helen had taught her what she needed to know. Ilana learned quickly. When I finally discovered their subversive activity, Ilana was already working the equivalent of a full-time job. I had not noticed because

I was busy with my work. Once I learned what she was doing, I began to assign her tasks directly. However, her work created a problem. Ilana wasn't documented in the U.S.A. I couldn't pay her. Charlie had promised to help her obtain a green card, but all he got her was a temporary visa. And after our last disagreement, he apparently had forgotten about her green card. My calls to his office went unanswered. It was obvious Charlie was not happy with me. My decision to work with Nue was not what Charlie desired. Charlie had other plans for Nue.

So, I had this problem. Ilana was working for me, but I couldn't pay her. We talked about it. I told her I would establish a bank account in Belize to compensate her instead. While we were in Belize, I planned to set up the account. I hadn't told her how much money would be in it, and she hadn't asked. She said it was fun to learn to do the work and to help me. She did not care about the money.

I decided depositing a hundred thousand US dollars in her account would be a good start. And ten thousand more would flow into it every month after that. I assumed this would make her happy. Although, I had one concern. It crossed my mind that the money might change our relationship. I decided it was worth the risk. She had given to me without asking. I would give to her in the same manner.

Finally, beers and travel caught up with me. I was suddenly dead tired. I collected my empty bottles and headed to bed alone. As I lay awake trying to sleep, the low rumble of commercial airline travel continued to buzz in my ears. We had traveled all day from Charlottesville. The sounds of flying droned into my brain even though I was no longer in a plane. I couldn't get the sensation out of my head. And I could not go to sleep. The nightmares I had when I first came to this island began to rumble around in my thoughts like an approaching thunderstorm, like the dreams that seemed so real. Like when I would relive the night she died in my arms. In other dreams, she would be alive and well as if nothing had happened. I would tell her I was dreaming and explain to her that she could not be real. She was dead. But she would simply nod and say it was okay, don't worry about it. We would talk for a while, and the dream would end when I woke up. I seldom remembered what she said. Only remembered the dream ending and how it felt to be alone again.

Finally, I slipped out of bed. It was no good trying to sleep. Too many bad memories from my past, too many tragedies. Too many dead-staring eyes were looking at me in the dark night.

Ilana's absence was on my mind. Had the man from the jewelry shop who threatened to kill her found her and dumped her dead body off a boat into the sea? Had I returned to Belize to spend more sleepless nights learning to live alone? I wondered if I could do it a second time. This time, without a pretty island girl to lift me out of my despair.

A book lay on the dresser. I picked it up, hoping it would take my mind off Ilana. She had to be alright. This was her home, after all.

I turned on the light beside the couch and began to read.

TUESDAY, DECEMBER 8, 7:25 A.M.

JOHN

Massive waves, the progeny of a tropical storm, rise into giant walls of fluid glass before curling over and rushing toward the shore in foaming exuberance.

It is spring break, and in another life, I am a teenager standing on a Florida beach with friends, watching the waves in awe. I enjoy swimming in Lake Michigan when the surf is big. The ocean break doesn't look that different. Still, something ominous seems to be lurking in the power and beauty of this surf. Perhaps something beyond what I have experienced.

'Bet ya a dollar you don't dare go in the water, ' one of my buddies probed.

The surf looks awesome. Beauty resides in its power. I love to body surf, and these waves definitely look like a challenge. They are ocean waves – storm waves. They will be great to surf. I can't resist. I take the bet.

Diving in, I swim to the break, ducking my head under waves as they rush towards shore in all their white-water fury. I am not scared. I am a great swimmer, and I love the water. But I am a northerner. I have no experience with ocean waves. I am ignorant. They are different. I do not know that they run up the shore much longer than any Lake Michigan wave and turn to rush back down the shore into the ocean at great speed.

I wait and watch, swimming beyond the break, looking for the right wave, a big full wave, one I can body surf to shore. Finally, a promising wave rises up, and I swim furiously toward shore, allowing the wave to pick me up, my body riding down its face. I skim over the glassy surface in elation, flying on the water, gliding towards shore until the power of the wave becomes wasted. Lazily, I begin to swim the remaining yards to shore.

It's then that the wave turns on me, flowing swiftly down the shore, returning to its home in the ocean. I pick up my pace, swimming against the current, trying to reach the beach as the flowing water drags me towards the ocean. I can see the beach. I can see my friends. I am close to being safe. I swim faster, faster than the current, but I fear I cannot swim at this pace for too long. I must make it to shore soon, or I will get tired, and the wave will win and drag me out into the ocean to drown. I begin to understand I have made a mistake and I have only one chance to live. I do not have the strength to fight this current a second time. I am not making much progress and I'm quickly becoming exhausted. I have one chance and one chance only. I pick up my pace, kicking furiously, arm over arm, breathing with each stroke. One chance to live or die in this ocean. One chance to make it to shore before I am too exhausted. Furiously, I stroke for shore until the tips of my fingers brush the firm sand under the water and I stand up quickly with the rushing water pulling at my ankles as it rushes back into the ocean.

I am safe, no longer subject to the will of the water. I take some deep breaths while standing in the water and smile meekly at my friends who are on the shore. They are totally unaware of what I have experienced. I hear them talking loudly, laughing about something. They did not see me struggling in the water. They were not afraid of me. They don't know I almost died.

A wave rises up behind me, rushing towards me. I am unaware of its intentions until it knocks me over into its foaming, white-water fury and drags my tired body into the ocean to fight one more time to return to the safety of dry land.

My eyes opened.

I was dreaming, a never-ending memory from my youth. I sigh, relieved to be awake.

The morning sun greeted me, reflecting off the waters of the sea, streaming in through the open windows off the balcony, flooding the couch where I was sleeping. My back was sore and stretched from laying in an odd, uncomfortable position. I groaned, remembering my nightmarish dream. The light beside the couch was still on. I clicked it off.

Ilana, her image instantly interrupted my morning contemplation with a shot of adrenaline-induced panic. Suddenly, I was scared for her. Maybe it was because of my dream, my never-ending nightmare from hell, which had disturbed my mental equilibrium. But more than anything else in the world, I wanted to see her.

It occurred to me that perhaps she had come to the condo while I slept on the couch, simply gone to bed without bothering to wake me. I remembered leaving the door unlocked for her.

Please, God, let her be in bed, I repeated to myself as I walked to the bedroom.

The bed was empty.

I was now very scared. I did not expect her to be gone all night.

My shorts lay on a chair in the bedroom. I quickly put them on and headed for the door in a T-shirt while somehow struggling into my tennis shoes without falling, stopping only to tie the laces. I needed to find her and fast. My mind visualized her dead, her body turning gently in time with waves washing up on some forgotten shore. Angry laughing men had abused her still small body while she had cried somewhere not far from me in a place where hatred lived. On a night when I had slept, not looked for her, not tried to find her, not until it was too late.

I desperately tried to exorcise these terrible thoughts from my brain as I walked, but my imagination was too great. I had seen too much pain in the last year. It was too easy to assume the worst, expecting tragedy, sadness never far behind, crying not yet simply a memory.

A blackbird sat on a nearby fence post as I rounded a corner of the condo. Instinctively, I headed for the beach while eyeing the bird. Never liked blackbirds. They are bad omens, signs of death.

I briefly considered going into the town, walking along the shore, hoping to see her coming towards me. I knew approximately where her brother lived, somewhere near the old section of town, down where the native fishing boats docked, but I had never visited their house. Ilana had always kept us apart. I didn't really know why. Truth was, I hadn't spent a lot of time thinking about her brother.

Now I needed to find him. He could help me look for her. He had been with her last night. He would know what to do. But I didn't know what her brother looked like and where to find him.

Perhaps I could ask around. His name was Enrique. Or was it?

Out of the corner of my eye, I saw a familiar form sitting at the end of the Condo's dock: a woman getting a suntan dressed in a white bikini. I stopped to look; I didn't know why. My clouded mind would not allow me to assume anything, but the scene was oddly familiar. Still, it couldn't be her, or could it? Seeing a woman sitting there was like stepping into the past. It made me curious. I headed for the dock slowly, hopefully, yet afraid, ready to turn, fearing disappointment.

The young woman on the dock had her back to me, content to face the sun, gazing over the gently rolling blue-green sea. Only her silhouette against the shining waters was visible in the morning sun. She could be anyone, I told myself. Do not hope. You will be disappointed. Panic pounded in my chest.

My boat was moored to the dock on my right as I passed it, but I didn't look. The image of the woman in a bikini was my focus. She brushed back her black hair with a familiar gesture. Her hand was resting on the dock when I walked up behind her. A pink sapphire ring that I had given Ilana was on her finger.

'So, Mr. John,' she turned and smiled at me. 'Can we go for a sail today?'

HONG KONG, WEDNESDAY, DECEMBER 9, 11:45 P.M.

JASON

Jason leaned into his office chair, turning his head from side to side to ease the tight, sore muscles in his neck.

He had been staring at a computer screen on his desk all morning.

He was too tall for the furniture in his office, especially the local variety designed for shorter Orientals. He had been forced to work hunched over, intensely staring down at his screen, looking slightly uncomfortable when working at his computer. Despite his angular frame, he was a nice-looking kid with short red hair and big dark-rimmed glasses, the kind that slid down his nose and made him look like a college kid. Skinny and not particularly athletic, his vocabulary was colored with a Virginia twang, which slowed his naturally intense thought patterns, seeming to indicate he wasn't very smart. Not true, though. He was very intelligent.

Outside his office windows, the lights of the Hong Kong sky blinked in constant confusion as he worked. The Hong Kong Distribution House had been officially closed for hours. Jason was still working. The intense nightlife outside his office walls held no allure for him. His only interest was his job, and tonight, his job was to solve a puzzle he had recently discovered in inventory.

But his eyes were not cooperating, slowly losing their ability to focus. He rubbed them, attempting to put some life into his visual senses. It was late, and he should have been in his apartment getting ready for bed, but at this moment, he had no interest in sleeping. He only wanted to solve his puzzle.

A business major in college, he was not an accountant by training, but he was good at numbers. This was one of the reasons John first noticed him. Jason seldom made a mistake. The other skill he acquired over time was understanding the complexity of computers. It was an innate ability, one he had been born to enjoy. He had received no formal training, but he had tinkered with computers from the time he was a kid. A nerd was the term normally used to describe him. He knew this, but he didn't care. Computers fascinated him, and why not? Look where his skills have taken him. He was running a multi-million dollar business in Hong Kong, far from Richmond, Virginia, his hometown. All this was good, but the puzzle he had discovered was not good. Something was wrong. Although, he wasn't completely sure it was a problem. He couldn't be certain until he could identify the source of the problem. What was causing it? It could be simply a figment of his imagination. So far, he had discovered no concrete evidence he could take to John. He had only his intuition telling him something was wrong. But intuition alone was not enough. He didn't want to alarm his boss unless and until he had clear evidence of a problem.

He rubbed his eyes again. He needed sleep. He wasn't going to solve his puzzle tonight. It was too complex. He moved the cursor on his computer to the shut-down button and watched the screen go blank. Stuffing his notes in his briefcase, he decided to work on his puzzle again tomorrow night. An idea might come to him in the meantime, something which would help him solve his puzzle.

Placing his pens in his desk drawer, he neatly arranged the papers on his desktop as was his normal habit and adjusted his tie. He didn't like dressing in a suit and tie every day, but it was a requirement of his job, unlike in Charlottesville, where he could go to work in jeans and a shirt. John didn't care how he looked. John only cared his work was done well. But John had warned him. Chinese are very conscious of social position. And social position is often defined by dress. Therefore, a suit coat and tie were necessary if he wanted to work in the Far East.

He sighed, threw his suit coat over his shoulder, and grabbed his briefcase.

He had been working on his puzzle for several evenings now. A small number of gemstones seemed to be disappearing into the system. Not many, not enough to make a real difference, but enough for Jason to be curious. However, to date, he had only questions, unanswered questions. Like how many gems were gone, how their trail was being covered, and where they were going. It was as if they were in his computer one day and gone the next, all evidence of their existence evaporating into thin air.

It was exasperating.

11:55 Pm. Night Janitor

The night janitor watched Jason walk a dimly lit hall towards an elevator.

Americans were strange, he thought. They worked long hours, days, and nights. Did the young man not have a family and wife, someone who waited for him at home? Still the American's actions in the last few nights had been odd even for him. He usually did not work this late at night.

The janitor had been asked to report any strange activity of the American. He was promised money for such reports if the information was useful. So far, the janitor had noticed nothing worth reporting. But this new behavior, staying so late at night. This might be useful.

He made a mental note to communicate the information to his contact, hoping he would get paid for it.

BELIZE, 6:40 P.M.

JOHN

Sea water sprayed off the dark blue bow of my sailboat as it cut easily through the clear waters of the Caribbean Sea between the shore and the reef.

Sheets of white, sunlit sailcloth stretched high into the sky, held by a tall mast, and spread into a cloudless blue sky. Trimmed to a fine curve, the sails bent the wind's will, pushing the sailboat effortlessly through the water toward shelter for the night. Her gauge showed a steady four to four and a half knots. Swim fins and masks lay in a corner of the cockpit, still wet from use. They would be put away later after we docked. At this moment I was content to relish in the power of a warm wind, the rhythm of the sea bringing comfort. Tired, I was tired, but it was good tired which flowed through my body like the gentle currents of the sea.

Ilana sat in the front of the cockpit, the breeze blowing through her straight black hair. She seemed more at peace than I had seen her in a long time. This was her ocean. These blue waters were her friends. The lowering sun warmed her slim brown body as she leaned against the cushions. Her eyes closed momentarily as if she was dreaming.

In her bikini she was darker skinned than me, even though she had lost some of her previous deep tan during months of indoor office work. I thought she was even more beautiful now, and I told her so. I also warned her and said she needed to use suntan lotion now. Her body was not accustomed to being outside in the sun, not like before when she was constantly outside. I even offered to assist in applying some lotion by spreading it over her back where she couldn't reach. I didn't mind. It was a delight to run my hand over her body. She had beautiful, flawless skin. She agreed at first but took the lotion from me when I began to apply it to more areas than her back. I laughed.

My sailboat had needed to be thoroughly cleaned before we could take her out. Most of our morning was spent scrubbing and washing her decks. Below was a mess. Nothing had been touched for months. We didn't clean the boat properly before leaving it in Cancun. We were in a hurry to get out of Mexico at the time. Dried food had to be dislodged from corners of the kitchen by hard scraping, floor washed, toilet cleaned, etc. When we were done, she looked good again. More work was required, but we had time to finish the job before returning home.

Helen called while we were working and reported no major catastrophes looming on the horizon, nothing that required immediate attention. She said she would e-mail a few items for my attention. I thanked her, deciding to wait until tomorrow to look at my email. Manana, this was Belize. Whatever can be put off until tomorrow can be done tomorrow. If tomorrow ever comes.

The chrome wheel turned instinctively in my hand, easing a slight luff in the jib. The forward sail smoothed, and the boat speed increased. Waves splashed against the bow. Our dock came into sight. One more tack, and we were home.

Ilana and I had not yet discussed why she didn't come to the condo on the first night of our stay. I had not asked her and she had not volunteered the information. So, I guessed we needed to talk, but neither of us felt inclined to initiate a conversation.

I stretched while leaning against the cushions, feeling muscles in my back that I had not felt in some time. Cleaning the boat in the morning, then swimming and diving in the afternoon, was more physical activity than I had experienced for months. Our favorite diving spot over a reef was as I remembered. Alive with color and movement. A sense of another world always seemed to come to me as I swam in these warm waters filled with complex coral designs and scurrying fish swimming in streams of red, yellow, and purple, their colors flashing over the soft white sands of the sea floor.

HONG KONG, THURSDAY, DECEMBER 10, 11:05 P.M.

JASON

One more late night and Jason was still no closer to solving his puzzle.

Exhausted, he took a minute to rest, but the computer screen on his desk was not interested in resting. It continued begging him for attention, demanding answers. He always enjoyed working with computers, but not tonight. Tonight, his computer had been acting more like a demanding mother than a friend. He was getting nowhere.

His day had been busy, and he was not able to work on his computer puzzle until well into the evening. And now it was already past eleven at night, and he was no closer to a solution than when he started. Whoever had created this problem, this person was really good. Jason thought he knew what was happening, but he still had no concrete proof.

Two floors down below Jason, another employee of the Hong Kong Distribution House, was also working late into the night. This wasn't unusual. Employees often stayed late to fix problems or to finish a task, like a rush delivery to a client. The Hong Kong Distribution House was well known for being the most efficient and customer-friendly Distribution House of the three. John had often attempted to have the other two Houses duplicate its practices. But his efforts were not rewarded. It wasn't because the methods of the London and the New York Houses were very different. It was their corporate culture. Hong Kong employees were more devoted to their jobs than the employees in the other two Distribution Houses. John finally gave in and allowed each House to work within the confines of their own discipline and culture. He couldn't change them.

Jason decided he needed to change his approach if he was going to solve his puzzle. It was not possible to solve it using his current methods. He would have to try another way. He knew that all gemstones were carefully cataloged in Sri Lanka after cutting and before shipping. He decided to ask Sri Lanka to send him this information separately in a sealed document by courier. This would give him an independent paper trail he could use to track the stones through his computer. He knew this method would take methodical, detailed work on his part, but he could think of no other way to understand what was happening. He had to do it the hard way. Satisfied for the moment, he packed his papers and shut off his computer for the night.

Two floors below Jason, an employee watched the screen on his computer go blank. He had been monitoring Jason's progress through the computer's inventory programs. Alerted by his superiors that something unusual was going on in the boss's office, he had been tracking Jason's activities. The man discovered exactly what Jason was doing, and he thought he knew why.

When Jason turned off his computer, the employee also turned off his computer and, like Jason, prepared to go home.

He would prepare a report for his superiors and send it out in the morning.

BELIZE, 8:40 P.M.

JOHN

'My brother wants to meet you,' Ilana said.

Lost in thought at the time, sitting next to her on the balcony of our condo as a warm, gentle breeze washed over me, I was quietly relaxing in the limited light of evening. The view off the balcony was mesmerizing, almost hypnotic filled with shadowed beach sand dissolving into the glassy dark waters of an anxious sea, painting a living monument to the beauty of this island.

Dinner at one of our favorite restaurants had been good. Conversation, on the other hand, was limited. We both knew something needed to be said, but neither of us was willing to begin. Maybe it was because we were in Belize. Everything was slower here. The rapid pace of the modern world reduced to only a fraction of its normal intensity. I couldn't put my finger on the exact reason. It just was. In Belize, what appeared initially to demand immediate attention often melted away quietly into the realm of insignificant. It could wait for another day, a day which might be forever lost in the relaxed attitude on this island.

And it was just possible if she had never brought it up, I might never have asked her about what happened the night she disappeared and did not come to the condo until the next morning. It would have been far easier to let that question simply retreat to a forgotten memory where it wouldn't matter anymore, than to bring it up.

I had spent very little time thinking about it; more interesting other activities. We went sailing the day she greeted me on my dock in the morning. The next day, I worked in the morning, made a few phone calls, and spent some more time cleaning the boat in the afternoon. When I became bored, I had gone for a swim. Today was more of the same, except this evening when we walked into town for dinner. It was a good day, easy and relaxing. I didn't see any reason to spoil the mood.

She looked beautiful at dinner, a warm glow of the sun in her cheeks, her black hair silky smooth from the soft waters of the sea.

I briefly wondered why I was so enamored with her. Was it because I thought I had lost her forever that night she disappeared? Was this the reason she seemed extra special now? I found myself staring at her throughout our meal, almost unable to keep my eyes off her.

Finally, she asked me what I was doing.

Nothing, I lied and looked away.

The gentle lapping of the waves on the shore were the only sounds that accompanied us as we strolled along the beach to our condo after dinner. I turned the key in the door and held it for her. She found the light switch in the room. The moon was low on the horizon, shining across the sea outside our balcony. I suggested we go outside and have a nightcap. Not because I wanted to talk but because I didn't want this night to end.

'He wants to talk to you,' she said with more than a hint of determination.

'Okay.'

The moon cast a long white tail of light across the smooth waters of the sea. The wind had calmed, and it was a beautiful evening. It brought back all the good memories of this place. The last thing I wanted to do was to talk about her brother. But it was obviously a conversation she desired. I took a sip of wine and resigned myself to listening.

'My brother is my only family. I have told you this,' she began.

'Yes.'

'He feels responsible for me,' she continued. 'After the joy of greeting me passed, he became very angry. He asked why I had disappeared without talking to him. He had been worried about me. He said he was glad when I finally called. But then I did not call him again for a long time. He wondered why I had not called again. He asked me why it was so difficult to call.'

She was silent for a moment, I suppose, trying to decide how to continue. It gave me time to think about what her brother said. I could understand why the last few months had been difficult for him. Not knowing where his sister was or if she was okay. Truth was, I had never considered him. My relationship with Ilana seemed to exist in a world apart from anything or anyone else. Her brother never entered my mind.

She continued, 'I tried to explain to him why I had to leave, but he didn't want to listen. He said I was stupid to take money from the man in the Mayan Jewelry shop who paid me to spy on you. He said it was the cause of my problems. I told him he would not have a new boat if I did not take the money. He became angry and threatened to sink the boat.'

'Ilana, you need to make this right with your bother,' I offered.

'I tried. I told him I was sorry,' she explained. 'I should have called him more often... But I am not my brother's only problem. Mostly, he has a problem with you. He wants to meet you, and he wants to know what your intentions are for me. I am sorry for this, John. But he is my brother. We had a big fight.'

I looked at her. A small tear reflected in the soft light of the moon before falling from her cheek.

'Look, Ilana, I will do whatever you want me to do.'

'No, John, that's not it. I don't think you understand. He says it is not right I sleep with you like a whore.'

I was stunned. I should have seen this coming. But our relationship had come so naturally. And it had happened in the middle of so many other problems, my selfish problems. She was the only person who kept me sane. I needed her. Therefore, it seemed only right she was with me. Beyond this, I had not thought.

'Okay, I get it. I will talk to your brother,' I agreed.

She smiled. 'What will you tell him?'

'I will tell him what he wants to hear. I will tell him I intend to take care of you. He does not need to worry.'

She was silent before continuing, 'When he became angry, I tried to run away from him. But he grabbed my arm and would not let me go. I yelled at him and said he did not understand anything. He said that was not true. He said he did understand. He asked me how I could be so stupid. He demanded to know where I was going. Was I going back to be your whore? I told him I was not a whore...' She paused, 'That is why I did not go to you that night, John. I was afraid of my brother. I slept in his house.'

The moon dipped behind a palm tree before disappearing

into the sea. The night became intensely dark. I could not see her face in the shadows, but I could feel her small body tremble when I reached to touch her arm. I knew I needed to say something, something to make it right for her. All I could think about was my blind, utter, self-absorbed attitude. I wondered how I could have been so stupid. And this woman, this wondrous person who had come into my life when I needed her most; I knew how important she had been to me. How badly I needed her. I had taken her as if I deserved her because I needed her, nothing more. This made it right in my mind.

The gentle sound of waves washing up on the shore soothed my anxious brain, which was intensely absorbed with desperately trying to find a solution to my indefensible position. The sound of the sea, the gently lapping waves, reminded me of the nights when this relaxing sound was the only thing that kept me from going insane, the nights when the loss of Monica was more than I could bear. That was another time. It was before Ilana came into my life. Now was a different time. Now, I needed to put Monica behind me and move on.

'You should not have to be afraid of your brother,' I said, my words coming from deep inside. 'That is not right. Your brother is your family, and you should not have to choose between your brother and me. Tomorrow, I will make this right for you.'

I paused before saying. 'If you will have me, I will marry you, Ilana.'

She slipped off her chair and fell into my arms, her tears flowing quietly in the night.

I held her for a long time without words.

LANGLEY VIRGINIA, SATURDAY, DECEMBER 12, 10:30 A.M.

CHARLIE

Charlie looked over a report while sitting at his desk in the bowels of CIA headquarters.

It was Saturday, and he had come into his office to clean up some loose ends. One such loose end was John Van Laan. He had not given much thought to John for over a month, but he had not forgotten. He still received reports from Thailand. The latest report indicated nothing interesting. Everything was happening as John had said it would. Still, Charlie didn't trust it. He thought about calling John and asking a few pointed questions. But why? He had nothing new to tell him. Besides, their conversation would probably evolve into an argument like the last time, which would do neither of them any good. Truth was Charlie wanted to be friends with John, but he could never make it work. Something always seemed to get in their way. It was frustrating, but so was his investigation. He was getting nowhere nearer to building a case against the man from Thailand, Mr. Nue, the man whose actions had led to the death of his friend, Monica.

He thought about trying a different approach. Instead of concentrating on Nue, perhaps he should concentrate on some of Nue's known associates. Perhaps this would lead him to some concrete evidence. He took out a sheet of paper and wrote a message to a buddy who worked at the U.S. Embassy in Thailand.

Charlie thought again about John as he folded the message and put it in an envelope marked for encoded transmission. Perhaps the barrier to his being a friend of John was Monica. But she was dead.

She should not matter anymore.

BELIZE, SUNDAY, DECEMBER 13, 10:05 A.M.

JOHN

A large Catholic Church dominates the main courtyard in the small town of San Pedro on the island of Ambergris.

Its tall, faded pink stucco walls seem to lord over the old, humble wooden homes and shops that spread out from the church's shadow as if they are dependent on the church's dignity for their existence. When the church was new, its deep red stucco must have fairly glowed in the bright sun of a Sunday morning. But now, like an old woman who was once beautiful, the church looked old and tired; its color dull and faded with only a hint of its past elegance. A few notes of somber, uninspired music crept guiltily out of the church's open-air doors as we approached the church from the road. Its organ was no longer capable of full, rich cords of heavenly music. The notes from its pipes sounded more like a whimper, an excuse coming from the wrinkled lips of the old woman.

I wasn't really concentrating on the music as we walked the hot, dusty road past the church. I was rehearsing the conversation I hoped to have with Ilana's brother. It had been playing in my head for the past few days. In a few minutes I would be meeting him for the first time. I was nervous. But I knew what I had to do and we were on our way to do it. I was glad the time had finally come.

Her brother had put us off. When Ilana called him to arrange a time for us to meet, he said he was busy. He had to work and go fishing. The only day he could meet with us was Sunday. He would not be fishing on Sunday. We had to wait.

The delay, however, didn't seem to bother Ilana as much as me. In fact, I don't think I had ever seen Ilana look so happy. Even though I knew she wanted to settle the situation with her brother, she didn't seem to mind waiting. I assumed it was because we were in Belize. As I have said before, time moves at a slower pace here.

I assumed her good mood was mainly because I had

proposed to her. A proposal of sorts, not your conventional proposal, but still, I had asked her to marry me. I told her I would get her a ring when we returned to Charlottesville. I wanted it to be special. I remembered a blue sapphire I had shown her in the vaults. I thought it would make a wonderful engagement ring.

Ilana had a bounce in her step today as we walked into town. I was having a hard time keeping up with her pace. Breakfast had been a bowl of cereal and some fresh fruit. We had overslept. Contentment had come over both of us the last few days and nights as if our world had finally settled into its rightful place. Our relationship, my work, it all seemed to be in step, as it was meant to be. The tragic memories from the past were slipping away. Terrible times now forgotten, replaced by the beauty of red bougainvillea climbing onto a deck off our bedroom and soft, warm nights of refreshing sleep with Ilana by my side. The clear waters of the Caribbean were filled with endless glorious mysteries to explore. Fresh breezes in our sails and her smile filled my days.

I had not dreamed in the last two nights. Instead, I had slept a deep sleep, which bordered on being completely unconscious. And when I woke, I was refreshed and looking forward to another day. I had no second thoughts about my decision. In so many ways marrying her was what I had needed to do. I was actually looking forward to meeting her brother. I assumed he would be happy when I told him our news.

Ilana stopped as we were passing the church and hesitated. 'I want to go in,' she suggested.

'Okay,' I replied, even though I was anxious to meet her brother. This was her day. If she wanted to go to church before we saw her brother, it was fine with me.

As we approached the church, singing voices swept softly outside from the open wooden doors of the church, inviting us in. Worn stone steps led down a short hall to a large auditorium with a high ceiling supported by wood beams and dusty stucco walls. An empty row of pews near the back of the dimly lit church seemed an appropriate place to sit, but Ilana had other ideas. She led me by the hand up the aisle to a pew near the front. As I sat on an old, worn wooden seat, Ilana immediately knelt on the stone floor and crossed herself before sitting next to me as the congregation continued to sing. A few of the locals looked our way. It was obvious I was a stranger. Only a few other foreigners were in the church. The congregation was mostly native islanders and people of Spanish heritage like Ilana.

The priest was dressed in a typical black robe with a white collar. He spoke very fast, interspersing Latin blessings with a few intelligible words in English. Ilana knelt along with the congregation at appropriate times. She knew the liturgy. I did not. I was raised Protestant. I remained self-consciously seated during the service. The priest began to administer the sacrament of the Holy Supper as I observed the ceremony. Eventually Ilana went up front for her blessing as I sat wondering if I should join her. I did not.

Strangely, as the service progressed, I began to feel more comfortable. Peace lingered in this church among these simple people. In a way, I envied them. They lived and worshipped in one of the really beautiful places on earth. No one could take their island from them. They had their God, their sun-filled sky, and their warm sea. For most of them, this was all they required of life. I knew I was romanticizing, and I knew life on this island was not easy, but at this moment, it seemed complete.

I began to contrast my life, wondering why I was always rushing around the world searching for something to make it better, something that I hoped would save me. What was I missing? Was everything I required right here in this place surrounded by natural beauty? Did I really need to be anywhere else? I rested, lost in meandering thoughts, while Ilana waited in line. When it was her turn, she took the sacrament from the priest and crossed herself before retreating to where I sat.

I took a moment to ask God for help and wisdom. I told Him I was on my way to talk to her brother. Make things right for him.

When the service was over, we exited the church with the congregation. A few people said hello or waved a greeting with a smile.

'This is my church,' she explained. 'I am glad you came with me this morning.'

'No problem, I enjoyed the service.'

'I thought I might see my brother in church. I didn't.'

We continued walking the dusty main road through town past old wooden houses. The marina used by the local fishermen was ahead. I assumed this was where we were headed. I followed a step behind Ilana, letting her lead.

Memories of the morning when I feared I had lost her ran through my head as we continued. If I had not found her on the dock that morning, I would have had to come here by myself, desperately looking for her brother, asking if anyone knew him. Could they tell me where I could find him? And when I found him, what would I have said to him? I would have had to explain to him who I was. And why I was looking for his sister. And why she was not with me. And why I had let something bad happen to her.

As I continued behind Ilana, I was very happy I did not have to do that. It would have been awkward and terrible. I would not have been very civil, hell-bent on finding his sister. It would not have been a good way to meet her brother.

Stopping by the marina, she spotted her brother on his boat. Taking my hand, we approached his boat from the dock. He was working on his lobster traps. When he heard us, he turned to look up.

Her brother was not a big man, maybe older than his sister, but it was difficult to know. He had spent most of his life outside on the sea. His work had taken its toll -- made him look older than he was. A weathered canvas hat covered a full head of curly, uncombed black hair. His scruffy beard was unshaven and he was dressed in an old shirt open at the neck and a pair of dirty jeans.

He returned to his work after seeing us as if he hoped we would simply go away and not bother him. Ilana stood silently on the dock, waiting as her brother continued working on his traps in the back of the boat as if we didn't exist. It was clear he had done nothing special to prepare for us.

Our meeting was not off to a great beginning.

Finally, Ilana spoke. 'Ricky, stop mending your traps and come up here. I want you to meet someone.'

When he continued to ignore her, she stepped lightly off the dock into his boat and gave him a shove. 'Ricky, you cannot ignore me. I am still your sister. You promised to meet with us today. Now stop working so I can introduce my friend. He has something he wants to tell you.'

Enrique, or Ricky as Ilana liked to call him, turned to me where I stood above him on the dock, watching their sibling drama unfold. 'Is this the man?' he asked her.

'Yes, this is the man and he wants to talk with you,' she said.

Ricky slowly took the tools he had been using to mend his traps and placed them in an old rusty metal box. He intentionally did not look at me, continuing to clean his boat while his sister impatiently waited for him to finish. Finally, he stood and spoke to her. 'I will talk to this man now.'

After he helped Ilana off the boat and got off himself, she introduced me. 'Ricky, this is John Van Laan.'

I put out my hand. 'It is good to finally meet you.'

He brushed his dirty hand on his jeans and shook my hand hard, looking me straight in the eye. 'John Vandelin...' he spoke hesitantly, mispronouncing my name. 'I am Ilana's brother, Ricky.'

'Van Laan,' Ilana said clearly, trying to get him to pronounce my name correctly.

'I will call this man John,' he said defiantly to his sister.

'John is fine,' I replied in an effort to smooth over their minor dispute. Having a conversation while standing on a dock under the hot sun was becoming awkward.

'Maybe we could go somewhere and have a cup of coffee,' I suggested.

Ricky looked at his boat for a moment as if he was trying to decide if he had time to do this thing for his sister. He sighed, like he was making a big sacrifice, and walked off the dock without saying another word. Ilana took my hand. We followed behind.

A small, old wooden house stood near the docks on the beach, serving as a restaurant for local fishermen. Strips of curling white paint peeled off its gray, weathered wood siding before collecting on the sand. The front of the house had two large shutters, which opened in good weather, revealing a small kitchen inside. A faded green canvas awning covered the opening, sheltering a wooden counter from the hot sun. The smell of greasy, spicy food filled the air. Next to the house was a large black chalkboard nailed to two poles buried in beach sand. On the board was a menu with prices for the food the kitchen served. White plastic tables and chairs had been casually placed randomly outside the house under green umbrellas in the sand.

Ricky wandered up to the house approaching a large old woman with gray hair working behind the counter. He greeted her with a nod. She smiled at him. I could not hear what he said, but he pointed at us and gave her some folded bills. She nodded.

'Good morning, Mrs. Hernandez,' Ilana said politely.

'Good morning, child,' she replied. 'It is good to see you again. What would you like?'

'Just coffee, please,' Ilana said nervously.

'And you?' the old woman asked me with a smile.

'Coffee, please. How much is it?' I reached for my wallet.

'No, no,' Ilana corrected me. 'Ricky has paid for you. Go have a seat now, and I will bring your coffee to you.'

I put my wallet in my shorts.

Ricky sat at one of the tables under an umbrella, sipping hot coffee. Our meeting was not happening as I imagined. The sun was high in the sky, late in the morning, and it was getting hot. I tried to position my chair in the shade, but Ricky had taken what little shade the umbrella offered. I was forced to sit in the hot sun, feeling more and more like this was going to be an inquisition rather than a celebration.

When I'm in Belize, I always wear a straw hat for protection from the sun. I am a tall, blonde-haired, pale-skinned Caucasian, not like the natives. I burn easily. But my hat only protected my head. My arms and legs were exposed to the sun and I had forgotten to put on suntan lotion in my enthusiasm to meet her brother. I had not anticipated being out in the sun. I could feel my skin begin to burn. On the other hand, Ricky seemed content to sip his hot coffee under the umbrella's shade and let me sweat in the sun. I began to wonder if he was doing this on purpose.

It was time to get right to the point. 'Ricky, Ilana told me about her conversation with you. I think I need to explain our relationship.'

He continued to sip his coffee as if I did not exist, sitting very straight in his chair. It was obvious he was a proud man. I liked him almost immediately, even though it was clear he did not like me.

Ilana came with hot coffee, put my cup on the table, and sat down. At the time, I badly wanted something cool to drink. I was getting hot in the sun.

'I have asked your sister to marry me,' I began.

Ricky looked shocked as if these were the last words in the world he expected me to say. Immediately, he turned to his sister. She gave him one of those little sister looks that says; see, I told you so.

I don't think he knew how to react. He was not prepared for this outcome.

'I'm going to build a house on this island,' I continued. 'This house will be our home. We will spend time here every year. I hope you and I can become friends. I know I have done some things which are wrong in your eyes. And for this, I apologize. I hope I can make it up to you in the future.'

He looked again at his sister. She just stared at him.

I continued. 'However, my job requires I spend considerable time in the States. It would be great if you could visit us sometime.'

I stopped, didn't know what else to say.

'Well, Ricky, do you have something you wish to say to my friend?' Ilana demanded.

He ignored her as if he was trying to decide something in his mind. Then he nodded as if he was agreeing with himself before saying. 'John, you should have come to me first if you wanted to marry my sister... I am her brother. Her father is dead. You should have asked me first.'

I didn't know how to react. In some cultures, older cultures, a bride's father is asked before the bride. I knew this, but it wasn't my custom. I never considered it.

Ricky turned to his sister. 'And you, Ilana, I have never been able to control you. I have tried to be a good brother for you. But after our parents died, even when you were very young, you went your own way. I could not control you then, and I cannot control you now... I am sorry... I am sorry I cannot feel good about what has happened to you. But as always, you do as you wish. You do not listen to me.'

He continued without giving her an opportunity to respond, 'John, I hope you treat my sister well, and I hope you are happy. But you need to know I am not happy. I am sorry... Now I think I have work to do.' He stood from the table with his coffee in his hand, hesitating for only a second.

Looking at Ilana, he bent down and gave her a kiss on her cheek and walked away without speaking another word.

BANGKOK, THAILAND, TUESDAY, DECEMBER 15, 12:15 P.M.

NUE

While sipping tea at his favorite restaurant, Nue read a report from Hong Kong that had arrived on his desk that morning.

An unoccupied, empty chair on the other side of his table was Nue's only companion at lunch. Nue valued his time alone, his solitude. There was enough time to talk during the day. Lunch was his time to think and plan. When he was in Bangkok, he always ate at this restaurant at this very table, which was reserved specifically for him. Made from the finest deep-grain mahogany polished to a glossy dark finish, the table was set flawlessly with expensive hand-painted china and heavy silverware. This was no ordinary restaurant - only the very rich ate here.

An immaculately landscaped garden on the banks of a quiet pool sat next to his table. Hard-edged granite rocks were strategically placed throughout the garden as a natural contrast to the soft, delicate flower pedals and lush flora, all for the viewing pleasure of the restaurant's patrons.

A waiter standing next to his table respectfully waited for Nue to remove his report before placing plates of steaming food in front of him.

'Are you in need of anything else, sir?' the waiter asked.

'No, that will be all,' Nue replied.

The waiter bowed and backed away.

Nue frowned to himself as he ate, unhappy with what he was reading in the report from Hong Kong. The tall, red-haired young American named Jason, who had been appointed by John Van Laan to manage the Hong Kong Distribution House, was searching for something. It was possible he was attempting to trace the gems which were being sent to Phillip. This was not good. However, it was also clear the young man was not yet convinced he knew what was happening.

Nue still had time before he would have to deal with the young man.

58

BELIZE, TUESDAY, DECEMBER 22, 8:55 A.M.

JOHN

A bright red glow of flowering bougainvillea blossoms climbing into the balcony outside our bedroom momentarily captured my attention that morning.

I knew I would miss seeing this wealth of red flowers each morning. And the blossoms would not be the only thing I would miss. I would also miss my boat. We had used her almost every day during our stay in Belize. And for long moments at sea, I was able to completely forget about Charlottesville. I had just returned from checking on her, one more last look inside the cabin to be certain everything was stored neatly and securely. It would be months before I could sail her again.

Although it was not my favorite duty, I had habitually called my office and talked with Helen each morning. She gave me a list of tasks which could not wait and I spent a couple of hours on my phone or computer dealing with these issues. But I knew she was holding back some items and the pile was probably getting higher. It was time to return to Charlottesville.

Ilana was humming in the bathroom of our condo as I packed for our trip home in the bedroom. We had walked the beach after dinner last night. Light from nearby buildings and street lamps allowed us to see where the white sands of the beach met the glassy dark waters of the sea. Dinner had been delicious, and we were weary from another day of sailing and swimming. The night air was warm without a breeze. Shorts and tee shirts were all we needed. And sandals, we needed sandals. Broken glass and rusty cans were buried in the sands, marring the otherwise pristine beaches.

It had become our habit in the evening to sit for a short time on the outside balcony in the dark before bed. Usually, we talked about happy things but last night's conversation was strained.

'You don't have to return with me,' I had said to the shadow of her profile against the moonlit sea. 'You could stay here in this condo or look for something more permanent to rent.'

Ilana started to respond, 'I don't...'

'No, just listen to me, please, for a moment. You have the money I deposited in your bank account.'

One hundred thousand dollars had been placed in a bank account in Belize City in her name. I showed Ilana how to write a check and where to sign her name. And a credit card came with the account which she had used to purchase a few items. She also had cash from a check she had written. However, only a few dollars have been spent to date. Every time I urged her to buy something nice, she refused. 'No, John,' she would say. 'I don't need to buy this.' Or she would buy something cheap instead. I smiled and let her do as she wished. It was her money.

'You could look after the construction of our new house,' I suggested.

Earlier in the week, I had taken a day away from sailing and spent it with a builder. The man had been very kind and told me he could start my house as soon as I sent him blueprints. In the meantime, I instructed him to remove the old burned house and prepare the land for new construction. I gave him a check as a retainer, and we shook hands.

'Someone needs to decide what goes into our house,' I said to her. 'It will be a lot of work. I could fly here every chance I get and visit you. And you could come up and see me anytime you wanted, stay for a few days, then return home.'

A breeze passed through the balcony as she thought about what I said. I sipped some whisky while waiting for her answer. I knew the answer I desired, but I had prepared myself for the other possibility.

Hastily folding and placing my clothes in a suitcase in preparation for leaving, I was almost done. I was bringing only few items with me on the plane so I didn't have much to pack. Earlier, I had stored most of my clothes in my boat for our next trip.

The boat was in much better shape than before we arrived. When we weren't sailing or swimming, I spent time working on the boat. The winches had been polished and oiled. The deck was scrubbed and washed. Ilana had done most of the work in the galley. She seemed happy to be busy. Even though she had not talked about it, I think it helped take her mind off her brother. He was the other subject which I had tried to talk to her about last night. It was obvious he had hurt her but she was a stubborn woman. She didn't want to talk about him. Her brother could do what he wanted, she said.

While I packed in the bedroom, she was busy in the bathroom, putting items into a case and zipping it closed. I was happy she was coming with me. She had told me last night I could not be without her at the office. She had become indispensable in her mind. She used work as an excuse to return.

'Do you need any help packing?' she asked me after she was finished.

'No, I'm almost done.' I threw a few remaining items into my bag and zipped it closed without too much concern for being neat. Almost everything was dirty and would have to be washed when we arrived home.

Seagulls floated past the open balcony in the morning breezes. In about an hour, we were headed to the airstrip on the island. It was already getting windy. I was worried we were in for one more stomach churning, bouncing flight in a single engine turbo prop to Belize City. Ilana had not weathered the last flight too well. However, she seemed unconcerned at the moment as she was cleaning our condo in preparation for departure.

'You don't have to do that,' I said to her. 'Someone will clean this place after we leave.'

She didn't respond, so I sat down on a couch to watch her work.

She looked good. Although her smooth skin was not as dark as when I first met her, she had regained some of her tan. White slacks and a tight pink t-shirt fit her slim figure and showed off a healthy skin tone. Her black hair flowed gently over her shoulders as she worked.

'Aren't you going to help?' she asked as I sat on the couch.

'No, I told you that someone will clean this place after we leave. Let it be.'

'I will feel better if I do this. I don't want this place to be messy when they come.'

'Just like a woman. You're worried the maids will talk about you behind your back when you are gone.'

'John, I know these people. This is my home.'

'Okay, okay.'

I stood up to help her. I had nothing else to do. I could have called the office, I suppose. But calling might force me to become involved in some work I didn't want to do.

'There is something we could do.' I suggested as she continued to make herself busy.

'And what is that?'

'We could finish talking about your brother.'

She stopped working. 'I am sorry,' she said. 'But you know my brother has upset me.'

I said nothing.

'I think I need to give him time to decide he has made a mistake.' She looked at me. 'John, I want to marry you. You know I do. I want to be with you for the rest of my life. But I also want my brother to be with me when we marry. I hope you understand. I want to wait until my brother is ready... Is it okay with you to wait?'

'Of course.'

CHARLOTTESVILLE, VIRGINIA, TUESDAY, JANUARY 5, 1999, 10:35 A.M.

JOHN

His letter arrived a few days ago, along with the other mail. Helen spotted it immediately and brought it directly into my office, where she had put it on my desk, unopened. I occasionally looked at it while answering phone calls and reviewing incoming reports, but I wasn't really interested in opening it.

Ilana and I have been home from Belize for almost two weeks and already our tans are beginning to fade. It had been a particularly cool and rainy Virginia winter; no sunshine, mostly cloudy days. It reminded me of some West Michigan winters, except it didn't snow as often in Charlottesville.

I had skipped going home for the holidays. I couldn't exactly leave Ilana behind. And taking her with me would have invited too many questions from my mother. I wasn't ready to face her inquisition, not just yet. Instead, I called my folks , wished them well and told them I was busy with work and maybe would come home for a visit soon. They sounded disappointed, but this wasn't the first time I had missed the holidays for work. They said they understood, but I knew they didn't.

Routine had taken over our life since our return. Ilana worked assisting Helen and doing some of the domestic chores, which Arny used to do. A sick feeling churned in my gut every time I hurried past the door to Arny's apartment. I missed him. It wasn't the same without his laughter echoing through the halls. It was much drearier or maybe it was simply the weather. Or it could have been because we had only a small crew working in the office. My current office environment didn't feel anything like my old office and probably never would.

The unopened letter on my desk had a fine, gold embossed line around the envelope. The return address was Thailand. It was addressed to me personally, not to my company.

Work was progressing well. My company was continuing to recover and sales were rising rapidly. Mr. Nue was helping. The cutting we transferred to Thailand was being completed to our specifications. No complaints were heard. In addition, emeralds were beginning to arrive from mines in Columbia. Nue's contact in this country was proving to be very useful. I suggested putting the man from Columbia on our Board. Nue agreed. Manuel Ortega was his name and we had been talking. If everything went well, Manuel suggested that perhaps all Columbian emeralds would someday be marketed by my company. I thanked him.

But somewhere in my brain, I sensed it had all come too easy. Even Bob was finally returning my calls. I assumed because he was happy and the pressure was off him, and his New York Distribution House was making money again. I'm sure this had something to do with his new attitude. Money and perhaps because I had decided to leave most of the company's employees under his direction in New York. Bob liked being a boss. In his defense, he was a good manager, and modern means of communication allowed easy access to information from New York, almost as fast as I could get it by walking down a hall, and in some cases even faster. To return these jobs to Charlottesville would have been expensive and very disrupting for our employees. The only exceptions were a few key marketing and advertising people. They had moved to Charlottesville since their work was something I wanted to monitor closely.

A silver letter opener easily slit the official-looking, gold-lined envelope.

It was time.

I had put off reading the letter long enough. Still, I was reluctant. I didn't know why. The letter looked innocent enough. Even so, I scanned it quickly, hoping it was not a problem.

It was a personal invitation from Nue to visit the Thai sapphire mines. He had previously asked me to come, but I had put him off and said maybe someday. I had told him I always wanted to see the mines, which was true. They were legendary in the world of sapphires. Some of the finest rubies and sapphires in the world had come from these mines. Most of the mines were now depleted. After years of sifting through the same dirt over and over, the local miners had extracted almost every valuable gemstone that ever existed from the mines. And this was Nue's big problem.

Thailand had, for hundreds of years, depended on these sapphire mines as a major source of income. When the mines began to become depleted, the Thais looked to other countries to fill their markets. Sri Lanka was one of the places they exploited. However, when my company began to purchase most of the gemstones from Sri Lanka, Thailand lost access to them. This was one of the root causes of our problems with the Thais.

Still, some Thai mines continued to produce limited quantities of sapphire. Nue's letter asked me to visit these mines and offer advice on how to increase production. I didn't know if I had an answer to his question. If the mines contained no more stones, there was nothing anyone could do to increase production. Sapphire mining was not magic.

However, Nue's letter added one new contingent. He said he would consider marketing Thai gemstones through my company if it would help him increase production. Nothing like this had ever been suggested before. I knew the output of these mines was weak, and his country depended on the income generated from these mines. I never asked or expected him to let me market them. Yet, this was what he was suggesting now. And as a first step, he was requesting me to visit the mines. He knew it was something I would have difficulty refusing.

Ilana poked her head through the open door into my office from the apartment. I motioned for her to come in, welcoming an opportunity to think about something other than Nue's letter. She looked great in tight jeans and a big green sweatshirt over a black turtleneck sweater.

'Want some hot coffee?' I asked her, knowing she was having difficulty staying warm.

'Okay.'

'Look at this letter,' I suggested on a whim as I got up to get her a cup.

She took the letter and carefully read it. 'So, are you going?' she asked after she was finished.

'I suppose.'

'Can I come?'

'No.'

'Why?'

'It could be dangerous.'

'Then why are you going?'

'Because I have to go. It wouldn't look good if I refused Nue after all the help he has been giving me. It would show bad faith.'

'Isn't this the man who tried to kill you?'

'Yes, but everything is different now.'

She pondered my reply while I sipped coffee, curious to see how she would react, thinking her opinion would add creditability to my innate fear. But all she said was, 'I don't like to be away from you, John.'

'That's it? That's your only reaction?'

'What do you want me to say?'

'Do you think I should go?'

'I know you will go,' she answered. 'Why ask me?'

'Because I value your opinion.'

'Okay, I don't like you to go.'

'What don't you like?'

'I have decided I don't like this...this Mr. Nue.'

'That's it? You just don't like him?'

'Will you take someone with you?' she asked, ignoring my question.

'I think I'll ask Tim to come along. It's winter and he isn't busy now. He can help me analyze the mines.'

She didn't say anything, obviously disappointed.

'Say, the sun is shining,' I suggested to cheer her up. 'Why don't we go to the club for dinner?'

'I don't like your snooty club.'

'Okay, some other restaurant then?'

'I think I will make tacos.'

She turned on her heel and walked out of my office.

HONG KONG, THURSDAY, JANUARY 7, 7:15 P.M.

JASON

A package containing the requested information arrived from Sri Lanka, hand-delivered by a courier. Jason did not open it until after he had completed all the other multitudinous tasks required of his job. His work was exhausting at times. As a result, he did not have time to look at the contents of the package until it was late.

The information in the package he received was very thorough. Every single stone in the next shipment from the Sri Lankan cutting factories had been detailed in the report. It was exactly what Jason wanted. The reported shipment was scheduled to arrive shortly. It would be entered into the Hong Kong Distribution House's computers like all the other shipments from Sri Lanka. Nothing in regular protocol would be changed. Nothing except this time, Jason would personally double-check to be certain every single gemstone in the shipment was entered into the Hong Kong computer. He wanted to be certain that not one gem got lost in some sort of statistical mystery. The document on his desk gave him the information he needed to accomplish this task.

All shipments were normally logged in, and samples were checked for quality as soon as they arrived. Most newly arrived gemstones were immediately shipped to customers to fill existing orders. The remaining gemstones went into inventory. But somewhere between initial logging and inventory, some of the gems went missing. It was as if they had never been logged in, or they simply disappeared once they were in inventory. Not many, in fact, only a small fraction of the total was disappearing. This is what made his task so difficult.

The value of the lost gemstones, if they were in fact lost, didn't amount to much money, not compared to the gross sales of the house. It wasn't like they would really be missed. But after several incidents of missing stones were reported, Jason had become concerned. He was an exact numbers guy, and he wanted his company to run on exact standards. He was determined to discover if a small number of gemstones were being siphoned off on a regular basis. And if they were, where were they going? And why? This was his puzzle and he didn't like the fact that he had been unable to solve it.

And yet, the quantity was very small. It could be nothing more than a statistical or systems error. If he sounded an alarm and nothing was really wrong, he would lose face with his Chinese employees. He had to be certain.

Two floors below Jason, an employee waited for his computer screen to indicate Jason was again searching through the inventory. However, the employee's screen indicated no new activity this evening. In fact, Jason had not been working long night hours on his computer recently. The employee wondered if Jason had finally given up.

The recent reports filed by this employee to his boss had indicated no new activity. Days had passed without anything new to report. But still, his boss asked him to continue. The employee wondered when he would be allowed to go home at closing time. He was looking forward to returning to a less tiresome schedule. He was tired of maintaining the same hours as his boss.

Two floors above the employee, Jason put the documents from Sri Lanka in his briefcase and turned out the lights in his office. The documents would remain with him now, day and night. He would not let them out of his sight. If he lost them, he would have to start over.

He sighed to himself. In a way, he hoped it was just a systems error. This would make his job much easier.

THAILAND, FRIDAY, JANUARY 29, 9:20 A.M.

JOHN

Whirling helicopter blades sent fine particles of dirt and dust spinning into the atmosphere as we waited for the noisy flying machine to settle on the tarmac of a local helicopter pad. Another day of visiting sapphire mines in Thailand was our destination.

A door to the mechanical bird opened and I ducked my head, following Nue inside. Tim came behind me, carrying his backpack. Mine was small, a lightweight backpack which could easily be thrown over my shoulder while visiting mines in the interior of Thailand. We weren't staying long so I didn't need a large suitcase, just a few changes of underwear and some shirts and pants enough for three or four days.

When I informed Nue our visit would be short, he sounded disappointed. He wanted to show me Bangkok and the cutting factories after we were finished seeing the mines. But my shit detector had been going off ever since I received his letter.

It was what I called my subconscious sense of alarm, which rang in my head like a smoke detector whenever something did not smell right. I knew I couldn't refuse Nue's invitation to visit the mines, but I reasoned I didn't have to make it a long, extended trip. I informed him I would enjoy visiting Bangkok someday when I had more time.

Ilana was in Australia. She had unconditionally informed me she would not be left behind in cloudy, cold Charlottesville while I traveled. So, a compromise was reached. After flying to Melbourne, Ilana agreed to stay in Australia, where she was now sitting on a warm beach at the subtropical resort of Noosa. Tim's wife Sarah was with her.

Tim and Sarah always took a vacation in the winter. He earned it by putting in long days at the Montana sapphire mine, which he managed in the summer months. Tim never took time off during the few weeks of warm weather when his mine was operational. He felt he needed to be on-site in case something went wrong. Winters in Montana were long, cold, and dark. He needed to get away. By January, all the mining equipment had been repaired, and everything was ready and waiting for spring. There wasn't much for him to do. Accompanying me to Thailand was a perfect excuse to get out of a cold and windy Montana. I convinced him by saying he could mix business with pleasure. And as an added incentive, the company would pay for his trip. This sealed the deal. It appealed to his fiscally conservative nature. He said he would be happy to go along. When I told him I was flying Ilana to Australia before traveling to Thailand, he asked if Sarah could stay with her. I agreed.

The main reason I asked Tim to accompany me was because he was hands-on when it came to mining. He would be a big help in evaluating Thailand's sapphire mines.

We were encouraged with what we saw in Thailand. Suggestions were made which we thought might help the Thai improve production from their depleted mines. I hoped Nue was happy. However, he didn't show it, not much in the way of appreciation. He simply took in the information as if it was what he expected. The man was a hard read.

After Thailand, Tim and I planned to spend some time together in Australia and enjoy some sunshine with our ladies on a beach for a few days. Ilana and I were then scheduled to fly to the interior of Eastern Australia to visit Clarence. The new color enhancement lab had been in operation for over a year, but I had not seen it. Tim and Sarah planned to travel to Hawaii for a couple of weeks.

Wind from the helicopter's blades stroked the air in a whirlwind of anxious noise and commotion, making it almost impossible to hear as we boarded the vibrating machine. I found a seat in the rear next to Nue.

A chartered private jet had flown us from Australia to Bangkok, Thailand. It was scheduled to return this afternoon to fly us to Australia. This was the last day of our four-day visit. Each day, we flew by helicopter to different mining sites. The town of Chanthabur was our base. The city had a nice hotel, D Varee Diva

Rimnaan. The name of the hotel was a bit long, but it was comfortable, and everything was paid for, compliments of Nue.

Our stay had been pleasant. In the evenings, we shared dinner at the hotel restaurant. Tim and I used the time to discuss with Nue and his associates what we saw. Specific suggestions were made and methods we thought would improve the output of their mines were shared. The subjects of mine, safety and the environment, were constant topics of conversation. Our working dinners at the hotel lasted several hours each night. We had a lot to discuss. Some of Thailand's mines were a safety and ecological disaster. The use of water cannons washing soil through jigs was efficient, but the method clogged streams and made erosion a major problem during the rainy season. Absolute lack of land reclamation changed once pristine green valleys into ugly scarred brown patches of dirt and wastelands completely unsuitable for farming.

Nue and his people politely listened to our daily suggestions and dutifully wrote down everything we said. But I wondered if we were wasting our time. It would be difficult for the Thai to change decades of mining practices in the near future. Plus, it would be expensive. Our suggested methods involved the use of new heavy equipment and extensive engineering, which would give them the ability to dig deeper and extract more gemstones. We also suggested putting in place land reclamation practices to repair damage. I told Nue we would assist him financially, but only if he included reclamation as part of the program. It was the same deal we made with miners in other areas of the world. Nue had nodded as if he agreed, but I wasn't sure we had a deal.

Apart from business, the dinners gave us an opportunity to become acquainted. As I expressed earlier, Nue was a hard read. His conversational skills were sadly lacking. He did tell me a few stories from his life in Bangkok and described a restaurant where he always dined. It sounded nice. I guess he hoped I would change my mind and come with him to Bangkok after our visits to the mines. I declined even though I was intrigued.

Our trip had proved to be hard work. The daily tours of the mines were exercises in self-discipline. The conditions the miners lived in were primitive and depressing. I wondered if today would be any different.

As our helicopter flew over tree covered hills, I let my mind wander. By late afternoon, we were scheduled to be on a plane flying to Australia to see Ilana and Sarah. I told myself I could make it through one more day.

Today, we were traveling into mountainous areas. It was supposed to be cooler and more pleasant. A mine in the Trat Province close to the Cambodian border was our destination. The nearest town was Bo Fa Mai, a small mining village. It was the farthest distance from the city of Chanthabur of all the sites we were scheduled to visit. According to Nue, this was a relatively new mining area. It had only been worked for about two decades.

Dirt brown roads curving through the hills below were the only evidence of human civilization in the lush green forest canopy below as I looked out of the window of the helicopter. These dusty, meandering scars on the land represented the only means of travel other than air. They hugged the hillsides and followed twisting streams through the valleys. There seemed to be no real logic to their placement, more like an artist's exercise in random symmetry than an honest attempt to travel from one place to another. Occasionally, where the twisting roads intersected in the forest, villages with straw roof huts could be seen near a stream with children playing in the water.

The helicopter made a pass over the town of Bo Fa Mai before landing. From the air, I could see an earthen dam above the town holding a man-made lake. A large area of brown dirt intersected by a muddy stream wandered through the tree-covered valley below the dam. Both sides of the waste area were encompassed by hills. The dirt was pockmarked with small black holes, which appeared to be blemish-filled scars in the middle of the lush green forest. Local villagers could be seen digging in these holes, hoping to find gemstones. Farther into the valley, a rusty old bulldozer belched smoke, pushing over trees, taking life from the forest to enlarge the ugly brown scar and create new areas for the villagers to search for gemstones.

Tim pointed through his window and yelled something at me, but I couldn't really understand what he was saying over the noise of the helicopter's engines. I assumed he was seeing the same things I was seeing. I nodded and looked out the window.

Nue sat next to me as if he was in a trance. He never looked out his window, just stared serenely straight ahead.

He had seen it all before.

11:25 A.M. John

Dust spun in violent aerial swirls as I watched our mechanical bird rise in a rush, barely missing a tall tree before disappearing over the lush green forest. We were left behind as the distant roar of its jet turbines echoed through the valley.

Every day of our trip, our helicopter stayed behind with us after landing, ready to take off as soon as we were finished.

Today was different.

'The pilot has to fly an injured miner from another village to a hospital,' Mr. Nue explained, reading my mind. 'It will return before we are to leave.'

'Thanks,' I responded, trying to sound unconcerned.

I was already looking forward to boarding the bird and heading to the airport. But not just yet. First, we had work to do. Still, if we were lucky, I thought we might be able to leave Thailand as early as late afternoon. I told Tim we would see how our day progressed and make a decision later about when to leave for the airport. However, seeing the helicopter take off seemed like a sign that we might not be destined to leave as soon as I had hoped.

A grassy plateau above the village where we landed was serviced by a dirt road along the shore of a man-made lake enclosed by a dam. The lake looked pleasant from what we could see, except the water was a dull brown color. I assumed its color was from mining activity farther up the valley. Nue explained that the dam had been built to provide water for the village and was essential for the mining. He seemed proud of this accomplishment.

We continued past the dam and down a hill towards a village. A stream from an opening in the dam cut through the village, which was bordered on both sides by the high banks of a gorge.

Questioning faces of children playing in the streets of the

village were difficult to avoid. I wondered what they were thinking, watching our curious party travel through their world toward the brown, pitted, scarred earth we had seen from the air. Three days of unsmiling faces were beginning to have an effect on my mind. I missed Ilana's smiles.

Unfortunately, our trip had been only partially successful. One of my main goals was to establish a bond with Nue. In this I did not feel very successful, but not for lack of trying. On a few rare occasions, I was able to get him to discard his stoic mask. Tim was far better at breaking through his reserve. Few people on earth can resist Tim's charisma. Even Nue was not totally immune. Tim would make a humorous remark with a twinkle in his Irish eyes. Nue's face would crack like it was made of stone, and he would actually smile. Then, as if a cloud had passed over him, Nue would once again assume an expression resembling an inhibited frown and settle into a Zen-like trance as if the cares of the world bounced off an invisible shield around him.

In a way, I admired his discipline and self-control. I was personally much more transparent. And lately, I had been having a difficult time hiding the fact I wanted to leave this place as soon as possible. I decided to try mimicking Nue's composure to disguise my discontent.

'You okay, boss?' Tim asked as we passed hastily constructed wood shanties.

From Tim's question I concluded I was failing to hide my feelings. 'Yea, I'm alright,' I whispered. 'I'll be a lot happier when we board our plane and head to Australia.'

Tim nodded.

I searched for any building which might resemble a school or a medical facility in the village. I saw none. A few vegetable gardens had been planted near the huts, no flowers. Children could be seen playing with makeshift toys made from sticks and balls of tape.

A rickety stair made of wood allowed us to get down a bank that bordered the streambed where villagers were working. What remained of our morning was spent viewing the work of these miners. Hand-made jigs and water cannons were their tools. Most of the gemstones we saw had good red color and natural rubies, but they were not particularly valuable due to their small size. I was told some fine large stones had come from this area, just none recently. It was possible, although no one said it, that all the good stones had already been found. Perhaps greed and hope were all that remained.

I turned to Nue and suggested doing some exploratory drilling before destroying more of the forest beyond the area which was being worked. If the drilling samples proved that only very few small gemstones remained buried in the soil, then perhaps they shouldn't continue to desecrate the land by clear cutting trees. He nodded as his assistant wrote my suggestion on a pad of paper. I wondered if he had any intention of doing what I recommended.

After a few hours, Nue excused himself, saying he had to confer with one of the village elders and make a telephone call. He informed us he would return in an hour. He suggested we continue viewing the mine in his absence and that his assistant would be our guide and translator. And so, we continued on our own, covering approximately a mile or more in the valley, walking around a bend in the river bed. Unfortunately, we didn't see anything new or different. Just more villagers working a muddy river valley. It was dirty and heavy work that included digging holes and washing the mud in hand-made jigs with the water supplied from the nearby stream. The villagers appeared determined. The lure of finding a fine ruby was their motivation, as if the riches were only a shovelful away.

Talking to the miners was possible through Nue's assistant. He seemed nice, although I was never really sure he translated our questions accurately. However, that may have been more difficult than I imagined. Cultural differences make any form of communication problematic. Add the barrier of different languages, and it is almost impossible to communicate beyond very simple concepts. Despite this, the miners were cooperative. Even though I sensed a certain reluctance in their mannerisms, miners everywhere are naturally suspicious of strangers. The people in this valley were no different.

Someone touched my arm from behind as we continued. A

young miner in a straw hat smiled and proudly held out a small dark red stone for my inspection. The gem looked like most of the other rough rubies we had seen that day, perhaps a little bigger than most with a good red color. As I was examining the stone, a loud explosion echoed through the valley.

We were not immediately concerned. Explosions are not unusual in a mining area. It wasn't until the native miners turned to look suspiciously upstream towards the village that I began to suspect something wasn't right.

A low rumble quickly followed the explosion, like the resonance of distant thunder that seemed to pass through my body, so low it was almost easier to feel it in my bones than hear it. I couldn't identify the noise although something in my memory banks registered. It just didn't come to me immediately.

'Sounds like an avalanche.' Tim said the word I had been trying to remember.

'See any snow?' I replied, half in jest, as an involuntary shudder coursed through my body. The word 'avalanche' immediately brought back memories of a painful experience in the Alps when I almost died.

'I know, but it sounds like an avalanche,' he smiled.

The low noise gained intensity as we listened, coming from somewhere upstream. Initially, we were blinded to its source because we couldn't see anything beyond the bend in the river except the tops of tall trees beside the river valley, which began to sway as wind rushed through their branches in the clear blue sky with no clouds. With no reason for the threat of severe weather, no reason for a sudden wind which bore down on us ahead of a wall of dirt-brown water rushing around the bend, hurrying through the valley, swiftly attacking everything in its path like a devouring animal; a massive wall, an unstoppable heavy brown shroud of raging ugly moving liquid fury, splashing glassy tons of heavy wet mayhem rushed towards us. The wall of water had to be at least ten feet high, maybe more, as we watched in detached, paralyzed fascination; no time to run more than a few steps before the churning fluid anger descended on us, filled with pulverized bits of wood from broken trees and demolished village shacks. Bodies were carried in the raging water, helpless, screaming, weeping bodies beneath its consuming wet roar. Unheard cries for help, gasping wide-eyed figures sucked into the liquid death, coated with brown grime, unrecognizable anguish, many already dead.

Instinctively, I ducked my head into the curling jaws of water as I had done a hundred times swimming in the surf. The compressing wall of water instantly buried me in its violent, rushing madness, hitting my body as I fought to dive below its fury only to be caught up in its uncontrollable swirling, angry, brown liquid violence, taking me in its grasp, twisting and turning in a black place. The water hit me so hard I instantly exhausted all the air in my lungs which I had instinctively inhaled seconds before the high wave crashed over me.

Fighting with every ounce of willpower to hold my breath and avoid sucking the ugly brown swill into my lungs, my helpless body was tossed around like a rag doll in the river. Briefly, light appeared through the swirling wet haze when I was momentarily thrown above the splashing fury, sucking greedily for air before once again being forced below the surface of the water, engulfed in its wet passion, held under the water by invisible arms of liquid steel. Pain, my body was constantly pelted by invisible projectiles, traveling through the watery violence. Long minutes underwater were followed by too few brief seconds of gasping for air, exhausted, crying for hope, starving for air, muscles aching in exasperation, drowning slowly, not ready to die, but losing the will to live as my body was weakening in the struggle.

Then thankfully, if by a miracle, the raging river unexpectedly quieted as if it had spent its anger and needed a moment to rest before continuing its orgy of carnage. I breathed deeply, swimming on the surface, gasping for life-giving air like it was my last meal.

The river turned and rushed over the side of a hill, increasing in speed again, churning and turning and flushing me down a mountainside. I rode the white water rushing through trees, which broke like twigs from the power of the furious rapids, narrowly missing protruding branches that reached out to cut and grab my helpless body. The splashing mass of water tossed me helplessly in its untamed current, trying vainly to see above the surface of the water but only occasionally able to discern anything in the watery confusion, swimming for my life, hoping to avoid invisible rocks in the swirling liquid.

I couldn't be sure if it was Tim, but when the river marginally slowed again, just a little, I spotted a body floating in the water wearing a plaid shirt like his. The body in the shirt was about twenty feet from me. He didn't seem to be swimming, just paddling weakly, floating in the water next to other lifeless, limp bodies washing down the river. Perhaps it wasn't Tim at all. Just only another victim caught in this nightmare.

I needed to be certain, swimming in his direction, trying to breathe but inhaling some of the ugly brown swill that was carrying me. I coughed the muddy liquid from my lungs when I could, fighting to remain above water as the current dragged me, clenched in its white water teeth. I'm a good swimmer, but it was taking everything I had to keep my head above water.

I watched as the body wearing Tim's shirt rose up, rushing over a big boulder. After bouncing off the top of the rock, it went limp, thrown into a swirling tornado of brown water below the rock like a rag. I thrashed madly to avoid hitting the rock, narrowly missing it, and grabbed at the plaid shirt as I passed. The man in the shirt wasn't moving; he was no help. It was all I could do to keep his head above the rushing water, which seemed to have a mind of its own, a mind determined to bury both of us beneath its violent rush. I held on to the shirt, pushing its owner's head above the water when I could, kicking and thrashing for air. I was wearing down fast as my arms were growing weary and heavy. I couldn't hold his head up much longer. It was all I could do to maintain my hold on the shirt as he drifted beside me like a heavy log.

I feared I would have to make a decision soon. I could not hold on to the shirt much longer. The time for a decision was coming fast. I might have to let him go to save myself. I could not last much longer. If I didn't let go soon, complete exhaustion would eventually make me another victim of this angry water.

But it's odd what thoughts pass through your head under intense stress. I actually began to question letting Tim go; I reasoned it would be better to die with him. Then, I wouldn't have to explain to Sarah how I let her husband drown in the water. Let him die while I saved myself. So, I held his shirt and pushed his head above the water when I could, coughed, and breathed when I was able. We washed downstream in the wet grip of the water, holding onto his shirt. Every ounce of energy in my body was slowly dissipating as we were flushed down a gorge in the mountain side. A rock under the water hit my side; pain was instant, lungs exhausted precious air from the sharp blow to my rib cage. Still, I continued churning in the brown wet mass, somehow holding Tim's shirt as if this piece of cloth was my salvation, not just his, but mine also while spitting gritty water from my mouth with every hurting attempt to breathe.

Like a greedy animal devouring its prey, the water began to swallow me alive, holding me in its fluid steel teeth, twisting and turning the life out of me like an alligator twists its prey. I was dying. I knew I was dying. I couldn't hold my breath much longer. Still, I held onto Tim's shirt, not so much to save him, but because I didn't want to die alone. I could see his smiling face in my mind as I drifted into unconsciousness. I cried out to God for help. But it was no good. I gave up. I couldn't make it. My strength was gone, and I was slowly drifting into a semi-conscious state.

In a dream, the gentle, warm waters of the Caribbean washed over my body. Small, colorful fish from a reef glided past me in streaking infusions of elusive reds and golden yellows. I was at peace at last. I looked for Ilana and saw her ahead of me, swimming effortlessly, gliding peacefully. I swam towards her even as my lungs screamed for air. But I couldn't get to her. My strength was gone. She turned to me and smiled as if to say it was okay. Go up and breathe. You need to live. It is not yet your time to die. I understood and kicked furiously to the surface, while holding the shirt of my friend. My head finally broke through the surface of the water in a rush, and for reasons I did not understand, I was alive, coughing and breathing while somehow still holding onto Tim's shirt.

I wondered if I was still dreaming because the stream was calmer than before. I could rest, swimming on my back and breathing deeply in gently rolling water. I turned Tim's head over so he was upright in the water, his nose in the air. The stream had entered a wide valley between the mountain's hills, momentarily spreading its violence stretched over a larger area. We were drifting near the edge of the river. I wrapped one arm around Tim's head and began to drag him behind me, using a life-saving technique I had learned many years ago. I feared that the river would eventually take us down another rushing, twisting gorge in the mountain after we passed through this plateau. We would again be engulfed in a more white-water fury and I had only barely enough energy to stay afloat. The next gorge would be my death - our death. I had to get to the shore if I wanted to live.

My strength was fading. Even though the water was gentle, I was making only modest progress. Dry land was close. I could see dry land. I was getting closer, but I was not there. The stream was traveling at a reduced pace, although it was still moving relatively fast, just not the raging, white-water fury I had experienced through vertical drops down the mountainside. Trees near the shore passed as I swam towards them. Somehow, I had to drag myself and Tim out of the moving water before we were through this valley. I reached for a branch of a tree coming towards me. It twisted in my hand when I tried to grab it, ripping my flesh and slipping quickly away. Another branch appeared. I held on to Tim's shirt, and this time, I was able to hold onto the branch by wrapping my arm around it.

The river pulled at me, dragging us like a mother who didn't want to let go of her children. Slowly, I was able to inch my way toward shore while holding onto Tim's shirt. When I finally felt my feet touch solid ground, I stood up in the water as the thumping of helicopter blades rang through the forest. After dragging Tim's unconscious body out of the river under the cover of trees near the shore, I sat down to rest.

I couldn't explain why I crawled under those trees while the helicopter was flying over. I obviously wasn't thinking clearly. But somewhere in my semi-conscious mind, I feared Nue was looking for us for the wrong reasons. Although we needed help, my brain wanted to think about what had happened before deciding if it was wise to seek his help. The sound of an explosion was still rumbling through my subconscious brain like an unwanted guest at a funeral.

Something was not right with all this. The earthen dam, the one we had seen earlier above the village, must have collapsed, causing the rushing water down the stream bed. But why? Why did it collapse? And why did we hear an explosion which sounded like dynamite.

Rolling Tim over on his back, my buddy didn't look too good. I checked his throat for obstructions. It was clear. He was still breathing, but he didn't sound good. His breathe was raspy and irregular. I bent over him, breathed hard into his mouth, pushing my hands on his chest, breathing and pushing, breathing and pushing until finally he coughed and coughed some of the fluid from his lungs. He was still semi-conscious, but his breathing was regular.

And then I was done.

I could do no more.

I literally fell over and lay next to Tim under the trees to rest. My body hurt everywhere from the beating it had taken in the river. Especially my side, where a boulder had crushed my ribs. It was a mass of pain. When I was fighting for my life, I felt no pain. But now my chest tightened, and the pain made it hard to breathe.

I lay on the forest ground of decaying leaves, exhausted. Checking occasionally on Tim, I was relieved to see his chest was moving in a slow rhythm with his breathing.

I closed my eyes.

AUSTRALIA, NOOSA, 4:10 P.M.

ILANA

Cool water washed gently over Ilana's gleaming body as she stood under a simple open-air shower in brilliant sunlight.

The leaves of a nearby palm tree wistfully swaying in a warm breeze were accompanied by the sound of lapping waves rolling up a nearby shore creating a calm underlying rhythm for this place by the sea; a musical beat that swept subliminally through her mind as she showered.

The shower by the beach was simply a rusty old nozzle attached to a wood wall, used by weary beachgoers to wash salt and sand off their bodies before returning to their rooms. The clear, fresh water from the nozzle washed through her gleaming black hair and cleaned the sand off her legs and feet as Ilana closed her eyes for a restful moment of quiet satisfaction as tender streams of water cascaded over her shoulders and ran down the soft curves of her tan body. The sun was hot. The cool water felt refreshing. Finally turning off the faucet, she dried her body with a towel and stepped into her sandals. A wood bark path led to her condo, where Sarah was resting in their room after an afternoon tanning session on the beach. Fairer skinned than Ilana, Sarah never stayed at the beach as long as Ilana in the hot sun.

It had been a good day for Ilana, except she missed John. Sure, it was nice to be outside on a warm beach again. The salty air had refreshed her and given her a sense of well-being. But just being on a beach wasn't enough anymore. Not like before. Now, she seemed to need John to make her life complete. She wondered how this had happened. She was no longer the carefree girl who lived on an island in the Caribbean Sea and roamed its beaches alone. Now, everything was different.

She and Sarah had gone into town earlier for lunch and some shopping. They enjoyed each other's company even though their relationship was still somewhat strained. They came from different worlds. A natural barrier existed between them. But despite this quiet void, they made the best of their time together and actually began to become friends. The last few days had been especially good.

Ilana thought about John as she walked slowly up the path. She wondered where he was. She knew he was coming sometime soon, maybe even tonight. She didn't know exactly when. John wasn't sure when he would be able to leave Thailand but had told her not to worry. She wondered if he was traveling now, heading by plane to Australia. She hoped so. She missed him.

A sea breeze swept her long black hair into her eyes as she walked. Instinctively, she brushed the offending hair aside with her hand as flashes of brilliant sunshine reflected off a blue sapphire engagement ring on her finger.

THAILAND, 6:55 P.M.

JOHN

Slowly, the river began to recede. No longer fed by a mass of rushing waters flowing from the lake above the damaged dam, the river returned to its normal banks as if nothing unusual had happened.

For short periods, a few minutes at a time, I would wake up before again falling back into an exhaustion-induced semi-coma. One of these times, I turned my head to look at Tim. He was beginning to show signs of life. I hoped the worse was over. We were lying on the forest floor where I had not moved since falling over in exhaustion. My strength was completely wasted.

Tim opened his eyes during one of these times when I was awake and turned his head sideways to look at me. His face assumed his usual cocky grin. I couldn't believe he could smile at a time like this, but he was actually grinning like always. I started to laugh, but then I stopped as a sharp pain rebelled in my side.

'So, John,' he said. 'Where are we?'

'Thailand.' I tried to smile.

'Still?'

'Yes.'

'And where's our helicopter?' he asked, grinning at his own

joke.

I had to laugh this time, even though it hurt. 'I think we missed it.'

He closed his eyes. Exhausted, I closed mine again. Night walked into the forest as we slept side by side in darkness under a sheltering canopy of trees while I dreamed of a warm beach somewhere in another world.

THAILAND, SATURDAY, JANUARY 30, 6:55 A.M.

JOHN

Streaming light filtered down through openings in the high forest canopy, capturing ghostly films of pallid moist air floating through the dark forest of craggy old trees on a misty cool morning.

Eventually, one shaft of golden sunlight broke through a small opening in the green leaves high above where I was sleeping and covered my face with light so dazzling that I blinked instantly into consciousness. Turing over to avoid the sunlight from burning my eyes, I groaned audibly. Every inch of my body hurt, and when I tried to get up off the ground, the muscles in my side screamed in painful rebellion as I involuntarily settled into a submissive kneeling position on the damp ground.

My departure from the world of sleep was so sudden and violent that I didn't immediately understand my current predicament. However, after taking time to sort through a mental newsreel of recent memories, it all returned to me in a panicked flash. All the pain, the swirling waters, the blank-eyed, dead bodies, and the remnants of village shacks, all floated mercilessly through the waters of my confused brain. The cool mountain air quickly convinced me my memories were correct. I was shivering. My clothes were damp from the morning dew. Brown grit appeared to have penetrated every crevice of my body, covering my hands and face.

Tim looked far more content than me, lying on the forest ground with his eyes closed like he was sleeping peacefully. I didn't want to wake him, but I couldn't help wondering if he was simply unconscious or dead. Thankfully, he stirred when I nudged him and immediately opened his eyes. He sat up easily and brushed the dirt from his face while I was forced to continue on my knees, afraid to move with a pain in my side begging me to be still. Tim seemed to be in better shape than me. He had not struggled in the river as I had. Instead, his limp body had been more passive, and as a result, he had sustained fewer injuries except for an ugly bruise on the side of his head, which looked red and swollen.

'I seem to have taken quite a hit to my head,' he instinctively raised his hand to touch it.

'Good thing you didn't get hit anywhere important,' I replied in jest.

'Yea, good thing,' he smiled. 'So where do you think we are?'

'Some place downstream from the village we were visiting yesterday.'

'Oh yeah, I remember now. What do you think happened?'

'Dam must have broken. Water from the lake swept us away.'

'Seems right,' Tim paused before adding. 'I don't remember climbing up on this bank?'

'You can thank me for that.'

'Really?'

'Yes, you hit your head on a rock in the water and became unconscious. I grabbed your shirt and held on to you.'

'So, I wasn't much help.'

'Out cold like a log floating in the water.'

'So, you saved me?' he questioned.

'Dragged you up on this bank and gave you mouth to mouth. I didn't want to do it, but it seemed the only way to save your ugly puss.'

'Yuck.'

It seemed almost impossible he had survived. We guessed he was out cold after the rock hit his head, but he hadn't stopped breathing, and I must have kept his head above water enough for him to keep him alive. Anyway, if it was a miracle, then it was a miracle. I was just happy he wasn't dead.

'I thought we were goners,' I said. 'I didn't want to die alone, so I held on to you. It was a selfish act, really.'

'I see. Well, in that case, I'm happy to have been of assistance.'

'Oh, you weren't much help.'

'I was there for you, wasn't I?'

'Yeah, you were there,' I smiled.

'What now?'

'Well, first, you can help me get into a sitting position. I think I have a few broken ribs.'

'Oh yeah, you look kind of uncomfortable.'

'You noticed.'

'Yeah, I noticed, but then you are always doing something odd.'

'Just help me, will you? My side is killing me.'

He helped me turn over. My side hurt like mad, but it felt better to sit. After I had a chance to rest, I asked him the question which was on my mind, the question which must have been processing in my subconscious as I slept.

'You remember the noise we heard a short time before the river hit us?'

'Oh yeah, I remember.'

'Do you think that was an explosion?'

'Sure sounded like one.'

We sat and talked about what we heard for a while. I questioned whether the dam breaking was an accident. The engineering of the thing didn't look all that good when we had passed it in the morning. So, it was possible that the dam simply broke. But then, what about the sound we heard? Was it an explosion, and did the explosion cause the dam to break? And if it did, that begged the questions of who or what set off an explosion and for what reason.

'I see what you mean,' Tim responded. 'Maybe it happened on purpose.'

'Yes, it could be this time Nue attempted to remove me from office using a less conventional method, like a natural disaster. Think about it. He is a stockholder and a board member now. He would be an obvious suspect if something happened to me. Like if I was murdered, he almost certainly would come under suspicion. But if I died from an accident, natural causes... well, that would make it easier for him to take over the company without suspicion. Remember, he already controls thirty percent of the stock he got from Phillip and Lin. With my shares in limbo, he would be a shoo-in to take control.'

'Nasty, nasty,' Tim replied.

After a pause, he added, 'A lot of villagers were swept away like us. Do you think Nue would kill all those people just to get rid of you?'

'This is Thailand, Tim. Life is cheap here. I'm not sure poor villagers matter much to someone like Nue.'

'Seems outrageous.'

'Maybe not.'

Tim didn't respond, so I continued. 'And Tim... what does he do if he finds us here alive?'

'Think nice try. Better luck next time.'

'Or kill us and claim he never found our bodies.'

'You have a very suspicious mind.'

'I have learned to think this way.'

'Trying to stay alive?'

'Yes.' I paused. 'So, if he is behind what happened to the dam, then I don't think we should return to the village.'

'Not worth taking the chance, is it?'

'No.'

'So where do we go.'

'I remember seeing a town called Pailin on a map. It is across the border in Cambodia. Mines are in the region. I have never visited them, but I know the name of the man who runs them. If we can get to Pailin, I think we can get some help.'

'How far is the town from here?'

'I don't know.'

'Do we have any other alternatives?'

'None I can think of.'

'Okay, let's go.'

Tim always made decisions quickly, and he almost never second-guessed himself. He simply got up on his feet and stretched as if he did this every day, ready to start walking.

I, on the other hand, gingerly rolled over on my knees again and slowly lifted my hurting body to a standing position. Every muscle in my side screamed bloody murder when I tried to move, but after some effort, I was finally able to stand upright while Tim surveyed my feeble efforts.

'You don't look too good.'
'Hurts like hell.'
I walked slowly to the stream and bent down in agony, trying to ignore the pain in my side. After washing my hands and face with water from the stream, I paused, wondering if I should take a drink.
As much as I needed water, I could not drink that brown muck.

HONG KONG, SUNDAY, JANUARY 31, 12:10 A.M.

JASON

Intense phosphorescent lights hummed on a myriad of flashing colorful signs attached to buildings at street level far below the high windows of Jason's office.

He had no interest in the cool jazz tempo of these pulsating lights. Jason was too deep into his work, double-checking inventory figures on his company computer screen and comparing them with numbers on the documents he received from Sri Lanka. His work was extremely laborious. After waiting for the documents to arrive from Sri Lanka, he once again was deep into solving his inventory puzzle, hoping this time he had the information he needed to verify his suspicions.

At Jason's request, before every new shipment of gemstones arrived at his office, the cutting factories in Sri Lanka delivered documents to him personally, detailing absolutely accurate numbers: the exact quantity, cut, and color of every single gemstone in the shipments sent to his Hong Kong Distribution House. For several weeks, Jason spent a substantial amount of time comparing these numbers to the numbers in his Distribution House system. To his chagrin, the numbers initially checked out and he began to think he had made a mistake, assuming all his suspicions were nothing more than a statistical error.

He stopped checking for a few weeks until yesterday, Saturday, on his day off. He had some free time and decided to take another look. This time, he found what he was looking for. A small quantity of gemstones from a recent shipment had disappeared into his system. They were noted as being shipped in the inventory, but they did not show up on any outgoing shipping manifest; no invoice, no manifest, just gone. Then again tonight, he discovered that gems that were supposed to be in his inventory yesterday had strangely disappeared from his screen, evaporating into thin air in the last twenty-four hours. No indication of having been shipped, no nothing... simply gone. He began to wonder how many variations of the disappearing gems puzzle he would discover.

Rubbing his eyes after staring at his computer screen for long hours, his sight was getting blurry. Enough for tonight, he thought. Jason shoved his papers into a briefcase and shut down his computer.

He would check again tomorrow to be certain he had not made a mistake.

12:15 PM.
EMPLOYEE

Two floors below him, an employee watched his computer screen go blank. He had been monitoring Jason's activity in the system. The blank computer screen meant his boss was done for the night. The employee was glad because now he could go home.

He wondered why his boss was again looking at the inventory program after stopping for weeks. Oh well, the employee thought. His after hours work meant more money for him, overtime pay. He would make his report and send it in as he had been advised. But that didn't mean he wasn't getting tired of the late hours. He hoped the men who were receiving his reports would tell him his work was no longer needed. Then he could go home to his family at night and on weekends instead of staying at work, but only if the men at the top agreed. Until then, the work was something he knew he had to do. The men who received his reports were very powerful.

He turned out his lights and waited a few minutes. He did not want to be seen leaving the building at the same time as his boss.

THAILAND, MONDAY, FEBRUARY 1, 2:40 P.M.

JOHN

'I need a break,' I said weakly after half stumbling over a small rock.

A tree next to where I was standing was the only thing that kept me from falling over. I held onto it while resting. My feet felt like they were made of stones, and I thought my knees might buckle at any moment. I was dead tired and hungry and thirsty. We had been walking for two days now.

Tim lived in the mountains in Montana. Compared to me, he was completely at ease. He knew how to navigate with the sun, which meant we were fairly confident we were walking in the right direction. But without a map, we could only guess at where we were headed.

That morning, we found a clear mountain stream running through the forest. The water was cold and clear. It tasted good, like receiving the best gift in the world when you are thirsty. We drank greedily until we could drink no more, but we had nothing to carry water, so we couldn't take any of the good stuff with us.

Apart from constantly being thirsty and hungry, my major problem was walking. Not Tim; he was having no problem. But my side hurt every time I took a step. Twisting and turning through rough forest terrain was difficult. I was afraid I was holding Tim up. And the farther we went into the hills, the more water became an issue. At times, we found water, but then, we would go for hours without seeing any streams, just rocks and dirt. And food, eventually, we would need food. We had not eaten since the day before yesterday. More than once, I second-guessed our decision to head for Cambodia. If I was wrong and Nue had not been trying to kill me, then we were needlessly causing ourselves considerable grief.

'Maybe I should go on alone. Come back and get you after I find some help,' Tim volunteered as I leaned against a tree with my head down.

'How are you going to find me again on these hills?' I asked.

'I'm pretty good at this sort of thing.'

'Pretty good isn't good enough.'

I felt guilty holding Tim back, but I wasn't ready to quit, not yet. Besides, he owed me. I had saved his life in the river, didn't I? Although I didn't say this to him, I knew it was true. Plus, I didn't like the idea of being left behind and lost in these never-ending hills.

The terrain was becoming rockier. I hoped this meant we were getting close. I knew the mines at Pailin were somewhere on the other side of the border, but I didn't know exactly where. Our other problem was we weren't sure which way to turn once we were over the border into Cambodia. The mines could be either north or south of our position. It was a fifty-fifty shot. And when your life is in the balance, those aren't great odds.

Tim and I had talked about this. I thought the mines were north of the border. My memory of a map showed them northeast of the village we had visited with Nue. For the last two days, we had traveled east into the hills. Once we were over the border, I thought we needed to turn north toward the mines. But we had one problem. We had no idea how far the river had taken us from our original position. Everything depended on our starting position, and our starting position was a guess.

The other problem was I had badly underestimated the distance we needed to travel to arrive at the border. It didn't look far on a paper map. But short distances on maps don't always translate into a few miles in reality; especially if you are walking through hills covered with trees and rocks.

Pressing slowly away from the tree to test my balance and strength, I mentally prepared to move on, that is, if I could tolerate the pain in my side. A few minutes of rest didn't seem to be of any help. The more I rested, the more my muscles tightened. And the more I tightened up, the worse the pain got. Tim watched me as I tried to disguise how badly I was hurting.

'You sure you want to go on?' he asked. 'We could stop here for the night. I could look for water while you rest.'

'Let's go a little farther.'

'You sure?'

'Yeah,' I said gamely, attempting to lift my foot over a rock that was only about a foot high. I didn't quite make it and was forced to hold on to the tree again to avoid falling. Tim reached over to help.

'I'm okay,' I said in frustration.

'You don't look okay.'

'Let's go.' I forced my feet to move.

My side hurt the most, but then almost every part of my body ached. I walked slowly and deliberately bent into the hill, looking for places to securely place my feet. Occasionally, I had to reach down with my hand to maintain my balance. The last thing I wanted was to fall. If my side hurt now, it would hurt a lot more after a fall. I didn't even want to think about how much pain a fall would cause my broken ribs.

Fortunately, the hills were not really high. But they were steep in places. More than once, we had to double back and look for a better route. That was discouraging, mostly because it is more difficult to walk down a hill than up.

We had been following a trail in the woods for some time, although we weren't really sure it was a trail. It was overgrown in places, but we always managed to pick it up again. Tim said it was probably a trail used by deer or goats. We stayed on the trail because it seemed to be going in the right direction, and it was easier than making a new trail.

After walking for I don't know how long, I had to stop again. I couldn't take another step. I was too tired. After I sat down to rest, Tim went on ahead as a scout so we wouldn't have to double back. My hand didn't look really good when I checked it. I had badly cut my hand grabbing a branch when we were in the water. The flesh was red and oozing blood with black dirt encrusted in coagulated blood in the wound. I had to use it to steady myself and got it dirty. When we found a stream, I washed out the wound with clean water, but it was soon full of dirt again from hanging onto trees and stones for balance. Picking dirt out of the wound only caused it to bleed.

My mouth was dry from breathing hard. I couldn't go much farther, even though I didn't want to stop. Nothing but trees, steel gray rocks, and brown dirt lay ahead on a hillside. Occasionally, the sun beat down on us when the forest opened when we walked in a rocky area. My heavy eyelids temporarily closed as I rested. Whether I wanted to admit it or not, I knew I had neither the will nor the strength to go on, much less stand up again. That's when I felt something touch my shoulder.

Startled, I opened my eyes. An old mountain man with deeply tanned skin and a scrubby beard in a faded gray shirt was leaning over to look at me curiously.

I had nothing to defend myself. I sat very still without saying a word, looking up at him. He took one step back while retrieving a rifle in a leather sling over his shoulder and pointed the barrel directly at me with his finger on the trigger.

NOOSA, 8:50 P.M.

ILANA

Ilana put down her bedside phone as tears formed in her eyes, even though she was trying to hold them back. The news she had just received was worse than anything she could have imagined.

When John and Tim did not arrive as expected in Australia, after the first night and the next day, she couldn't wait any longer. She called the company which owned the plane chartered to fly John and Tim to Australia. John had given her the number. Unfortunately, the charter company could tell her nothing except the plane had landed safely in Bangkok. When John and Tim did not show up the next morning, the plane took off. It couldn't stay. Other flights were scheduled. The man assured Ilana another plane would be sent as soon as Mr. Van Laan called for it.

The next morning, Ilana tried calling Mr. Nue's office. Again, no help, no news. His assistant in Bangkok told her Mr. Nue had not been in contact with his office recently. The woman said she was sorry and could tell Ilana nothing. Ilana left her a number to call in Australia, and the woman promised to call as soon as she had news. Ilana thanked her.

All day yesterday and today, she and Sarah had checked their phones for messages, anxious for any word from their men. They learned nothing. Their phone was silent.

They had eaten some food, but not much. Spent some time walking the beach, little else. All the joy of staying at a resort on the Pacific Ocean was gone. Mostly, they spent time inside their condo, living with terrible daydreams filled with imagined tragedies. Still, they didn't really know anything was wrong. A thousand possible explanations could be responsible for their silent phones. They tried to stay positive.

Some good did come from this time. They got to know each other better. They told stories they may not have communicated on an ordinary day. Ilana began to like Sarah, who was a pretty girl with light brown hair and an easy smile like her husband. Sarah told her about life in the mountains, about how she worked hard on her father's ranch as a child, where there were always chores to do. Births happened when the snow melted, and water began to run in icy mountain streams. Calves were born in the spring and needed to be fed.

Ilana told Sarah stories about her warm island in the sea, which Sarah said she found hard to imagine. These stories helped the women pass their time. They also talked softly about what could be innocently keeping their guys in Thailand. Hopefully, it was nothing more than something like the helicopter had become disabled, and the guys were stuck until it was fixed.

Ilana had tried to believe this was the explanation, but sometimes her heart beat fast to images of their helicopter burning with pieces of torn metal caught in tree branches in the high forest mountains and bloody bodies lying on the ground, dead, hidden by trees. She wondered why she had to be born with such a vivid imagination. At a time like this, it was a curse.

Another day passed. The evening turned into shadows, and their phone finally rang. Ilana now knew the truth, and it was awful. Although it was almost a relief to know, almost easier than living with imagined tragedies... still, it was unbelievably terrible.

Sarah came into Ilana's bedroom when she heard Ilana talking on her phone. She saw her tears, and this was all she needed to see to know the news was bad. Tears began to flow down Sarah's cheeks, and the sight of Sarah's tears only made Ilana's vain attempt to keep her own tears in check... impossible.

Ilana took Sarah's hand, sitting across from her on a bed.

'That was Mr. Nue on the phone,' Ilana said, still hearing the man's calm, dispassionate voice in her ear, speaking as if it was a normal phone call. He said he was sorry to have to tell her over the phone. And when he finished, he asked if she had any questions.

'I asked him if their bodies had been found,' Ilana explained to Sarah. 'He said no, but he thought they would find them in the next few days. He said he was very sorry. They could not have survived the flood waters.'

Sarah sobbed, unable to accept the news.

'Something about a dam breaking,' Ilana explained. 'Water from behind the dam rushed through a river valley where they were walking. They were carried away in a ravaging flood. Hundreds of villagers were also killed,' Ilana paused.

Sarah stared at her in a trance, tears flowing down her rigid face.

Ilana hugged her while Sarah sat with her arms stiff at her side, crying inconsolably.

THAILAND, 5:55 P.M.

JOHN

Out of the corner of my eye, I saw Tim standing a short distance from where I was sitting.

He could do nothing to help me. He didn't have a weapon, and even if he did, I'm not sure Tim could have done anything. The old Cambodian mountain man was standing only a few feet from me with his gun pointed directly in my face.

The truth was, I wasn't much of a threat to anyone. But the old man didn't know this, not in the beginning. But after a minute or two of observing my weakened condition, he put his weapon over his shoulder and took a water bottle from his pack. Opening the bottle, he stuck it in front of my face. I took the bottle from him and thankfully drank some of his water, finally handing the bottle to him. He took a few sips and offered the bottle to me again. I turned my head from side to side in an effort to say no. I didn't want to drink all his water.

'Come here slowly and show your hands,' I said, loud enough for Tim to hear but not so loud it would startle the old man.

The man looked around quickly, saw Tim, and went for his gun again. Tim stopped dead still in the forest and held out his hands. The man motioned with his gun for Tim to come closer. Tim walked slowly, standing in front of the man as if he was on inspection. The man looked at him and then offered him his water bottle. Tim took it and drank. He then bowed to the man and returned his bottle.

While this ceremony was in progress, I was sinking slowly to the forest floor, unable to sit up any longer without support. The two of them turned in unison to observe me. Tim bent over and helped me adjust my position on the ground so I was resting comfortably with my back against a tree trunk. The ground was rocky, damp, and cool, but that didn't matter; I couldn't stand up any longer.

The mountain man looked at Tim and began to speak. We could not understand a word he said. Tim silently turned his head from side to side to indicate he did not understand. Finally, the man stopped talking and pointed at us. I thought he was telling us he wanted us to stay here. He then made some motions with his hands, pointing up a hill, which seemed to indicate he would go somewhere and come back. Tim bowed to him and smiled his irresistible Irish smile. The man smiled in return. At least they had this in common: the universal language of smiles understood by all men.

'Let him go and do whatever it is he is trying to tell us he wants to do,' I said to Tim. 'I don't think we have much choice. As you can see, I'm all done for today.'

Tim smiled again, and the man returned Tim's smile with a smile of his own. I would have found this ceremony comical if I had not felt so awful.

NOOSA, WEDNESDAY, FEBRUARY 3, 7:45 A.M.

ILANA

Mr. Nue was on Ilana's mind all day yesterday, waiting for him to call, hoping he had news about finding the bodies of their men.

To pass the time, she and Sarah had wandered the beach of Noosa to get some fresh air. In the afternoon, they went to a restaurant when it seemed they should be hungry, but they only picked at their food. The people around them looked happy. Why not? This was a resort, after all. It was late summer in Australia, and activity was high. Kids played on the sandy beaches while Ilana and Sarah sat quietly in their condo waiting for their telephone to ring, hoping someone would tell them that bodies had been found in the forest before being put in boxes to fly home to the States for burial.

They waited because they didn't want to go home alone. Somehow, that didn't seem right. They wanted their men to go with them. Finally, Nue called late in the afternoon and told them as if it was a scientific fact. He said the bodies might never be found. The forest may have absorbed them, or the river could have carried them out to the sea.

Dreams of decaying bodies lying in a forest and partially devoured skeletons floating down a river filled Ilana's mind during the night. In the morning, she and Sarah decided to go home. There was no reason to stay. The concierge at the condo complex had been kind. He helped them arrange for airline tickets.

Slowly folding her clothes, Ilana placed them neatly in her carry-on suitcase. She had decided to pack in the morning even though they weren't leaving until late afternoon. Packing was something she could do to take her mind off John's death. Stopping for a moment to look at her suitcase, she remembered the first time she had seen the case. John had purchased it for her in a luggage store in Cancun, Mexico. She had put all her new clothes in the case that day, more new clothes than she ever had in her life. Tears formed in the corners of her eyes as she remembered how happy she was then. Now, she wondered where all her sad tears came from.

Ilana could hear Sarah crying in the other bedroom. Sarah cried often, alone in a strange land, a land far from her home. Fortunately, Sarah had family. She had talked to them on the phone several times. Ilana thought about calling her brother, but she decided he probably would not understand her grief. He might even be glad John was dead. She did not call him.

Ilana went into Sarah's bedroom to console her, putting her arms around her. They had each other to lean on. Ilana wondered what she would have done if Sarah had not been with her.

CHARLOTTESVILLE, VIRGINIA, TUESDAY, FEBRUARY 2, 5:50 P.M.

HELEN

The big varnished oak doors to John's office were closed.

Through an open door in her office, Helen observed the polished silver handles on the doors, expecting to see the handles click and the doors suddenly open. But the imposing doors remained stubbornly closed... silently waiting... waiting to be opened... waiting for John... waiting for clients or partners to arrive... waiting...

Helen wondered if she would ever see the doors open again. Probably not. The person who took John's job as the CEO of the company would probably work from a different office, such as an office in New York or London. This is what Bob Anderson had done. So, this was the end of Helen's career with the company. She tried not to think about that, about losing her job, but it was hard. Her job was her life.

No real work had been accomplished at the Charlottesville office in the last few days. Although employees had arrived each day and assumed the posture of workers doing something, in reality, almost nothing was accomplished. Helen knew why. They, like her, were worried about their jobs. Now, with John gone, they knew everything would change. It had happened before, and it would be worse this time because this time, there was no chance John would ever return. So, there was no reason to hope conditions would ever be the same again.

Helen knew about John's death because Nue had called her and told her to keep the news confidential until it was decided what to do. She had initially tried to hide the news from the other employees, but rumors from their New York office began to circulate, indicating something was terribly wrong. Finally, she had to tell them.

Inside John's office, a small lamp on his desk cast a pale gray shadow over the furniture in the receding light of the afternoon. It was the same light John often used late at night or in the early morning. Helen couldn't bear to turn off the light and leave John's office completely dark. Turning off the light seemed somehow like giving up.

She had entered his office in the morning to close the drapes and turn off the computers. She pushed the chairs neatly around the conference table. Papers on John's desk were arranged by her in well-ordered stacks. The small kitchen behind the black glass doors was cleaned. Helen washed everything, placing clean dishes, cups, and glasses on their proper shelves. It felt good to be doing something. But at the same time, the work felt wrong somehow, almost as if she was washing away an era in time that would never ever return. It was as if she was removing all physical evidence of John's existence.

Off to one side of his desk, she found a notebook which she had never seen before. She would never have opened it if John was still alive, but now... well now, it didn't seem to matter.

The wire-bound notebook had a University of Virginia logo. The word 'JOURNAL' was handwritten with a black marker on the cover. She opened it carefully and began to read. After only a paragraph or two, she realized it was John's personal journal. Reading it felt like she was intruding into his life. Still, she was fascinated, but at the same time, she knew she should stop. Maybe later... maybe when all this was over... not now. She placed his journal on the corner of his desk where she found it. After taking one more glance around his office to be certain everything was in its place, she closed the big oak doors, listening to the silver handles sullenly click shut.

It was time.

Helen had waited all day to do this one final task and still, she waited a little longer, hoping for news which would make it unnecessary. A few days earlier, she had been invited to participate with Bob and Clarence in a conference call with Mr. Nue. Together, they decided to wait three days before sending an announcement. It read:

We regret to inform you that John Van Laan, the Chairman and CEO of Gemstones, Inc., is missing and presumed dead after an accident at a mining site in Thailand. Bob Anderson of New York City will temporarily assume the duties of the CEO of the company pending an election at the next scheduled board meeting.

The announcement was signed by three members of the Board of Directors. Helen had been instructed to send it by fax in the morning, but she had waited hoping for a miracle.

No reprieve had come, and it was time. She couldn't wait any longer. She picked up the announcement and walked to the office fax machine. She had earlier programmed the machine to send the fax to numerous locations all over the world, to all present and past board members of the company, as well as others who were involved in the company and would want to know the news.

Hesitating for a few extra seconds, she stared at the SEND button before finally pushing it.

LANGLEY, VIRGINIA, 6:05 P.M.

CHARLIE

Somewhere deep in the bowels of CIA headquarters, Charlie was exhibiting his normal high energy and high-intensity work ethic. Although it was late in the day, he was still at his desk, laboring over yet another series of the endless reports his superiors demanded. He wondered how he would ever be able to accomplish any real work again if all he did all day was fill out reports, which, in his mind, were nothing more than an endless and meaningless exhibit of institutional nonsense leading nowhere.

The reports took time. They looked and felt like work. And surely, they were work. But what did they really accomplish? Nothing. The reports seemed to be designed for no other purpose than to make everyone feel they were doing something, some work, when, in truth, they were actually doing nothing of importance. The real work was accomplished in the field. Charlie knew this from experience. But now, as a result of being promoted, he felt literally handcuffed to his desk doing nothing except these endless reports. He wondered briefly if he should ask for a demotion so he could return to doing something important again.

In the background, his fax machine buzzed. However, Charlie had by now become so accustomed to the sounds of office machines that he didn't respond to them anymore as he worked at his desk. Finally, after sending enough time and energy on useless reports, he decided it was time to leave his office and get a drink. His buddies from the Agency were probably already at their favorite bar. He clicked save on his computer and shut it down, thinking he could review the reports one more time in the morning before turning them in.

That's when a paper curling out of his fax machine caught his eye. The logo of John Van Laan's company was on the cover page. A quick scan revealed the word 'Announcement.' Helen's signature was at the bottom. Charlie never ignored news from Helen. She sent him copies of all the company's confidential faxes. This slightly unethical behavior was the result of an agreement between the two of them. Helen kept Charlie informed about what was happening at John's office and Charlie agreed to keep Helen informed of any information he thought she should know. Charlie wondered if John knew about Helen's slightly subversive activity. Charlie assumed he did, but he wasn't sure.

After reading the announcement, he quietly laid the fax on his desk and leaned back.

So... it had finally happened.

He had tried to warn John more than once but the man was stubborn. And in the end, Charlie decided it was his attitude which cost John his life. He decided to open an investigation into John's death through his Far Eastern contacts in the morning. No hurry now; John was gone.

Charlie read the fax one more time, this time allowing remembered images of Monica's dead body to run through his mind in the background like an old movie: a memory he normally shut down before it began because he didn't want to think about her anymore.

He wondered if he would ever be able to forget the night she died.

HONG KONG, WEDNESDAY, FEBRUARY 3, 6:10 A.M.

JASON

Jason absentmindedly reached back with his long arm and picked a fax off his machine without looking at it, placing it on top of a pile of papers he would deal with later.

He had come in early in the morning for one reason only: he wanted to finish the work he had begun late last night. After becoming too tired to concentrate last night, he had gone home to sleep. Now, he was once again in his office, deep into a new variation of the 'missing gems' game.

This was what he called his project lately. It was like a high-stakes game. His opponent's task was to make the gems disappear without a trace of evidence. If they won, they could keep the gemstones without paying for them. For Jason to win the game, he had to discover how his opponents were making the gems disappear. His reward would be to send the criminals to jail.

At this particular moment, he was discovering one more way gemstones were disappearing from his Hong Kong Distribution House. This time, the gems had been shipped to a new client. But the invoice for the shipment had apparently been deleted from the system sometime in the last twenty-four hours. And since no trace of the invoice remained in the system, the new client was not obligated to pay for the gems. No invoice, no payment. And even if the invoice existed, it wouldn't matter because the client's name was probably phony. The client's address was a P.O. box in Singapore and it was probably a dead end.

Jason wrote detailed notes on this new variation of the game. He had a lot of notes: quantities and descriptions of the gemstones from the original documents sent to him from Sri Lanka, copies of original invoices that had disappeared, copies of missing shipping manifests, and finally, the names and addresses of the phony clients. He leaned into his chair and stretched while wondering what John was going to do when he received the evidence of fraud.

He was pretty sure he knew.

Heads would roll.

6:15 AM.
Employee

Two floors below Jason, an employee was making equally copious notes on all of Jason's activities. However, he did not have the Sri Lanka documents supplied to Jason. As a result, the employee could only speculate about what Jason was trying to accomplish. But even so, he could see something was not right.

After looking at his notes from the previous day, he remembered an invoice Jason had looked at. A search for this invoice in the system today was a dead end. Odd, he thought. Maybe the shipment had been canceled. That was a possible explanation for a deleted invoice. However, there was another explanation, but he didn't want to consider it. None of this was his business.

His only responsibility was to report Jason's activities in detail, nothing more. And he was doing the work. But if his suspicions were correct, someone might get hurt. Now, he wished he had never volunteered for this job. The extra money he was earning would mean nothing if he was fired. Maybe it would be better to simply ignore everything and tell his superiors he had discovered nothing.

He didn't have to file another report until tomorrow. He had time to think about what to do. He noticed Jason had turned off the inventory program on his computer. The employee was glad. He had other work to do this morning.

6:20 A.M.
Jason

Before moving on to his normal work routine for the day, Jason glanced at the pile of faxes on his desk. The one on top was an announcement. Helen's name was on the bottom of the cover page. Curious, he decided to read it before doing anything else. A tremor immediately ran through his body as he reread the fax for a second time, still trying to understand what shouldn't be possible.

Immediately dialing Charlottesville, he waited impatiently for her to pick up. 'Helen. Please...'

'I know Jason. I have been expecting your call. I'm surprised you got through. Everyone has been calling.'

'What happened?' Jason asked.

Cold fear ran through his body as he talked to her. All of a sudden, he felt very alone in a faraway city that was not his home, surrounded by foreigners who were not his friends.

And the game in his briefcase, who was going to help him with this now? He could ignore it for a while. It wasn't as if the number of gems that were disappearing was of any great consequence. They barely showed on the radar screen compared to the total sales of his Distribution House.

But still, it was something he could not ignore forever.

NOOSA, AUSTRALIA, 3:20 P.M.

ILANA

A family dressed in brightly colored bathing suits and t-shirts, carrying towels and shovels, strolled a path surrounded by waving beach grass leading to the shore. After arriving at the beach, the father spread a big blue towel on the sand and sat down to relax. His children, a boy and a girl, aged eight and five, grabbed shovels and ran laughing to where gentle waves splashed on the shore in monotonous regularity. The Pacific Ocean looked warm and inviting. The boy immediately dropped his shovel and ran into the water, screaming with delight.

His mother looked up in alarm. 'He's in the water, Henry. Go down there and make sure he doesn't drown.'

Henry, the boy's father, had been busy surveying the beach for pretty young ladies in skimpy bathing attire. At the sound of his wife's voice, he looked up at her frowning, insistent demeanor and determined it would do no good to argue. Dragging his overweight body off his beach towel, he yelled at his son.

Inside a nearby condo overlooking the sea, none of this happy activity was of any interest to the inhabitants. Sarah was finishing her packing after one more good cry. Ilana was helping her. They were almost done putting Sarah's clothes in her suitcases. Soon, a resort van was outside their door, and it was time to leave for the airport. Their bill had been paid, and they had checked out of their room. The only task remaining was to go to the airport and board a plane for a long journey home, flying first from Noosa to Melbourne, then taking a trans-Pacific plane from Melbourne to San Francisco. From there, Sarah would fly to Salt Lake City and then to Copper, Montana, where her father would drive her home.

Ilana's itinerary had her flying from San Francisco to Atlanta and then to Charlottesville. It promised to be a long day and night of travel for both women. Ilana was not looking forward to her eleven-hour flight to San Francisco. But even more, she dreaded having to say goodbye to her friend Sarah. They had become soul mates in the last few days, and so she was not looking forward to leaving the one person who had been a comfort.

That's when their evil telephone rang.

Ilana looked at Sarah. Both of them had gotten to a point of mental exhaustion where they had no desire to answer the phone - only bad news came from this phone. Ilana briefly toyed with the idea of ignoring it.

'Hello,' she reluctantly picked it up out of habit as much as anything.

'Is this Sarah?' an older man's voice with an obvious Australian accent asked.

'No, I am Ilana.'

'Yes, Ilana... of course. My name is Clarence Aldridge,' the man said. 'I met you in Montana last spring. You remember, at a cabin in the mountains? John Van Laan is my friend and business partner.'

Clarence paused. He couldn't get himself to say John 'was' a friend. But it would have been correct to use the word 'was' since John was presumed dead.

'I live and work in Australia,' Clarence continued. 'I wanted to offer you my services while you are in my country. If there is anything I can do to help you, please ask.'

'No... I mean, thank you, Mr. Aldridge. But we are leaving in a few minutes...'

'Oh... okay then. I wish I could ask you if you enjoyed your stay in my country, but this must be terrible for you.'

Ilana didn't know what to say.

'I'm so sorry, Ilana,' Clarence repeated.

'It is okay, Mr. Aldridge. I will return to Belize now.'

'I wish I could do something for you.' He waited for a reply, and when it did not come, he asked, 'Could I talk to Sarah, please?'

'Yes, here she is.' Ilana handed the phone to Sarah, who had been listening to Ilana's conversation.

'No,' Sarah turned away, refusing the phone. 'I don't want to talk to anyone.'

'It is Clarence Aldridge.'

Sarah looked at the phone briefly and finally took it. Ilana listened as Sarah talked softly into the portable white phone.

Clarence and Tim were buddies. They had frequently consulted with each other on mining matters and their operations were not very different. Tim had been to Australia to visit Clarence's mining operation, and Clarence had visited Tim and Sarah in Montana. Sarah liked Clarence. She began to cry again while she talked. Eventually, she put the phone down and went into the bathroom to wash her face one more time.

Ilana finished her packing and closed Sarah's luggage, dragging her suitcase to the door with a sigh. Sitting down on a couch in the living room, exhausted from mental stress; she absentmindedly stared out of the condo's window toward the beach, momentarily distracted by a family outside on the beach, playing and laughing as she watched. A young boy was in the water, splashing his father, who was splashing back. The boy soon became bored. After getting no satisfaction from splashing someone who could splash him back, he decided it would be more fun to splash on his little sister, who was playing innocently near the shore. The girl instantly screamed when the cool water hit her warm body, and although Ilana could not hear his father, she could see the man yelling at his son.

Ilana envied the family. She would have liked to have been the girl on the beach. Illana's parents had died when she was young. And they were seldom home even before they died. Her mother's days were spent working and cleaning resorts. And her father was always gone fishing.

Now Ilana's chance for a family of her own had disappeared with the death of John. Ilana wanted to pity herself as she sat looking out the window, but she could not. John was dead. She could do nothing to change this fact. She needed to move on. Still, she briefly wondered why it always had to be this way. Why other people seemed to find happiness, if not in their youth, then maybe when they were older? Why couldn't she? As images of her unhappy childhood ran through her mind, she questioned why, when you are older, even then, the child you left behind never completely leaves you. Why did the young, lonely girl of her youth still live inside her mind, deep in her darkened memories of the times when she played alone on sad, empty beaches?

As she sat looking outside her window while no longer interested in the beach activity, she remembered how the waters surrounding her island would retreat down the shore, leaving behind small interesting remnants on the beach for a poor young girl to find. Tiny bits of sea life, such as empty sea shells or brittle brown carcasses of horseshoe crabs and soft, tan, leggy sponges; these gifts from the sea were given to her, a poor, lonely girl. Or smooth, round black and white stones and pieces of sculpted driftwood, they were the toys of her childhood.

She had so many hopes for a better life after meeting John. He had taught her so many new and wonderful things. It was as if life, like the sea, had offered her a new set of wondrous toys to examine. The most important was the love of a man. It was something she never had before.

Now, everything had changed and she had been forced to return to being a lonely girl again, the same lonely girl she had been as a child. It was as if life had taken her full circle, back to weeping by a seashore.

She wiped her eyes. It was time to leave.

The cursed phone rang again.

Ilana's first instinct was to find Sarah so they could get out of their room quickly before she had to answer any more phone calls. All she wanted was to be away from this place of grief and tears.

The phone rang several more times.

Ilana stared at it. She didn't really want to talk to anyone, and she knew Sarah was in no shape to take another call. They needed to be gone.

The phone continued to ring.

She picked it up. 'Yes?'

'Ilana, it's John. Can you hear me?'

'Who?' Ilana asked. The connection was bad, and she could not really hear the voice very clearly through the static.

'It's me, Ilana, John Van Laan. I am in Cambodia. Tim is with me.'

Ilana hesitated, listening to her heart beat wildly, afraid to believe what she was hearing.

'Ilana?' John repeated into his phone, which had inexplicably gone soundless.

'John, is it really you?' Ilana asked so silently John could almost not hear her.

'It is. Now listen very carefully. Don't tell anyone where I am or that you have talked to me. I am calling from a pay phone. We are traveling to Australia to meet you, but it will take us a few days. I will call you again when I can. Please, it is important you don't tell anyone I called. Do you understand?'

'I understand.'

'Okay, are you all right? I can't hear you very well.'

'I am now,' she replied louder.

'Okay, good. Tim wants to say hi to Sarah. Is she there?'

'Yes.'

'Can you get her? And remember, tell no one.'

'Sarah,' Ilana yelled into the bathroom in her excitement. 'Sarah, Tim is on the phone!'

Sarah appeared in the doorway, looking at Ilana wide-eyed.

'It's Tim. Here, take the phone.'

HONG KONG, SATURDAY, FEBRUARY 6, 9:40 A.M.

JASON

Completely oblivious to a mess of neglected, stale beer bottles and broken potato chips scattered over a table next to his favorite lounge chair, Jason slept in the living room of his apartment. Only a few feet from where he rested, out of sight, lying hidden beneath a low wooden coffee table covered with dated American newspapers and a few old magazines, was his brown leather briefcase. It had not been opened for several days.

Thirty stories below the windows of his Hong Kong apartment, pedestrians weaved around each other, strolling to the tune of their internal music - Saturday errands to do, places to go, and items to buy. It was a nice day, cool but pleasant, with a warm winter sun casting active shadows in step with the pedestrians on the sunny side of the street.

However, Jason was unaware of the human confusion below him. In fact, Jason was seldom a witness to any activity in his neighborhood during the day. Jason was mostly familiar with the empty gray streets near his apartment building at night. Streets illuminated by lamps and colorful neon signs. He had very little interest in his apartment or its neighborhood. He only required a bed for sleeping, a kitchen for food, and a closet to hang his clothes. He had rented his apartment primarily because it was located not far from his office. It meant he could walk to work.

He had tried to make his place reasonably comfortable. A Washington Redskins football poster and a few framed photographs of the Shenandoah Valley, picturesque views of the mountains near where he was raised, were taped on his walls, reminding him of his real home. But most of the time, his apartment was an ignored wasteland, filled with unwashed pans lying scattered on the kitchen counters and in the sink. An unmade bed was in another room. Jason didn't care. He never spent much time there. He was always at work.

However, in recent days, he had become less motivated to go to work. He wasn't putting in long hours at his office as before John's death, although he knew he should. When a new CEO was appointed by the board of directors for the company, Jason would have to prove to the new guy he could do his job. He would no longer have John in his corner. He had proved himself to John. He wondered if he could prove himself to a new CEO. But then, he wondered if he really cared. With John gone, it would all be so different.

His other problem was in his briefcase. He had ignored this problem because it didn't seem important anymore, not compared to John's death. Besides, he didn't know who to tell even if he wanted to. Who in the company could he trust with the information? Obviously, someone in his Distribution House was stealing gemstones. That much he had proved. But he did not know who or even how many employees were involved. It was possible everyone in the Hong Kong Distribution House was involved. And until he knew who was responsible, he didn't know who he could ask for help. Asking the wrong person could get him killed.

A videotape of a recent American movie was playing on his TV, flashing lights across the dark room where he slept. The shades in his apartment had been drawn to make the picture on his TV screen come alive with color. But the images had not held his attention for long. The movie didn't have much of a plot. It was an action thriller, one mad fight scene after another. Jason had fallen asleep after about half an hour. His body badly needed rest after all the late nights at the office.

NOOSA, TUESDAY, FEBRUARY 9, 7:05 A.M.

ILANA

In the half-light of a predawn morning, Ilana lay in bed, staring at the silent white portable phone on her nightstand, hoping and wishing it would ring.

Turning over, she closed her eyes, hoping to think about something else. Waiting and listening for their phone to ring had become slow torture for the ladies in the last few days. Time stood still. Seconds turned into minutes, minutes into hours.

The first phone call from John and Tim made them feel as if they had been reborn. Their men were alive, and their life renewed. But no one else knew, and the women soon began to feel isolated, their world seemingly not real. They needed a phone call from their guys to reassure them that they were really alive. The truth of their survival in the river needed to be validated. Perhaps it was only a cruel hoax. They had not seen John and Tim with their eyes, not held them in their arms, lingered with them in smiles. This they needed. They wanted physical contact urgently. So, when the white telephone was silent for hours, or recently for more than a day, fears slithered inside their minds like tiny worms. And in the dark place in their hearts, the place full of tears and sorrow, panic took control of their emotions and it was difficult to fight off their fear.

As Ilana rested on the side of the bed nearest to the sliding glass doors of her condo, she could see past her balcony to the beach and the big blue Pacific Ocean. Mornings were usually special - the ocean was alive, running in long rows of giant waves breaking in a crescendo of crashing water on the shore. Except some days, like today, were different. Today, the languid blue waters of the ocean rested in an eerie, still, glassy calm. Only a few low lumbering waves rolled undetected beneath the surface of its smooth waters, barely breaking the placid calm surface of the ocean near shore, washing harmlessly onto the beach before sliding ignominiously back into the sea.

She thought about a morning walk on the beach. The sun would be rising soon, turning a gray morning sky into a new blue day. She had been awake for hours. She needed to be out of bed. Still, it was nice to rest beneath warm sheets. And she could see the ocean from where she lay. So why not remain in bed where she felt shielded from the world? It might not be the same outside. On the beach, she would become entangled with the commotion of life. In bed, she was simply an observer. Outside, she would be forced to feel the wind flowing over her body, watch the shore birds scurrying on vibrating stick legs, picking at invisible food in the sand, and sense the ocean restlessly seeking her attention, drawing her to its constant agitated motion. That was not true when she was in her bedroom. In her bedroom, she felt safe from all this needless confusion.

Rolling over, she looked at her phone, again feeling a scared longing for it to ring, fighting a still small voice inside her head that said that it would never ring again... not ever. Maybe something had happened to John, something bad. She had been trying to convince herself he was alive, fighting off a panic of his assumed death. She woke up early that morning, suddenly afraid his phone calls were a dream, an illusion created by a deep need inside her to be with him.

But their men were alive.

They are alive.

She repeated this phrase over and over again to fight off her doubts and fears. She knew they were close to Phnom Penh because John had told her. He said their journey was difficult but not to worry. They were making progress. He explained he was injured and beaten up by the river, but he would be alright. He would heal. Don't worry.

She closed her eyes and rested for a moment, almost falling asleep again before once again opening her eyes and staring at her phone.

Outside her balcony, the sun rose out of the ocean, filling the sky with an orange glaze that frosted the low gray clouds near the horizon in color. Ilana did not see the clouds. She had closed her eyes. In a dream, she heard a knock on her door. Then she heard it again.

She thought she was dreaming...

Wasn't she?

She ignored it.

Footsteps in the hall; Sarah walking to the door of their condo from her bedroom.

Ilana waited; her eyes closed and her heart beating wildly in the stillness of her fears.

CHARLOTTESVILLE, MONDAY, FEBRUARY 8, 5:07 P.M.

HELEN

It was way too early to go home by Helen's standards. She seldom left work early, normally not until well after six. Some days, she never left the office until after eight. Helen was John's in-house secretary, and John always worked late. So, it seemed only natural for Helen to work the same hours.

Besides, her apartment was not an exciting place. It was far more interesting to be at work. New York, Hong Kong, and London were on the line at work. Someone was always calling at work. Something was always happening at the three Distribution Houses or the mines. People in other parts of the world apparently did not care that time zones existed or that the employees at the main office needed to eat and sleep like ordinary people. They were expected to be constantly available to problem solve, twenty-four hours a day.

As a result, she and many other employees put in long hours, John more than anyone else. Plus, Helen knew that John also fielded calls late into the night from his apartment long after he left his office. Most days, she would come to work early only to find him already in his office, dressed in casual clothes, talking to someone. She wondered if the man ever slept.

Now she wondered why. What did all his hard work accomplish? All those long days and nights, had it done him any good? Or had it all only brought him more trouble than it was worth?

And for her also, trouble.

Soon, she would have to find another job. She wondered how she would be viewed by a prospective employer. Would he see a woman who could out-work almost anyone? Or would he see an old, broken-down woman? But then... why did she care? She knew she would never find another job like this one, nothing as interesting with the same set of characters she had met at this job, people who had come to be her friends, people who lived all over the world. It had been great. But now it was coming to an end; no real reason to stay in the office past five anymore. She should go home.

Turning off her computer, she straightened her desk. Force of habit, she thought, neat and tidy to the end. She couldn't help herself.

Her telephone rang.

She instinctively reached for the receiver.

NOOSA, FEBRUARY 9, 7:10 A.M.

JOHN

'You okay, old man?' Tim asked me with a smile.

'I'm fine. Thanks for asking.'

In truth, I was anything but fine. I was tired. I was sore. I smelled bad. A week's growth of stubble constantly itched on my face. I pitied the guy who had the airline seat next to me on the last leg of our flight. My smell must have been pretty awful for him, which was good in a way because the guy had slid to the opposite side of his seat as far from me as he possibly could. He gave me plenty of room. He didn't try to monopolize my armrest. For this, I was grateful, and I understood. I must have looked bad.

But despite the extra room and no matter how hard I tried to find a comfortable position, sitting in an airplane seat, which was not designed for comfort, I couldn't. My side hurt. Constantly adjusting my position didn't help. Nothing worked; no matter how much I tried, I hurt. Finally, I gave in and tried to ignore the pain, something I had been doing for a week but with only a limited degree of success.

Tim didn't look much better than me. He was a mess. His clothes looked like they had come from a Salvation Army store, and he spent a month sleeping on city streets.

A week ago, we had both looked pretty good. But ground-in mud from the flooded river had never been washed out of our clothes. And our journey down to Phnom Penh had done nothing to improve our appearance. We didn't stop for long in any one place. We kept moving after short rests, so there was no time to clean up.

When we arrived at the airport in Phnom Penh, the red-eye to Melbourne was at the gate and ready to leave. We ran for the plane, which was not a great idea for someone in my condition, but we made it. However, this meant we did not have an opportunity to call our ladies before our flight took off.

At Melbourne, we caught a red-eye flight to Noosa. And we didn't call their condo in between flights because it was late at night.

We didn't want to wake them. The net result was we hadn't talked to them for more than a day, and they didn't know where we were. They didn't know two scruffy, dirty, dead tired, hurting, smelly, and a little horny guys were standing outside the door of their condo.

Not that I was overly concerned about being horny. Sex was not a high priority. All I really wanted... badly wanted... was a warm bath and a week of sleep. And I never wanted to ever see my dirty, smelly clothes again.

Tim knocked on the door. Not too loud; he didn't want to scare the women inside. They could be sleeping. It was early in the morning. However, we had no idea what time it was.

'Go ahead and knock a little louder,' I said. 'I can't stand here all day.'

The open hallway outside their condo was interrupted by closed doors. A railing was a safety barrier on the other side. It was not an attractive area; the side of the building opposite the ocean. It was a sad, empty place to be waiting for a door to open. I hoped that wonder and love lived on the other side of the door. I had dreamed about this moment for a week. It had kept me going. A beautiful woman who, I hoped, still loved me resided inside the room on the other side of the door. She was my world. My last brush with death had made this even clearer than before. I thought of Ilana often as we bounced and banged down uneven roads in a jeep. Every turn, every bump in the road hurt. Tim had asked me several times each day if we should stop and rest for a while. And rest was exactly what my body was aching to do, but I couldn't stop because she was not with me. I wanted to rest where she was.

I wondered what she had been thinking. I wondered what Nue had told her. She had probably been told we were dead. I hoped she wanted me as much as I wanted her. Our phone calls helped, but they were not enough. I needed to see her, hold her, kiss her tender lips.

Standing outside her door, my body began to feel as if it was finally breaking down, no longer able to hold up. It had made it this far, fueled by a mixture of adrenalin and hope. Now, I could go no farther. My side was a mass of pain. I felt like I was going to fall over any second. My face itched; I needed a shave. I smelled; I needed a bath. I was a tired and broken man. But I had made it. I smiled to myself, knowing I had accomplished what seemed almost impossible in retrospect.

'What are you smiling about?' Tim asked.

'You... you don't look too good,' I replied.

'Yeah. You look like shit,' he countered.

'Thanks for the confidence booster.'

He smiled and knocked on the door again.

'Who's there?' a weak voice I recognized as Sarah's asked through the closed door.

'It's Tim, Sarah. Open the door for God's sake. I need a kiss.'

7:35 A.M.
John

Hot, soapy water breathed into every pore of my dirt-encrusted, badly abused body as I leaned my head on the side of a big white bathtub, resting in warm luxury. Ilana was somewhere in the bedroom. I could hear her moving around. She had helped me undress while I sat on the side of her bed and listened to hot water filling the bathtub. I wanted to sleep badly, but I told her I needed a bath first... although... I wondered if I could stay awake in the tub.

'What do you want me to do with your clothes?' she called from the bedroom.

'Burn them. I don't ever want to see those clothes again,' I replied from the bathtub.

My side ached, but it hadn't felt this good since the flood. I closed my eyes and let the memories of my ordeal come over to me, thinking about how we had pushed to get out of Cambodia. It was all worth it now. I was glad I had kept moving. The old Cambodian man, I could still see him in my mind. We had not been able to speak to each other. I could not understand a word he said, and he could not understand us, but we communicated with a language composed of smiles and gestures. He helped us through the hills and found a jeep and driver for hire. I wondered if I would ever be able to thank the old man properly. Someday, maybe, I would find a way. I think he knew from my smiles how much I depended on him during those days of walking in a forest with no trails. I wondered why he did it. He could have left us. It would have been easier for him. I doubt we would have made it without him.

'May I join you?' she asked.

I opened my eyes, relieved to be out of the forest. She was still dressed in her pink pajamas, a colorful bird embroidered on her pink t-shirt top with matching boxer shorts. I wanted nothing more at that moment than to lie in the tub and luxuriate in its warm, cleansing embrace, but I couldn't deny her.

'Sure.'

She undressed slowly, looking at me several times as if she was wondering if it was really me. Slipping naked into the water facing me, she sat down carefully between my legs, her small feet wiggling up along my side. I held her feet to keep them from hitting my sore ribs. Slowly, I massaged her toes in the hot water while trying to ignore a growing desire. My body needed rest, nothing more. But the lady was so beautiful. I smiled when she slipped gingerly toward me, touching me in a place that made me groan, this time with pleasure.

'I see you are still alive, John Van Laan.' she laughed.

'I am hurting, but I'm not dead.'

'Does it hurt down here?' she said, holding me where it didn't hurt at all, where it felt so good. It had been too long, and even though I knew this would not be good for my side, I had no choice.

'No, that does not hurt,' I replied honestly.

'Where does it hurt?'

'My side. I think my ribs are broken.'

'I will be gentle with you.'

'Okay,' I submitted, leaning back and closing my eyes.

Rising up out of the water, she stood over me, lowering her naked body down gently until I entered her. Slowly at first and without ever leaning on me, she moved rhythmically as I reached up to touch her firm young breasts and ran my hands down her sides in the warm, gentle water, finally letting it happen. All the pain and fear of the last few weeks were released in one anguished moment of extreme pleasure as if my recent sad adventure had never happened.

Then she rested, lying on my chest, her tears blending in with the warm bathwater.

HONG KONG, WEDNESDAY, FEBRUARY 10, 6:05 A.M.

JASON

A cup of coffee steamed on the kitchen counter in his apartment as Jason dialed a long-distance number. He didn't really know why he had chosen to call her. It felt more like he was calling his mother than making a business call.

His briefcase was still on the floor in his living room, out of sight, having not been moved for days. Dust had begun to accumulate on it, camouflaging its appearance, disappearing into the floor of his apartment beneath a wood table covered with magazines and old newspapers. It had not traveled with Jason to his office. He did not need it anymore. His work had become routine, eight to five like any other ordinary manager. He had a job to do, and he did it well. But he was not comfortable. His future was uncertain, and his neglected briefcase was bothering him. Something needed to be done with its contents. He knew he had a responsibility; he couldn't let it sit forever.

But what to do? Who to tell?

He didn't know.

John... John would know what to do. But John was dead.

He thought about telling Bob. But that did not seem like a good idea. Bob was an old fool. If he told Bob and Bob gave the information to the wrong person, it could put him in danger. No, Bob was not an option. In fact, the more he thought about it, the more confused he became. Round and round he went, trying to decide who to call, getting nowhere fast. And as a result, he did nothing because he did not know what to do.

Maybe he could tell Helen? he wondered. No, she wouldn't know what to do any more than he did. In fact, why was he calling her? He wasn't sure even as he listened to his phone ring her number. Just wanted to talk, he concluded; he just needed to talk to someone he trusted.

When they were working together in Charlottesville, Jason

and Helen talked all the time. Their offices were close to each other. It was easy to walk over to Helen's office and get the latest company news. Helen knew everything. Jason sometimes concluded Helen knew company info even John did not know. People confided in her. She was the company's mother.

'Hi, Helen. It's Jason,' he heard himself say into his phone after she answered. 'Yes, I just thought I would call and... you know... like old times... have a chat, only from a few thousand miles away.'

Helen returned his greeting. It didn't take much to get her started. Helen liked to talk. And it had been quiet at the office with John gone. Helen was not receiving as many phone calls as before. Company buzz was probably circumventing Charlottesville since the notice of John's death. So, without any urging from Jason, Helen was only too happy to rattle on to Jason's amusement and contentment. He listened even though he was only vaguely aware of what she was saying. It was pleasant simply to hear the sound of her voice. It made him feel as if he was home.

'Nothing new concerning John?' he finally asked when she took a breath.

Helen answered his question by telling him about preparations for a memorial service in Michigan. Other than this, she had nothing new to report. She did say the company was in no hurry to select a new CEO. Bob had told her it was decided to wait until the next quarterly board meeting.

Nonetheless, she had heard some discussion about a successor to John. She also mentioned that a man named Phillip Palmer had called. Mr. Palmer had asked her some rather odd questions. Helen had tried to answer Phillip's questions, but only briefly.

Jason remembered the name Phillip Palmer. Wasn't he a member of the board of directors for a short time? Jason wondered silently what had happened to him and why he had now resurfaced.

'Okay, thanks, Helen. It's been good talking to you,' Jason hesitated, briefly wondering again if he might tell her about the contents of his briefcase. He decided not to.

'Let me know if anything new surfaces.'

NOOSA, FRIDAY, FEBRUARY 12, 11:50 A.M.

JOHN

Voices swept over me like music from a mellow jazz ensemble, blending their notes into sweet melodies as I lay in bed. I neither cared nor heard what the voices were saying; just content to know they were nearby.

A framed picture hung on the wall in the condo, a beach scene painted with impressionistic pastels, blending colors in faded patterns of light. The picture briefly held my attention, but not for long, as I listened to the music of their voices coming from another room. After a while, I rolled over on my side in bed because the muscles in my back were beginning to ache from lying in one position too long. My ribs were still sore, but they were beginning to heal. I could breathe now without too much pain, and I could turn over in bed. It was still painful to stand, but the pain was manageable, not sharp jabs like before. Over the last few days, I had mostly dozed on and off in bed, getting up only to relieve myself. But the truth was, I didn't really need to sleep much anymore. Yet I had very little desire to leave my bed.

Ilana had been spending most of her time either resting with me or caring for me, bringing food and water. She told me her story about when she learned I was dead. Nue's phone call had been difficult to hear; a terrible emotional trauma for her and Sarah. I felt guilty and responsible for their pain. I wondered if I could have avoided it. Should I have been smarter? Should I have seen catastrophe coming and done something different?

Collectively, we decided only a few people should be told Tim and I were alive. Tim called his family, Sarah hers; no one else. Ilana called David, who called my family. Everyone was instructed to say nothing to no one. As far as anyone in the company was concerned, I was still dead. I hoped this would buy us a few days of peace, a few days of rest so I could heal.

The bedroom in the condo had become my security blanket

in a way. It was like a warm cocoon sheltering me from a painful world. It was a place where no one knew about John Van Laan, and no one wanted to kill John Van Laan.

Ilana, Tim, and Sarah were close. I had food and drinks and a safe place to rest. I cared for nothing more.

My eyes closed, and my only wish was to sleep without dreams, no rushing waters... no glass-shattering bullets out of silent air. I wanted nothing, just to be still, inert... my mind a void.

My only problem was that I had little to no control over the images that were constantly racing through my subconscious, like pictures of Arny and Monica lying uncomfortably dead in pools of their blood. Or Monica's funeral filled with red rose petals silently falling like blood past the soft round edges of her polished wood casket. I constantly wondered how long before death would be my fate like theirs: my body lying in a padded casket, trapped and dead, confined to fear and terror, buried forever in a dark place with no light.

A shiver of cold fear washed over me whenever I thought about how close I had come to dying. When my eyes involuntarily closed, I would relive my horrible experience in the river. As a result, I had been trying to keep my eyes open and look at nothing. The white walls of the condo bedroom suited me fine. I spent hours looking at these white walls. I did not look outside. The beach outside my bedroom windows held no joy for me. I did not see playing children or a blue ocean. I had nothing in common with them. They existed in another world, the real world, a place full of pain and fear, a place where terror ruled. A place filled with shipwrecks lying on the seafloor next to the old gray boots of dead sailors deep in black ocean waters. I wondered if I had died in the river, would my boots now be lying on the sand at the bottom of the ocean?

By all logic, that should have been my fate. I should have died in that river, my body floating relentlessly out to the sea, slowly disintegrating into skull and bones, caught in tides of restless activity until only my boots remained, stirring on the shifting sands of some tidal pool.

I wondered why life was full of tears and anger. Dark days

filled with red rose petals falling from funeral wreaths lying on a wood casket? I remembered walking past Monica's closed casket on the day of her funeral. Her parents had wanted it closed. I was glad. I didn't really want to see a lifeless smile on her dead face.

A red rose wreath had covered her casket. I had wondered why people thought flowers were appropriate for funerals. Flowers are full of life and color. Death is cold and dark. Wouldn't it be more appropriate to send vases of dirt or dust to be scattered on the grave site? Dust to dust; aren't we just dust in the end?

One of the rose petals from the wreath had slowly fallen to the floor as I passed her casket. I picked up the soft, delicate petal and put it in my pocket. Now, a dull red, dried, brittle rose petal was hidden between the pages of a book somewhere in my library. I made a mental note to find that petal when I returned home and place it where I could see it.

Home... just thinking about home sent a shudder of involuntary panic running through my body. When I got home, it would all start again: all the problems, all the pain. I held my breath thinking about home, my heart pounding as I waited for the frantic tremors to slowly subside, to ease so I could think clearly again.

Perhaps... I wondered. Perhaps it would be better to stay in this place by the sea. It was better than going home. It was warm and comfortable here. No one knew I was alive here. No one would come looking for me here, wanting to kill me.

I closed my eyes and tried to sleep without dreaming.

HONG KONG, 1:15 P.M.

THIEF

His shoes crept over the carpet without making an impression. A martial arts master at the highest level, the thief could enter a room and leave it again as if no one had ever been inside, as if even the air in the room had been undisturbed by his presence.

His task was to find a brown briefcase and remove its contents, papers which would then be photocopied before being replaced in the briefcase again; all accomplished before Jason returned to his apartment after work. It was a simple job. Not one which required the skills of this man. Still, he had been paid well, and an important person had hired him. He accepted the job without comment.

The man looked quietly around the room taking his time, allowing the furnishings to filter through his consciousness. Finding an object in a room was often easier if you let it come to you rather than furiously searching for it, your eyes darting from one object to another. A logical flow was present in most rooms, a flow created by the routine activities of its inhabitants. In the end, the object he was looking for would come to him if he followed the flow. It would reveal its location.

The apartment's bedroom was the first room he searched. If something was important, it was usually hidden in a bedroom. Most thieves come at night and it is difficult to take something in a bedroom at night without its owner knowing. But the briefcase was not found in the bedroom. Next, he searched a room used by Jason as a spare office. The martial arts expert assumed the briefcase would be in one of these two rooms, but it was not. He then searched the living room, waiting for the briefcase to come to him, and it did. Finally, under a low table, only partially hidden, it was an object that did not logically fit with the other objects in the room. It was a distraction. Something which should have been in a more appropriate place.

The man slid the briefcase from under the newspapers which partially hid it, slowly so the dust which had accumulated on the outside was unmarked. Opening it carefully, he took a mental picture of how the papers appeared in the briefcase before he lifted them from the case.

This was important because he would return the papers to the case exactly as he found them.

NOOSA, WEDNESDAY, FEBRUARY 17, 10:20 A.M.

JOHN

Murky water rushes over my open eyes. I can't see. I can't breathe.

Strong currents hold me under the discolored water as if a hundred hands are reaching up to pull me into its liquid hell. It was just like when I was in the river in Thailand, not knowing if I was swimming up or swimming down. My lungs cry for air. Out of nowhere, a large, jagged rock appears in the moving gray abyss. I cannot avoid it. It hits me, hurting me deep inside. I curl up in agony as my blood passes slowly through the murky waters. Small black rocks like gunshot pellets sting my body. I don't see them until it is too late.

That's when she appeared, gliding through the troubled waters almost as if she is lazily swimming for pleasure in the clear, warm waters of the Caribbean, sliding up beside me, her long red hair flowing in the water.

'It's okay, John,' Monica says calmly.

'How can it be okay?' I ask. 'I'm dying here. Can't you see that?'

'I can, but I'm telling you everything will be alright.'

Seeing her, I'm both terrified and elated at the same time. I search her face for a clue, wondering if she is a dream? I touch her. I can actually touch her face. She must be alive. She smiles.

'Why have you returned to me?' I ask her. 'Why now?'

'You seem so unsure of yourself,' she replies. 'I wanted to assure you that you don't need to worry. You will be fine... or maybe...maybe... I just wanted to see you again. Is that so bad?'

'No, of course not, but can you help me get out of here?' I ask, twisting and turning in the swirling waters, slowly dying, needing air to breathe.

'Don't worry,' she says again. 'This will pass. I know it has been very hard for you, but it is time for you to move on now.'

The white phone on my bedside table abruptly rings, waking me.

Sweat covered my face. I realized I had been dreaming, a dream so terrifyingly real, and yet, I almost preferred my dream to being awake. Monica was with me in the dream. I was dreaming about her again. Something I did often in the past but not lately. So why now?

My bed had become my refuge. I had only been out of my bed a few times in the last week, and then only at the insistence of Ilana. I always retreated back to my bed after only a short time because fear lived outside the walls of the condo where we were staying. Every time I thought about leaving this place... panic passed through my body like a shivering lightning bolt. But in this bed, I was not afraid. I didn't want to be anywhere else. I was becoming a recluse, and I knew it, but I didn't care. Fear didn't reside in this bedroom. This was a place of peace, a place where the soft, warm body of Ilana rested beside me.

She brought me everything I needed: food, water, and comfort. I had no reason to brave the terrors which lived beyond the walls of this room. My dreams and memories were enough pain. The images of my time in the river were never far from me. The raging river lived with me constantly.

Except for this morning, my dream this morning was different. Monica came to me this morning in my dream. I wondered why.

Tim answered the call on his phone in the other room. I heard him talking. I assumed he was having a conversation with someone in his family. He and Sarah were thinking about traveling home soon. I couldn't stop them. They had been here long enough. It was time for them to leave. They had a life outside these walls.

Not me. I did not want to think about leaving. Not yet anyway. I wondered if I would ever be able to go. Mostly I wanted to sleep but not to dream. Lately my nights had been full of dreams. I slept in fits and spurts. There were times when I simply rested with my eyes open, hoping to think about nothing.

Tim came into my bedroom with a cordless phone in his hand. 'I think you should take this call,' he said calmly.

'No. I don't want to talk to anyone,' I said and looked away.

'It's Clarence.'

'Why are you talking to Clarence?' I said, getting angry. 'I thought we decided not to talk to anyone in the company.'

'I'm sorry,' he replied. 'The phone was ringing. I picked it up. Habit, you know. Anyway, Clarence recognized my voice. What was I going to do?'

I looked at the phone in his hand. If I had to talk to anyone in the company, I would have chosen Clarence. So why not talk to him? Plus, I had no reason to be mad at Tim. Someone was bound to find us sooner or later.

'Come on, John. Take the phone.'

'Okay.'

'Hi, matey,' Clarence said calmly over the phone, his low voice resonating with rare strength and warmth.

'Hi Clarence,' I replied hesitantly.

'So, Tim tells me you are not dead.'

'Yeah, we had a close call, but we escaped.'

'You are in one piece then?'

'Yeah. I'm beat up around the edges, but nothing fatal, at least nothing that I can determine to be fatal at this time.'

'Tim told me what happened. It's quite a story.'

'Yes.'

'Say, I have an idea. Why don't you spend a few days with me?'

I heard his words, and I wanted to see him, but I wasn't sure I was ready. Several excuses ran through my head, and I was having a difficult time deciding which one would best cover my fear of leaving this bedroom.

'I can send my company plane for you,' he offered in my silence.

'I don't know, Clarence. I'm still recovering.'

'You will be safe here, John. Someone will eventually find you where you are. I think it would be safer for you here.'

'I don't know Clarence. Thanks... but, I think...'

'John, I can protect you, and I promise not to tell anyone where you are.'

'Well...I'm not sure...'

'Good. Get packed. I will send the plane in the morning. And I will come myself.'

'Okay... I guess.'

'See you in the morning, John. We have a lot to talk about. Now get some rest and get packed.' He hung up before I could object.

I laid the phone on my bed while listening to Clarence's conversation replay in my head. Okay, maybe it was time to go, but the thought of leaving was something I dreaded. A brief wave of panic ran rampant through my limbs.

Then, I remembered my dream of Monica. She had told me it was time to move on. Her words gave me strength. But then fear struck back, panic totally out of control this time.

These bouts of fearful panic happened often in the last few days, only briefly at first, but more each day. Every time I thought about leaving this room, fear would take over, sometimes worse than other times. By now, I had come to expect panic to hit me whenever I thought about going into the real world. At that moment, I wanted more than anything to call Clarence and cancel his plane, anything to make this panic stop.

At the same time, I knew I couldn't. I knew my retreat from reality needed to end. No matter how hard it was going to be, it was time. I needed to go. Monica had told me I needed to move on. And Clarence was right. Someone would eventually find me if I stayed here too long. I had no choice.

I rested again, allowing the panic to subside. I let fear slowly slide from my body, accepting it, understanding it, and not resisting it this time, just letting fear wander away. It was important to recognize my fear and accept it for what it was. I had to learn to live with fear, not as a friend, but as an unwanted guest. I assumed it would be traveling with me for a while whether I wanted it or not. I couldn't ignore it. But I did not have to let it rule my life.

Slowly, my jagged nerves began to calm. I rested, finally closing my eyes while allowing my fears to rest with me, allowing my unwanted guests to rest at my side. My body was healing, but the scars in my mind were different. They were deep and still hurting. It was obvious it would be some time before they healed. I had to accept my mental wounds. I knew this. But it was hard...hard to do.

I began by trying to think about something else, something other than the fear that lived in my memories of the river. Perhaps it would be good to make a few calls. Activity might help, giving me something else to do and think about other than my predicament. In a way it had felt good talking to Clarence. Instead of making the fear worse, he had seemed to make it better.

Jason... I don't know why he came to mind. He just did, and I wondered how he was doing. I had not thought of him for some time. It occurred to me he was all alone. The report of my death must have left him feeling isolated. I was his closest confidant. Since I had taken the first step in communicating with the outside world, I decided I could make one more call. And Jason would be who I would call. He should still be awake in his office, this side of the world. It was three hours earlier in Hong Kong.

I found my company telephone directory on a table in the bedroom. Jason's telephone number connected me directly to his desk phone. I hoped he was in. If not, I would hang up. I didn't want to leave a message. I was afraid someone would accidentally hear my voice and I wanted to stay dead for a few more days.

Fortunately, he answered immediately. His voice, with its slight Virginia drawl, was easy to recognize.

'Jason, listen to me carefully,' I said quickly. 'Don't talk. Just listen. This is John Van Laan. I am not dead. I am alive. Now close your door so we can talk.'

'Yes sir,' he replied. The click of his door shutting was audible in the background.

'Boss, are you really okay?'

'I am, and you? How are you doing?'

'I'm fine, but I have a problem.'

He talked fast like he had been holding something deep inside, something he needed to get out, or he would burst. 'I'm so glad you called. I don't know what to do about this problem I have. Can I tell you?' he rattled on like he was in a big hurry.

'Yes, of course, what is it?'

Jason described in detail his problem with the missing gemstones and how the documents he received from Sri Lanka verified everything. He had evidence, but he didn't know what to do. He didn't know who to trust. After my death, well, the company was disorganized. So, he didn't know what to do.

I did not interrupt him. Just let him talk until he was finished. When he finally took a breath, I cut in, 'Jason, how long has it been since you made your discovery?'

'Oh, I don't know. I guess it was shortly before you died. I mean, about the time the announcement of your death came over the fax,' he quickly corrected himself, remembering and reliving his feeling of loss.

'And you haven't told anyone else about this?'

'No. I... I know I should have told someone, but...'

'Okay, good. You did well. And now you must do exactly as I say.'

'I will.'

'Do not say another word over the phone. I want you to hang up and leave your office immediately. Do not return to your apartment. Take only your wallet and your cell phone. Then call Clarence after you are safely out of your office. Do you understand?'

'Yes, I guess.'

'Good, and make sure you are not being followed.'

'Okay.'

'I will call Clarence and tell him about your situation as soon as I hang up with you. We will decide what is best for you, and you must do exactly what he tells you when you talk to him. Do you understand?'

'But all the evidence, it is at my...'

'Jason, nothing more over the phone,' I said as loud as I dared without trying to scare him.

He hesitated for a moment, 'Okay, I'm leaving now.'

'Good, and Jason...'

'What?'

'Be careful. Make sure you are not followed.'

'I will.'

A shudder of panic shot straight through my body as soon as the call ended with an empty click. It was as if Jason was now in the swirling river, and I was swimming next to him. He was in serious trouble. I quickly found Clarence's number. My hands were shaking. Wave after wave of panic took possession of my weak mind. My fear had returned, this time not as an unwanted guest but as an aggressive enemy. But I didn't have the luxury of dealing with him. Now I had to concentrate on Jason.

Any lingering doubts that the river disaster in Thailand was only an accident were quickly dissolving in my mind. A pattern of violence and deceit was becoming painfully evident. The problem Jason described involved employees working in all phases of his operation. A well-organized criminal operation such as what he described could not have gone undetected for long without the cooperation of many of his employees. I, of course, assumed Nue was probably directing it. And if this was true, then Jason's discovery was a strong indication Nue had never given up control of the Hong Kong Distribution House as I had demanded.

So, it wasn't just my paranoia, which was pointing the finger at Nue. Jason's testimony would tell the story, a story the Board of Directors needed to hear. A story that could put Nue into a world of trouble. But this also meant Jason might become a target. If Nue became aware of what Jason discovered, he could not allow Jason to leave Hong Kong.

'Clarence, yes, it's John again. Sorry, but I need a favor. Where is your plane?'

I listened while he told me it was returning to Australia after delivering rough gemstones to the cutting factories in Sri Lanka.

'Can you divert it to Hong Kong? I asked. 'I think Jason is in trouble. We need to get him out of there and fast.'

After discussing the situation, we decided that after landing in Hong Kong, his pilots would personally go into the city to retrieve Jason. Jason might not be safe alone at the airport without an escort. I wanted the pilots to personally escort him out of Hong Kong fast, today if possible. Clarence was in full agreement.

'And please, keep me informed,' I begged Clarence.

'I will contact you as soon as I have any information,' he

responded.

'Thanks.'

'No need to thank me. I'll get your lad out. Now, don't worry.' He hung up.

Tim was standing in the bedroom doorway, listening to my conversation. 'I see you are back to work?' he commented.

'Doesn't look like I have a choice.'

'We were worried about you.'

'I know.'

'You alright then?'

'Not really, but I can't let it affect me because we have a problem.'

'Jason?' he asked, having heard my side of the conversation.

'Yes.' I explained briefly what Jason told me.

'What's next?'

'Got to call Charlie and eat some crow,' I said. 'We are going to need his help.'

'That should be fun.'

I had previously explained Charlie's opinion of Nue to Tim, about how it was different than mine and more critical. So, Tim knew everything. And now, well... it was obvious that circumstances indicated Charlie was right and I was wrong.

'Want to call him for me?' I asked.

'No, I think you need to talk to him yourself,' Tim said, smiling.

I dialed Charlie's number. Fortunately, he was away from his desk. In my haste to call him, I had forgotten it was fourteen hours earlier in the States. Charlie was probably home in bed. I would have enjoyed waking him up, but I didn't have his home phone number. After leaving a message on his office voicemail, I sat for a moment against the headrest of my bed.

Fear breathed cold air down the back of my neck and I shivered even though it was warm inside the condo.

10:20 P.M.
John

Tim handed me a phone. 'It's Charlie,' he said. 'Good luck.'

It was night, and by this time, I had been out of my bedroom for hours. A walk on the beach with Ilana and two good meals contributed to my reentry into the world of the living. Ilana seemed especially happy with this new development.

Concentrating on something other than my fears, moving beyond my needs to the needs of others, took my mind off my personal problems. My concern for Jason woke me up and forced me to get back to work. I knew my fears weren't gone. They still roamed around inside my head breathing a chill in the warm air, forcing me to look away at times. But I was managing far better than before, and for this, I was grateful.

I had explained to everyone the potentially dangerous situation Jason might be in. We were worried about him ever since. Phone calls from Clarence provided constant updates on the progress of his plane. And Jason had called a couple of times during the afternoon. So, we knew Jason was fine until sometime later when he stopped calling, and his silent phone stirred my imagination into full panic mode. After the horrors I recently experienced, it was too easy to picture Jason surrounded by Nue's men, shot dead or worse. Waves of panic engulfed me out of nowhere for no reason. Calm one minute, then filled with fear the next. To compensate, I tried to be positive. I had no way of confirming Jason had been captured. I told myself I needed to assume he was okay, but that was not easy.

Tim said I looked pale. I told him it was nothing. I was worried about Jason, that's all. I did not want to be responsible for one more death, one more funeral, one more casket. I wasn't sure I could handle it.

Luckily, Clarence called around this time and told us he had talked to Jason not too long ago. He said Jason was camped at a restaurant in the city, waiting for the pilots to arrive. After we learned the plane landed in Hong Kong, we were waiting for the pilots to call and say they had Jason. Once the plane was in the air with Jason as a passenger, we could relax.

Due to my worrying about Jason, I had forgotten all about my earlier call to Charlie.

'Good morning, Charlie,' I answered, remembering it was fourteen hours earlier in Washington DC... early in the morning even for Charlie.

'Mr. John Van Laan, world-renowned entrepreneur. I thought you were dead?'

From the satirical tone of his voice, I knew Charlie was not interested in letting me off easy. It was obvious he was still pissed at me for ignoring him.

'Regretfully alive and you?' I answered, hoping some humor would lighten the mood.

'Great, life has been good,' Charlie replied. 'No one has disagreed with me lately.'

'I guess that's because you haven't been talking to me?'

'You think there's a connection?'

'Could be. But doesn't the CIA know everything? So why would anyone disagree with you?'

'I'm glad you have finally seen the light, John.'

'I have seen the light,' I said. 'And now I'm afraid I will have to make your life difficult again.'

'Why is that?'

'Because you will be dealing with me again.'

'Not if I don't want to.'

'Oh, you will want to.'

'And why is that?'

'Because you like me.'

'John, I'm sorry to have to tell you, but I don't like you that much.'

'Really?'

'Really,' he said with some finality.

I knew he had to be smirking behind his phone. At least, I hoped he wasn't serious.

'Look, Charlie, we could play this game all day,' I responded. 'And that would be fun, but I called to tell you that I think Nue was responsible for trying to kill me. And I guess that means I have to admit I was wrong, and you were right.'

'You guess?'

'Okay, you were right. Satisfied?'

Charlie had to be smiling now, and he could have made me grovel, and I would have deserved it, but he didn't. He simply let me tell him everything that happened without interrupting. He had a few questions, of course, but for the most part, he listened. It was as if he had been waiting for me to call, and this made me wonder, did he know I was alive? Did someone tell him? Give him some evidence of my travels? The CIA has its sources. But he didn't say a thing. Maybe he just never thought I was dead. The CIA requires proof and never accepts anything as fact until all the evidence is in.

After finishing my story, I asked him if he had any questions.

'Not right now,' he replied.

His abrupt end to our conversation surprised me.

'Okay, let's talk more when I return to the States,' I suggested.

'Do we have to?'

'As I said, you will want to.'

'Oh yeah, I forgot that part.'

'One more thing,' I said, ignoring his comment. I told him about our current mini-drama concerning Jason, and he didn't disagree with my assessment. He said Jason needed to get out of Hong Kong immediately. His opinion made me feel better. I had been wondering if I was overreacting, but Charlie confirmed my fears. He thanked me for the update and, without any additional editorial comments, said goodbye.

I was relieved. He could have been harder on me.

HONG KONG, 7:30 P.M.

MAN

A taxicab pulled to the curb of a busy Hong Kong street.

'Airport and hurry,' the man said, handing the cabby cash.

After listening to the information he was given on his phone, the man instinctively sensed it might be too late. He was told the American had left his office early in the afternoon without talking to anyone. This was odd because the American was a man of habit. He spent all his time working in his office and seldom left until sometime late into the night, going directly home to his apartment. He almost never left his office during the day, except today, for some unknown reason. Without saying a word, he had abruptly deserted his office. He did not speak to his secretary or anyone else. He did not tell anyone where he was going. This was something he never did.

When the American did not return to his office in an hour, an employee was sent to his apartment, concerned something may have happened to him. His apartment was empty. A check of his office telephone records revealed he had received a call from somewhere in Australia before hurrying past everyone without saying goodbye.

His behavior was most unusual. The man's boss was concerned. It was possible the American was attempting to leave Hong Kong. The man's assignment was to prevent this from happening because the American had information which could not leave the island. The man was instructed to use all means necessary to stop the American.

Failure had no place in the man's mind. But first, he had to find the American. Fortunately, he was prepared for this possibility. He had previously been given a complete description of the American and instructed to search his apartment to photocopy papers from his briefcase. The man was informed that the American was a potential long-term problem, a person who might require a permanent solution. In preparation for this possibility, the man had followed the American on several occasions to observe him. He looked for clues to the American's strengths and his weaknesses, information that could only be gathered by watching and observing small details that could be useful in the future.

But not under these circumstances.

This was all wrong. It was not the right place or the right time. The man had not been given the necessary time to properly prepare. He would be forced to improvise which meant dealing with variables not weighed in advance. A high possibility of failure was likely under these circumstances. Worse, the situation could get out of control. But the man had no choice. If he was to succeed, he had to disregard his concerns. He would have to take chances. He would have to find a way. There was a pattern, a logic to everything. He would simply have to recognize this logic and act accordingly. The man was confident it would come to him if he was patient. He would know what to do when the time was right. It had always been this way.

After arriving at the main airport terminal, the man went inside the large, sprawling building while unconsciously running his fingers across the cool steel of a small caliber pistol in his pocket. He didn't like killing with a gun. It left behind clues such as spent cartridges. There were far better ways to kill: simpler, quicker ways with less possibility of detection. The feeling of the silencer on the end of his gun barrel was revolting. He took his hand out of his jacket. He hated guns. Guns were for amateurs.

The man assumed he would have only one opportunity to do the job cleanly without leaving evidence behind. And if he did not recognize the opportunity and take advantage of it instantly, he would fail. This thought, however, did not make him afraid. He had trained himself to understand every situation and react without hesitation.

Leaning against a tile wall near one of the men's restrooms along the main hallway, the man rested, attempting to sense his next move. The airport was the obvious place to leave Hong Kong in a hurry. Therefore, the American had to be here. It was simply a matter of finding him, and with this, he had help. He was not working alone. Several times he had been called on his cell phone by people who were attempting to track the American. But so far, they had not been successful. No one matching the American's name had bought an airline ticket. This was odd. He wondered if his boss was mistaken. Maybe the young man had simply gone for a walk or was doing a personal errand.

He quickly put this thought out of his mind. It was not helpful. It was time to concentrate. The man would need all his powers to find his prey in this maze.

Travelers scurried past him, all seeming to be in a rush, endless lines of people walking the hallway dragging suitcases behind them. The man wondered where they were going and why they felt the need to be traveling. Did some far-off destination hold promises of happiness or fulfillment? Was it not enough to be content in one place?

He searched the faces of the travelers, hoping to see the young American. Waiting patiently, he hoped to feel his presence. However, this method had not always been successful for the man in the past. Sometimes, he never found his target, never felt his presence. But today was not one of those days. Today, he sensed he had come to the right place. The American was here; he was sure of it.

Suddenly stepping away from the wall, the man hurried down the hall toward the entrance to the terminal. Of course, he thought. The reason the American had not bought a ticket was because he was not leaving by commercial flight. He was traveling by private plane. The man hurried, anxious to fulfill his task. The terminal for private planes was on the other side of the airport.

An automatic door swung open.

A taxi waited outside, parked at the curb with its backdoor open. A pretty young woman in a professional business suit stood ready to step inside. The man gently touched her shoulder. She grimaced in pain and turned to see who was causing her discomfort, wanting to complain loudly.

The man who had touched her said nothing. He simply stood very still, looking directly into her eyes with a cold and resolute stare.

The woman stepped back and let the man enter the cab without complaint.

NOOSA, 10:10 P.M.

JOHN

Night descended on the resort town of Noosa. As the sun slid down behind trees outside our condo, a dark world crept into my soul, a world full of fears and terror. It rested uneasily on the waters of my mind like a droning old rusty ship, relentlessly searching the seas for sunken lost tragedies.

When we heard nothing for too long, we called Clarence to get an update. He told us the pilots had gone into the city to get Jason. Clarence was waiting for them to report. He promised to call as soon as he had news.

For too much time, the phone on the table had been silent. It was unnerving, sitting and waiting. The longer the white phone was silent, the less I liked it. My fears began to take control of my mind as we waited. I decided I needed to get out, get away from the phone, do something... anything other than worrying and waiting for the phone to ring. I asked Ilana if she would like to go for a walk. She said yes, and Tim agreed to find us as soon as he heard any news from Clarence.

The shore was deserted. The sea was calm, a shimmering mirror of rolling glass under the moonlight. A myriad of stars were eclipsed only by the moon's tail of white light dancing across the water. I was drawn to the ocean, to the water's constant movement. The wind was down. Waves slowly rolled monotonously on shore. I reached down to touch the sea's fluid and its soft essence.

So much had happened.

Everything was different now. Only a short time ago, I was a recluse resting in bed, alternately sleeping and dreaming...afraid to face the world. Now, I was outside, exposed to the elements. But like a prisoner recently released from jail, my mind was still locked up inside a self-imposed prison, my thoughts confined by my fears. I needed to find a way to fully reenter reality. Just being outside was not enough. I needed to make physical contact. A gentle wave ran up the long sandy incline of the shore, washing over my hand, cool to the touch, coming to me solely; it seemed for the purpose of extending the long reach of the sea to me, to offer me its energy. A sense of peace, more peace than I had felt in a long time, came over me, a gift given to me by the waters of the vast sea.

I wondered if this place by the shore, this time, was a prize for not dying a watery death in Thailand. And was this enough, just being here, witnessing this one moment of peace by the sea? Nothing more required or needed?

Ilana stood silently, watching over me. I took her hand, and we walked slowly along the shore under the light of glassy beams of moonlight.

'You okay?' Ilana finally asked quietly.

'What do you mean?'

'You have been hurt badly, John.'

The pain in my side walked with me. It was still difficult to move easily, but most of the other lumps and bruises from my wild ride in the river were healing. Ilana had taken good care of me since I arrived in Australia. She had fed me and cleaned me, dressed my cuts and scrapes. My strength had returned. But I knew what she was asking. She wanted to know if I was healing mentally. It is harder to heal wounds in the mind than cuts and bruises on the body.

'Yes, I guess I'm okay,' I answered without much confidence.

The truth was, I was up and walking, but I wasn't really feeling very good.

Ilana's hand, her soft, warm fingers felt good, and somehow, just having her with me was enough in that moment.

HONG KONG, 8:20 P.M.

JASON

The pilots sat in the back seat of a cab with Jason stuffed in the middle, still nervous.

They had found him sitting in a restaurant anxiously waiting with fast food on his plate, hamburgers and fries. But he wasn't hungry. He had ordered the food to kill time. When the pilots arrived, Jason was sipping a cup of coffee and trying to read a newspaper not comprehending the words, too worried to concentrate.

His last call to Clarence had failed. His cell phone was dead, and the batteries ran down. Apparently, he had forgotten to charge his phone last night. Worse yet, he didn't know Clarence's number. It was programmed into his phone, not his memory. He couldn't call Clarence even if he found a payphone. And he couldn't call anyone else. The numbers were all in his phone and the stupid phone was currently useless.

Time stood still. It seemed to Jason that it was taking forever for the pilots to show. Maybe their plane was delayed, didn't land, or they weren't coming.

What would he do then?

Eventually, they came.

Even though it seemed to have taken a long time, it had only been several hours since he last talked to Clarence.

When he saw the pilots, two blue-uniformed Caucasians walking into the restaurant wearing visor hats, he assumed they were his guys. He waved, and to his relief, they returned his greeting. Their cab was almost at the airport now. His Aussie companions sensed Jason was uptight. They had been trying to get him to lighten up, have some fun, kidding him, talking the talk with their patented Australian accent, telling him one joke after another. They helped. He laughed at their jokes, but Jason was not so sure he was out of danger. John had certainly been afraid for him, and Jason had been kicking himself mentally ever since his conversation with John. He should have seen what John had recognized immediately. Of course, he was in danger. Why had he not known? He had been so intent on solving the puzzle of the missing gemstones that he had completely ignored its implications. And worse yet, after hours spent solving his puzzle, the evidence was in his briefcase under a table in his apartment, not with him. He wanted to show it to John. But John had told him no, don't worry about your briefcase, just go.

He would have to deal with the evidence later. Obviously, John had been more worried about him than the information in his briefcase. And if John was worried, then Jason felt he had every reason to be afraid.

And the more he thought about it, the more scared Jason became.

HONG KONG, 8:35 P.M.

MAN

The man stepped out of his cab, scanning the area quickly for every detail, nothing overlooked; nothing which told him he was wrong. The young American was near. He could feel it. He had come to the right place.

The terminal used for private planes was a long, wide building. Its interior was divided into sections, each section containing a large hanger and a passenger lounge. Upscale in every detail, the building's abstract design was defined by a muted red and gray brick design that swept across the exterior, interrupted by flowing curved expanses of glass. Modern furniture, dark red leather, and chrome gave the waiting rooms a bright, upbeat appearance. A set of glass doors served as the entrance to each section of the building. Next to the door, written in chrome block letters, was the name of the company or individual who leased that section. A simple concrete pathway connected a sidewalk to each set of entry doors. Long black limos were parked outside along the curb, either delivering or waiting for wealthy travelers.

The man stood motionless, surveying the scene, looking for signs of an American. Seeing nothing, he suddenly became alarmed. It was possible the young man was already inside the building in which case he needed to move quickly. The man handed cash to the cabby and asked him to wait. Walking the sidewalk past the entry doors, he attempted to sense the American's presence. Nothing came to him except a confidence the American was not far away. He stopped to survey the various sets of doors leading into the interior sections of the building, this time more slowly, more carefully. None of the doors seemed right to him. Slowly, he resumed walking, confident something would come to him. He simply needed to be patient.

The day was clear, with only a slight breeze. The weather would cause no delayed airplane departures. He had to find the American before he was on his plane. He stopped to lean against a signpost, attempting to understand his next move.

Not far away, a cab pulled to the curb. The man watched intently as an old gray-haired Oriental in an expensive business suit exited the cab. The man relaxed.

A second cab arrived. Two pilots in blue uniforms stepped out of the back doors. One of them leaned inside to pay the fare. Nothing unusual, still the man tensed. Something told him this was the cab he desired.

The steel gun hidden in his pocket touched his hand. He still hoped to find another way to kill; a quicker, cleaner way to accomplish his mission, a way that left less evidence behind, was preferred. Walking briskly, he needed to find the young American quickly if he hoped to accomplish his task without using a gun. His instincts would show him the proper method: a quick blow to the throat, a twist of a neck, a thousand ways to kill a man at close range, so fast it would be over before anyone suspected.

A tall young man with short red hair and big glasses stepped from the cab along with the pilots. Everything was suddenly as he assumed it would be. The young man was his target. The man moved, taking long, athletic strides, feeling his muscles tense, preparing to kill. His prey was only a few yards away. It would be over in seconds.

The young American turned toward the man and looked directly at him. The man hesitated, slowed, puzzled, and unprepared for this development. The young American seemed to recognize him. This had never happened to the man before. His cover and his camouflage had always been more than adequate.

They locked eyes.

It was a moment of instant recognition.

The American turned to sprint for the doors inside the building. His pilot friends looked confused and unsure. The man reached for his gun, running after the American past the surprised pilots. Raising his gun, he stopped and aimed his pistol. The pilots could be heard yelling behind him. Jason fell, rolling on the ground as if he knew a shot was coming. Stunned by this development, the man hesitated a few seconds before pulling his trigger, just enough time for his bullet to pass innocently over the American's head and crash into a brick wall. The American was up quickly, sprinting for a door and diving inside the building before a second shot shattered the door's window into a thousand pieces of cut glass.

A security guard came out of a nearby door, pulling his gun out of his holster and looking frantic. The man quickly pocketed his weapon and turned towards his waiting cab. The moment to accomplish his task had passed. It was time to leave. The guard looked confused. He could hear men yelling at him, pointing and screaming. But he observed nothing suspicious, just a man walking briskly to a waiting cab.

The man got in, shut the door, and the cab drove off.

8:55 P.M.
Man

The silver Gulfstream came to life with a high-pitched whine. Slowly, the noise of its engines ramped up in intensity, blowing hot dust into the night air. In front of the plane, a workman wearing a black and yellow slicker waved orange flashlights, signaling to the pilot to turn hard left. The plane's small black-rubber front wheels dug into the rough concrete as it turned to begin its arduous journey, bumping and bouncing over a barren landscape toward a departing runway.

Several minutes later, from a window inside the main terminal lounge, the man watched as the plane appeared like a miniature toy, thundering over a runway, disappearing beyond the man's sight behind some buildings before reappearing again. Its engines threw a hot orange draft behind, lifting into a dark gray, hazy night.

The man had discarded his coat, his hat, and, more importantly, his gun had been placed in a wastebasket of a restroom soon after entering the main airport terminal. Spent cartage at the scene of the shooting could be traced to the gun. The weapon of death was now a liability. He did not like using guns. He was glad to be rid of it.

Disappointment walked with him when he turned to leave. He had failed in his mission, but he knew it was not his fault. The mission had failed because it could not be successfully completed.

Fate had intervened for reasons the man did not need to understand. He needed only to know the American had an advantage the man had not anticipated. The young American's time to die was not today. It was not meant to be. It was not logical. The man discarded his disappointment as easily as he had discarded his gun. It was unnecessary mental baggage now. It was time to move on. All things were as they should be. He had new problems to solve and already his mind was working on those problems. Slowly and confidently, he walked the wide hallways of the airport, blending in with the other travelers.

Once again, he wondered where they were all going and why they felt a constant need to travel when everything they required from life was here.

NOOSA, THURSDAY, FEBRUARY 18, 9:15 A.M.

JOHN

I helped her pack my bag quickly and efficiently, taking clothes out of dressers in bunches and placing them hurriedly into a suitcase. We didn't have a lot of time. I was anxious to get to the airport. When Ilana saw what I was doing, she gave me a gentle shove in the side. I winced as a pain shot through my ribs. She didn't notice.

'Let me do this,' she reopened the suitcase and took everything out. Neatly folding the clothes, one item at a time, she replaced everything. 'You are so messy.'

I stood aside, very aware that it is sometimes wise to give in to a woman.

'Our plane will be here soon,' I commented. 'We need to get going.'

'The plane won't leave without us,' she replied without looking up from her task.

She was right, of course. It was Clarence's plane. It wasn't going anywhere without us on board.

Tim was at the resort's main reception desk paying the bill using his wife's credit card, hoping to throw off anyone looking for us. We didn't want to leave a paper trail. I told him I would reimburse him after returning to my office. Sarah was humming in the other bedroom, packing her things. She was glad to be leaving. Although Australia had been initially fun, in the end, she had endured too many bad nights here. She was looking forward to going home.

I decided to take a short walk to get out of Ilana's way.

Palm trees swayed in ocean breezes near the beach. It was another warm day of Australian summer. The wind had strengthened overnight. Waves broke in monotonous crashing regularity on the shore. I found a bench and sat down to rest.

The news from Clarence last night had been good and bad.

The good news was Jason and the pilots were safe. The bad news was Jason had almost been killed by a lone gunman. This incident gave further credibility to the fact that we were all in danger. The attack on Jason was too pointed. No one else was targeted, only Jason. When the gunman realized he could not succeed in killing Jason, he fled.

I wondered if Nue thought I was alive. If he did, he had to be looking for me. I now believed, more than ever, that Nue was guilty of attempting to kill me. But I also knew he would deny any involvement in either my mishap in the river or in Jason's attack. I could accuse him, but to what good? Without direct proof, he would calmly look at me in his usual unemotional state of mind and ask why I would say such a thing.

I had to have solid evidence. Hopefully, Clarence had an idea, or Charlie could help because it was going to be difficult to prove Nue was guilty. And without proof, I could do nothing to get rid of him.

Clarence's plane was currently in the air. It had been flying continuously, never staying long in any one place. Arriving in the early morning in Australia, it had delivered Jason safely to Inverell, the town where Clarence's office was located. After general maintenance and refueling, a new crew was assigned. They were coming to fly us to Inverell, where we would be joining Jason and Clarence. I was looking forward to seeing all of them.

'Our taxi is here,' Ilana touched my shoulder.

'Okay.' I took one more look at the blue Pacific Ocean.

It was time to go.

INVERELL, AUSTRALIA, 1:45 P.M.

JOHN

I gave Jason a big hug when I met him at the airport.

'You okay?' I asked.

'A little shaken up, but otherwise fine,' he answered.

Seeing him again after a long absence made me acutely aware of the fact that the kid was my responsibility, and I had let him down. Sure, I was happy he was okay, but I also knew it could have gone very differently. He could have been killed.

The truth was, I honestly liked having Jason around. I never really admitted that to him, but I missed having the kid in my Charlottesville office. Even though he could be a pest, like when he was bugging me about something he thought we should be doing differently to improve office efficiency or constantly asking me why we were needlessly spending money on something we didn't need or why we had not fixed a problem he told me about last week. It was always something with the kid. While I was busy trying to run a multi-national company, I had this kid constantly jabbering in my ear.

Now, that wasn't completely his fault because it is my policy to be receptive to employee suggestions. The big oak doors to my Charlottesville office are normally open for a reason. Employees like Jason were encouraged to walk in and discuss whatever was on their minds.

That was not always true. There were times when the doors were closed. When I was busy and wanted some peace, I asked Helen to close the doors so no one would bother me. However, whenever I shut Jason out, he would bug Helen instead. He would bug her until she bugged me about whatever it was he had been bugging me about in the first place. I say all this because I also have to admit that most of the time, he was right. When I had bigger issues to solve and didn't have time for details, Jason helped make the office more efficient.

From the local airport, we drove to Clarence's office in the Nullamana Mining Company complex in Inverell, where he offered us a tour of the facilities for the first-timers in our group. His tour began in the office complex. I kind of hung back. I had seen it all before. Jason, however, was apparently very interested. I could hear him chattering constantly, asking Clarence a thousand questions. I was certain if Clarence would let him, Jason could increase the efficiency of the Nullamana Mining office by a factor of ten. However, it appeared the old Aussie was about ready to boil over; Clarence was old school. He had a good technical mind, but when it came to getting things done, Clarence's management style was to, more or less, let things take their course. He had often told me that rushing to conclusions often creates more problems than it solves.

I decided it was time to rescue Clarence from Jason.

'Hey, Tim,' I said. 'Why don't you show Jason and the ladies the production area out back.'

'Sure, boss,' he replied. Tim had been here many times. He knew the layout almost as well as anyone.

Ilana looked at me. She had been holding my hand whenever she could after leaving the condo. Clarence's mining company was one more new experience added to a long list of other new places she had visited recently. She seemed insecure. I knew I should be sympathetic, but I had my own issues. I was still coming out of a funk. Although I was feeling stronger both mentally and physically, I wasn't a hundred percent.

And while I was improving, Ilana seemed to be getting weaker, becoming more insecure. The nightmare that the women had experienced at the condo must have had a deeper effect on them than I realized. Tim and I had talked about it when we were alone. He said Sarah was reluctant to let him out of her sight. And when he had kidded her about it, she had become very angry. She told Tim he wasn't there when she was told he was dead. He didn't know how that felt. And if she hadn't gotten over it all just yet, well, so what... it had been hard, real hard. So maybe he, Tim, should be a little more understanding.

I suggested to Tim that perhaps our experience may have been easier in one respect for us than for them. At least we knew what was happening. They didn't. Tim agreed.

I smiled at Ilana. 'I need to talk with Clarence. Let Tim show you around. It will be fun.'

Ilana reluctantly let go of my hand and wandered off next to Jason. They looked kind of funny together. Jason was so tall he had to lean over to talk to Ilana.

'Is there someplace we can talk?' I asked Clarence.

'Let's go to my office.'

The Nullamana Mining Company occupied the biggest building in Inverell, Australia, which didn't say much because the town of Inverell was a small town. High in the mountains and much cooler than Noosa. Forests covered the land surrounding the town, similar to my native Michigan. However, some really different animals, koalas and platypuses, lived on this land. This was Australia, after all, not Michigan.

The executive offices for the mines were housed in a brown brick, flat-roofed structure connected to a sloped roof, white metal building. Clarence was the CEO of the company. I liked to kid him about his office. Half his décor consisted of aboriginal artifacts. The other half looked like an old English library full of mining engineering books.

He settled into an old, big brown leather desk chair that looked like it had been around for years, evidenced by worn indentations in the cushions, which perfectly matched the shape of his back. No other chair would ever be as comfortable as this old thing for Clarence. The top of his desk top was scratched and covered with dust and mine reports. I had never seen his desk look any other way. I assumed it was his practice to enter his office after visiting the mines with his clothes covered with dirt and grime, not bothering to clean up first. I suspected he simply settled into his chair, unconcerned about the mess he was creating. In his mind, more important issues needed attention than a dirty desk.

'So, what's on your mind, matey?' he asked.

'Oh, I don't know,' I replied hesitantly, sitting down on an old, varnished wood chair on the other side of his desk.

'Just want to talk then?'

'I guess.'

He didn't say anything at first, and I didn't really know where to begin. I hoped Clarence could help me decide what to do, but the truth was, I wasn't sure that was possible because I really didn't want to talk about any of it. All the bad shit, the recent painful memories; subconsciously, I was trying to bury that stuff deep in the far recesses of my brain so I wouldn't have to relive the experiences ever again.

'I think Nue tried to kill me.' I finally aired the most important issue on my mind.

'What do you plan to do about him?' Clarence replied calmly.

'I don't know.'

He looked at me, probably trying to determine my mental state of my well-being or lack thereof. I'm sure he had been informed about how I had turned into something of a recluse at the resort, staying in my room, licking my wounds. He was probably wondering if I had fully recovered.

'I guess you heard I had some problems at the resort,' I admitted.

'I heard.'

'I'm better now.'

'I'm glad you're alright, John.'

'Well, mostly better. But I have this problem, and I don't know what to do about him.' I paused, wondering if I looked or sounded even close to being healthy again. I didn't know if I could fake it. All my insecure fears and terrors were still in the back of my brain, out of sight, maybe, but not out of mind.

'Did Tim tell you the details?' I asked. 'About what happened in Thailand?'

'He told me his side of the story. Anything you want to add?'

'No. I'm sure he did a fine job.'

'Okay.'

'Well, do you agree? Do you think the bastard tried to kill us?' I asked too loud.

'It's hard for an animal to change his fur, John.'

I smiled. 'Sorry for my foul language.'

'It's not like you.'

'Yes, but do you agree with me?'

'It's possible he tried to kill you. But you don't really know, do you? From what Tim told me, you don't really know if the dam broke because Nue wanted to kill you or for some other reason. Maybe the explosion was an accident. Or the dam just broke because it was old, and the noise you heard was the retaining wall crashing down. The truth is, you don't know for sure what happened, and you may never know.'

'You're right... I don't know.'

We were both silent for a moment.

'Okay, but what's your opinion?' I asked.

'Nue will deny any involvement. And without proof tying him directly to a crime, you have no case against him.' Clarence sat back in his chair.

I didn't respond. The case against Nue was a sure bet in my mind, but obviously, I was prejudiced.

'Are you afraid Nue will try to kill you again?' Clarence asked.

'I am.'

'Maybe you need to get out of the business?'

'What do you mean?'

'Is it worth dying for, laddie? Is your job worth your life?'

'You want me to just give up?'

'How many close calls do you have to have before you accept the fact your time on this planet may be short? Isn't that what you were thinking about when you were hiding out in your condo?'

'I was trying not to think, just rest.'

'But were you resting?'

'No, I guess not.'

'So, it wasn't really working?'

'What?'

'You not thinking?'

'Not so much.'

'Were you thinking about dying, maybe?'

'Maybe.'

'Look, John, whether you are willing to admit it or not, the truth is that life is fragile, easily washed away in a raging river or with a bullet to the heart. Am I right?'

'I guess.'

'So, is it worth it?'

I didn't know how to respond. A few minutes of anxious silence followed before Clarence asked, 'Do you want to see the new lab?' He instinctively knew it was time to move on. We were accomplishing nothing.

'I don't know,' I responded. 'The last time I visited that place, I came close to dying.'

I was referring to the time when Clarence and Monica were injured in a fire at the lab. I saved them, but not without taking a big risk. The cause of the fire had never been determined, but Clarence and I strongly suspected sabotage.

'I'm not worried, mate. Let's have a look,' Clarence said. 'I think you will like what we have done.'

He led the way down a series of white antiseptic hallways past a number of rooms used for sorting and shipping. In the middle of the building was a big vault where the gemstones were protected each night. Clarence held open a door at the back of the building.

A sidewalk behind the warehouse ran parallel to a fifteen-foot-high cement wall, which separated the warehouse from the lab, protecting the warehouse in case the lab exploded. It was the one safety feature that had worked during the fire. It still stood exactly as before the fire, although it was now tainted in places from black smoke.

'Thinking about the fire?' Clarence asked.

'Yes.'

'Have I thanked you lately for saving me-'

I interrupted him. 'If I had been smarter, I would have stayed behind the wall where it was safe.'

'Well, here's to your lack of intelligence then,' he smiled.

The sidewalk took us around the back of the warehouse, where it turned towards the lab and passed a red water tank. The tank had helped in saving the lives of Clarence and Monica by leaking water, which kept them from burning. A new, larger tank built of stronger metal replaced the old one. Images of two bodies lying under the old tank flashed through my memory as we passed the new tank. At the time of the fire, I could only vaguely see them through the smoke. The water in the tank didn't look like it was going to last much longer. I wasn't sure I had time to run for help. Someone needed to rescue them immediately and I was the only one around at the time. I had gone, probably a dumb act, but fortunately, it turned out okay.

Rows of new furnaces inside the reconstructed lab were arranged in four long lines, surrounded by white-coated lab technicians busily checking gauges on control panels. Looking like large white metal cylinders, the furnaces stood five feet high by three feet in diameter. Attached to the top of each cylinder was a series of electrical lines and pipes. Inside the furnaces were ceramic cylinders. A blanket of tubing surrounded the cylinders, covered by a metal shield that made the furnaces appear larger than they really were. The tubes fed a constant supply of cool water monitored to control the temperature inside.

When we found Jason and the group, he was holding a particularly fine sapphire given to him by one of the technicians. After handing it to Ilana, he asked her, 'Tell me what you see.'

'What do you want me to see?' Ilana eyed the oddly shaped stone.

'See any flaws?'

'No.'

He then gave her a magnifying glass, knowing what the glass would reveal.

Although most of the flaws in the stone had been cured by the furnaces; still, some flaws remained which could not be altered. The stone's color had been greatly improved. Before entering the furnaces, it only had a hint of blue. Now, it radiated with a deep blue, equaling the color of the sky on a clear day.

The gemstone would be beautiful in four or five carats when cut.

BANGKOK THAILAND, 12:40 P.M.

NUE

Elegant orchids offered a soft visual contrast to the hard-edged granite rocks that defined the borders of the outdoor garden. The flowing lines of the flowers, their fragile petals filtered dreamlike through Nue's mind as he rested, observing pale orange and sweet pink blossoms nestled under the shade of towering palm trees. The flowers were breathless in their grandeur, their colors blending together in ways unmatched by human artwork.

Mr. Nue's self-assigned task for lunch that day was to ponder his next move, but at that moment, he was simply enjoying the flowers. It felt good to have returned to Bangkok. He had been gone too long in the mountains. He missed the quiet patterns that consumed his life when he was home. He fell easily into his old habits. Lunch at his favorite restaurant was special. He loved to sit at his reserved table while viewing the outdoor rock garden through the restaurant's open windows. The flowers always offered him a special feeling of contentment. Deep red and sun-bright yellow blossoms of hibiscus plants reflected in the glassy waters of a pond. Their expansive petals opened up for only one day before quickly closing into faded limp decay, eventually breaking free and floating harmlessly on the surface of the water, shriveled memories of their brief, colorful glory.

Nue slowly sipped his tea, allowing his mind to wander while his eyes unconsciously scanned the garden, searching for lovely images to fill the black holes of violence that dominated his thoughts.

Something in his world was wrong, and he suspected the cause of his concern. He sensed John Van Laan was alive. John's body had not been found even though they had searched long and hard. The young American, John's former assistant, had escaped Hong Kong after it was discovered the young man had been talking to someone in Australia. Phone records indicated a call had come from Noosa, the town where John's girlfriend had been staying. It was the same number Nue had called when he told her John was lost and presumed dead. That was not good news. The girl should have been gone. She had no reason to stay. And even if she had stayed for some unknown reason, why would a call from John's girlfriend cause the young American to simply leave in the middle of the day? Nothing made sense. That is, it didn't make sense unless John was alive to make the call.

All evidence pointed to one obvious conclusion. Mr. Van Laan had survived his experience in the flood.

Nue took out his cell phone.

He was not overly concerned with the current situation. Life was a series of variables. He couldn't control all of them, and it did no good to agonize about what could not be changed. He simply needed to consider the situation as it was today and make proper choices for the future.

Calculating the time of day in Columbia as he listened to his phone ring, he knew he should have determined the time before calling. He hoped it was not night. He did not wish to disturb his friend, but regardless, he allowed his phone to continue ringing.

He would leave a message if the man did not answer his phone.

HONG KONG, FRIDAY, FEBRUARY 19, 12:25 P.M.

JASON'S SECRETARY

She unlocked the door quickly, hoping no one in the hall was watching and wondering why a strange woman was entering a man's apartment. Chinese in origin with translucent white skin and straight black hair cut efficiently short, her eyelashes held a tint of mascara. Although she had been out of school for almost ten years, she could have easily passed for a teenager. She was a beautiful young woman.

Jason had not hired her as his secretary because she was pretty. He hired her because she was very competent, bright, and eager to please. After giving a number of young women a tryout, he finally settled on her. The others didn't seem to understand the importance of their job as she did. It had helped, he supposed, that she was pretty, but what he really needed was someone he could trust. And now he was trusting her with a very important task.

She did not want to disappoint him.

Afraid to turn on the lights but more afraid to search in the dark, Jason's secretary forced her fears deep down inside her where she could control them. After closing the apartment's door, she determined that enough sunlight was filtering through the closed drapes of Jason's apartment, enough light to observe vague images of furniture, doors, and rooms. She could do this without turning on the lights, which she worried might lead to someone questioning her. She told herself to be brave.

Jason had called her last night when she was home. He waited to call her because he didn't want their conversation to be overheard by someone in his office. He told her he was fine and said he hoped to return to work shortly. He needed a favor. Would she please do this for him and tell no one? Could he trust her to keep a secret?

She had said yes.

It was her lunchtime. She had waited to go to his apartment until now to do what he asked: retrieve his briefcase, remove the papers from it, and mail them to him. He gave her an address. He had warned her to be careful. If someone discovered her in his apartment, he suggested she say she had been asked to pack some clothes and have them sent to him. He gave her a list of the clothes he needed. He said to use the clothes as a cover for being in his apartment. A spare key to his apartment was on his desk at work.

The pretty secretary liked Jason. Her boss worked hard, and he didn't harass her like some of her former employers. Jason had been very professional. She felt she owed him a favor for being a good boss. The papers in the briefcase must be important.

But now she was not so sure she should have agreed. It had seemed so easy when he asked her. Now it was very scary. His dark apartment was spooky.

A shadow slid across a wall, scaring her. Or was it simply a product of her imagination? Was her heightened sense of fear sending false signals? ... Perhaps the wind was blowing a drape across an open window? She told herself to be calm and concentrate.

She had never been in his apartment before, although she had fantasized about coming here. The truth was she had a crush on Jason. She had never told him. But perhaps doing this task for him, perhaps this would change how he thought about her. She wondered briefly why he had left Hong Kong and whether he would really return. Everyone at the office had been talking. Nothing concrete. Rumors were floating.

Concentrate. She told herself to concentrate and pack his clothes first. Then, if someone came, her excuse for being in the apartment would look legitimate. It was true, after all. The clothes were to be shipped to Australia.

She found his suitcase, which he had told her was in his closet. Laying it on his bed, she began to pack. As expected, Jason's bedroom was well organized. Everything was where he told her it would be. It seemed odd to be touching his clothes. She diligently folded each item before placing it in the suitcase. A slight rustling sound came from another bedroom, almost unrecognizable. Was it her imagination again? No, she had heard something. Or did she? She stopped to listen. Only the sound of her pounding heart worried her. Finally, unable to control her fears any longer, she threw the remaining clothes in the suitcase and closed it quickly. Only one more task remained. Find his briefcase. Jason had told her to look under a coffee table in the living room.

She needed to grab it and run.

A shadow passed across the door to the bedroom in the half-light. She stood perfectly still, holding her breath, waiting and listening. Nothing.

She relaxed.

The blow was not hard, not intended to do any real damage, well placed to the back of her neck. She fell, immediately unconscious. The man caught her in his arms before she hit the floor. Carrying her limp body into the bedroom, he laid her across the bed and efficiently searched her clothes, finding nothing of importance.

The man looked down at the pretty young girl, considering his options. It was bad luck she had come to the apartment when he was there, but it was fate.

Nothing could change fate.

GRAND HAVEN, MICHIGAN, WEDNESDAY, FEBRUARY 24, 5:40 P.M.

JOHN

Lake Shore Avenue near Grand Haven, Michigan, was not a very hospitable place that evening. The air temperature had dipped into the lower teens, aided by a strong northwest wind that arrived on land after blowing over the icy plains of Western Canada and whipping uninhibited across flat expanses of Lake Michigan. Sucking ethereal mists of water vapor from the lake, clouds rose like pale ghosts dancing across a blue sky over the lake before eventually linking together when approaching land into massive dark monsters which hid the sun and showered sheets of snow across a frozen landscape. Where the wind was impeded by natural barriers of trees and sand dunes, huge snowdrifts accumulated. Massive orange machines attached to high metal plows threw showers of the icy stuff into the air, working desperately to keep the roads open. Unfortunately, the snowplows were only a temporary fix. Gusting winds continued to relentlessly blow, accumulating snow over the roads as we drove slowly into the descending darkness of evening.

We were making progress; my car's traction control was helping, but its wide, high-performance tires were not designed for deepening tracks of snow. I had to proceed very carefully or suffer the consequences, such as a hasty slide off the road into a ditch... stuck, with no help in sight.

Ilana didn't look too happy as she sat in the passenger seat of my Mercedes 550 SL. Her problem wasn't the snow. She liked playing in the stuff. She just didn't like driving in it. I, on the other hand, was a Michigan-bred boy accustomed to ugly winter weather. I had driven many times in conditions far worse than this. I was determined to not let the snow slow me down.

Our flight from Australia to San Francisco had been long. Jason went home to Virginia from California. I gave him my approval. He had family in Richmond and had been gone for months in the Far East. He was anxious to see his parents. I told him to talk to no one at the company and be careful. I would call him when I had returned to my office. In the meantime, relax.

Sarah was very happy to be returning with Tim to Montana. Every time I saw her, she was holding Tim's hand. When we parted ways in San Francisco, Ilana and Sarah hugged for a long time. A few tears flowed. A bond had been established between the ladies. It was not easy for them to separate.

An incident concerning Jason's secretary in Hong Kong was very problematic. She had called Jason while we were still in Australia from her cell phone. She said she was safely out of his apartment. He did not need to be concerned, but she thought he should know that someone hit her from behind when she was inside his apartment and knocked her unconscious. They talked while I listened. He sounded very concerned.

Finally, I asked him about his briefcase because I had to know.

She told him the briefcase was gone. Whoever hit her probably took it. She grabbed Jason's suitcase as soon as she regained consciousness, locked his apartment, and left. She wondered if Jason wanted her to contact the police.

Jason looked at me.

I asked him to ask her if she was alright.

She said she was a little sore, but she would be fine.

We decided to avoid involving the police.

As soon as Jason got off his phone, he said he was sorry. All the evidence he had painstakingly gathered to trace the missing gemstones was gone. He knew it was important. The look on his face indicated he was devastated. I told him to let it go. However, inside, I was pissed. I needed that evidence to deal with Nue.

Jason said he should have done a better job of hiding the evidence. I told him not to blame himself. If anyone was to blame, it was me. I should have warned him to be more careful. But everything seemed to be going well at the time. I never considered spies in his office. Apparently, I should have and my ineptitude only compounded my growing frustration.

I asked him why his briefcase was in his apartment and not in his office. Jason said he took it home and forgot about it after my death was reported. He didn't know what to do about its contents, so he just left it under a table. Someone may have been sent to his apartment after he disappeared. Perhaps they were wondering if he was sick and needed help. They could have found his briefcase and took it. Perhaps not because they knew what was in it, but because he was gone, and they were looking for evidence of where he went.

That was his explanation. It was a possibility, but it didn't explain why someone injured his secretary.

With Jason's evidence missing, a new plan was required, and I had one that I thought was good, but I wanted a second opinion from someone other than Charlie. Since it was Charlie who had suggested the plan to me in the first place, therefore, I assumed he would agree. So, I needed someone else, someone who would look at the plan with more objectivity. I decided my friend David would be perfect for the task and this was why we had traveled to Michigan, specifically to talk to him. David's office in Grand Haven was our destination this evening. Afterward, Ilana and I were invited to have dinner with him and his wife, Mary. And that's why Ilana was with me, not because she wanted to come. She would have preferred to stay at the cottage, but I had talked her into coming, which was not easy, given it had been snowing all afternoon, sometimes so hard the lake disappeared in a fog of white outside the windows at the cottage. 'Why?' she asked while watching one of these frequent snow blizzards obliterate the landscape. 'Why would anyone want to go out in weather like this?'

I told her it would be fun. She had looked at me like I was crazy.

Now that we were on the road, I was beginning to wonder if she was right. My windshield iced over almost immediately. Turning the defroster on high fan helped, but the road soon disappeared in a blowing haze of snow. Vague shadows of trees on the side of the road filtered through the growing darkness, the sun disappearing behind clouds. Fortunately, we weren't far from David's office in town at the time. I kept going, knowing that attempting to turn around might be impossible in the deepening snow. It was better to keep moving forward. Stopping could mean getting stuck. Luckily, when we got to town, the roads were somewhat better. The wind was less fierce, its force inhibited by trees and buildings.

'You okay?' I turned to Ilana, hoping I wouldn't see her 'white-knuckling.' This was the term I used to describe her state of mind when she was riding in my car: her eyes staring blankly at the road ahead, lips pursed in soundless expletives, and hands gripping the dashboard like it was a life raft. I had seen her this way too many times. Speeding cars was not her thing.

'I'm fine, John,' she said with a genuine lack of enthusiasm.

'Say, what was that phone call about?' I asked, mostly as a distraction, something to take her mind off the road.

'What phone call?'

'You know, the one you got earlier this afternoon. You looked kinda unhappy.'

'Oh, it was nothing.'

'It didn't sound like nothing.'

She didn't respond at first.

'Okay, if you must know,' she finally admitted. 'I was speaking to my brother.'

'Do you want to talk about it?'

'No!'

BELIZE, AMBERGRIS ISLAND, 6:45 P.M.

MANUEL ORTEGA

Pastel watercolors, pictures replete with colorful birds, waving palm fronds, and pale blue seas were set in simple wood frames to embellish the plain white walls of the restaurant. The tables were covered with yellow and white tablecloths, surrounded by simple wood chairs. The restaurant was located in the older section of the resort town of San Pedro, Belize. Nothing new and fancy; traditional spicy food had been served here for years. The Columbian liked this place. He had come here often in the past.

A waiter handed him a menu. Manuel thought he would have some fish. Even though it was early for dinner, his work for this day was done. So why not enjoy something good to eat?

A phone call to his friend and business partner had been his final task. The call had solicited no unusual response, no surprises. His partner had sounded almost uninterested when he was told the news. It was as if the man already knew what the Columbian would tell him. He only wanted the information confirmed.

Getting the information had been easy; simply a matter of asking the girl's brother for help. The Columbian knew where her brother lived. He had located him on a previous trip in case he needed to talk to him in the future. The Columbian had waited at the dock for her brother to return from fishing. When his boat arrived, the Columbian went out on the dock and informed him that he was an acquaintance of his sister. And yes, the Columbian had replied when asked; he was the man who had paid her money for information in the past. And oh, by the way, did her brother like his new fishing boat? Then he suggested that perhaps now it was a good time for her to fulfill her obligations.

The Columbian knew he had a talent for communicating with people. His method was simple. He simply looked people straight in the eye when he talked to them. He had a gift. Most people became instantly aware of the menace in his heart. It was as if a bloody barbed wire fence was wrapped around his aura. His method worked with most people, although a few people had not been very wise. They had chosen not to listen to him. The Columbian tried not to think about them now, about their lifeless bodies decaying under leaves in a dark forest or the sight of their red blood mixing with salt water, rocking listlessly in the surf on a lonely beach. He thought they had brought their fate on themselves, and it had been their decision. There was always a peaceful way to do things and an ugly way. He had simply fulfilled their wishes.

Fortunately for her brother, he cooperated when requested. He dialed several phone numbers on a cell phone which was handed to him before finally connecting with his sister. He asked his sister if she remembered the man from the jewelry shop, the man who had paid her money. She had answered yes after her brother described the man who was standing in front of him. The Columbian took the phone from her brother and walked down the dock to a place where their conversation could not be overheard.

The Columbian asked Ilana if she was well.

'Yes,' she had answered curtly.

He asked her if she now understood he knew where her brother lived.

'Yes,' she said she understood.

He asked her if she understood why this was important.

She had hesitated and then answered she did.

He then asked her one question. Was her boyfriend alive?

After a considerable pause, she said, 'Yes.'

Manuel thanked her and told her to tell no one about their phone call, especially not her boyfriend. She did not want something unfortunate to happen to her brother, did she? The Columbian said he would call her again in the future when he needed more information. Until then, he wished her a good day and turned back to give the phone to her brother, once again retreating a reasonable distance down the dock so he would not interfere in a family conversation.

He had what he needed.

GRAND HAVEN, MICHIGAN, 6:05 P.M.

JOHN

'How are you going to explain why it took you so long to get out an announcement? You know, let the people in your company know you are alive and didn't die in Thailand as had been reported?' David asked as if this was the most important question on the table.

I had other things on my mind, more important things. 'I don't know. I'll think of something,' I replied.

He nodded as if he fully expected my mindless response, making notes on a yellow pad of paper before moving to the next topic for discussion. 'Do you have hard evidence to prove your experience in the river was anything more than an accident?'

'No, I don't.'

David, as usual, was being his legalistic self. Shelves of law books lined the walls of his office. The books were an imposing sight to anyone sitting across from him at his desk. I have often wondered if any lawyer knows even a fraction of what was written in the books that line their offices. I assume the books are nothing more than a guise to impress clients. And as for David, I often told him to lighten up. Life is difficult enough without trying to understand it in terms of legalism. However, I don't think he ever totally agreed.

'But you suspect it was a deliberate act to kill you?' he continued.

'I do.'

'And you have only told a few people that you survived?'

'I already said that.'

'Why not?' he demanded again.

'Why should I?' I replied, this time in frustration.

'John, you run a multi-national corporation. Thousands of people depend on you. You have a moral if not legal obligation to keep them informed.' He said all this while giving me the look lawyers often use after asking their witnesses a leading question, a question which can be answered only one way, the way they intended. Today, I was his witness. No matter how I answered his questions, I was guilty as charged until proven innocent.

'Okay, David,' I replied. 'So maybe I don't have a legitimate excuse for not contacting my company. And it's true, I'm not sure the incident in the river was anything more than an accident. But I also think it's highly possible someone tried to kill me, namely Nue.'

I paused. When David said nothing, I continued. 'Truth is, I'm afraid of Nue. I didn't want him to know I was alive because I was worried he would try to kill me again when he learned I had survived. And I'm much happier being alive than dead...' I paused again, waiting for what I assumed would be a new accusation. When he remained silent, I finally gave in. 'Okay, I get it. It's time for an announcement. Do you think you can write one that doesn't sound like I have been derelict in my duties?'

'I'll work on it,' he said, apparently having accomplished his immediate goal and this was to put me on the defensive so he could get what he wanted from me. 'I'll have an announcement ready in the morning,' he said. 'I assume you will want to review it first before it goes to Charlottesville for release.'

He said all this as he was furiously writing on his legal pad. I assumed he already had the bulk of the text written. The man was that good.

Ilana was sitting quietly beside me in a leather armchair across from David during this exchange. She didn't appear to be interested.

'By the way,' I interrupted David after turning my attention back to him. 'I didn't come here so you could get on my case. I came here because I have a plan to deal with Nue, and I want your advice.'

Ilana stood up.

'Where are you going?' I asked her.

'I think I am bored. I want to take a walk.'

'I would like you to hear this.'

'Why?' she asked curtly.

Now, that seemed an odd question, especially coming from her. Usually, she wanted to know everything about anything. And she normally had an opinion on all of it.

'Because I assumed you would like to know,' I replied.

She sat down, looking miserably resigned to her dubious fate. I looked at her again. The woman was obviously unhappy. Something was bothering her. I gave in.

'Alright,' I said. 'Why don't you go for a walk?'

An important piece of the puzzle that defined this woman was missing, but I didn't have time to think about her. I let it pass and began telling David my plan after she left the room.

'Phillip has been purposely excluded from the company,' I explained. 'I know because Nue excluded him at my request. I don't think it made Nue unhappy. I don't believe Nue trusts Phillip. He was probably happy to oblige me. Phillip, on the other hand, must have been pissed...' I paused. 'Is any of this making sense?'

'I'm with you so far,' David leaned into his chair.

I looked at where Ilana had been sitting a few moments ago. It seemed odd she was absent.

I continued. 'From everything I've heard, Nue has downgraded Phillip's participation in company business. His name did not surface in any recent conversations I had with Nue. I have to assume Phillip is not a player at this time, and Phillip must hate this. He likes being at the seat of power.'

'Okay, say I agree,' David replied. 'So what?'

'So, I think I can use Phillip's dissatisfaction to convince him to help me take down Nue.'

'Why would Phillip ever help you?' David interrupted. 'You and I both know he despises you.'

'Look, David, his weakness is his ego. You know that. It's where he's most vulnerable. If Nue has cut him out of the company as completely as I assume, then more than anything, Phillip's ego has been bruised. And I think I can use that to my advantage.'

'How?'

'I'm working on it. But before I can proceed, I need to know if I am right about Phillip. Can you find out what he has been doing? Because if his situation is what I think it is, I will use it to try to recruit him.'

'Okay,' David replied simply.

'Thanks, now can we get something to eat? I'm starved, Kirby Grill alright with you? Ilana doesn't much like Fricano's pizza,'

'Sure. Just give me a few minutes.'

'Okay, I'll meet you at the restaurant.'

Ilana was sitting in the waiting room reading a magazine when I found her.

'Hungry?' I asked.

For some reason, I don't know why, it was just something about how she got out of her chair, turned, and walked toward the door with her back to me without saying a word.

9:10 P.M.
John

Where the land was open between sand dunes and towering pines, the headlights of my Mercedes illuminated windblown streams of dry snow, crossing the road like white dust. A layer of crusty snow still coated the surface of the road, but fortunately, the worst of the snowstorm was over. Stars were shining in a night that had turned bitter cold, with bright moonlight reflecting off the snow's windswept surfaces. Heavy winds still howled off the lake, and the air was gun-metal cold. Temperatures were forecast to fall to near zero. A big Artic high-pressure system had arrived from the northern plains to cover the area with a blast of dry, frigid air.

I drove cautiously as we slid slowly down the road to my cottage after dinner. This was not a night to become stuck in the snow. It would probably be hours before an overworked tow truck could come to our rescue.

The passenger seat heater was on high for Ilana, who was buried beneath an old warm parka Mary had given her at dinner. I had previously mentioned to David that she didn't really have a good coat for this weather. He had Mary bring the parka. The hood of the coat was over her head, making it impossible to see her face. She was quiet, not complaining about the cold as usual. The lack of chatter coming from my normally talkative companion was worrying. Only a few sentences had escaped her mouth at dinner. When Mary asked her how she liked Australia, Ilana had listlessly remarked that it was a nice place, nothing more. The only time she showed any real interest in joining our conversation was when we were discussing the weather. She said she couldn't believe anyone really lived in this cold winter place. Unfortunately, her remark did nothing to endear her to David and Mary, who lived here, but I don't think she noticed their reaction. I countered by saying it wasn't so bad in the winter, and I promised to build a fire for her when we returned to the cottage. I said it would be great. The blank expression on her face in response to my remark was that of a person who was not easily swayed by arguments that did not pass her reality check.

Big piles of newly plowed snow lined the driveway to my cottage when we turned off the main road. As I waited for the automatic garage door to open, Ilana opened the car door and took off, running for the cottage, apparently not interested in spending any more time in the cold than necessary. After parking the car, I hesitated for a minute outside, listening to the brutal wind rushing through the trees, sounding like a runaway freight train.

The cottage was cool when I entered. The furnace was making noise, meaning the heat was on, and hot air was rushing from the registers. Everything was working fine, but it wasn't very warm inside. Apparently, the furnace was having a difficult time preventing the frigid wind off the lake from invading every available crevasse in the cottage's exterior. Remembering my promise to Ilana, I returned to the garage to get some firewood along with a brown paper bag of old newspapers. My fingers were numb from the cold by the time I got back inside.

As soon as I had a fire crackling in the stone fireplace, I went to look for Ilana. I found her sitting immobile on a chair in the bedroom, still wearing the big old brown parka Mary had given her. The hood was pulled over her face, making it impossible to know if she was sleeping or just trying to stay warm.

'Hey you,' I said. 'I have a nice fire burning in the living room. Why don't you join me?'

She didn't respond. Even when I knelt down in front of her,

she did not move. Her face was buried so far inside the hood I could not see her. I reached inside to pull her face to me so that I could look into her eyes, and that's when I discovered her cheeks were wet from crying. Pushing the hood back revealed two red and puffy eyes which avoided looking at me.

'What's wrong?' I asked.

She didn't answer, just closed her eyes tight, tears washing down her face as she silently cried.

She was not heavy. It was easy to carry her into the living room and set her in front of the fire. A warm glow soon spread through the room as she stared at the glowing flames. I got up to get a few more logs from the garage, which I added to the fire after returning inside. When everything was blazing bright, flames leaping inside the open pit of the stone fireplace, I sat down behind her and held her in my arms as the fire crackled and sizzled, red hot coals casting warmth over the room.

The front curtains had been closed to hold heat inside the cottage. An imperceptible dark night lay unseen behind the curtains. Now that the room was warm, I decided to open the curtains to the expansive world that lived outside. A vast night scene greeted my view after I pulled the cord. Illuminated by a full moon casting eerie gray shadows over the treeless scene, the beach resembled a phantom snow desert dominated by ice dunes. The dunes had grown high from winter winds persistently splashing ice-filled water, which froze solid on the dune's surfaces. Beyond these dunes, waves could be seen constantly rolling toward the shore, like foaming ghosts in the moonlight. The elegant rushing water climaxed in showers of wet spray, cascading over the dunes in splashing confusion before disappearing forever, their glory lasting only a few fleeting seconds in time.

Ilana had, by this time, removed her parka and was sitting on it in front of the fire, mesmerized by hot flames of golden red licking the air. I sat on the floor beside her and kissed her cheek. She did not respond but did not pull back either.

I wondered if her problem stemmed from being far from home for extended periods of time. Had this become too much for her? Perhaps her telephone conversation with her brother made her homesick. I personally have traveled most of my life. I was used to it. But she was a woman from a small island who had never traveled before. Perhaps it was just too much to ask her to adjust to my lifestyle.

She rested her head on my shoulder. 'It's okay, John,' she said after an extended silence. 'It's not your fault. I am sorry...'

I touched her lips to stop her from talking. I needed no apology. I only wanted her to be happy. I kissed her slowly while searching under layers of sweaters before finally touching the smooth skin of her belly.

I laughed. 'You have so many clothes on. I wasn't sure there was a body under all that material.'

'I am warm now,' she said. 'Would you like me to take some of these sweaters off so we can be more comfortable?'

'Do you like the fire?'

'Yes, it's nice. It makes me happy.'

'You sure? You didn't seem too happy this afternoon.'

'I'm fine now. Please forgive me. I was just being selfish, thinking only of myself.'

She watched the fire burn for a few minutes in silence before getting on her knees and lifting my sweater over my head. Next, she unbuttoned my shirt and took it off. The fire felt warm and good on my skin as she played with my belt. Finally unhooking the button on my pants, she removed my remaining articles of clothing with a little help from me. I pulled her down on top of me, kissing her eyes as she giggled in happiness. The woman I loved was back, and I was happy and horny. She had a beautiful, almost elfish smile when she was teasing me. She knew I could not resist her big brown eyes sparkling in the reflected light of the fire.

Friday, February 26, 11:35 A.M.
John

Before I could meet with him, I needed to know that Phillip was still working out of his old office in Grand Haven, and there were no noticeable changes in his lifestyle.

My friend David confirmed this to be true. According to the

natives, the same old Phillip was inhabiting his office, and nothing had changed, nothing that could be interpreted as a difference in lifestyle.

Okay, so the next move was mine. I had to call Phillip to request a meeting. On the phone, he asked me why. Why would he want to meet with me? I told him I would make it worth his while.

'Okay, fine, but aren't you dead?' He said he had heard a rumor I had died in Thailand.

I replied, "If that rumor was true, he would be meeting with a ghost."

He responded by saying he would be disappointed if a real person showed up. It had been a relief to learn of my demise.

"Very nice," I replied and asked him where he would like to meet.

He said he preferred meeting in a public place, his favorite restaurant. 'The Delight' was the name of his chosen emporium of fine dining. Hardly an appropriate name in my mind, given he was always there.

After asking him for a time, I hung up my phone.

What remained of my morning was difficult. It took great self-discipline to meet with him. Scenes from the Plaza Hotel in New York kept running through my head like an old black-and-white movie. That was where I saw him last, the place where Monica died. He had disappeared from that gas-filled hotel room in a confusion of gunfire and his escape had been a particularly bitter pill to swallow. I could still taste the acid in my mouth when Charlie told me Phillip got away. Worse yet, no one was still alive who could swear to his being in the hotel room that night. No one willing that is, no person except me, and I was not enough. My testimony would surely be challenged in a court of law as prejudicial. It would be my word against his.

Charlie and his guys were there, but unfortunately, they were no help. They could not be certain. After firing gas into the room, everything became fused in a vague blur of gunfire and screaming. None of them could remember seeing Phillip clearly enough to identify him.

I spent all morning dreading my meeting, my thoughts frozen in anger. Yet, he was the key to my plan, and meeting with him was the first step. Without his cooperation, I didn't have a plan. Still, my hatred for him lay like an icicle dripping cold venom on the edges of my mind.

When I arrived at the restaurant, I caught his profile out of the corner of my eye across the dining room: familiar long nose and gray curly hair tied into a ponytail. He was already seated at his favorite table. I could hardly look at the man, and it was difficult to resist an instinctive desire to cut and run.

Dressed in his normal black attire, black shirt open at the neck and black pants, all very neat and sexy. In his mind, he was a gift to women and a blessing to the rest of us. But the odd thing about Phillip was, for all his careful attention to fashion detail, he always neglected one item of his apparel... his shoes. His dirty, old shoes were a clear giveaway to his less-than-orderly brain. This small gaffe in his otherwise fancy attire was a sign that something was not right with this man; something inside his brain was not clean and tidy. Something was missing, a connection not made, a section of his gray matter stagnant and septic, without blood.

He looked up briefly when I sat down. 'Ah, the ghost has arrived,' he quipped.

A half-eaten burger and a few fries lay on his plate. He was almost done with lunch. Good, it meant I could avoid eating with him. I wasn't sure I could stomach the idea of breaking bread with the man. It was symbolic, I knew, and I would have, if necessary, but I was happy I didn't have to eat with the man.

A waitress came to the table. I ordered a cup of coffee. The restaurant was not busy. It was still early for the lunch crowd. Phillip liked it this way. He always came early. It assured him he would get his favorite table.

He continued his meal as if I didn't exist. My coffee came, steaming in the relative cool of the restaurant. The booth where we sat was near a window. I took the opportunity to look outside as I waited for him to finish. The wind was blowing down Washington Street past shops lining the sidewalks. A few pedestrians caught outside were in a hurry, briskly moving through the cold. It wasn't snowing, but it looked like it might start again soon. Gray clouds scurried overhead, blocking the sun. Inside, the restaurant's decoration was highlighted by large framed pictures of old Parisian poster art. A small gas fire burned in one of those metal fireplaces behind closed glass doors on a wall. I didn't particularly like the décor. It seemed fake somehow, but the restaurant was always busy.

'Are you just going to sit and watch me eat?' he finally asked without looking up.

'I thought it would be polite to let you finish first.'

'Aren't you going to have anything?'

'No, coffee is good.'

'What's on your mind?'

'No niceties first?' I asked. 'Like, how are you? Or I'm glad you're alive.'

'I don't really care, John.'

'I didn't think you did. But I thought I would give you a chance to be human for once and prove me wrong.'

'Look, John, if you came here to insult me, just do it and leave.'

'Actually, I came here because I need a favor.'

He looked up. My statement caught him off guard.

'Well, this should be interesting,' he said. 'How can I possibly help you?'

'I have this problem.'

'And what would that be?'

'I don't really like Nue.'

Phillip said nothing.

I let my statement sink in before continuing, 'You don't like him either, do you?'

'No,' he replied.

'Why?'

'You tell me,' he challenged.

'Because he ditched you.'

'You noticed.'

'Yes.'

'Why don't you like him?' Phillip asked.

'That's not important. The important thing is, I think you can help me as much as I can help you.'

'Really, and how can I do that?'

'Look, Phillip, I'm getting tired of running my company. I had a year off, and I learned to like the lifestyle. I have enough money, as you know. I don't really need to work. The point is I'm not sure I want to do my job anymore.'

'Why a change of heart?' he asked. 'Does it have anything to do with almost dying in Thailand?'

'Near-death experiences do that to you sometimes.'

'I see.'

'Look, Phillip, I know you have been cut out of the company by Nue and I assume you are not happy with your current situation. Am I right?'

He looked at me kind of funny, like, why would I care? 'Okay,' he said. 'Let's assume you're right. What can you do for me?'

'Everything. Remember, I'm the CEO and the Chairman of the Board. And I'm not dead. I'm still in control.'

'But why would you want to help me?'

'Because I need something from you in return, why else?'

His beady black eyes seemed to be trying to stare right through me. I wondered if someone like him, who lied most of the time, had a special ability to know when others were lying to him. You know, it takes a liar to know a liar. And if this was true, then he would know immediately that I was not telling the truth. Or could it be that pathological liars are as blind to other people's lying as they are to their own lies? Either way, I was about to find out.

'I don't want to give control of the company to Nue,' I continued. 'I don't mind partnering with him, but I don't really trust him. I'm afraid if Nue takes over, he will transfer everything to Thailand. And under no circumstances do I want that to happen.'

This part was true. I wasn't lying to him when I said it.

'So how can I help you?' his eyes were now completely focused on me.

It was obvious I had gained his attention. I continued, hoping he could not see through my façade. 'I know we have had our differences in the past, Phillip. But I also know you, more than anyone else, understand this business. And more importantly, you understand the Thai. I need someone to be my Chief Operating Officer. I need someone to run the day-to-day operations. I will remain the CEO, but I want to have someone to be my second in command. Now, I have given this considerable thought, and I have decided you are the only logical choice. You alone have the skills to do the job.'

There, the bait was set. If he sensed I was lying, he would say so now. If not, well... just have to wait to see.

He took his time, looking down at his food. A few French fries lay getting cold on his plate. He ate one while continuing to look down as if the answer to his puzzle was written on the table. The waitress came and poured us each fresh coffee. He took a sip.

I waited.

Finally, he responded. 'This is quite a change of heart on your part. I'm not sure I really trust this idea of yours.'

'I'm tired, Phillip. This is simply a matter of practicality. I have no one else to turn to.'

'What about Bob?'

'Bob is incompetent. You know that. You saw what he did with the company in my absence.'

'How about your young assistant, Jason?'

I thought it odd he brought up Jason's name. I wondered how he even knew about Jason, but I let it pass.

'He's too young and inexperienced, maybe someday, but not right now,' I replied dismissively. 'Look, Phillip, this is our chance to bury the hatchet. Plus, you know you are the only person who can do this job besides me. I have no other choice.'

'You don't trust the Thai?'

'No, do you? You know what they will do when they get control, and so do I.'

'That's true.' He sat quietly, pondering the situation.

I felt like a fisherman waiting until the very last moment to jerk the line and set the hook, fearing if I pulled too early, Phillip would spit out the nasty hook and swim away. The hook was in his mouth. He had taken the bait, but he hadn't swallowed the hook, not yet.

'Nue told me it was you who had me kicked off the board. Is

that true?' he asked.

I knew he might bring this up. I was prepared, but I also knew that it would be a tough sell.

'That's true,' I replied honestly. 'And I don't have to tell you, we have had our differences in the past. But the past is over. Today, I have a problem I need to solve, and you can be part of the solution if you choose... or not. It's up to you. But please understand that you will work for me on my terms and not yours. I will still be the CEO, and you will answer me.'

I let him think about this for a moment. Then I continued, 'I'm sure you understood my reasons for kicking you off the board. I needed to regain control of the board. I couldn't do that with you on it. And I'm not giving up control now. But I am giving you a chance to share in the benefits of the company. You will run everything... under my guidance.'

He thought for a moment. In his mind, he had to know what I said made sense. Even if he didn't like agreeing with me, this time, he had to.

'What do you think?' I asked, tugging gently on the hook.

It was time for him to decide. Either he would swallow the hook... or he would swim away. Was his current fate dismal enough that he would accept my offer on my terms? Could he work for me? Did he see any long-term advantages to my offer? Could he make it work for him in the end? Those were the questions he alone needed to answer. I had to be patient. I knew how his brain worked. He was never one to concede anything until he had considered all possibilities.

I waited.

'Okay, say I accept. What do you want me to do?' he asked almost penitently.

'Nothing for now. I will need time to float the idea past the directors and get their reaction. You will have to be patient, but I don't think I will have any trouble if I do this right.'

We talked a while longer. I could tell he was still considering the idea. I had put the hook in his mouth and given it a tug. He seemed to have taken the bait, but I wasn't completely convinced he had swallowed. Our conversation reminded me of old times when we were friends. And the odd thing was, in reality, I felt I could work with him. But only if he would allow me to keep him on a leash. As I have said before, he was brilliant, and he understood the industry. This was what made my proposal plausible. Except for one thing, of course... I hated his guts.

I blamed him, more than anyone, for Monica's death.

2:50 P.M.
John

High waves, remnants of last night's storm, broke up and over the red concrete house at the end of the pier, splashing high in a frenzy of whitewater madness.

As I watched, the wind and waves fought against the man-made structure that had been unnaturally inserted into their world, a world of constant movement interrupted now by a hard, inert intrusion, a place where two worlds lived in conflict and occasional violence.

A short drive after my meeting with Phillip had taken me to a parking area along the channel in Grand Haven, where I could see the end of a pier jutting into Lake Michigan. As I sat mesmerized by an awesome display of nature's anger, I couldn't stop thinking about Phillip, about why I had not lost it at some point in our conversation, jumped up and yelled at him, 'Can't you see I'm lying? I hate you, and I will always hate you.'

Dark mounds of water rolled up the channel and over the pier, as I continued to watch. The weather was frigid, bitter cold in a heavy wind. I stayed in my car where it was warm and comfortable, even though I badly wanted to be outside to live in the violence of the storm, feel the wind and splashing water hurl against my face. I was angry. I wanted to release my anger and fling it into the wind. I wanted to be a wave billowing up and over Phillip, engulfing him in a cold, wet shower of icy hate, drowning him in a grave deep in the bottom of the lake. But I didn't. I had kept my cool. Good, because now the first step in my plan was in place.

I started my car and headed to David's office for a postmortem of my meeting with Phillip.

CHARLOTTESVILLE, VIRGINIA, MONDAY, MARCH 1, 2:20 P.M.

JOHN

Helen gave me a hug and kiss on the cheek as soon as we arrived at my office in Charlottesville. She had never before expressed this kind of emotion. With her, it was always business as usual; proper decorum was required. Adjusting her glasses and stepping back, embarrassed, she smiled broadly at me. 'It's good to have you back, John. This time, I thought we had lost you for good.'

'The notice of my death was premature,' I said, quoting a line from Mark Twain.

Employees came out of their offices and workstations when they heard us talking. Inviting them into the lobby, I gave a quick impromptu speech, said I was happy to be back, and apologized for any problems my extended absence may have caused them. After I expressed my appreciation for their continued loyalty to the company, they filed back to work.

Ilana immediately headed for the apartment, followed by a couple of the security guys carrying our luggage. I went to my office for what promised to be a day filled with answering e-mails and stacks of correspondence. I wasn't going to see the light of day for some time. It was pay-back time for hiding out in Australia.

The drapes in my office were closed when I entered. Of all the dictates Charlie demanded, closing my drapes was the one I hated most. But I did as I was told because Charlie was all business again. His guys were waiting for us on the tarmac as soon as our private jet came to a halt in Charlottesville. Black SUVs transported us to the office. I turned on every light in my office to compensate for the closed drapes, but even with an expansive high ceiling and lights, it still felt claustrophobic. Nothing to be done about that. I had to adjust. No solution existed except to put it out of my mind and concentrate on work.

Intercom rang.

'Clarence is on the line,' Helen said. 'And Jason called. He wants to know when you want him back in the office.'

'Tell Jason now. And I will take the call from Clarence.'

I mentally calculated the time in Australia. It had to be close to five in the morning. Clarence must have wanted to talk to me badly.

I picked up the phone. 'What is it, old buddy?'

'Couldn't sleep. Just wanted to make sure you got back okay.'

'I'm back, but I don't know if I like it here. Nothing but work is staring at me.'

'Have you decided what to do?'

I had told Clarence I wanted to consider my options while flying to the States. We discussed a few ideas while I was still in Australia, but nothing that seemed workable, even though we both acknowledged something needed to be done. If I was right and Nue had really tried to kill me, it would only be a matter of time before he tried again. And the worst part was we agreed that he would eventually succeed. If not the next time, then the time after that. After I died, Nue would find a way to take control of the company. He already controlled most of the stock. He could buy the votes he needed to gain complete control. And that, we assumed, would be disastrous for Clarence. My friend from Australia needed my company to be independent. He needed a reliable distribution chain to market his Australian gemstones. He also needed the rights to the proprietary color enhancement formulas the company loaned to his lab. If Nue had control of the formulas, they would almost certainly have been pulled from Australia and given to a laboratory in Thailand. When this happened, Clarence and his mines would be at Nue's mercy. Gone would be Clarence's profits from the lab. And more importantly, gone would be the high prices I paid him for his gemstones. Nue would never pay the prices Clarence was currently getting from me.

All this would spell the demise of the Nullamana Mining Co.

'I presume you are talking about Nue,' I replied.

'Yes.'

'I have a plan, but I can't tell you the details right now except to say it involves Phillip. I went to see him when I stopped in Grand Haven before coming here. He is not happy with how Nue has been treating him. I think I can use that to our advantage.'

'You saw Phillip?' he questioned. Clarence knew I hated Phillip. So, when he questioned why I had gone to see Phillip, he did so with good reason.

'Yes, trust me on this. I think he can help us.'

'If you say so, matey.'

'Look, Clarence, I don't know exactly how, but more about that later. Right now, I want to talk to you about an emergency session of the company's board. Can you come to the States soon? I don't want this to drag out any longer than necessary. Every day that goes by, my life is in danger.'

'Of course. You name the time.'

4:30 P.M.
John

After entering the last number of the combination into the lighted display on the vault door, I felt the iron handle click in my hand.

It turned slowly with increased pressure, and the big, thick stainless-steel door began to open, powered by an internal, humming motor. After turning on the lights inside the vault, I looked around the room.

It had not been easy to get away from all the commotion. Everyone wanted to talk, ask a question, and hear the story of my last escape from death one more time. The phone didn't stop ringing off the hook until late that afternoon. I finally had some time to get some real work accomplished. But before attempting to dig my way out from under a ton of paper, I had one task I wanted to accomplish first. It was something I had promised myself I would do as soon as I returned home. When no one was looking, I quietly slipped away from my office.

Prior to going to the vault, I had used my computer to search through the vault's inventory for one particular gemstone. The last time I saw the stone, Ilana had been with me, and she loved it, dancing around the room with the stone sparkling in her hand. The computer told me where to find it: drawer 17, parcel number

17457. After entering the vault, I located the parcel paper holding the stone. It was a bluish-green emerald from Columbia, which gleamed under the vault's bright overhead lights.

Quickly rewrapping the paper around the stone, I put it in my pocket. It was going to a jeweler in New York. The man was an artist who made exquisite rings out of gold. I planned to send him a general design to follow. The emerald would be the central stone in the ring, surrounded by diamonds.

The ring was for Ilana.

Thursday, March 4, 4:55 P.M.
John

Charlie arrived late in the afternoon with a big smile plastered on his handsome, dark face.

Apparently, he was a happy man. And why not? He was once more in control. I had to do what he said. My options were few. If I didn't cooperate, I couldn't count on his help.

In a way, I didn't mind. I liked the guy. I just wished I could see the world through his eyes. It would make everything so much easier. Good guys and bad guys. No gray areas.

Deal with it, as Charlie liked to say.

Ilana and I had been home for less than a week, but already, our days were settling into a routine. Charlie was rotating his guys through the office. Someone from the CIA was here day and night. I told him they weren't necessary. A security firm worked for me. Two of their men were in the building at all times. The firm had originally been hired to protect the gemstones in the vault. I assumed they were capable of handling other issues, like watching out for my safety. But Charlie insisted on having his men here. He told me we were dealing with something way beyond the ability of a local security firm. I didn't argue.

Helen had alerted me and warned me that Charlie was on his way in. Good, I was ready. It was time to pay my debt to him in person, and I assumed he would want me to pay. I had been wrong before when arguing with Charlie. I said Nue genuinely wanted to cooperate. Charlie had disagreed and said that was hogwash. Said

Nue was a bad actor who had one objective, which was to gain control of my company using whatever means were required. Now, after what happened in Thailand, I had to agree. Charlie was right, and I had been wrong.

'So, Charlie, how much crow do you want me to eat?' I asked as soon as he sat down across from me at my desk.

'No need, John,' he replied with a smile. 'It's enough for you to admit that my intelligence is superior to yours.'

I smiled and bowed my head.

'No need for that, John. Just a little adulation will do.'

'Thanks for being so humble.'

'Me, humble? I have no reason to be humble, do I, John?'

'None I can think of.'

'Good,' he said, smiling broadly. 'Got anything to drink?'

He swiveled in his chair to watch me open the wet bar hidden behind black glass doors in the wall of my office.

'I'll have a beer,' he announced. 'It's late, and I think I'll spend the night here with my boys. See how they are set up.'

'Why don't you have dinner with Ilana and me? I can have something brought in, or you can take your chances with Ilana's cooking.'

He looked surprised. 'So, she does your cooking too?' he smiled mischievously.

'Don't get personal. But since you asked, let me tell you how it is. She doesn't like the food I eat. So, she cooks her own food, and she gives me a choice. I can have some of her food, or I can make my own.'

'Not much of a choice.'

'You have that right. Shall I tell her you are staying for dinner?'

'Sure.'

I picked up the phone and dialed the extension to my apartment. Ilana answered after a couple of rings. 'Charlie is here. He would like to have dinner with us. Is that okay with you?'

'Yes,' she replied. 'When do you want dinner?'

'Give us a couple of hours. And oh, by the way, he likes his food real spicy.'

Charlie started to yell something in the background. 'Just kidding,' I said softly into the phone. 'Can you hear him yelling?'

'Yes, I will make his food like yours.'

'Thanks, Ilana.'

I smiled at Charlie. 'I thought you black guys liked spicy foods.'

'I like spice in some things, like women, but not food. And I don't like to be categorized.'

'Point taken.'

I took the tops off a couple of beers and handed one to him along with a glass. After sitting down on one of the leather couches, I took a long swig. To me, the first taste of beer is always the best. I enjoyed the moment.

'Can we get down to business now?' I asked.

'That's why I'm here.'

'I'm planning to call for an emergency board meeting later next month. Let me tell you what I hope to accomplish.'

6:50 P.M.
John

Hot air tinged with a hint of spice immediately greeted our senses when I opened the door to my apartment.

Ilana always kept the thermostat in the apartment turned up. She wasn't happy unless it was at least seventy-eight degrees. After growing up in Belize, she couldn't tolerate anything cooler. As was my custom, I immediately took off my sweater, threw it in a closet, and rolled up the sleeves of my shirt. Charlie followed my example by taking off his suitcoat, which I hung up.

'Sure, you don't want to give me your tie?' I asked.

He looked reluctant. Apparently, he didn't feel completely dressed unless he was wearing a CIA-issue uniform, starched white shirt, and ugly tie.

'Please go to the dining room,' Ilana yelled from the kitchen. 'Food will be ready in a minute.'

Since returning, Ilana and I had received no visitors. Charlie was the first. My time had been spent in my office and Ilana was either in the apartment or working with Helen in the office. Our days were all work and no play. I assumed having a guest for dinner would be a welcome change for Ilana. But when Charlie and I arrived in the dining room, I was surprised to see only two place settings.

Charlie also noticed. 'Isn't Ilana eating with us?' he asked. 'I certainly don't want her to think she will be intruding.'

'Let me ask her.'

I found Ilana in the kitchen working over the stove. Sweet smells of spices and fried fish mingled among the stronger odors of onions and pepper. Two bowls of chopped lettuce for a salad sat ready for serving on the counter.

'You're late,' she said without looking up. 'I have been ready for half an hour.'

'Sorry, we got to talking and...'

'I know, I know, you forgot about dinner.'

'Well, yes, I guess... Are you mad at me?'

'No.'

'So, why just two place settings? Aren't you joining us?'

'No, I'm not feeling well tonight. I think I will go to bed and watch some TV. I hope you don't mind.'

'Charlie would really like it if you joined us.'

She looked up. 'Oh, I am sorry. I will tell him myself.'

'You sure you're not mad?'

She looked up at me again. 'No, John. I am not mad. I know you have your work and you are busy. I am happy to help you. Now go to the... what do you call it, the dining room, and let me bring you your food.'

She turned her back to me and continued working at the stove as I watched. Something was wrong. I didn't know what. Maybe it was just being a woman and a Latin woman at that. And I was just a guy. Maybe I was never meant to understand.

'Is she going to join us?' Charlie asked when I returned.

'No, she says she doesn't feel well.'

Ilana brought salads and placed them on the table, returning to the kitchen to get the main dishes. The food was steaming and smelled delicious. It was late, and I was hungry. Charlie and I had talked longer than I intended.

'Charlie,' she said after putting the food on the table. 'Please excuse me. I would love to have dinner with you, but I am not feeling well. I wish to go to bed early. I hope you don't mind.'

'Of course. It's good to see you again, Ilana.' He stood and gave her a hug.

The food was delicious. Fish was tasty, lightly sautéed in butter with some spice that I could not identify. Ilana had found a market in Charlottesville that sold fresh fish. I personally was not accustomed to eating seafood. I'm a Midwestern boy raised on beef, but I was beginning to like her meals.

'This is really good,' Charlie said after eating in silence. 'Does she always cook like this?'

'Yes, I guess so.'

When he didn't speak right away, I sensed he had something on his mind.

'You're a lucky guy,' he finally said, sounding more like an accusation than a compliment.

Or maybe it was just how I understood his statement like I had done something wrong. I didn't think I had, but if I looked at it from Charlie's point of view, our relationship might appear slightly seedy or improper: a rich white guy like me shacked up with a poor girl from a poor country. She living in my house, cooking my meals, and sleeping in my bed... That's what I thought Charlie was thinking, and he deserved an answer.

'You're right, Charlie. I am a lucky guy...'

'Look, John,' he interrupted. 'You don't owe me an explanation.'

'I know, but in a way, I think I do. From the outside, it looks like I just went from one girl to another, a poor girl this time, picked up off the street. And with Monica dead and quickly forgotten, it was easy. Right?'

'I didn't mean anything like that.'

'Maybe not, but I still think I owe you an explanation. Maybe you more than anyone else.'

'John, you don't owe me anything,' he said with emphasis, sensing he had stepped on something awkward, and it was time to back off.

I could have stopped, but I didn't. I needed this conversation, maybe even more than he did. 'Charlie, it may look now like Monica didn't mean much to me. But that's not true. I have already told you I loved her, but I don't think you know how much.'

'John, please don't...'

'Just listen,' I interrupted him. 'You need to hear this. The truth is, Ilana helped save me when I was in Belize. Emotionally, I was a wreck when I arrived. Drinking was out of control,' I continued, wanting the words out in the open, words that had been cooped up in my heart for a long time, words I needed to tell someone. Charlie just happened to be in the way.

'Without Ilana, I could have easily turned into a drunk recluse,' I continued. 'Or dead, in which case no one would care. It was that bad. Monica's death really brought me down.'

'Okay, John. I can see Ilana is special. I guess some guys just have all the luck.'

I thought about what he said, about it being good luck for me that she came into my life. But that wasn't the whole truth, and I knew the truth. The truth was it wasn't luck she showed up... or my good looks... or money. The reason she showed up on my dock one day was because some guy was paying her to keep an eye on me. I hadn't told anyone this. It was our secret, Ilana's and mine.

I made a quick decision. I decided Charlie needed to know the whole story. He listened as he continued to eat. He didn't say anything; he just listened.

'Have you been back to Belize?' he asked when I was done.

'Yes, once. She wanted me to meet her brother.'

'Did you?'

'Yes, but he didn't like me much.'

'I can understand that,' he smiled.

'Why do you say that?'

'Because you took his sister away from him.'

'I suppose you're right.'

'Has she had any contact with him lately?'

'Yes, he called not too long ago.'

'How did it go?'

'Not well.'

Charlie didn't respond.

'So, do you think my plan will work?' I asked, changing the subject.

'I don't know,' he paused. 'A lot of things have to come together in order for it to succeed.'

'Aren't you the guy who originally wanted to set up Nue so we can get rid of him,' I argued.

'Yes, but...'

'But what? Why are you disagreeing now?'

'I'm not sure.'

'But you do agree. Nue won't stop until he kills me.'

'Yes.'

11:10 P.M.
John

Ilana was sitting up in bed.

The TV was on when I walked in, but she didn't seem to be watching it.

Charlie was gone, spending the night with his guys in Arny's old apartment. He told me he would be returning to Washington early in the morning. The final details of a proposed plan had come together while we were eating dinner. Initially, he didn't think much of my idea, and he didn't think it had a reasonable chance of success. But after some discussion, he finally agreed to give it a try, mostly because we couldn't think of a better alternative. He made some changes, of course, but only technical stuff. If everything went as hoped, he said we might have a slim chance of getting what we wanted. At least, this was Charlie's take. My expectations were higher.

It was a cool night in Charlottesville. I was tired. As soon as I got in bed, Ilana turned off the lamp on her side of the bed, slid over, and rested by my side.

'You okay?' I asked after turning off the TV. 'You said you weren't feeling well.'

'I am fine,' she replied softly.

'You sure? You don't seem too happy lately. Is everything alright?'

'Yes.' She snuggled closer to me.

'Have I done something wrong?'

'No.'

'Anything I can do to make you feel better?'

She didn't respond, her body trembling slightly as she lay against my side.

I whispered. 'Have you been crying?'

She wouldn't answer, but when I kissed her on the cheek, her wet tears caressed my lips.

The night was silent as I held her; the bedroom windows closed to a cold winter air. I don't like closed windows, and I don't like silent nights. I like to hear the sounds of summer nights, the crickets singing their love songs. These are sounds of life. Death is silent. As I lay in bed, only the sound of an occasional whimper escaped her lips. Eventually, she fell silent, sleeping beside me, curled up like a small animal.

I wondered how I had been able to sleep alone for so many years in an empty bed. Just being able to touch her shoulder at night, knowing she was with me in the darkness... she gave me comfort.

Sleep finally washed over me, accompanied by anxious images of shimmering waters floating through my half-conscious brain, accompanied by dreams of Monica's shiny wood casket with brass handles, covered by red roses and carried by faceless men from a long black hearse. Damp brown dirt slipped silently through my paralyzed fingers into a deep hole dug at a cemetery to hold her casket. I rubbed my hands on my pants in a vain attempt to clean them, making an ugly brown stain on the cloth.

Waking up in a sweat, the night was black. I lay in bed, wondering how long it would be before these images finally stopped appearing in my dreams. How many years before I could finally rest in peace? Maybe when I was an old man, maybe then? Or maybe never... maybe painful memories were destined to play over and over again forever in my dreams, like old movies that could never be erased?

And what about this beautiful young woman who lay at my side with her long black hair falling over a pillow? A woman so seemingly full of joy... yet, now filled with sadness, tears coming from something she would not tell me, a mystery which I could not solve.

In time, I drifted off again to another world where memories meshed with fantasy. Arny, my dear departed friend, visited me in a dream, smiling and laughing at my melancholy sadness.

'Did you think life would be all peaches and cream?' he asked with a wry smile.

'Where do you think the jazz singer gets his blues? Did you think his music was created simply for your entertainment?'

Wednesday, March 10, 10:10 A.M.
John

I put down the phone.

Charlie and I had just spent an hour going over details for the board meeting, mostly items that applied to my plans for Nue. In particular, we discussed the location. Our plan required controlling as many variables as possible. And what could be a better place to do that than on an island?

The location for the meeting occurred to me a few days ago. I had visited the island in the past. Some of my golfing buddies convinced me to take a quick trip, four days of solid golf. A private jet was chartered to fly us to Hilton Head, South Carolina. From a dock at Harbor Town, it was a short boat ride to the Melrose Inn on Daufuskie Island. The trip had been in early spring, like now. After considering the place, I called Charlie to ask his opinion. He liked it.

I immediately buzzed Helen after talking to Charlie and asked her to come into my office.

'I'm working on a letter you said you wanted,' she replied. 'Can it wait?'

Sometimes, I wondered who worked for whom. 'Helen, the letter can wait. I need to talk to you now.'

She opened the oak doors into my office as I was madly searching for any information I could find on the island, a golf magazine, a brochure. I found nothing.

'Do you remember when I went to Daufuskie Island to play golf? I think it was a few years ago,' I said to her as she sat down across from my desk.

'Yes. I remember it well. It was during a crisis we had with Adam's Jewelry,' she replied. 'I spent my time dealing with them while you were on the golf course having a good time.'

'Yea, yea. You saved my ass... again. Thanks.'

'And I thought you had completely forgotten,' she said with a smirk on her face.

'I never forget, Helen. Now, if you would be so kind, see if you can find a number for the Melrose Inn on Daufuskie Island. If I remember, they were building a conference center across from the Inn when I was on the island. It should be completed by now. Call and ask if they can accommodate a board meeting. Say around the first of April.'

'Why not just go to New York?' she asked surprised. 'Wouldn't that be a lot easier?'

'No, and I will explain why later. Now please just call and ask if they have enough rooms for our members. You know the drill.'

'Doesn't leave me much time to make all the arrangements, especially since I have never been on this island of yours.'

'I know, but I have confidence in you. Besides, you will like the place. I'll send you down there a few days early. You can sit on the beach and get a suntan.'

'Oh sure, you want me to plan a board meeting in a little over two weeks at a place where I have never been. And you think I'll have time to sit on the beach.'

'Sure, piece of cake. Now, off you go.' I smiled at her.

If looks could kill, I think she would have killed me right then and there.

'Get Jason to help you... and Ilana,' I suggested before she got out the door. 'And now that I think about it, schedule a room for Nue early, say on March thirty, the other members of the board for the thirty-first. I want to go early to meet with Nue... got it.'

'Sure,' she was furiously taking notes.

'We can talk about the details later.'

My mind was working at warp speed. So much to do. I made a mental note to call Phillip as soon as Helen confirmed the dates. He was at the top of my list.

I had been making frequent calls to him since seeing him in Grand Haven. Mostly because I knew that's what he required - constant attention, kind of like a big baby, only happy when he was getting attention. I did it because I had to. Because if calling him was what it took to keep him in line, I could do it. For my plan to have any chance of working, he had to cooperate. So, I called him every day.

Helen waited at the door, wondering if our conversation was over.

'That's it, Helen,' I finally said without looking up. I knew she would come through.

She always did.

BOGATA, COLUMBIA, MONDAY, MARCH 15, 8:20 A.M.

MANUEL

The Columbian hung up his phone.

His Thai friend had not sounded concerned, but Manuel was not happy. He had been trying to discover what was planned ever since he and Nue learned about the emergency board meeting. Unfortunately, his recent conversations with the woman revealed nothing of value, and the board meeting was coming up soon. She had told Manuel she didn't know anything. Even after he called her and threatened to harm her brother if she did not cooperate, even then she gave him nothing. And to make matters worse, recently, she had stopped answering her phone.

Manuel had a man in Belize. The Columbian was being informed. The woman's brother was doing nothing unusual. It appeared he had not been warned. So, it was possible she was telling the truth, but this did not help him. He needed information, and he needed it fast.

He wondered if he should put more pressure on her. Perhaps he should go to Belize and visit her brother himself. If a trip to Belize was what it took to make her understand he was not a man to be ignored, he would do it.

The truth was, she made him mad. She was arrogant, like the American she lived with. But then, all Americans were arrogant in his mind. They thought they had all the answers and the rest of the world simply needed to take their advice.

But Manuel knew Americans had troubles of their own. And some of these problems badly affected his country. Drugs were the problem, the main cause of conflict with his country. Drugs and money, money and power, power and violence; a natural chain of cause and effect caused by drugs. Drugs that were easy to produce and worth too much money. Drugs that brought the American military came to his country with helicopters and guns to stop the flow of drugs as if this would do any good. They just made it worse.

Violence causing more violence, more killings, escalating the problem.

Americans should stop interfering in their country.

Columbia was not the problem.

America was.

America was full of dope addicts. If it was not for all the money Americans were paying for drugs, then maybe his country would not be so bloody. But it was also true that Americans came to his country to buy his beautiful emeralds. So, finding a solution was complicated. Not all Americans were to blame.

However, one American in particular was a big problem - the American who wanted to take control of the international trade in emeralds. This had been the subject of a recent telephone discussion with Nue. Manuel told Nue this could not be allowed. The Columbian would not tolerate American control. He would rather work with the Thai than the American.

Nue agreed.

Manuel thought again about the woman.

He would be seeing her soon. He was coming to the board meeting. He assumed she would be there with her boyfriend. She would be surprised to see him. Perhaps in person, he could convince her to cooperate. He would have to think about this possibility and how to make it work to his advantage.

The Columbian frowned, thinking again about the girl, about how she was living with an American. Someone like her, someone who was born in Central America. How could she stay with this American? It was disgusting.

It was wrong, but he would make it right.

CHARLOTTESVILLE, TUESDAY, MARCH 16, 6:15 A.M.

JOHN

I had been dreading this call, putting it off for as long as I could. Although I had talked to Nue recently, it was only in short conversations. They were not long or involved. Nothing that could give him a clue I suspected him. Nothing that would allow him to penetrate my masquerade of pretended calm. I couldn't let him see the anger which seethed deep inside me. I couldn't let that happen under any circumstances. It would ruin my plan.

So, I had purposely kept our telephone conversations short, business only, almost to the point of being impolite. But this next conversation needed to be different. It would take time and require finesse. I wanted something from him, but it wouldn't be easy to get. I would have to be patient if I wanted to be successful. The board meeting was coming up fast. I couldn't wait forever.

There was an eleven-hour time difference between Charlottesville and Bangkok. This meant the call would have to take place in the morning, my morning, and his afternoon.

I don't like morning calls. I am never at my best in the morning, especially early morning. But it couldn't be helped. I woke up at about 4 A.M. I couldn't sleep because the phone call was on my mind, and I needed to be mentally prepared. I played the conversation over and over in my mind as I lay in bed. Like a dress rehearsal, I tried to prepare myself for every eventuality. I assumed he would try to fight through my defenses. He would want to know if I suspected him and what I was planning. His future plans depended on this knowledge.

I knew the smallest inflection in my voice might give me away. Or it could be my choice of one word instead of another. Attempting to be too cool might also be a problem, my conversation seemingly too choreographed. It might not sound natural, too reserved, too indifferent. There are a thousand ways to read a man's mind, even when he is trying to be impenetrable.

I wondered if I had already made a mistake in a previous conversation. I didn't think I had, but I wasn't sure. Nue was a very smart man. He was a master of seeing through the mind of an adversary. This was his game, after all. A game he played better than I did. But I couldn't let that stop me. I needed to play his game if I wanted to win.

All these thoughts ran through my head like a broken record as I lay in bed somewhere between sleep and restlessness; too much to think about, too many dangers, too many potential problems.

Finally, I got out of bed and got dressed. It was time. I dialed his number.

'Mr. Nue,' I said after he answered. 'I wonder if you have a few minutes to talk.'

'Of course, I am always happy to talk to you, Mr. Van Laan,' he answered formally.

'Thank you... I called to talk about the board meeting?'

Our conversation went well at first; at least I detected no problems. I began by explaining to him my reason for choosing South Carolina for the board meeting. I said I had considered several locations, such as New York or London. But late winter is never very pleasant in these cities; it is usually rainy and cold at this time of year. I decided we should meet where it was warm. Plus, I wanted the meeting to be close to my home, somewhere on the East Coast of the United States. I had recently traveled across the globe. I was exhausted. I hoped he and the other board members would understand.

He listened patiently, as was his usual manner before asking me why I felt I needed to call an emergency meeting.

'I have been thinking about making some changes to the company.'

'And what might those changes be?' he asked as if the question was insignificant; when, in fact, he knew they could affect everything.

'I don't want to discuss it on the phone. I hope you understand. This is why I called for a meeting. I think it would be best to discuss it with you and the other members of the board in person,' I replied, hoping to keep him on a string.

He was silent for a moment. 'I would be happy to help you with this matter, Mr. Van Laan. It seems to be of great importance to you. But I cannot help if you don't tell me what you are planning.'

I knew he would want to know, but I couldn't tell him. It was the bait.

'I understand,' I said. 'But the situation is complex, and it would be difficult to explain over the phone. Plus, I am still considering some aspects of the plan. I'm not quite ready to discuss it.'

'As you wish,' he said without emotion.

I assumed he was frustrated, wanting to know more. I was almost certain he would agree now to meet with me early to get the details. Still, I had to ask.

'Thank you. May I ask you for a favor?'

'What is it you wish?'

'I was hoping we could meet before the meeting. I can have my secretary schedule you in early. I hope you don't mind. I would like your opinion on a few items before I present the plan to the board.'

'I will meet with you,' he responded.

'Thank you.'

'Would you prefer to meet sooner?' he suggested. 'I have been thinking of traveling to your country before the meeting. I could come to your office.'

'That is not necessary.'

'Very well,' he didn't argue.

'I'll have my secretary call your office with your hotel reservations.'

'Very well.'

'Thank you.'

I was done. I got what I wanted from him. I was ready to hang up.

"May I ask if you have recovered fully from the injuries you sustained in the river?" he interjected coolly before I could end the call.

Apparently, he now wanted something from me. I had to be careful. It was his turn. Like I said, it was a game. He asked an innocent question, but I immediately sensed a trap. He knew that mentally dragging me back into the river where I almost died was a good way of exposing my real emotions. And I sensed he had the ability to see through the thinnest veil of deception. I needed to answer his question as simply as possible, hoping that would satisfy him.

'I'm fine. I cracked a few ribs, but they are healing. Thank you for asking.'

'I must apologize for what happened,' he continued.

'You have no reason to apologize. The dam broke. It was an accident. Nothing more needs to be said.'

'I was in the helicopter picking up a badly injured villager. He cut his hand and needed medical attention and many stitches. If I had not been in the helicopter, I too could have been killed.'

'I understand.'

'Do you want to know why the dam burst?' he asked.

Again, this is a simple question, but it touched off an alarm bell in my head. I realized I had never asked him why the disaster happened. He must have wondered why. It should have been the first question out of my mouth, a seemingly logical question from anyone who had almost died in the swollen river. That is unless you already thought you knew the answer. And, of course, I thought I did. I thought he caused the dam to break so I would be killed. But I could not tell him that, and as a result, I had never asked him.

So, what he was really asking me was why I had not asked him why the dam broke. I immediately knew I was in trouble. My mind raced.

'It is over, and I survived,' I replied, attempting to sound unconcerned. 'I don't have time to dwell on events I cannot change.'

This was probably the one answer he hadn't anticipated. It was, after all, the sort of answer he might offer in a similar situation. At least, I hoped he would accept it for this reason.

He waited for a moment before continuing to dig into my mental wounds. 'Many people died when the dam broke. It was a great tragedy for the village.'

'Perhaps I can do something to help?' I suggested. 'I can have our foundation contact your office.'

Nue understood how the foundation worked. It had been explained to him as a new member of the board. I always had the feeling he didn't approve. It didn't fit with his view of how an international corporation should work. The little people in his world were of no consequence to him.

'Thank you,' he finally said without emotion.

'I will make the call today. Thank you for bringing this to my attention. I should have thought of helping the villagers before. I'm afraid I have been too involved in my own problems.'

This was true. I had not considered the people of the village who had died, even though the images of their dead bodies constantly circulated in my subconscious. I guess I was trying not to think about them. They were caught up in the river's furious waters, just like me. I pictured the children I had seen playing by the banks of the river. I wondered how many had died. I assumed most. Now, I was ashamed. I had been lucky. The dam's collapse had affected the people of the village far more than it affected me. I wondered again if Nue was really responsible for such a tragedy. Could any man really do such a thing? And if it was true Nue was guilty, as I assumed, it made me mad. I had to be careful. Nue was playing with my emotions.

'We searched for you and other survivors for hours in the helicopter,' he said as if he was not listening to me.

Every word out of my mouth was important now, every inflection of my voice significant. I felt my heart rate rise.

'Were you able to rescue many villagers from the river?' I asked, trying to divert our conversation away from me.

Nue didn't answer immediately. My guess was he had searched for Tim and me, hoping to kill us if we were alive or recover our bodies so they could be shipped home in body bags, evidence of the fact we were dead, thus avoiding any delay in his plans to take over the company at the next board meeting. He had probably spent no time in his helicopter trying to rescue villagers.

He responded, 'We attempted to help, but it was difficult because the river was moving fast. So many died, it was very sad.'

This was a true statement. I knew. I was in the river. I had seen the bodies float past.

'We looked for you and your friend, but we did not find you,' he continued. 'Finally, after a few days of searching, we had to give up and assumed you were dead.'

I didn't comment.

'You were swept away by the river just like the villagers?' he persisted. 'I find it hard to believe you lived. So many others did not.'

'I was in the river,' I said as calmly as possible, feeling him probe my mental wounds like a surgeon with a sterile knife. 'I have the scars to prove it.'

'I am so sorry for your troubles,' he answered without sincerity. It was as if he was challenging me to call his bluff, wanting me to force him to admit he was lying. I couldn't let that happen.

'It's over,' I replied simply,

'A mountain tribesman found you. That is what I have been told.'

'We were very lucky. If it was not for him, I do not think we would have survived. I was injured, and walking was very difficult.'

'You were found in Cambodia, a long distance from where you started.'

'We got lost,' I said truthfully, mostly true anyway.

'Why did you not follow the river back to the village?'

'We got lost looking for help,' I said simply.

Nothing else I could say. But even to me, this sounded like a lie. It was the one place in my story where I was most vulnerable. He knew this as much as I did. It made no sense. It would have been far easier to follow the river back to the village.

He waited as if he was giving me time to admit my lie. When I remained silent, he asked in a tone that made it obvious he wasn't convinced. 'Have you healed?'

'I'm fine,' I said without comment.

He was silent again, and I wondered if he would mount another attack. But it seemed he was satisfied. He had accomplished what he wanted. He knew I was lying.

'I look forward to seeing you at the board meeting,' I said with finality.

'Yes.'

I hung up my phone, disappointed with my performance. Sure, I had held him off. I didn't get mad and give away my true intentions. Still, I knew he was right about our journey. It made no sense unless I suspected he was responsible. But, so what? Even if he did think I was lying, he didn't know for sure. And he did not know what I was planning.

It was a game, after all. It's our game now. And what choice did he have? Like me, he had to play. He had to come to the meeting. He knew the board meeting was too important to miss. So, I accomplished my goal, which was to make sure he came to the meeting. Everything depended on him being there.

I turned around in my desk chair to face my closed curtains.

It occurred to me that if Nue could read signs, then he would know these closed curtains meant I was afraid of him. The closed curtains were a dead giveaway.

As I thought about my curtains, I thought of Charlie. I wondered if maybe I should call and ask him about the curtains. But I already knew what he would say. He would tell me to keep the curtains closed. I, on the other hand, thought it was more important not to risk being too obvious.

I walked over to the windows and held the cord that opened the drapes in my hand for a moment before making an executive decision. The curtains opened to an expansive valley view and this simple act gave me a temporary sense of triumph. It was as if opening the curtains signified that I was willing to risk whatever it took to make my plan work.

. It was all on the line now.

Friday, March 19, 3:20 P.M.
Ilana

It happened when Ilana was alone.

Lately, she had stopped answering the phone. She had no real reason to answer it; she had no friends in Charlottesville; no one she really wanted to talk to. Plus, most of the phone calls that came to the apartment were not for her. They were for John. Occasionally, he called, but not that often. Only when he wanted something. And most of the time, it was just as easy for him to walk over and ask her in person. Helen called a few times, asking for help her in the office. And Charlie's guys called her sometimes to check on her. But if she didn't answer their calls, they would walk over to her apartment. So, she didn't really need to answer the phone.

Besides, she saw no real reason to answer the phone. It was much easier to let the machine take a message. And more importantly, this meant she could avoid talking to the man who had paid her money. This was the real reason she had stopped answering the phone. After talking to him several times, she decided she didn't want to ever talk to him again. Hopefully, he would stop calling if she didn't answer.

However, when the phone rang that day, she was bored, and she answered it without thinking.

'Hello,' she said tentatively, hoping it was not someone calling for John. She never felt completely comfortable talking to John's friends. She tried to disguise her foreign accent. Even though she could speak English very well, she felt self-conscious when she talked to strangers. She knew Americans thought people who spoke with a Latin accent were low-class workers. She knew she should not feel ashamed, but she did.

'Ilana,' a familiar voice answered.

Ilana immediately recognized the voice of her brother. 'Yes, Ricky. Is something wrong?'

Ricky had been working on his boat. The sun was warm. An old brown canvas hat protected his head from its burning rays. A gentle breeze floated through the marina as he toiled. The weather was not too hot. He had gone fishing in the morning, but he had not been very productive. The fish were not biting. He decided to return to the docks early to do some maintenance. He had been working on the boat's motor for a couple of hours when a man approached. Ricky was leaning over to pick up a tool at the time. His head jerked up when a heavy black leather boot landed in his boat. Fishermen didn't wear heavy leather boots. And when a fisherman steps onto a boat, it is with a gentle stride that comes from years of trying not to rock the boat. So, when the boot jarred the boat, Ricky was surprised.

The man wearing the boot did not look familiar. He had a craggy face partially obscured by a mane of black curly hair covering his forehead and a thick mustache over his lips. And when he spoke, it was with a heavy Spanish accent Ricky did not recognize. The man was a big man and slightly overweight. He looked lazy, but there was a hidden strength in his build. And the appearance of a heavy metal revolver under his belt inside his open shirt was disturbing.

He smiled at Ricky, quickly covering the gun with his shirt. 'You are Ricky Emula,' he said as if it were an accusation and not a question.

Ricky thought about denying his identity, but he decided to tell the truth. 'Yes.'

'Good, we need to talk. I have a favor to ask of you.' The man sat down in the back of the boat, looking tired and wiping his brow with a white handkerchief.

'What do you want?' Ricky asked.

'I want you to call your sister. My boss tells me she has not been very helpful lately. Perhaps you remember my boss? He is the man who recently came to see you.'

Ricky remembered the man. How could he forget? 'Is he the man who gave my sister money?'

'Yes.'

Ricky did not reply; he just stared at the man.

'I have a phone you can use.'

He retrieved the cell phone from his shirt pocket while again exposing his shiny pistol to the gleaming sun. Ricky wasn't sure the man did this on purpose or it was an accident. Either way, Ricky was keenly aware of the gun.

'And what do you want me to tell her?'

'It is very simple,' said the man calmly. 'Just tell her the man who gave her money will call her in a few minutes. She is to answer his call. He has a few questions he wants to ask her. She must answer truthfully. Tell her I will be waiting here with you until he has talked to her. When he is done talking to her, he will call me. He will tell me your sister has answered all of his questions truthfully. Then I can get off this boat and go have a nap before dinner. This is what I wish to do. I want to have a nap. But if my friend is not satisfied and your sister has not answered his questions truthfully, well then... He will tell her you and I will go for a boat ride. It will not be a pleasant ride for either of us. And I will not be able to take a nap.' He leaned back and rubbed his hand over the gun in his belt.

Ricky hesitated for a moment, considering his options. The gun gave him no choice. He sighed and nodded his head in agreement. 'What if she does not answer?' he asked.

'You will leave a message. You will tell her to call you. You will say it is an emergency.'

The international telephone number to an apartment in Charlottesville had been programmed into the black cellphone. The big man only needed to touch a small button on the phone with his large, meaty finger. The phone automatically dialed the number while the man listened. He then handed the phone to Ricky.

Ilana had been sitting in the dinette next to the kitchen when Ricky called. The drapes over the windows were closed. John could keep his drapes open in his office if he chose, but Ilana decided to close the drapes in the apartment. She vividly remembered the sounds bullets make when they shatter glass windows. Some things are not easy to forget. This sound was one of those. She felt safer with the drapes closed.

A Washington Post newspaper lay open on the table. John had the paper delivered to the office daily. Ilana was in the habit of getting it from Helen mid-morning. She usually read it with a cup of coffee when she took a break. It was spread out on the table because Ilana had not finished reading it.

The last few months had taught her that she knew very little about the world. Traveling to Australia, searching maps of Thailand, wondering what had become of John, taking trips to Michigan to see a great cold lake, and living in Charlottesville, all of these experiences had made her realize how little she knew of the world and how much she wanted to know more.

She had recently visited the campus of the University of

Virginia in Charlottesville. She went on sunny days when it was a joy to roam the grounds. White pillars, antique red brick buildings, the sweeping green lawns of the old campus; vestiges of Thomas Jefferson's architecture were everywhere. She felt a certain kinship with the students. They looked happy. She assumed they were smiling because they were learning. She was eager for this knowledge. She wanted to be like them.

Dressed in jeans and sweaters, she took walks around the campus with one of Charlie's guys in tow. It was something to do during the day when she was not busy. She peppered her CIA bodyguards with questions as they strolled. The guys had been to college. They told her what it was like to go to class and study. She knew she was older than most of the kids she saw on campus. Going to school was something she should have done when she was younger. But now she knew things she did not know then. Now, she wanted to know more. She had not talked to John about this yet, but she was planning to ask him. She wondered if the college would let her take classes. Charlie's guys had told her the college might have a program for someone like her. This had given her hope. She made the guys swear not to say anything to John. She would tell him when she was ready.

'Ilana, nothing is wrong,' Ricky said curtly.

'What is it then? Why are you calling me?' she asked, feeling a growing sense of dread.

After what happened in Belize between John and her brother, she no longer had a good feeling about her brother. And the last phone call she received from Ricky, the one when she had been forced to reveal John was alive, she knew she should not have done this. She had decided she did not want to talk to her brother anymore.

Ricky heard the reluctance in his sister's voice. He knew she was mad at him, and it was usually no good to try to talk to her when she was mad. His sister was very strong-willed. But this time, it didn't matter. He had to do what the fat man asked. The man had a gun in his belt, and he could hear every word Ricky said.

'A man will call you in a few minutes,' Ricky said before she could object. 'You know this man. He is the man who paid you money. You must answer the man's questions.'

'Why are you talking to me like this, Ricky?'

'I am sorry, Ilana. But you must do this thing.'

'You cannot tell me what to do, Ricky. You know that.'

'Ilana, a man is sitting on my boat with me. He is a big man, and he has a gun. I have no choice. Do you understand?'

Ilana's fear and dread were instantly verified. She had been afraid for some time, afraid her brother would call her again with a request such as this. She had answered the man's question the last time. She knew that was bad. John did not want her to tell anyone he was alive. But later, when she thought about what she had said, she decided it was not so bad. Sooner or later, everyone would know John was alive. She didn't think she had said anything which would hurt John. But she had also not told John about her call. She was afraid he would not like it. Plus, he had recently warned her to talk to no one.

It made her feel bad not to tell John. She did not want to keep anything from him. But what could she do? She had to protect her brother. And she had taken money from this man. She had made him promises. It was something she regretted, but it had happened. She could not change it.

At the end of the last phone call, she had told the man not to call her again. The man promised nothing, just thanked her for the information and hung up his phone. Ilana had hoped this was the end, but it was not. The man had continued to call, and now this. Her nightmare was continuing. It had to stop.

'I cannot do this thing you ask Ricky,' she reiterated.

'But you must. The man sitting in my boat is not a good man. He has threatened me. Do you understand, sister?'

'You must get away from this man, Ricky.'

'Where am I to go? I have nowhere to go, Ilana. I am not like you. I have my boat and my fish. I have nowhere to go. No, you must do this thing they ask.'

'I will come and get you.'

'I will not go with you. This is my home.'

'But Ricky, I cannot do what they are asking.'

'You have to. What is this American man to you anyway?

Soon, he will throw you out like trash on the beach. You owe nothing to this American.'

'Ricky, I love this man, and he will take care of me.'

'You are a fool, sister. You have always been a fool for men. No, soon you will return to this island.' He paused before saying, 'Now you must do as I say because I am your brother.'

'Ricky, I cannot.'

'Goodbye, sister. Remember, if you do not do what I ask, you will not talk to me again. I think I will be dead, swimming with the fishes.'

3:35 P.M.
Ilana

'I don't know,' Ilana told the Columbian repeatedly.

She was beginning to think Manuel did not believe her, but the truth was she didn't know. She had purposely avoided being anywhere near John when he was talking about his plans. She was afraid this might happen, and she didn't want to know anything that could potentially hurt him.

She was telling the truth.

Manuel was getting angry. He had received a call a few days before from his friend in Thailand. It was a persistent request for information. His friend, Nue, wanted to know what John Van Laan was planning for the emergency board meeting. His request had an urgency to it. And they agreed; the information was available from only one source, only from John's girlfriend. The Columbian was told to increase pressure on the woman. That's why his man in Belize had visited her brother. He hoped to make it very clear why she needed to answer all of his questions.

But for some reason, it wasn't happening. He was getting nothing from the woman, and he was becoming increasingly irritated. She was not being helpful and it was making him mad.

'You know I have to make a phone call after I am finished talking to you," he said to her while sitting at his desk in Columbia, thousands of miles south of where she stood fidgeting in the apartment's kitchen.

She was so agitated that she could not sit; she was afraid John might walk into the kitchen at any moment and overhear her conversation. He would know instantly something was wrong. He would hear it in her voice if nothing else. She had almost been screaming.

Do not talk so loudly, she told herself repeatedly. But it was hard. She wanted more than anything else to be done with this conversation. But first, her caller must understand she was telling him the truth. Otherwise, she feared for her brother's life.

'Yes, I know you will call your man in Belize. You must believe me. I have not talked to John about these things. I know nothing about the meeting. I do not know what he is planning.'

'You are not helping me. Do you understand?' Manuel reiterated.

'Why don't you ask him yourself?' Ilana interjected boldly.

'No. I want you to tell me.'

'I don't ask him about his plans. Do you not understand? I have spoken to you as clearly as I can. I can't tell you what I do not know!'

'Then you must find out.'

'No, if I ask him now, he will be suspicious,' she said with resolve, which made her feel suddenly strong.

'Do not play games with me, little woman. I am not a man who plays games.'

'I also don't play games,' Ilana said, finally letting her frustration turn to anger. Even though she knew getting angry was not good, she could not help it. She had been honest with this man. Now, he needed to believe her.

'I have told you everything I know,' she explained one more time. 'I do not want to talk to you anymore.'

The Columbian could think of nothing more to say, nothing which might persuade her to tell him what he wanted to know. She was either being stubborn, in which case she was putting her brother's life in jeopardy, or it was just possible she was telling him the truth. Enough for now, he thought. He would see her at the meeting. She would be surprised. He did not think she knew he was coming. He would get what he wanted from her then. Now, it was time to do what he had to do to make sure she cooperated the next time he talked to her.

'Okay, little woman.'

'So, now you will make your call?' Ilana asked hesitantly.

'Yes, now I will make the call about your brother.'

'You will not have him harmed,' Ilana said as forcefully as she could. 'I will never help you again if you harm him.'

'I am not sure you have been truthful. So now I must decide what to do about your brother.' He hung up his phone quickly.

He would let her worry.

4:40 P.M.
John

Against all odds, Phillip and I had actually become quite cordial.

For one thing, Phillip liked to talk on the phone. He was one of those people who would rather talk on a phone than converse face to face. He liked to talk at length, and he liked to talk often. That's why I made a point of calling him at least once every day. Somedays more than that.

I was hoping these conversations would keep him from talking to Nue. I did not want Nue to know Phillip and I were talking to each other. Of course, I couldn't prevent Phillip from calling Nue, but as long as Phillip had me as his phone pal, I hoped he wouldn't find it necessary to call Nue.

Phillip admitted to me that he wasn't happy. Nue had cut him out of the company. Of course, I knew this because I was the person who asked Nue to do it. Phillip knew that, but oddly, it didn't seem to matter much to Phillip. We had talked about it, Phillip and me. We agreed that Nue should not have done what I requested. Why? Because, as Phillip said, Nue owed him. After all, Phillip had helped Nue. Without Phillip's assistance, Nue would not have been involved in my company in any capacity. So, when Nue told Phillip he was out, Phillip felt more betrayed by Nue than me.

Plus, Phillip admitted he didn't blame me. I was simply doing what Phillip would have done if he had been in my shoes. Phillip understood this.

The situation with Nue was different. Phillip had done nothing to Nue to deserve being booted from the company.

Of course, this didn't completely stop Phillip from feeling I had betrayed him. But it was something that happened a long time ago. And with Phillip, the guy who betrayed him recently was Phillip's current enemy.

Phillip was someone who needed and wanted an enemy. It didn't really matter who they were. He just needed someone to hate. It made his life interesting, gave him something to talk about on the phone. And as I said before, he loved to talk on the phone. It was what he liked to do more than almost anything else. He liked to talk on the phone, mostly complaining about his perceived current enemies.

Okay, I knew all this when I initiated my plan. It was what I relied on to keep Phillip in line. This was our game now, Phillip and me. Phillip loved intrigue, and he loved to play games. And to play this game, I had to call Phillip every day, sometimes several times a day, just to keep him in the game, this time with me as his ally and Nue as his enemy.

'Daufuskie Island, South Carolina,' I said to him over the phone. 'A resort on the island has a conference center. You will like the place. It has a beautiful inn which overlooks the ocean. It will be great.'

'I thought we were going to New York. Wasn't that what you told me?' Phillip protested.

'I told you I was considering New York, but I have decided to go to South Carolina instead.'

I knew Phillip, and I knew he liked New York. When he was in the Big Apple, he always pretended to be a famous actor. He wore a tweed coat, a colorful scarf around his neck, with his gray ponytail blowing in a stiff wind, accelerating through the high canyon walls of city skyscrapers. New York is a city where money and art coexist in an uncomfortable marriage. He was right at home in New York. But a southern barrier island off the coast of South Carolina... Daufuskie Island would be a completely different experience for Phillip. Just thinking about having his spindly white legs extended from shorts while wearing a colorful Hawaiian shirt made him uncomfortable. I knew he was having a difficult time picturing it. It wasn't his scene.

'Look, I want you to come early to the island before the board meeting so we can talk.'

'How early?'

'Maybe a day or two, I'll have my secretary send you plane tickets. Everything has been prepared. A room at the Melrose Inn on the island has been reserved in your name.'

Phillip loved this kind of attention. He was in the big time again. He was in his element: intrigue, a chance to run a big international gem company. Planes and fancy hotels were like valuable treasures for him. I had tugged on the line and had him hooked. I didn't think he could get away now. In addition, I had given him an enemy: Nue, Phillip's required enemy. He didn't need many, just one at a time, and this time, it was Nue. I had given him everything he wanted and desired in life. It was all too good for him.

I put down the phone after saying I had work to do. I knew, given the opportunity, he would talk my ear off. I always had to cut our conversation short at some point because the truth was, I couldn't stand to talk to the man any longer. It made me ill.

I sighed and turned in my desk chair to look outside. It was a bright, sunny day in Virginia. A promise of spring was in the air. Maybe, I wondered, when this nightmare was over, maybe I could return to something that approximated a normal life.

I thought about Ilana, assuming she was in my apartment next door. Or perhaps she was in the office helping Helen. I hoped so. Work was good for her state of mind. She needed things to do. However, lately, she has not seemed very interested in working. I wondered why. Maybe it was because I had not been spending enough time with her. My fault, but I couldn't help it. Company business was absorbing my days. Hopefully, we will be able to spend more time together soon.

I opened the dark glass doors that covered the wet bar built into the wall of my office and poured a glass of bourbon. I felt I deserved a drink after talking to Phillip. Besides, it was late, and most of the important work was done for the day.

Helen came into my office.

'Want something to drink? Wine, bourbon?' I asked with a smile.

She looked at me, kind of funny. I had never asked her to join me for a cocktail before. It was always business with her.

'Sure, I guess,' she said hesitantly. 'Wine.'

I poured her a glass and sat down on one of the couches in my office.

'I want to talk to you,' I requested.

She must have wondered what was up. I never talked to her like this. And we always sat at my desk when she was in my office; she on one side, and I in my desk chair. It was a proper business setting, the way she liked it. Decorum was very important to her.

She carefully took a sip of wine, cautious not to spill on the leather. 'May I first tell you why I came in here?' she inquired.

'Sure.'

'I have made all the preparations for the meeting. Fortunately, the Inn was not too busy. It's not their busy season. They had enough rooms.'

'I was depending on that.'

'You are so smart, Mr. Van Laan,' she replied with a hint of sarcasm.

'I have my good days.'

BELIZE, AMBERGRIS ISLAND, 2:50 P.M.

RICKY

Far from where Ilana sat anxiously in the cool stillness of her kitchen, a gentle, warm breeze drifted through the old docks of the fishermen's marina near the town of San Pedro, Ambergris Island.

Brightly colored fishing boats tied to the moorings rocked to the calm rhythm of the sea. Overhead, a gray pelican swooped down to settle on a nearby dock pole. After folding his long wings into its body, the bird suddenly flapped again and rose slowly into the air, but not before letting out a loud squawk of protest; the big bird's tranquility irritated by the annoying ring of a nearby cell phone.

A heavy-set man leaned over to pick up the offensive ringing technological gadget he had carelessly laid on a seat cushion in Ricky's fishing boat. Ricky looked up from his work, warily eyeing the phone. He knew the reason for the phone call. He had been anxiously waiting for it. He stopped working to listen when the man put the phone to his ear.

A heavy wrench caked with dried black oil and grit lay on the floor of his boat not far from where Ricky sat, listening to the man talking on the phone. If Ricky could get the wrench in his hand without the big man noticing, maybe...

Ricky hesitated, hoping he might not need the wrench. If the man left his boat without bothering him, then the wrench would not be needed. If not... well... the wrench might help him avoid being killed. Patiently, Ricky knelt down on one knee. With his back blocking the man's view of the wrench, he slid the weapon under his shirt while using his other hand to gather some old rags from the floor. The man was not talking as Ricky sat up to listen. Mostly, the big man was nodding his head as if the caller on the other end of the line could see him. Apparently, the other person was doing all the talking.

'Si, senor, I understand,' the big man finally nodded, slowly pointing his fat finger at a small button on the black cell phone to end the call.

Ricky looked at him suspiciously. The truth was, Ricky was never really nervous about the outcome of the call. He was confident his sister would do what he asked. But when the man looked strangely at him, Ricky began to suspect something was wrong.

The big man smiled through his mustache. 'It seems we must go for a boat ride,' he said. 'I had hoped to take a nap, but a boat ride will not be so bad. It is a nice day, and the waves are not too high.'

'But,' said Ricky. 'Surely, my sister answered your friend's questions.'

'I am sorry. My friend told me we needed to do this thing. Now it is time for us to go for a ride in your boat,' the man said as he reached inside his shirt and placed his meaty hand on the handle of the gun under his belt.

Ricky looked at the man. Surely, this was all wrong. The wrench was in his hand behind his back. He had no choice now. It was time to stop this madness. With his free hand, he pointed toward ropes that held the boat to the dock in a half gesture of surrender, asking the big man to untie the lines so they could leave the dock. Then, while pretending to start the engine, he warily watched his opponent, looking for an opportunity. When the big man leaned over the back of the boat to untie a line, he raised the wrench high in the air to crash it down on the back of the man's skull. But the big man moved away just as Ricky swung and the heavy wrench had too much inertia for Ricky to change its direction quickly.

The big man was nimbler than he looked. With one quick motion, he ducked under Ricky's intended blow, the wrench passing inches from his head. Crouched in an almost cat-like position, the big man pounced. Swinging with all his strength, the pistol in his hand landed a blow, hard metal against soft skin and brittle bone just under Ricky's chin. Ricky went down quickly and hard, blood spurting from an open wound to his jaw, slowly seeping into small cracks in the old wood floor in his boat, unconscious and helpless.

The big man quickly hid the pistol under his shirt while searching the docks for anyone who may have noticed their brief fight. Seeing no one, he prepared to get underway. The engine started after several attempts. The big man let it run slowly in neutral while he released the lines until the boat was free from the dock. After a quick glance to be sure no one was watching, he leaned with all his heavyweight against a dock pole, pushing the boat away. The transmission clicked easily into forward gear. He turned the wheel toward open water while pulling the throttle back to accelerate away from the dock.

Waves rolled slowly through the harbor, rocking the moored boats in a confused rhythm as Ricky's boat disappeared from view.

CHARLOTTESVILLE, 7:25 P.M.

ILANA

Curled up alone on a comfortable couch in a dark room, staring at nothing, Ilana listened intently to a phone ringing in a far away bar in her hometown in Belize.

'Henry, is my brother in your bar? I would like to talk to him,' she half pleaded as soon as Henry answered the phone.

'I am sorry, Ilana. But he has not come here today,' the bartender answered.

In a previous call, she had asked Henry to go to the docks to look for Ricky's boat. Henry liked Ilana; she was very pretty. He had agreed. When he called her back, he told her Ricky's boat had not yet returned from the sea.

She waited several hours before calling again, hoping Ricky would be at the bar by this time. He was not. She thanked Henry and hung up. She could ask him to do no more.

It was then she began to worry in earnest. Up until this time, any number of reasons might explain why her brother had not returned to the harbor. But by now, his boat should have been tied up safely in the marina for the night. She knew her brother's habits like her own. He should have been at Henry's bar. He always went there after work.

Her earlier conversation with the South American man had been running through her head, over and over, ever since she talked to that awful person. Each time she replayed what she told him, it sounded worse to her. She had become angry with the man and told him off. It had felt good at the time. But now, she knew it was a mistake and she wanted to call him back, apologize, and beg for her brother's life... But it was too late. She couldn't call. She didn't know his number. She couldn't remember it.

On a table nearby, she had scribbled several telephone numbers on a sheet of paper next to a newspaper crossword puzzle she had been doing to pass the time. She had once memorized the telephone number of the man she worked for when she was in

Belize. But that was months ago, and she could not remember the number and none of the numbers on her paper looked right.

She had tried a few, but with no result. To make matters worse, she had no real idea where the man lived or what his name was. She only knew what he had told her when they were sitting together at the Jewelry shop, which was almost nothing. And now she knew why. He was smart. She was his pawn.

As she wandered through the apartment in a trance, Ricky's last words ran rampant through her mind. 'I will be dead, swimming with the fishes.'

His words had sounded funny when he first said them. Ilana didn't take him seriously, but now she couldn't help thinking about what he said. And it didn't sound funny anymore.

John's apartment suddenly felt big and empty. Talking heads babbling from a television screen somewhere in the kitchen disturbed her silence with their constant bitter banter. The transparent stream of ugly noise coming from the TV ground was like grinding salt into a fresh bleeding wound that was beginning to burrow deep into her skull. Without thinking, she rushed into the kitchen and angrily turned off the noisy TV.

Beyond the drapes that covered the windows of the apartment, a gray-maroon evening sky was setting over the valley. Stark black leafless trees contrasting with vague shadows of distant mountains blended into rich shades of charcoal as night took control of the sky and the rooms of the apartment became dark.

Ilana had neither the energy nor the desire to turn on the lights. Curled up in one corner of a couch, she wept bitter, acrid tears in silence while her mind traveled to a place where she imagined her brother's body splashing into the warm blue waters of the Caribbean. Gasping for air, he was dragged down by heavy metal weights to a place where his bulging eyes could see nothing; no light, only darkness. Eventually, when he could hold his breath no longer, he stopped fighting the ropes that held his wasted body and exhaled for the last time. Ashen, his skin paled as his body cooled in the deep dark water.

Alone now and convinced she had killed her brother, Ilana no longer wanted to be in this place with all these strangers. Rocking slowly back and forth, the sound of her brother's voice begging her to help him screamed in her ears.

Why had she not listened?

Hot air flowing from an open floor register ruffled the long white drapes, blocking her view of the outside world as she sat alone, crying in soft muffled gasps of despair.

8:05 P.M.
JOHN

It had been good to talk to Charlie on the phone.

He was doing his best to help—well, mostly helping... helping when he wasn't complaining. Too many things could go wrong, he complained, too many variables that could not be controlled. But still, he admitted, my plan had a chance of working—a small chance.

I argued that if he had a better plan to get Nue out of my life forever, he should tell me now. But the truth was, we had only one plan. And if it worked, we could get rid of Nue. Charlie could use the criminal evidence we gathered on recorded tapes to prevent Nue from ever again setting foot in the United States. Despite his diplomatic status, Nue and his affiliated companies would be prohibited by the State Department from ever participating in a US company, owning stock, or sitting on a company board. Hopefully, Nue would then retire to Thailand, where he belonged, and leave me and my company alone.

I reminded Charlie, the plan had been his idea in the first place; a fact he only grudgingly admitted. And I assumed he was complaining because it was my plan now, not his. I was dictating the place and time.

Anyway, we had a plan. It was a sting operation according to Charlie. He had agreed to bring the equipment we needed to pull it off. It seemed he was finally getting into the spirit of the thing.

The clock on my desk read eight after I hung up from my call to Charlie. It was later than I thought and I was suddenly tired and hungry. Ilana had not called yet to ask me about dinner, which was not like her. But lately, she had been trying to stay out of my way. She knew I was busy. So, I wasn't completely surprised. After

231

placing my hand on the palm reader in my office bookshelf, the door to my apartment automatically opened. It was dark in the hall. I searched for a light switch while listening to the door behind me click shut, locking me inside. A muffled whimper from somewhere near the stone fireplace sounded like a small animal had found its way inside the apartment. I hit the light switch, suddenly concerned. Bright lights flooded the living room. Ilana's hands immediately covered her eyes.

'What's the matter?' I asked, sitting down beside her.

She did not answer, continuing to cry softly. I put my arm around her shoulder to comfort her. She did not move away, but she did not respond to me either, simply sat bent over on the couch crying, tears flowing down her cheeks.

'Ilana.'

When she continued to refuse to acknowledge my presence, holding her hands over her eyes to shield them from the lights, I knelt down in front of her. 'Please talk to me... Ilana, please.'

Nothing.

I again sat down beside her and this time she moved slowly under my arm and nestled against my side, her only acknowledgment of my presence. I brushed her long black hair from her face and rested beside her. I don't know for how long. Eventually, her crying slowed. Yet, she was unwilling to talk. Nothing seemed appropriate. Time passed. A phone rang in the other room. I thought about letting it go to voice mail, but decided to answer it for no other reason than to stop its irritating noise.

'Hello...'

Okay,' I said, wondering if I should disturb her in her state of mind. 'Ilana, it's your brother. Do you want to talk to him, or should I tell him you will call him back later when you feel better?'

A light seemed to go on in her eyes. She looked up at me like I had given her a present.

'No, no. I will talk to him.' She leaped off the couch in one quick movement and literally grabbed the phone from my hand. 'Ricky, is it you?' she wiped her tears with her free hand, silently listening. After a minute, she said. 'Okay, Ricky, I understand. You are not hurt bad?'

She listened again without interrupting him. That was not normal for her. Usually, she interrupted everyone.

'I understand,' she finally said. 'We will talk later. Yes, I am glad you called... No, thank you... I love you, Ricky... yes, goodbye.'

Now, that was a strange, one-sided conversation. I waited for an explanation and eventually she looked at me as if she suddenly realized I was in the room, hesitating, seeming to be unsure. Finally, she explained, 'He had an accident on his boat. I ...I thought he was dead. His boat did not return to the dock today. His friend called to tell me. I am sorry, I was so worried. I thought he was dead.'

'He is alright?'

'Yes, he was not hurt bad.'

'What happened?'

'He didn't tell me exactly, some accident. He needed some stitches to his jaw, but he will be fine.'

'That's it. That's all he told you?'

'It was just an accident on his boat. These things happen to fishermen.'

'You thought he was dead?'

'Yes,' she replied with the phone still in her hand, standing rigid like a statue, her face red from crying, her eyes puffy, makeup smeared.

'You okay now?'

'Yes... I am okay,' she answered unconvincingly.

'You don't look so good.'

'I am fine.'

'You don't look fine to me.'

'John...'

'Why didn't you tell me what was wrong when I asked you?'

'I don't know, John... It is all so confusing... I mean... I don't know if I should be here. This is not my home. I sometimes don't know what I am doing here. You are always so busy, and I am alone. And... I make mistakes... sometimes... I don't mean to do these bad things. But I don't always do what is right. And... and I am afraid I will hurt you. I do not want to hurt you, John... Maybe I should go home where I belong. I am not sure I belong here anymore. I am sorry, John... I...'

Then she began to cry again.

Nothing she said made sense. It all came bubbling up from some unknown pool of confused thoughts. Like a faucet had been turned on inside her brain, and everything that had been bottled up flowed out at once. I didn't know what to think.

'Perhaps I should get you something to eat,' I finally suggested because I didn't know what else to do. 'Let's go to the kitchen.'

Soon the stove was sizzling with leftover enchiladas. It was the only food I could find in the fridge. I poured her a glass of wine and insisted she sit at the counter and let me serve her. Her eyes were still red and puffy from crying. I gave her a tissue to wipe her tears.

She sat silently as our food cooked. Sometimes, she looked at me.

And sometimes she just stared into space, to a faraway place in another world.

SAVANNAH, GEORGIA, MARCH 30, 9:10 A.M.

JOHN

My initial urge was to cut and run.

Seeing Phillip in all his three-dimensional glory was more difficult than I anticipated. Talking to him on the phone was one thing. Dealing with him in the flesh was a lot harder.

Tall and lanky with a slight hunch to his shoulders, he arrived at the Savannah Airport. I knew I should have been happy to see him. He was, after all, a major player in my plan.

He looked good, confident, and content, strolling down the sterile halls of the terminal building. I didn't like seeing him that way. I would rather have seen him looking hopelessly confused. Or maybe I was just frustrated; because, as usual, I was wrong about Phillip. He did know how to dress for the island. Instead of his normal avant-garde, big-city cosmopolitan look, today he wore a light brown polo shirt and white cotton pants with a lightly colored sweater thrown casually over his shoulders; more like someone stepping off the curb of Sunset Boulevard than Madison Avenue; like an actor outfitted for a play entering the stage, posture erect, with a confident smile on his face, his pompous ponytail swinging with his gait. Completing the look was his intense black eyes separated by a long, straight nose I had learned to hate. Only his scruffy, dirty black leather shoes disagreed with his upscale resort wardrobe selections and gave away the possibility that a few pieces were missing from this puzzle of a man. But I had to give him credit. He had obviously researched his role for the island and dressed accordingly.

I took a deep breath.

It was time to play my part in this drama. If I was to succeed, I couldn't do or say anything that might give away the real reason I had invited him to the island. I couldn't afford to give him even a hint of my true intentions. The man was very smart.

Fortunately for me, it was a bright, sunny day in Savannah, Georgia. I always seem to function better in good weather. I think this oddity in my character is a direct result of growing up in western Michigan. The weather in my hometown of Grand Haven is cloudy most of the year. The big body of water known as Lake Michigan that lines the shore of the town is the main culprit for all this dullness. Westerly winds flowing across its cold water gather water vapor rising to form billowing, sun-obstructing clouds. Endless days of gray skies can be downright depressing. A day of sunshine always gave me a lift, and fortunately for me, the low country of South Carolina had favored us with sunny skies since we arrived. Temperatures were in the seventies, and the forecast indicated more days of summer-like weather in early spring.

All preparations had gone well. Charlie and his guys had completed their setup. Nue had arrived on time, currently installed comfortably at the Melrose Inn. Helen called to tell me the news. Jason had gone to the Hilton Head Airport to transport him. This was my idea. I thought it would be a touch of irony to have Jason greet him since I assumed it was Nue who had been instrumental in putting a contract on Jason's head. As a precaution, a CIA agent accompanied Jason to make sure nothing went wrong. Jason informed Nue that I would like to meet him at about twelve-thirty for lunch. So, one participant in my plan was in place. Phillip was the only other important participant, and he was my responsibility.

I was ready. Ilana and I had been on the island for a few days. Coming early gave me time to prepare, both mentally and physically. Helen, Jason, and our CIA bodyguards accompanied us. Charlie met us at the airport with his people. Helen was very nervous about the preparations. She could hardly wait to hit the ground running. It was all I could do to restrain her. Jason, on the other hand, saw the trip as one more grand adventure. A month of living at home had renewed his spirits. The painful memory of his near-death assassination had faded and I was happy that he had not been mentally scarred by the incident in Hong Kong.

Before leaving Charlottesville, anxious anxiety accelerated as the emergency board meeting approached. Everyone wanted to know what I was planning. I attempted to be honest when board members called, asking everyone to wait for the meeting, and explaining that I wanted to discuss my plans with the board face to face. Most of the members respected my wishes with varying degrees of acceptance. Some wanted a minimum explanation before they would commit to spending time and money attending the meeting. I reluctantly offered some clues to those who were persistent and who I thought I could trust. But the real truth was, even I didn't know how the board meeting would go. Too much depended on today's meeting with Nue and Phillip.

Ilana had been my biggest challenge before traveling. I assumed she would accompany me to the meeting. However, as the time grew close, she made it increasing clear she did not want to go. Plus, I had caught her crying a few more times, like the first time. It didn't happen often. And it wasn't as bad as the first time.

Her crying spells followed a strange pattern. I would find her curled up on a chair or in bed. The room would be dark and the only reason I knew she was there was because I could hear her quietly sobbing. The only thing which seemed to help was to simply hold her. After a while, she would calm down, cuddle beside me, and stop crying.

I always asked her what was wrong, but she would refuse to answer.

'Anything I can do to help?'

'Sit with me,' was her usual reply.

We would rest in dark silence until eventually, she would stand up as if nothing was wrong and turn on a light, go into the kitchen for something to eat, or watch some TV. She would say everything was fine, but I knew it was not fine.

My hope was that this trip would be good for both of us; I thought that getting her out of the apartment with its closed drapes and into some sunshine might revive her spirits. If everything went as planned, I thought perhaps Ilana and I might stay for a few extra days after the meeting. She could enjoy the renaissance of spring on the island. Few places on earth are as beautiful as these barrier islands this time of year, filled with flowering azaleas.

This small mental incentive gave me a lift. In the last month, I had spent almost no time thinking about what to do after the meeting. Every ounce of mental energy was focused on the next few days.

After arriving by air from Charlottesville, taxis drove our contingent to the south end of Hilton Head Island in the Sea Pines Plantation. A scheduled ferry was at the dock in Harbor Town, waiting to take us to Daufuskie Island. Walking down a boardwalk to the boat felt good. The sun was bright and warm, reflecting in wind ripples moving across the flat water near the dock. A gentle, warm breeze filled the air and I could smell the sea. Ilana walked quickly ahead of me with a new-found joy in her stride and a shy smile on her face. She was near the water again, and the water was her home.

I suggested we find seats inside the passenger cabin of the ferry where Helen and Jason were already seated. Charlie and his men had followed inside, sitting opposite to each other with a green wooden table between them. Charlie was checking messages on his phone. Jason sat intently reading a copy of the Washington Post he had taken with him from the office. Helen stared at a list of tasks written in a notebook, preparing for work as soon as she stepped foot on the island. Ilana insisted on standing outside in the back of the boat, the wind blowing through her hair. The steward said he didn't mind.

A boatman released the dock line. The ferry turned and accelerated away from the protected harbor into the Calibogue Sound.

The Sound is a broad body of water that empties the tidal swamps of the low country into the Atlantic Ocean between the islands of Hilton Head and Daufuskie. It is a mile to three miles wide at different places. Hilton Head is connected to the mainland by a bridge. But Daufuskie Island can only be accessed by boat or helicopter. This was the reason I chose Daufuskie for our meeting. It was easier to control the environment, with fewer variables than in New York City or old London Town. Charlie agreed

The sun cast flashes of light off the glassy blue water as we slowly motored across the Sound. Ilana seemed momentarily happy, content to gaze out over the water, looking in the direction of the Atlantic Ocean. This wasn't her island of Ambergris, but it was an island in the ocean. She gave my hand an unexpected squeeze as if to say she was glad she had come. I leaned over and kissed her on the cheek.

Multimillion-dollar homes lined the banks of Daufuskie Island as we drew near. Some rising from behind stands of pine trees; tall and majestic, looking like mini-hotels. I wondered who built houses this big. Did the inhabitants spend their time wandering their enormous edifices to wealth, searching from room to room, looking for a place to rest? Or did they simply live in a small portion of their mansion, allowing the other rooms to languish in forgotten opulence?

I put these thoughts aside, content to observe Ilana as the wind swept her hair off her face. Her big brown eyes gleamed in the afternoon sun. She was a portrait of natural beauty. I put my arm around her slim waist and held her, satisfied to simply be in the presence of this beautiful woman.

Pelicans skimmed over the water near the ferry, rising with lazy flaps of their wide wings before gliding inches off the crests of choppy waters.

'Look, John,' Ilana said.

The back of a shiny gray porpoise briefly appeared, a spray of water rising from its blow hole before diving into the dark green waters of the Sound. A flurry of tiny sandpipers flying in formation skimmed the water with intensity and speed, their wings rotating at rpms too fast to see, darting in and out in unison over the ocean. The sun was warm on my face. The scent of the sea rested in my mind, and for a brief moment, as I held her hand in the back of that boat, I was at peace.

It was a moment I have remembered many times since then, a moment I wish I could relive.

10:50 A.M.
JOHN

Sitting next to me in the back seat of a taxi, Phillip seemed content while looking out a window as we traveled north on Interstate 95 from Savannah Airport to Hilton Head Island.

I-95 is a major divided highway that runs up and down the eastern coast of the United States. It was very busy that day.

'It really is different here, isn't it?' Phillip announced for no particular reason.

'What do you mean?'

'So flat and ugly, nothing but scrub forest and swamp.'

'That's why they call it the low country,' I replied, not wanting to contradict him.

But I knew he was wrong. Closer to the island, broad, expansive rivers flowed to the ocean. Spanish moss could be seen growing in abundance, hanging from sprawling branches of great live-oak trees. Tall pines cast their shadows over stately palms growing next to low-lying splashes of green palmetto bushes. Flowering azaleas were a visible treat to the eye. In a few weeks, they would be in their prime, the islands alive with the brilliance of their rich colors.

'Mr. Nue is already here,' I said. 'Since it might be awkward for the two of you to meet without my having previously told him why you were coming, perhaps we should get that out of the way today,' I suggested.

Phillip turned to me. 'Nue is here?

'Yes, I asked him to come early.'

'Why?'

'I wanted to talk to him before everyone else arrived. He's our biggest shareholder and deserves a little special attention.'

'Does he know I'm coming?' Phillip questioned.

'No, he doesn't.'

'Do you think it's a good idea to tell him now? Perhaps it would be better to wait...'

'Why wait? Nue is well aware of your talents. Why not deal with the issue of your becoming the COO now so we can concentrate on other issues later?'

'I suppose,' Phillip sounded unenthusiastic.

It occurred to me Phillip had expected me to announce his appointment at the board meeting. In this case, he would have the opportunity to enjoy Nue's displeasure in front of everyone. But this was not how I do things. I don't appreciate surprises at board meetings. I like everything choreographed.

'Okay then,' I said, 'I'm meeting Nue for lunch. Why don't you join us?'

'All right... I guess.'

I hoped he was satisfied. The idea of meeting Nue when Nue didn't know he was coming – I hoped this was more than enough drama to lure Phillip to the meeting. When he said nothing more, I decided to let him be.

It takes about forty-five minutes to drive I-95 to Hilton Head from the Savannah Airport. Cars and trucks speed at close to eighty miles an hour. Very nerve-racking, especially when not driving. I like being in control. I don't like sitting in the back seat of taxis, but there are times when it can't be helped. To take my mind off the road stress, I thought about something else, something peaceful like the first day Ilana and I arrived on the island, only four days ago.

The Melrose Inn, where we were staying, was a stately two-story, southern mansion-style hotel featuring tall white pillars. Green shutters framed the windows, and pale-yellow wood siding completed the appearance of this antebellum-style inn. A grand circular driveway at the entrance is window dressing because cars are not allowed within the Melrose Plantation Development. Stretch golf carts serve as transportation vehicles, outfitted to carry luggage and passengers.

Dinner at the Inn the first night had been good. A bottle of wine and key-lime pie for dessert topped off a meal of fresh seafood. Even Ilana seemed to like the cuisine. We went for a leisurely walk that evening over a large grassy area fronting the resort leading to a beach. Something about the island felt very relaxing, slower, and less intense. A gentle breeze was blowing in from the ocean. I suggested the walk to familiarize ourselves with the grounds.

A couple of Charlie's guys wandered along behind us at a comfortable distance, even though I didn't necessarily think they were needed. I had told Charlie that his guys weren't required to babysit us for the next few days. The resort had a very competent security staff. But, of course, he disagreed. Charlie reminded me again about how many times I had been wrong in the past. He said I was in no position to advise him on matters of security. 'Leave it to the pros,' he suggested. I humbly accepted his judgment, hoping the need for security would be over soon.

The sun was setting over our shoulders across the island in the west as we neared the beach.

'Just like your island,' I said to Ilana. 'Sun sets behind the trees.'

She smiled.

We stopped at the water's edge to search for porpoises. Every once in a while, one could be seen surfacing for air before diving into the sea, their smooth gray bodies sliding effortlessly through the choppy water. A few were swimming in tandem, probably a mother and child, a small porpoise swimming on the shoulder of its older parent.

Across from the Inn and over the Calibogue Sound, the southern end of Hilton Head Island was visible a couple of miles away. A few high-rise condos could be seen interspersed among one and two-story housing units along the beach. To the east was the Atlantic Ocean. Occasionally, an ocean-going freighter sailed up the river towards the docks in Savannah.

As we continued our walk, the color of the sea slowly evolved from steel blue to charcoal gray in the retreating light of night descending on the Sound. A great blue heron silently passed over us like a great black shadow floating in the twilight, spreading its expansive wings, gliding towards shore. Folding its wings into its body after landing, it stood tall on stick legs, facing the water like a lonely soldier, standing vigil as the sky slowly darkened and the air cooled.

When my thin summer sweater became insufficient to keep me warm, I suggested we return to our room. She nodded, and we turned towards the lights of the inn, shining through the darkness.

The interior decorating in our room at the Inn was typical of this part of the country, very traditional. We had a suite with a sitting area on an outside deck. One large window viewed the grounds toward the Sound.

'Do you like it here?' I asked her after pouring a couple of glasses of wine.

Sitting on one of the couches wearing a yellow sleeveless top under a blue canvas jean-style jacket, white shorts framed her beautiful long tan legs. A few days before we left Charlottesville, she had gone shopping. A nice complement of resort clothes had been purchased just for the trip. I think Helen must have gone with her. Helen knew where all the expensive shops were located.

'Yes, I think I like it here,' Ilana answered sleepily.

'I'm glad,'

'Can we talk?' I asked her, thinking this perhaps might be a good time to ask her about what had been bothering her. I had been unsuccessful in penetrating her defenses at home. She seemed more at ease on the island.

'We are talking, John,' she answered with a smile.

'You know what I mean. Can we talk about what has been on your mind lately?'

'I'm okay. There is nothing to talk about.'

'You don't seem too happy lately.'

'This is all so different, John. I am sometimes afraid... I am sorry.'

'Can I do anything to help?'

'No.'

'Do you want to go back to Belize?' I asked, afraid to pose the question but at the same time needing an answer.

'John,' she paused as if to emphasize the point. 'John, you know I want to be with you. How many times do you ask me this question? Do you ask me because you want me to go home?'

'No, you know I want you to stay. But I also want you to be happy.'

'I will do better. I am sorry. Please don't worry.'

A tear formed in the corner of her eye, which was difficult to see in the muted light of the room. I loved being near her. What was it about being with the woman you love, simply being close to her, absorbing the soft lines of her body into your mind as her black hair casually fell on her shoulders?

'What are you doing?' she interrupted, dissolving my moment of wonder.

'Simply loving you with my eyes.'

'You need to stop that.'

'Why?'

'Oh you, I know you. You are so bad.' She got up. 'I love you, John Van Laan.'

The glass of wine in my hand almost spilled when she descended on my lap without warning. Placing the glass on a table next to my chair, I brushed her hair from her face and bent down to kiss the tiny crease at the corner of her eye where moist tears had formed.

'So, you want to talk,' she smiled, pushing back so she could gain my full attention. 'Okay, I have something I want to talk to you about. And I think this is a good time to talk.'

'And what do you want to talk about?'

'I want to go to college. Now, let me finish before you say anything. Steve tells me they have classes for someone like me at the University of Virginia. I think I want to find out about these classes. And I would like to start in the fall if it is okay with you. I have been thinking about this for some time and I don't see why you should object. It will make me a better girlfriend for you. I will learn things and ...'

She would have continued if I had let her. It was obvious she had prepared a speech and waited until just the right moment to spring it on me.

'Whoa,' I said, breaking her momentum. 'You don't have to convince me. Of course, I would love to have you go to the University. I know some people in the administration. I can help you.'

'You don't mind then?'

'No. I think it's a great idea.'

'But it is expensive. No?'

'Ilana, don't worry about the money. You have plenty of money, remember. We will work on getting you enrolled as soon as we return to Charlottesville.'

'You don't think I am too old?'

'No, you are never too old to learn.'

11:05 A.M.
JOHN

The insistent ringing of my cell phone instantly shattered my pleasant daydream as our taxi drove to Hilton Head Island.

I almost dropped the phone in the back of the cab, awkwardly attempting to get it out of my pocket.

Phillip was sitting next to me at the time, seemingly content to observe the passing scenery. His silence was beginning to worry me. Normally, you couldn't shut the man up. He would talk about anything just to fill a void. But today, he was quiet as we drove down Highway 278.

'Hello.'

'John.'

'Yes, Helen.' I recognized her voice.

'I forgot to mention that Mr. Nue did not arrive alone.'

'You mean he brought his usual assortment of bodyguards?' I replied, hoping for no complications.

'Yes, yes, they are with him. But I thought you should also know one of our board members came with him.'

'Who?' I asked, now concerned. My orchestrated plan was a pretty tight deal. It wouldn't take much to throw it off.

'Manuel Ortega, you know, the man from Columbia with the emerald mines.'

'Have you told Charlie?'

'Yes.'

'Okay, thanks, Helen.'

'Is that it? Do you want me to do anything special for him?' she asked.

'No, just get him a room.' I hung up my phone.

Traffic noise on the highway was constant and hopefully loud enough to prevent Phillip from overhearing the other side of my cell phone conversation. However, the unnerving noise also made it hard to concentrate, which was exactly what I needed to do. Things were starting to go astray. First, Phillip's silence was worrying me. It wasn't like him. And now I had another problem, Mr. Manuel Ortega. He and Nue seemed like an odd couple. I wondered what their arrival together meant. Of course, they knew each other. Nue had helped convince Ortega to allow our company to market some of his Columbian emeralds as an experiment. This was the first step in a larger plan to make emeralds our next major product line. But I didn't think they were buddies. So... why were they traveling together, on my leased plane no less? And more importantly, why had Nue neglected to mention this detail to me in any of our previous conversations?

'Problems?' Phillip asked.

'No, just a few loose ends.'

'Who's Charlie?'

'Just one of the guys from the office,' I lied.

When Charlie arrived, he hit the ground running with a cell phone in his ear, complaining as soon as he was off the boat about how long it had taken to get to the island. Immediately, he put a helicopter on notice in case it was needed. Typical CIA nonsense was my take for this precaution, but I said nothing. I knew from experience it would do no good.

My determined buddy, Charlie, immediately went to work rigging the important rooms for sound and video. A room in the Conference Center across from the Inn was the first to get special treatment. This was the location of our all-important lunch.

Architecturally, the Conference Center looked similar to the Inn, with pale yellow painted sideboards and green awnings windows complimented by white pillars at the entrance. Inside the Center, long halls lead to banquet and meeting rooms. An operations center was established in one of the rooms down the hall from where we were to have lunch.

Nue's private room in the Inn was also rigged, as was Phillip's, in case lunch failed to produce the desired results. Charlie said we might get what we needed from a private conversation if my plan failed. I was doubtful. I thought we would be successful at lunch, but I didn't argue with Charlie.

He also installed equipment in several other rooms, including the bar in the Inn. Charlie said alcohol was a great agent for loosening lips. The CIA had, on more than one occasion, learned valuable information from surveillance set up in bars. All his equipment was portable. He could place it anywhere on short notice.

Seven CIA agents came with Charlie. In addition to Steve and Brad, who were my personal bodyguards for the week, three guys and two women arrived with Charlie. Four of them pretended to be couples on vacation, blending in with the other guests at the Inn. Their job was to back up security in case something went terribly wrong. The other guy was a hi-tech expert who spent his time hiding out in the operations center.

The room in the Conference Center, which had been prepped for lunch, was where I hoped to push Phillip into a confrontation with Nue. Three place settings, complete with glasses, plates, and silverware, were on a table surrounded by cushioned armchairs. Located near a large window, the table overlooked a small azalea garden outside. Upholstered wood furniture against the walls, complimented by a dark green carpet, gave the room a comfortable atmosphere, like being in a private clubhouse.

I wondered how comfortable Nue would feel when he encountered Phillip. I hoped not too comfortable.

DAUFUSKIE ISLAND, SOUTH CAROLINA, 11:20 A.M.

ILANA

Ilana had gone outside to relax in quiet contemplation while sitting on one of the Inn's outdoor lounge chairs.

Situated comfortably near the beach under the shade of a nearby live oak, she occasionally took a sip from a half-empty glass of iced tea, which had been placed on a glass-topped wrought-iron table next to her chair.

It was a beautiful morning. Ilana was having trouble staying focused. Even something as simple as reading a book was a difficult, considering all the wonders surrounding her. She loved being outside again. The cooped-up lifestyle she endured in Charlottesville was like being in jail. It was far better to be living under the sky with ocean breezes running through her hair.

Somewhere overhead, a small bird was chirping its plaintive love song. Ilana looked up in wonder, searching for the bird, enjoying its clear, gentle chirping but finding it difficult to locate the tiny creature among the green leaves of the giant oak tree.

Out on the Calibogue Sound, a white cabin cruiser sporting multiple fishing poles motored past the island, cutting through the placid inlet, creating a wake that marched across the glassy waters in lines of military precision until their momentum was broken as they lapped harmlessly on shore, splashing noisily, disturbing the otherwise gentle tranquility of her morning.

In a lounge chair not far away, Ilana's CIA bodyguard for the morning, Brad, had been keeping an eye on her while pretending to read a book. At the time, he was tracking the movements of a man approaching Ilana's chair from the direction of the Inn. The man was medium height, square-jawed, with the deeply tanned skin of someone who spent considerable time in the sun. His curly black hair featured a tint of gray in the temples. On the surface, nothing about this man looked disturbing. However, his sudden appearance bothered Brad, and there was something about him that did not fit a typical tourist casually strolling the grounds, something disturbing. Although he was nicely dressed in a polo shirt, khaki pants, and brown sandals and he was walking with the easy gait of someone in no hurry; Brad decided he had no real reason to be overly concerned, but out of habit, he scanned the man's short-sleeved shirt, looking for a bulge that might be hiding a gun. He saw no bulge. Even so, as a precaution, Brad sat up, waited, and watched with his hand on a hidden gun under his loose shirt, ready to move at the first sign of trouble.

When he came near her chair, his shadow fell over the book Ilana had been trying to read, surprising her.

'May I sit down?' he asked politely, taking a seat in a lounge chair next to Ilana before she could respond.

Instantly recognizing the man... the man from her nightmares, the man from the Mayan jewelry shop, she almost dropped her book and instinctively turned in Brad's direction for help.

He returned her gaze, silently asking if everything was alright.

A quick decision was required and she made it. She smiled at Brad and turned back to the South American.

'My name is Manuel Ortega,' he said very deliberately in a heavy Spanish accent. 'Do you remember me?'

Ilana nodded. 'You never told me your name before.'

'You know it now.'

She did not respond.

'Okay, now listen to me very carefully,' he whispered. 'What I am going to tell you is very important.'

She silently stared at Manuel as her heart raced.

'I am a member of your boyfriend's board of directors,' he continued. 'Mr. Nue is my partner in business. Do you know his name?'

Ilana did not respond, afraid to show any emotion to Brad.

'Don't answer if you don't want to. It doesn't matter.' Manuel shrugged his muscular shoulders. 'After you have had some time to think about what I told you, you will want to talk to me.'

Ilana was shocked. This man, this devil... What did he say... something about being a partner of Nue and a member of John's board? How was this possible?

She always knew she would hear from this man again, but she never imagined in her wildest dreams she would see him here, now, on this island. In fact, she had hoped he would not try to contact her again until after the board meeting. Maybe by then, she would find the nerve to tell John what this man had been doing to her and her brother.

Before coming to the island, she had made a decision to wait. She decided she did not want to do anything to distract John until after his meeting. She knew the meeting was important to him. She did not want to add her troubles to his other worries. So, instead of bringing her problems to John, she took measures that she hoped would buy her time. For example, she had made no effort to learn John's plans. She had left the room every time John was discussing important matters on his phone. If he casually asked her for her opinion, she said she was not interested and tried to change the subject. If that didn't work, she interrupted him and said she wasn't feeling well. Could they talk about this later? She hoped these measures would eliminate her problem until later. She assumed that if she knew nothing, she would be unable to tell this man anything important, even if he found a way to force her to talk.

Out on the Calibogue Sound, a cormorant duck struggled to rise out to the water, its wet wings shedding water as it flapped and paddled furiously to gain altitude, rising only a few feet into the air. Nearby, a young boy played on the beach, his dirty, wet hands working diligently to build imaginary sand castles in his future. But Ilana noticed none of these things. Her world was completely absorbed with an unexpected nightmare in the form of this ominous man, a devil in a man's clothing.

Running her hand through her long black hair, brushing it off her face, she momentarily gazed out to the sea, stalling for time... time to think, her mind whirling with possibilities.

The glass of iced tea next to her lounge chair sat temporarily ignored, water condensing in drops sliding slowly down the side of the neglected beverage glass, forming a puddle of water on the table.

And no one would have noticed even if they were looking because the movement of Ilana's trembling lips was ever so slight.

Brad didn't notice. He was not aware of the bitter thoughts raging through Ilana's mind like steel-driven spikes. This was all wrong. This was not supposed to happen to her. Everything had been going so well. Everything had changed dramatically since the day she arrived on this island. It was as if she had been reborn when she stepped out of the taxi and walked the boardwalk to the ferry boat. The smell of the sea stirred something deep inside her soul.

She couldn't explain it. She only knew everything was different. This island was not her home and wasn't as warm, but she loved being here. Maybe it was the undercurrent of sounds that seemed to fill the air, the waves lapping up on the shore, the birds singing in the trees in the morning. Or the wind blowing through the leaves of palm trees. She couldn't identify the difference exactly, but she could feel it in so many ways. Like how a cup of coffee smelled in the morning on the deck outside the Inn, its gentle aroma stirring in the crisp morning air. Or the promise of warmth from a morning sun shining through the trees and over the glassy waters of the Sound. The gentle reeds swinging in a breeze over the marshes. She loved it all. She loved being on this island.

And John, too, seemed more energized. They had gone for a walk on the beach the first night and had a discussion about her going to University. When it was time for bed, time to rest for another day, they had found it difficult to sleep. It was as if neither of them wanted this evening to end. She didn't know what it was, but somehow, she didn't want this night ever to be over.

She had rolled over in bed to run her hand through his hair, to touch the corners of his mouth while they rested in the dark. It was as if she wanted to know every part of this man and take all of him inside her where he could not escape. She had nestled up against his shoulder and ran her hand down across his chest and then down farther until she felt him grow in her hand, knowing she was bringing him pleasure in a way only she could. This made her happy. She removed her panties and got up on her knees over him while pulling her cotton t-shirt up over her head. Leaning down to kiss him long and hard, her tongue caressed his lips until he entered her. She held him in the night while returning to some innate knowledge of the sea, born from having lived by the water all her life. Moving slowly to the gentle rhythm of a night on a beach long forgotten, a night broken only by the sounds of rolling waves breaking in endless succession on the shore. Outside her hotel window, an unseen tree frog sang his furtive song in the night. A brown palm branch broke free and floated unnoticed in the breeze, falling gently on the cool grass.

It had occurred to her later, maybe it wasn't John who was different. Maybe it was her. She knew she was happy again, happier than she had been for months. Not just a relieved happy, but happy as if everything would happen as she hoped.

But now... This evil man sitting next to her made everything so wrong.

Ilana shivered involuntarily even though it was a warm day.

11:55 A.M.
JOHN

For reasons I did not understand, Phillip persisted in his streak of abnormal behavior, remaining very quiet while we drove through Sea Pines Plantation Resort on Hilton Head Island towards the dock at Harbor Town.

On the ferryboat ride to Daufuskie Island, he asked a few questions and made a few stabs at conversation, but he was not acting as I expected. I had been preparing for what I thought would be his normal barrage of questions, pumping me for information about the company and his new job. Even though we had talked through many of these details in our previous telephone conversations, I still expected him to continue his constant information assault. It was how he filled his time, running his mouth. But this morning was different. He was quiet... oddly, unnaturally quiet. It had me concerned.

Although I had to admit, I was also relieved. Not having to talk to him was a relief. It meant fewer chances to slip up and give away my real reason for inviting him to the island.

When we arrived at the Inn, I walked him to his room and told him to get settled. I would come for him in about half an hour. Lunch with Nue was next on our agenda. I promised to show him around the resort afterward.

In the meantime, I badly needed to talk to Charlie. Manuel Ortega's sudden appearance on the island had me even more worried than Phillip's behavior. Manuel needed to be neutralized. I didn't want him interfering. Everything depended on my luncheon meeting with Nue and Phillip, alone in a room.

The Inn was built parallel to the water, and the hotel rooms were connected by a long hall. It took time to walk from one end of the Inn to the other. Phillip's room had purposely been selected on the far south side of the Inn. Nue's room was on the north side. I had hoped this architectural feature would keep the two of them separated. It was important they not meet before lunch.

The carpeted hallway running lengthwise through the interior of the Inn seemed endless as I picked up my pace, wanting to talk to Charlie as quickly as possible.

'Charlie,' I said into my cell phone. 'Where are you?'

'Conference center,' Charlie replied. 'Where are you?'

'In the hotel, we need to talk.'

'Okay, come over. I will meet you at the door.'

Cutting across the circular drive, I hurried towards the entrance to the conference center, which was directly across from the Inn. Charlie opened the door as soon as he saw me. We found an empty room where we could talk in private.

'Did Helen tell you about Manuel Ortega?' I asked.

'Yes, is he important?' Charlie asked calmly. My friend could be unnerving at times.

'Possibly, I don't want anything to go wrong. Not now.' I was truly concerned about Manuel, but it didn't appear that my buddy, Charlie, held the same opinion.

'Look, John. We have talked about all this,' Charlie responded. 'Your plan may work, but it may not. Putting Nue and Phillip in a room and hoping they get mad and start talking nonsense is a long shot. You know it, and I know it. And even if they start arguing, which I sincerely doubt, what makes you so sure they will bring up past crimes?'

I had no easy answer for him.

'You know I went along with this caper of yours because we don't have any other good options,' Charlie continued. 'But the odds are long, my friend.'

'I know, I know, but it can work, Charlie. But not with interference from someone like Manuel Ortega.'

'What do you want me to do about him?' Charlie asked dismissively, looking like he was already resigned to failure.

I didn't get the feeling my friend Charlie was really trying to be helpful. He was telling me my plan was a long shot, but I personally had been convinced from the beginning it would work. I knew Phillip. And I knew Phillip wanted revenge on Nue for dumping him from the company. Phillip would naturally want to press his advantage when he met with Nue. And his advantage was that he knew what really happened in New York when Monica died. He knew Nue had threatened to kill me that night, plain and simple. Force me to sign over my company to him or die. Phillip could testify to this. He had a headlock hold on Nue. He could threaten to expose Nue if Nue didn't cooperate with him. Now, I didn't think Nue would like to be in a submissive position. So Nue would be obligated to fight my appointment of Phillip to the position of COO. He wouldn't want Phillip anywhere near the company and especially not in a position to run it. Phillip could put Nue in a world of trouble. All of which meant it could get ugly in a place and time where they thought no one was listening. The subject of the murders of my former partners, Arthur and Vidu, could easily come up without any help on my part. Or I could introduce them to the discussion myself if necessary. I was convinced Phillip knew all about how they both had been murdered by Nue. Therefore, Mr. Nue would need to neutralize Phillip quickly, and the one way he could accomplish this would be to let Phillip know that he had already acknowledged his part in the murders to me when we met in Hong Kong. It was not a secret.

But today's meeting would not be like my last meeting with Nue in Hong Kong, where there were no witnesses and nothing was recorded. This meeting would be different. Charlie would record every word in this meeting. And the evidence could be used to press murder charges against Nue. If I could get Nue to admit he had ordered the killing of my former partner, Arthur, who had been gunned down on the streets of New York, a case could be made against him. Even if his diplomatic passport allowed him to leave the country, the State Department could bar him from ever being allowed to return to the United States again. And exclude him from doing business in our country, meaning he would have to give up his stock in my company. He would be out, which is exactly what I wanted.

So... a lot depended on what happened at lunch. Phillip and Nue in a room alone with me. No interference. Let the fireworks begin, and let Charlie record it all.

'Just keep Manuel out of the way,' I replied to Charlie. 'Make sure he doesn't drop in on the meeting. I don't think Nue will talk freely with Manuel there.'

'And if Nue brings him, what then?'

'Have Helen call Manuel out of the meeting. Make up an excuse if necessary.'

The time for the meeting was getting close now. I had to calm down.

Charlie looked at me. He knew I was getting uptight. 'Okay, John. Look, I'll handle Manuel. Everything is set. Go make it happen.' He gave me a reassuring pat on the back.

'Thanks, Charlie,' I replied confidently. But I felt more like a kid in a little league baseball game who had just been patted on the back by the coach and sent into bat even though the coach knew he would strike out. Charlie was a pro. I was an amateur. Although the plan seemed foolproof to me when I first envisioned it weeks ago, now that the time had come, I wasn't so sure. Charlie knew, but he had been kind. He helped me even though he knew it was a long shot.

Still, I badly wanted it to work, and I hadn't considered what to do if it didn't.

Stones crunched in abstract distraction under my feet as I hurried back to the Inn to retrieve Phillip. The sun felt warm on my face. A golf cart passed me filled with laughing hotel guests having a good time. I wondered why it was always so hard for me to have fun. It seemed like everyone lived in a different world from me. They were always laughing. I was not. I wiped the sweat from my forehead and stopped for just a moment to gather my composure. I was walking too fast. I needed to calm down.

A child cried.

I turned to see a mother dragging the kid by his hand towards the entrance of the Inn. It was obvious the young boy wanted to stay outside and play. He had been running around having a good time. However, his mother had another agenda for the poor boy.

I could sympathize.

Life always seemed to have a different agenda for me.

12:10 P.M.
ILANA

Ilana sat inside her hotel room, staring longingly out of a window, her tears still wet on her cheeks.

She would have rather been outside enjoying the wonders of the island, but she didn't want to risk talking to that man again. And now she knew his name. She also knew the devil was a member of John's board and a friend of Mr. Nue. Bad, very bad.

A pink flower petal from a fresh bouquet on a nearby table broke free and drifted in the stagnant air, finally settling on the carpet of her hotel room. Ilana watched it fall with stone-dead eyes. Standing up as if in a trance, she wiped her eyes and went into her bathroom to wash her face, hoping to clear her mind. It was noon, time for something to eat. But she wasn't really hungry. The conversation she had with Manuel outside on the lawn was still running through her head, upsetting her stomach.

'No,' she had defiantly told him. 'I do not want to go for a walk with you.'

Manuel Ortega had looked at her as if his look alone could penetrate the soft, tender skin of her defenses like a surgeon's scalpel, cut her deep to the bone, and watch her bleed. This was what he wanted to do. He wanted to cut through her cocky arrogance until she screamed. She had become a headstrong woman. He remembered how she had defied him before. He wondered if she would try again. But that was before she had thought her brother was dead, killed by his man. Hopefully, that lesson had weakened her will.

'Then we will talk here,' Manuel replied in a quiet, confident tone as an ever-present off-shore breeze rustling through overhead trees covered the sound of their conversation. 'But first, I must warn you that if you tell your friend John about our conversation, your brother will go on another boat ride with my friend. This time, he will not return to the dock. Do you understand me?' Manuel waited for the impact of his statement to sink in. 'My man is watching your brother at all times. Your brother cannot escape.'

Ilana stared back at him without responding.

Manuel took this to mean she understood. 'You do not need to be concerned,' he continued. 'If you tell me everything you know about what your friend John is planning, you won't have to worry about your brother.'

'I don't know anything,' Ilana replied. 'I told you before, John does not tell me his plans. And I don't ask him. So, I am sorry, but I have nothing to tell you.' Ilana fairly spit out the last words before thinking she needed to restrain herself for fear of alerting Brad that something was wrong. Or worse yet, making the South American angry. She did not want to live through another time like the last time when she thought she had killed her brother.

She took a deep breath and rephrased her reply to Mr. Ortega, this time trying to sound like the young girl who had taken this man's money, the innocent island girl she had been in the past, a girl who didn't know any better.

'I don't know what to tell you, Signor. We are here for a meeting of the board. But you already know this.'

Manuel looked carefully at Ilana before pausing to look down at the grass beneath his chair, feeling uncomfortable in his new American clothes. He had been trying to look and act like a typical tourist. But a young man sitting a few yards away had been staring oddly at him, making him wonder if, despite all his careful preparations, he still didn't look like he belonged, didn't fit in.

Perhaps he would never fit in. Oh well, he thought. Americans are funny people. It is difficult to think and act as they do.

He smiled at Ilana. She certainly was a pretty girl. If circumstances were different, maybe he would have her. But not now. Now she was with a filthy rich American, and she was getting haughty again. He decided to deal with her later. What he needed now was information, and it was obvious she didn't want to give him any.

He tried a different approach. 'Who came to this island with your American friend?'

Ilana quickly recognized that Manuel had changed tactics. He was probing. She needed to be careful now. Charlie's name came to mind first. He had come with John. Certainly, this was something Manuel would like to know, but she couldn't tell him about Charlie. Instead, she replied as truthfully as possible without really giving him anything important.

'Oh, his secretary and some other office staff,' she said. 'They are here to help with the meeting. And we have our bodyguards. They always come with us when we travel.'

'I see. Do you have a bodyguard with you now?'

'Yes, the young man in the chair a few yards to my left.' Ilana smiled to herself. She was only too happy to tell Manuel about Brad. She was glad Brad was nearby. He made her feel safe.

Manuel glanced quickly at Brad and made a mental note of his appearance.

'And where is your boyfriend now?' Manuel asked her.

'Oh, John is picking up someone from the airport in Savannah,' she said without thinking.

'Who is he picking up?'

Ilana instantly regretted she had mentioned where John was going. She knew the answer. John had casually told her. He was picking up Phillip. Phillip would be here shortly. Manuel would know soon about Phillip. She didn't think it would matter if she told him about Phillip. Besides, if she lied, Manuel might kill her brother when he discovered her deception. She really didn't have a choice.

'I think he is picking up someone named Phillip Palmer,' she said. 'Do you know him?'

'No,' Manuel lied.

But, of course, he knew. He knew about Phillip because Nue had told him about Phillip. Manuel instantly recognized that this was important information. He did not think his friend from Thailand knew Mr. Phillip Palmer was arriving today. Then, he wondered why John Van Laan was picking Phillip up at the airport. According to Nue, Phillip was no friend of John's, not to Manuel's knowledge. All this was very interesting and more than enough information for now. He decided he needed to talk to Nue immediately. Ilana was going nowhere. He could probe her later.

He smiled at Ilana. 'I think I will go now. We will talk again soon.'

He stood before she could respond and walked unhurried towards the entrance of the Inn.

Ilana thought it strange their conversation had ended so quickly, but she was happy to see the man go. Immediately, she returned to her room to get away from this man. When she was safely inside, she tried to take a nap. But this was when the feelings of dread and sadness descended on her again like those strange, cold, white snowflakes that sometimes fell from the sky in the north, making everything inescapably gray. She had not felt like this since leaving Charlottesville. The place where they were staying was a warm place, an island of green trees and large expanses of water, which lifted her spirits. It had liberated her from these sad, ugly feelings. But now, an icy cold stirred again deep inside her soul. And this time, the warm sunshine and clean ocean air couldn't keep the cool mist of fear from rising out of the waters of her mind.

Tears formed in her eyes as somewhere out on the Calibogue Sound, a porpoise rose out of the water. If Ilana had been walking on the beach as she had planned earlier, the sight of the porpoise swimming in the Sound would have brought her joy.

But instead, she quietly cried in her room, alone and afraid.

CONFERENCE CENTER, 12:45 P.M.

JOHN

My coffee was getting cold.

Three place settings for lunch were neatly arranged on the table. White cloth napkins, dishes, and a full complement of silverware sat next to bowls filled with wilting salads. Water dripped down the sides of ice-filled glasses while a waitress dressed in a plain black and white uniform waited somewhere down the hall in the kitchen.

Phillip was standing by a window, seemingly content to stare outside while wearing some silly-looking, Hollywood-style, chrome-rimmed sunglasses even though he was inside the building – the same offending sunglasses that had adorned his face from the minute he exited the taxi on Hilton Head Island. His silly sunglasses were beginning to annoy me, but I said nothing, kept my mouth shut, and simply let him wear his stupid sunglasses. The man could find so many ways to irritate me. I sometimes wondered how he did it.

I took a sip of coffee and glanced at my watch, ignorant of the fact that my coffee was cold. I had other issues on my mind, more important issues, mainly, where Nue was. He was late. Over fifteen minutes late so far.

It had been difficult waiting for the day and hour of this meeting to finally arrive, especially after all the preparations. But now that the time had finally come, the unanticipated minutes of delay seemed to drag into an extreme discomfort. Helen should have been here by now, escorting Nue into the room.

Phillip and I had come early. I wanted to be in the room when Nue walked in the door. I wanted to see the expression on Nue's face when he saw Phillip. I expressly didn't want Nue to see Phillip before this moment. I wanted it to be a complete surprise. The element of surprise was an important aspect of my plan, catching Nue off-guard and unprepared.

An adjacent room in the building had been commandeered by Charlie to monitor and record the video feed from cameras in the ceiling. A couple of his people were ready in case things got ugly. Guns were loaded, and they were wearing flak jackets. The plan was for them to storm the room if I said, 'This meeting is over.' I had been instructed to say those four words if the situation got completely out of control. It was a last resort and only to be used if someone was going to die, someone like me. Only then, not before. Because the last thing I wanted was to have Nue discover that I had brought the CIA with me. Later, maybe, but not until I had everything I wanted from him.

'I don't think he's coming,' Phillip concluded smugly like he knew something I did not.

'He coming,' I replied. 'We just need to be patient.'

Helen knew enough of my plan to know I wanted Nue here on time. So why, I wondered, why had she delayed bringing him? I decided to get up to pour a fresh cup of hot coffee.

'I'm not sure why you invited me here today,' Phillip probed.

He had not been acting normal, not like I expected him to act. It seemed like he didn't really care if Nue showed up, and that's not how I assumed he would act. I had thought he would be looking forward to meeting Nue. I was anxious to see the expression of surprise, perhaps even horror, on his face when he came in the door. But at that moment, Phillip looked like he could care less.

I didn't know where his question came from or why he asked it, but I did know it needed an immediate answer. 'We have been over all this before, Phillip,' I answered. 'You know why I want you working at the company. I have had enough phone calls in the middle of the night and red-eye flights to all parts of the world. I have more money than I can spend. I want to slow down and enjoy life. That's why I need someone to help me, and you are the man. Besides, I think you deserve a second chance. So, what part of this do you not understand?'

I knew I was probably exhibiting more frustration than the situation warranted under normal circumstances, but I was annoyed. Annoyed that Nue wasn't here and increasingly frustrated with Phillip for asking dumb questions.

I took a deep breath while wondering what was going on inside Phillip's brain. He looked like it had just dawned on him what I was doing, but he said nothing. Hopefully, I was wrong, and he was thinking about Nue, looking forward to Nue's arrival almost as much as I was.

'Maybe we can do this later?' he suggested casually.

His statement surprised me even more than his question. I wondered if I had been wrong about him all along.

'Let's wait a little longer. I'm sure he will be here shortly. Normally, he's very punctual.'

'That's why I don't think he's coming,' Phillip concluded.

A phone rang.

<h2 style="text-align:center">1:10 P.M.
CHARLIE</h2>

It was easy for Charlie to watch the operation unravel. Sitting in a comfortable chair in the CIA control center on the island, he was aided by banks of video screens persistently operating in semi-darkness connected by wires laying twisted haphazardly across the carpet. Dials and switches, computer keyboards, and digital information collection devices. Multiple gadgets were spread over tables lined against the walls of the room – everything Charlie needed to do his job.

Since arriving with his team of professional spooks, he had worked day and night to set up the equipment. It had not been easy to convince the Inn that his equipment was necessary to make a video presentation to the board, but they had finally given in. Charlie's next challenge was the tricky matter of installing surveillance equipment in individual hotel rooms without anyone knowing. Invented excuses were used, such as the need to drop off information packets for the participants. Once inside the rooms, the sophisticated surveillance equipment had to be quickly installed and invisible to the occupant. No one except Charlie's people knew where the eavesdropping equipment had been placed. Incredibly small and lightweight, these monitoring devices were extremely sensitive.

Before lunch, Charlie observed Nue and the other new arrival, Manuel Ortega having a casual conversation. Nothing particularly interesting was recorded in their conversation. Manuel had suggested they go outside for a walk. This by itself didn't seem to indicate a problem, but Charlie had one of his guys keep an eye on the pair.

On a separate screen, Charlie had watched John and Phillip arrive early for the meeting. Phillip poured himself a cup of coffee and wandered over to a window wearing sunglasses. John seemed preoccupied at the time and for the most part ignored Phillip, answering him only when it was necessary.

Nue eventually returned to his room just before it was time to go for lunch. Manuel came inside with him. When Helen arrived in the hall outside his room to take Nue to the luncheon meeting, Nue had one of his bodyguards ask her to wait. Now, this had seemed odd to Charlie. It was the first clue to the plan's failure. It was impolite and uncomfortable, forcing Helen to stand in a hall.

Every few seconds, she changed position with her cell phone in her hand. On more than one occasion, she looked at her phone as if she wanted to make a call. After about twenty minutes, a guard opened the door. Nue exited briefly to inform Helen he regretted he would be unavailable for lunch. Urgent business required him to remain in his room near his telephone. He said he would call John later and explain.

Helen immediately retreated from her post outside the door of Nue's room. Holding her cell phone in her hand, she walked away at a brisk pace while dialing. Charlie watched John take her call. Disappointment was written all over his face. The man was so transparent.

In contrast to John's frustration, Nue simply sat in his room and had a pleasant conversation with Manuel. After a few minutes, a couple of white-jacketed waiters arrived outside his door, delivering a room service lunch. The two men talked as they ate.

What had been interesting to Charlie was that the conversation between Manuel and Nue discussed nothing of major significance. The Columbian's mine operation and his gross sales for the year were mentioned. Nue's new cutting facility in Bangkok was also discussed. Manuel suggested perhaps some of his emeralds might be sent to Nue's facility for cutting. Nothing important, nothing about John's company, about the board meeting, or speculation about why John had called the meeting; none of the things that Charlie expected they would be talking about. And certainly, nothing that seemed important enough to miss the lunch with John. Charlie wondered if they were carefully avoiding those subjects on purpose.

He turned to watch the screen showing John and Phillip eating lunch in the room down the hall. John looked upset even though he was trying hard not to show it. Clearly, John had lost his appetite, only occasionally picking at his plate, mostly looking out of the window. In contrast, Phillip seemed to be enjoying his meal, eating and talking, still wearing his sunglasses. John sullenly listened, forced to endure a constant flow of chatter coming from Phillip without offering much in return, which didn't seem to deter Phillip as he prattled on.

Charlie alternatively watched the two monitors for a few more minutes. When it was obvious that nothing important was happening, he demoted the boring conversations to background noise and stood to stretch. Next to him, Steve continued to listen to the conversation in Nue's room. One of his other agents, named Marisa, monitored John's conversation with Phillip, recording every word. Brad had been assigned to Ilana for the day. He was somewhere keeping an eye on her. The other two agents in the room, Tony and Dianne, were dressed in flak jackets, resting in a couple of chairs, occasionally checking their equipment.

'What do you think?' Charlie asked Steve.

'Not going to happen.' Steve turned away from a monitor to answer Charlie.

'Any reason why?'

'Not that I can see. Just bad timing, I guess.'

Not far away, Ilana was curled up in an upholstered armchair in her room, sleeping. She had cried until her body finally gave in, and she slept.

Charlie could not see her because John had insisted that no monitors be placed in their room. Charlie had briefly considered putting a video monitor in the room without John's permission, for

John's safety, if for no other reason. But he had decided, against his better instinct, to allow John his privacy.

1:15 P.M.
JOHN

Still wearing his offensive Hollywood-style sunglasses, Phillip picked up a white cloth napkin off the table and daintily dabbed the corners of his mouth in a theatrical fashion that was all about him.

I was beginning to wonder if the man would ever finish eating. I had been waiting politely. To leave the room prematurely was not good form. Phillip might wonder why I was anxious to go. But I wanted to learn what had gone wrong, hoping maybe a plan B could be put in place. To do that I had to get out of that room because I couldn't have him listening to my conversation.

'Perhaps I can arrange a meeting with Nue for later this afternoon?' I suggested to Phillip.

It was a long shot, but there was still time to get the two of them together before Nue discovered Phillip was on the island. Once this happened, the element of surprise was gone, and the conversation between the two of them would likely be much more sedate, not the heated confrontation I hoped would produce the evidence I desired.

'Okay, I guess,' Phillip replied without enthusiasm.

'Say, since you're not busy right now, why don't you spend some time with Jason in preparation for your new job?' I proposed.

I wanted Phillip occupied where he could be controlled. I had been trying desperately to think of something to keep him away from Nue. If he was out roaming around on his own, it was possible he would accidentally run into Nue. This wasn't a large resort, and I couldn't keep them apart forever.

'Jason manages our Hong Kong Distribution House. He can bring you up to date on what has been happening in the world of sapphire sales,' I suggested. 'I'll have him meet you here,'

I immediately headed for the door without giving Phillip a chance to say no. He was nibbling on some of the last remaining scraps of food on his plate at the time and didn't seem to be in a hurry to leave the room. My hope was Jason could stall Phillip long enough for me to set up another meeting. Although it seemed all wrong to leave him sitting by himself, I had no choice.

As soon as I closed the door, I dialed Helen and asked her to please find Jason and send him over to the conference center to spend some time with Phillip. Tell him I need him to stall Phillip, keep him in the room.' I knew I was sounding somewhat frantic, and I needed to calm down, but I was frustrated and in a hurry to get things back on track.

'You should talk to Jason yourself,' Helen replied candidly. 'You can better explain to him what you want him to do than I can.'

Now, that was not the reply I wanted from her. But then she was being her usual exacting self. Everything had to be specified in detail with this woman. I could have argued with her, but it would have taken more time than just calling Jason myself.

'Okay. Do you know where Nue is now?'

'He was in his room last time I saw him.'

'Thanks, Helen, what's his room number?'

As soon as she told me, I disconnected and immediately hit Jason's cell phone number, waiting anxiously for him to answer.

'Look, Jason. Do me a favor,' I started explaining. Get over to the Conference Center. I want you to keep Phillip company for a while. Talk to him, tell him how the Hong Kong Distribution House operates, tell him about your customers, anything, just keep him occupied. Don't let him go outside. Understand?'

'Okay, boss.' Jason was a quick study. He didn't need a long explanation.

I then called the hotel desk and asked for Nue's room. One of his bodyguards picked up the phone.

'Can I speak to Mr. Nue?' I asked.

'I'm sorry, but Mr. Nue is busy.'

'Tell him it's John Van Laan.'

'I am sorry. Mr. Nue cannot come to the phone,' the man said without acknowledging who I was.

'Okay, please tell him I called and ask him to call me.' I gave the man my cell phone number and listened as he hung up.

I was half tempted to go directly to Nue's room and demand to see him. But that might look like I was desperate, and the last way I wanted to look was desperate.

But the truth was, I was desperate. I snapped my cell phone shut in frustration. What if I couldn't get a meeting arranged today? Okay, tomorrow might still work. I had one more day before the board meeting. The directors weren't scheduled to begin arriving until tomorrow. But it could get messy in the meantime. No, it had to be today. Phillip was in place. All I needed was to get Nue to the meeting. But what if I couldn't? Too many questions kept circulating in my brain, too many variables, as Charlie liked to say.

A warm breeze played through my hair as I stood in the driveway fronting the Inn. My cell phone was in my hand. I wanted to make a call, do something, anything... but I didn't have a clue what to do next or who to call.

I thought about calling Charlie and asking him for help. But why? What would that accomplish? He would simply say I told you so.

I looked at my cell phone, hoping to hear it ring, hoping Nue was calling. But nothing, just frustrating silence.

Finally, I wandered aimlessly toward my room, not exactly sure why; I just didn't have anywhere else to go.

The room was quiet, feeling empty when I closed the door. I assumed Ilana was probably outside, somewhere, enjoying the sunshine. A small refrigerator contained bottles of cold water and assorted alcoholic drinks. I selected a water bottle and twisted off the cap while resisting the urge to open a stronger drink.

Something stirred in the bedroom. A silhouette that I quickly recognized was Ilana. She was sitting in a chair in front of the window. The lights were out, and the curtains pulled shut. It appeared she had been sleeping. The phone in her room rang. Her eyes opened quickly and got big.

I'm not sure she saw me at first. Not until I walked into the bedroom to answer the phone, hoping it was Nue. Needing it to be Nue.

'Don't answer it,' she said weakly.

'It's okay.'

'No,' she sounded frantic, like she didn't know who I was.

'Hello,' I ignored her and answered the phone. 'Hello,' nothing, empty silence.

I put the phone back on the receiver.

Something had changed. I didn't know what it was, but I knew the look on her face. It was familiar. She had reverted back to how she looked several times in Charlottesville.

'You okay?' I asked, even though it was obvious she was not okay.

She didn't reply, sitting curled up in a chair in a fetal position with her legs pulled up tightly to her body with a sad, hurt look in her eyes. I knew how she would act now. This had happened before. It would do no good to ask her questions. She would not answer. She would just retreat farther into her shell. I wondered why and why now. She had been fine since we arrived at the island. I had hoped she was over her problem, but obviously, that was not true. Something had gone terribly wrong again.

Problem was I really didn't have time for her. I had other tasks to do, more important tasks, like getting Nue into a meeting with Phillip.

Then I asked myself why? What was more important than her?

Putting my arms under her shoulders and legs, I gently lifted her out of the chair and placed her on our bed. I laid down beside her and ran my fingers through her hair. I wanted to ask her what was bothering her, but I did not. I knew she would not answer me. She lay quiet and silent, like a small wounded animal afraid to move.

My problems slowly drifted away as I lay beside her, unimportant in comparison to her situation. I closed my eyes and rested beside her, finding her hand in this place of silence, slowly caressing the small lines in her palm. She responded by closing her fingers over my hand and holding it tightly. I reached up and ran my fingers gently over her high cheekbones and across her moist lips, then down the long, soft line of her neck. It seemed good to be with her, touching her. Everything else at that moment was irrelevant. Images of Nue and Phillip passed fleetingly through my mind as we rested. I wondered briefly what they were doing, but these concerns quickly wandered away. My crisis was insignificant compared to the puzzle of this woman. All I wanted now was her happiness again, the way she used to skip down my dock in her bikini. I wanted Ilana to be free of anxiety. I wanted her wild spirit with me again.

Soft waves of remorse washed against the beachheads of my mind, wondering if I was the source of her problem. Had I done this to her? Searching through recent memories of the past few months, I tried to think of anything that could have caused her to fall into these deeply frightening episodes of depression.

The storm off the coast of Belize came to mind. The day we fled the island, the look on her face when she appeared on the deck from below, the smile she gave me as waves crashed up and over the bow. She had been unafraid, determined to help me beat the storm. We fought the wind and the waves together. Somehow, it had seemed right for her to be on the boat with me. She had given me the confidence I needed to get through the ordeal. Before she appeared, I feared for my life.

It was difficult to believe now that a woman who had demonstrated so much courage could be brought so low. When I touched the soft round curve of her shoulder, she turned on her side, still holding my hand, and buried her head in my chest.

This was not how I had imagined my afternoon would be. But it was painfully obvious I was not in control of my life. Everything was drastically different than I envisioned. In as much time as it took for the sun to retreat behind the shadow of a passing cloud, everything had changed. My meeting with Phillip and Nue, which I had so carefully orchestrated in my head, had not occurred, and the solution I hoped for was as elusive as ever. And now Ilana had fallen again into a depression she didn't deserve and could not escape.

Everything had gone wrong, gone astray. I felt like I needed to do something, but I had no clue what. I rested holding her, afraid to move, afraid that anything or everything I did now would be wrong. I must have slept for a short time, fitfully, in strange dreams of falling flower petals and rusty old fishing boats abandoned on the shore.

She got up out of bed first before I did. Without a word, she simply disentangled herself from my arms and sat on the edge of the bed for a moment before walking into the bathroom and splashing cool water over her face. After running a comb through her hair, she returned to the bedroom and smiled at me.

'Want something to drink?' she asked as if nothing unusual had happened.

'Sure.' Following her out of the bedroom and into the sitting room, I stopped to look out the window at the green grass lawn in front of the Inn spreading out to the Sound. I badly wanted to be outside, and I wondered if I could convince her to go for a walk, but I didn't ask, content that she was feeling better.

The phone rang.

'Don't answer it, please,' she asked, holding a couple of soft drinks in her hand.

This time, I obeyed her and let the phone ring.

3:25 P.M.
PHILLIP

Jason droned on, rattling off facts about the Hong Kong Distribution House, its best customers, the kind of gemstones they preferred, and the sizes, colors, and cuts.

His head was full of facts. He had a photographic memory. If Jason was capable of anything, he was capable of boring anyone to death with his encyclopedic repertoire of factual information. He was trying to do what John asked him to do, which was to keep Phillip occupied, and he was using the resources he had at his disposal, his crowded mind filled to the brim with facts.

Phillip was fascinated at first. Phillip was probably the only person who could outdo Jason in the category of factual information. For an hour or so, he and Jason had traded intellectual jabs in a game of factual up-man-ship. Phillip was winning, but this fact alone didn't amaze him. Phillip knew he could out-duel anyone when it came to material recall. Still, he was impressed with Jason.

But eventually, the game began to bore him. For the last five minutes, Jason has been doing all the talking.

'Look, Jason,' Phillip finally said. 'This has been very interesting, but I need to stretch my legs. Can we finish this some other time?'

Jason became instantly alarmed, acutely aware that his job was to prevent Phillip from leaving the room. 'I have just a few more things I think you will find interesting,' he said, hoping to hold Phillip's attention a little longer.

'Jason, enough already,' Phillip replied.

'But let me tell you...'

Phillip stood. 'Jason, it has been great getting to know you. I'm sure we'll be talking more in the future. Right now, I need some fresh air.' He smiled knowingly at Jason, who had remained sitting in his chair, reluctant to abandon his post.

Several strategies ran through Jason's active mind, but he knew none of them would work. Phillip was determined to leave. Jason finally gave in. 'It was great to meet you, Phillip. Do you want to return in a little while so we can talk some more?' he asked, even though he was quite sure he knew the answer to his question.

'No, I think this is enough for one day.'

'Okay then. I will be running along.'

'Good, run along.' Phillip smiled.

He shook Jason's hand, and they left the room together. Jason immediately headed down the hall, dialing John's cell phone number as he walked.

No one answered.

3:40 P.M.
PHILLIP

Patches of wind ripples glided over the gently rolling waters of the Calibogue Sound like miniature sand pipers flying in formation.

Sunlight reflecting off the disturbed water momentarily captivated Phillip's attention as he strolled the beach. It felt great being outside, stretching his legs. The warm sun on his face gave his skin a healthy glow after being cooped up for months in snowy Michigan. This trip was a nice change of pace for him.

He wore a stylish outfit: white pants and a black and white striped, short-sleeved shirt, which allowed the rays of the sun to warm his arms. The only element of his wardrobe that didn't fit his hi-fashion resort look was his old shoes. They were black leather, rather ordinary-looking scuffed shoes, the kind he always wore regardless of the weather, winter or summer. A small hole was beginning to form in one of the soles, but Phillip was a frugal man. He never bought new shoes until the old ones were literally falling off his feet.

As he stood on the shore, he thought it might feel good to put his bare feet in the water. But to do this, he would have to remove his shoes, and he was afraid his lily-white feet might look odd. To make matters worse, his new pants would become wrinkled when he rolled them up to avoid getting them wet, thus negating the time and money he had spent to create his new stylish, high-fashion resort look.

Somewhere inside the muddle that filled his brain, he knew his old black leather shoes didn't fit in with his new look. Yet, he was not comfortable taking them off. For now, he would just have to be content to walk the beach in his old shoes with the breeze blowing his graying ponytail back over his shoulders and his head held high as he strolled the shoreline, confident he fit in with the other rich folks in this resort.

It wasn't difficult for him to walk on the beach in his black leather shoes. The smooth gray beach sand on Daufuskie Island was composed of fine particles of broken sea shells. After ocean tides retreated down the shore, the beach sand would become quite hard and smooth. Bikes could easily be ridden on the sand. Although the beach was not so hard that you couldn't write your name on it, his leather shoes did not make much of an impression, and walking on them was very easy. All of this meant Phillip did not feel completely out of place walking the beach in his old ugly shoes.

The delay in confronting Nue at lunch had been disappointing for Phillip. He had been looking forward to seeing

Nue's reaction when he discovered Phillip would soon become the COO of the company. Phillip hoped it would be a shock for Nue.

Phillip understood Nue's game more than anyone. He knew Nue was plotting to take control of the company. As soon as Nue found a way to remove John, he would move quickly to take over the company. But with Phillip involved, it would not be so easy for Nue. Nue would have to deal with him. Not just John but also Phillip could be a major problem for Nue, an obstacle to his assuming control, something Phillip had been looking forward to making painfully clear to Nue because Phillip knew things that Nue would not want to be made public.

Phillip knew who had ordered the murder of Arthur, a deceased partner of John.

Only a few feet from where Phillip stood on the beach, a gray pelican dove head first into the ocean from a height of about fifteen feet, bouncing hard off the water before quickly surfacing as if nothing had happened. After resting for a moment, the big bird opened its wide wings and began flapping furiously, pushing against the water with webbed feet, running and flapping, lifting slowly, flying inches above the water while increasing speed before rising into the air.

After stopping to watch the pelican, Phillip continued his slow stroll down the beach, allowing the events of the day to sort through his cluttered mind. It was most interesting to notice how disappointed John appeared when Nue didn't show. Phillip knew why he was anxious to see Nue, but he didn't quite understand why John had acted so frustrated when the meeting was postponed.

Phillip was no dummy when it came to navigating the politics of a corporation. Layers of meaning could be interpreted with every gesture. However, he was new to this corporation. He couldn't possibly understand every nuance. Not yet, anyway, but he had time to learn. Once he was inside, he knew he had the skills to play the game as well as anyone. He only needed time to sort out a few things first, and it appeared John was willing to give him that time.

To Phillip, this only seemed right. Phillip was a trained geologist and an expert in the world of colored gemstones. Phillip had helped John learn the business. In Phillip's mind, John wouldn't have anything if it wasn't for him. Phillip also knew John had been born and raised in a church which coexisted with guilt. Phillip assumed John was feeling guilty for having left Phillip behind. This was the reason Phillip assumed he was being given an opportunity.

The more Phillip thought about his future prospects, the happier he became. And in some small way, he wanted to celebrate. Perhaps by removing his shoes, rolling up his pants, and sticking his feet in the water. What difference did it make if someone saw him?

Bending over, he rolled up his pants and loosened his shoelaces. In order to remove his shoes on the damp beach sand, Phillip had to stand on one foot while taking off his shoe and sock from his other foot without losing his balance and getting his sock wet. He knew he looked awkward as he worked to accomplish this balancing act, and awkward was not how he wished to appear, but he was happy, and the gently waving water looked inviting.

With two shoes and one sock off, while standing on one pale white foot with his other foot in the air still covered with a sock, he heard his name called by someone with a foreign accent who sounded vaguely familiar. Reacting awkwardly without thinking, he turned to see who was calling his name, and his unintended twisting motion caused him to temporarily lose his balance, which in turn forced him to place his still-socked foot on the wet beach sand to prevent a fall. Immediately, cool water from the damp beach sand penetrated his sock. Damn, he muttered under his breath while quickly raising his now wet foot to remove the offending soaked sock.

In no apparent hurry, two gentlemen dressed in resort wear meandered toward Phillip as he gathered his socks and shoes from the beach. Behind the men were two other men who looked strangely out of place, dressed in black suits, white shirts, and ties. One of these men had casually thrown his suit coat over his shoulder in the afternoon heat.

It had to be uncomfortable to be outside in the heat dressed in a suit, Phillip thought. Who are these guys? Unfortunately, he couldn't see them clearly because the sun was initially behind them.

Phillip could distinguish nothing more than black silhouettes coming his way.

While placing the offending wet sock inside an empty shoe, he instantly regretted taking off his shoes. His exposed feet and ankles looked ugly, lily-white under his rolled-up pants. But it was too late to put his shoes and socks back on his feet. He was obligated to greet these men while shoeless.

'Phillip,' Mr. Nue emerged from his shadowed silhouette, calmly extending his hand as if he expected Phillip to be waiting for him on the beach.

'Good afternoon,' Phillip replied calmly, trying to imitate Nue's tranquil composure; while thinking it was strange that Nue did not look surprised to see him.

'You remember Manuel Ortega from Columbia?' Nue asked.

'Of course, Manuel, it is good to see you again.'

'And you too, my friend,' Manuel replied.

'I see you are enjoying the sunshine,' Nue said innocently.

'Yes, and you?'

'It is a pleasant afternoon. Care to go for a walk with us?'

Phillip glanced over his shoulder and recognized immediately that the men in suits standing at a respectful distance were, in fact, Nue's bodyguards, and no doubt they were packing. Unfortunately, Phillip's gun was back in Michigan. After years of traveling with valuable gemstones, he always carried a weapon with him. He wished he had his gun now. He didn't trust Nue. Still, the beach where they were standing was near the Inn. Other resort guests were casually strolling nearby. Nothing was likely to happen in broad daylight.

Phillip quickly decided to go for a walk with Nue, walking slowly so he wouldn't go too far from the safety of the Inn.

'What brings you to this island?' Nue asked Phillip.

'I am to be the Chief Operating Officer,' Phillip proudly announced, finally feeling the satisfaction he had been anticipating.

Nue said nothing.

Phillip was initially disappointed with Nue's reserved reaction, but then Nue was Nue, a man who never allowed his emotions to show. 'Aren't you surprised?' Phillip suggested, hoping for some small reaction.

'No.' Nue spoke the word with so little emotion that Phillip wondered how he could maintain such an even composure.

When neither Nue nor Manuel appeared to exhibit the least hint of surprise, the actor in Phillip was disappointed with his audience's inattention to his dramatic announcement. Then, he became curious. He knew Manuel was on the board of directors.

'Did John tell you, Manuel?' he asked. 'Did he tell you I am to be the COO?'

'No, signor, I was not told.'

Phillip suddenly forgot to walk as slowly as he had planned. He picked up his pace as he contemplated a new complication he had not considered before. It seemed suddenly wrong for John to not have told Manuel about his appointment. Phillip didn't mind the fact that Nue had not been told. Nue was a special case. John wanted to tell him in person. Phillip was only too happy to go along with this plan because he had been looking forward to dealing with Nue himself. But hadn't John told him that he was going to consult with some of the other board members? Suddenly, Phillip wondered if John had told any of the other board members about his appointment. He didn't know. He had not asked John. He just assumed it was happening. Agitated now by the thought that perhaps John had not spoken to any of the board members, Phillip unconsciously increased his pace again. He was beginning to wonder if his appointment as COO was a sure thing after all.

Nue recognized immediately that Phillip was surprised to learn John had not informed Manuel. 'So, why do you think John has not told us about you?' he asked.

'How should I know,' Phillip replied.

'Do you suppose John has a reason?'

'I assume he does.' Phillip was now walking so fast the others could barely keep up. Something was wrong, and Phillip knew he had to figure it out quickly. But at the same time, he did not want to betray John's confidence. But what was he missing?

Phillip slowed his pace when he suddenly realized they had walked some distance from the Inn and were now standing on an uninhabited, lonely section of the beach. Stopping to turn around, he hoped to see the Inn, hoping the safety of the Inn was too far away.

The cut green grass lawn flowing from the Inn to the beach was still visible, but it was now several hundred yards down the shoreline. The beach where they were, fronted an uncultivated, old-growth forest. Vines grew into tall trees, searching for sunlight shaded by a canopy high above the dark land. Long, pointed leaves of palmetto bushes in clusters covered a forest floor of thick brown, decaying soil. Phillip did not want to be any farther away. The shady lowlands beside the beach looked ominous in appearance, like a place where someone could die and never be found; the damp earth slowly decomposed the corpse until nothing remained to tell a story.

'Maybe we should turn back,' Phillip suggested, suddenly feeling vulnerable, keenly aware of the black suits who were trailing behind.

'We need to talk.' Nue took hold of Phillip's arm ever so gently, preventing him from moving.

The Thai had surprising strength for such a small man. Phillip knew that Nue was trained in martial arts. It would do no good to resist. Besides, the black-suited tag-alongs standing behind Nue would probably prevent him from leaving even if he tried to get away.

'Okay, let's talk,' Phillip gave in.

'What does John hope to accomplish at the board meeting?' Nue asked.

'I don't think I'm the person to answer that question.'

'Who is?'

'John. You should ask him, not me.'

'I will, but let me ask this question before you go. Don't you think it is strange that John has not told us about you?' Nue probed Phillip's defenses.

Phillip had nothing to say.

'Phillip, when did you become so naive?' Nue continued.

'What are you talking about?' Phillip asked.

'You know Mr. Van Laan,' Nue continued. 'He is a very organized man. He rarely brings anything to a board meeting that he has not previously discussed with the members. He does not like dissension at his board meetings. Mr. Van Laan prepares his board members for all major issues. The meetings are simply a formality.'

'If you say so,' Phillip answered while immediately understanding the negative implications of what Nue was saying. Then he remembered something John told him. 'He has told me he wants to explain his plans to the board in person,' Phillip suggested. 'I am only one part of his plans.'

That's it, Phillip thought to himself, almost sighing with relief.

'So, signor, you think this is the reason Mr. Van Laan has not told us about you,' Manuel interjected at this point.

'He told me,' Phillip interjected. 'He wants to slow down and enjoy ...'

Nue never let Phillip finish his sentence. 'Phillip, do you really believe that? You know this man. Does slowing down really sound like something John Van Laan will do?'

'Okay then, you tell me what John's plans are if you know so much.' Phillip was getting angry. Enough of what Nue said was beginning to make sense. And if Nue was right, then maybe Phillip's future was not as certain as he thought it was. And this thought made Phillip very edgy.

'I don't know,' Nue said as if it didn't matter. 'But I know who does, and she will tell us.'

'Who knows?' Phillip asked.

Manuel interjected, 'His girlfriend will tell us.'

'He has a girlfriend?' Phillip was surprised. Of course, he remembered the woman who had died in the New York hotel room, but John had not mentioned any new girlfriends to him during their extensive telephone conversations.

'Yes, she is traveling with him,' Manuel explained.

'Why would she tell you anything?' Phillip inquired.

'You don't need to know why.' Nue stated.

'But we may need your help to force her to answer our questions,' Manuel finished his sentence.

'And why should I help you?' Phillip asked, suddenly curious if there might be something in this for him.

'Because you want to know the answer,' Manuel replied. 'Is that not true, my friend?'

Phillip thought about the logic of his statement. He didn't want to help. Nue was still Phillip's enemy at the moment, and John, his friend. But on the other hand, Nue had raised some rather interesting questions. And Manuel was right. Phillip needed to know as much of what John was planning for the board meeting as they did. So maybe he should help. Besides, his feet were getting cold, standing on the wet sand. It was time to end this conversation.

'What do you want me to do?' he asked.

6:20 P.M.
JOHN

Long spreading branches of live oak trees dripping with Spanish moss cast gray shadows across the vivid green grass of the Inn's lawn, diminishing the intense colors of the day, setting the stage for the calmer shades of the evening as the sun retreated behind statuesque pines and the afternoon air cooled.

Ilana had said 'No' to my idea of going to a restaurant for something to eat.

I found that odd, her refusing me. Normally, she was happy to go to a restaurant.

She had me worried, although she appeared to be fine, watching TV and smiling at me occasionally. The only exceptions were a few times when the phone rang. Her composure would change then, and a mask of worry would suddenly cover her face. She would demand that I not answer the phone and quickly disappear into her bedroom. I didn't understand these incidents of strange behavior because, apart from these few examples, she was acting reasonably normal. No new episodes of curled-up crying had occurred.

When I suggested a walk before dinner, she said she was tired. Would it be alright if we just stayed inside, she asked. I agreed, content to do whatever made her happy. A room-service dinner was ordered.

Although... I had to admit I was disappointed. I would have enjoyed being outside and taking a walk. It seemed wrong to be cooped up in our room when so many splendors existed outside. But for the moment, I was happy to accommodate Ilana. Something had happened to her again, and whatever it was, she was deeply affected by it. I tried to get her to talk about it, but each time I raised the subject, she would smile, flash her big brown eyes, and say it wasn't important.

Jason stopped in to tell me he had held Phillip's attention for as long as he was able. Eventually, Phillip became tired of talking and went for a walk. That was not good, but there was nothing I could do about it.

Mr. Nue never returned my call. I had hoped he would call, but my cell phone didn't ring and that was also something out of my control.

Out of frustration, I called Charlie. He told me Nue and Manuel were out of their room somewhere. And unfortunately, his surveillance equipment was currently useless when they were outside. He had no clue why Nue canceled lunch.

Thanks, Charlie, I said to myself after hanging up. You're no help.

However, I did mention to Charlie that Phillip was also out for a walk and asked him to send someone to keep an eye on him. Charlie agreed and called back later to report that my worst fear had been realized. Nue and Phillip had met and talked. It was on the beach near the Inn. Charlie's man had been unable to hear the conversation. Waves breaking on the shore made too much noise. So, Charlie didn't know what was discussed.

Okay.

All my carefully constructed plans had fallen apart, but oddly, I didn't care as much as I should have. Forces beyond my control had taken over my day. No matter how hard I tried to make things happen my way, something had interfered with my plans. The fact that Nue had gone for a walk with Manuel and accidentally met Phillip on the beach changed everything, but it had happened. I had to accept it. Nothing else I could do. Nue would no longer be surprised when meeting Phillip. That part of my plan was now history.

Slowly, the problems concerning Nue and Phillip slipped away as I changed course, concentrating on Ilana's problems instead. Room service arrived with a cart carrying our dinner. Shrimp for an appetizer lightly breaded fish for the main course; I think it was red snapper with asparagus and twice-baked potatoes. I had almost nothing to eat at lunch. I didn't have much of an appetite at the time. Now I was hungry.

Somewhere outside our room across the green grass lawn, a big blue heron arrived for an evening of fishing. Gliding on outstretched wings, the bird soared over the water like a sailplane. Extending its stick legs as it neared the shore, it gently touched down, folded its wings, and stood very still; like a gently curving black statue standing over the lapping gray water.

7:15 P.M.
JOHN

Ilana appeared preoccupied at dinner.

'Like the shrimp?' I asked to get her attention while remembering my first trip to Hilton Head, seeing shrimp boats trolling up and down the Sound with their poles and lines extended out over the water like the wings of a big bird. 'Are the shrimp as good as Belize?'

She smiled. I knew the answer to my question. In her mind, nothing was as good as it was in Belize, at least not when it came to seafood.

The doorbell rang.

'I'll get it.' I got up before she could object.

Phillip barged inside as soon as I opened the door wearing a yellow V-necked sweater, looking oddly different somehow. I couldn't ever remember seeing the man in yellow before. Black was his normal color of choice.

'Phillip?'

'Hope I'm not disturbing anything,' he replied, even though

it was fairly obvious he was interrupting our evening meal.

'Just dinner,' I politely responded while turning to look at Ilana, wondering if his appearance had a negative effect on her. 'I would like you to meet my friend, Ilana?'

'My pleasure,' he bowed slightly in her direction.

Ilana appeared initially unaffected by his usual theatrics. She simply stood and offered her hand.

'You are very lovely.' Phillip smiled one of his big, broad, engaging smiles which he was confident could sweep any woman off her feet. 'Why are you hanging around with this low life?' he laughed.

'Oh, I think I like this man,' Ilana smiled.

Phillip turned back to me, 'I thought I would drop in and see if you have any plans for me for the rest of the evening. If not, I'm off to dinner.'

'I wish I could tell you I have something, but I have been unable to contact Nue all afternoon. I'll try to set up a meeting for the morning. I still think it would be good for the three of us to talk before the board meeting.'

'Yes, yes. Just let me know... Oh, by the way, I saw Nue this afternoon. Went for a walk and happened to run into him.'

'Oh, did he have anything interesting to say?'

'Nothing, really. Strange thing was, he didn't seem a bit surprised to see me. I thought that was odd. You didn't tell him I was coming here, did you?'

'No, you know I wanted to wait.'

'Well, he didn't look surprised. But then you know Nue. Never shows any emotion... But let me ask you a question. Have you told any of the other board members? You know. Are any of the others aware of my appointment to the position of COO?' Phillip asked quickly.

Ilana had returned to the table to finish her dinner, but when Phillip started asking questions, she got up to leave the room.

'No, but....'

The phone rang.

Ilana looked at it anxiously, like she didn't want me to answer it. But personally, I was relieved to hear it ring. It gave me an excuse to dodge Phillip's question. I asked him to excuse me to go into the bedroom to take the call. If Charlie was on the line, I didn't want Phillip overhearing our conversation.

'Hello.' I closed the door.

'John, this is Mr. Nue. I was informed you have been trying to call me. Please accept my apologies. Unexpected and urgent business at home has kept me occupied.'

'Yes, that's what I was told. Is everything okay?' I asked, wondering at the same time why he happened to be out taking a casual walk in the afternoon if his business was so important.

'It's nothing which needs to concern you. Mostly family matters in Thailand.'

'I see.'

While talking to Nue, the sounds of a faint conversation between Phillip and Ilana in the other room vaguely caught my attention, wondering what they possibly could be discussing.

'I am sorry I missed our lunch,' Nue continued. 'Perhaps we can meet tomorrow morning for breakfast.'

'Sure. Same place, I'll have breakfast catered in.'

'When would you like me to come?'

'Nine o'clock. That okay with you?'

'Yes.' Nue replied in his normal, almost monotone voice as if nothing had ever disturbed the man. 'I met an old acquaintance of yours when I took a walk this afternoon,' he continued.

'Yes, I know, Phillip.'

'He told you we talked?'

'Yes.'

'He said you are planning to hire him to work in the company. Is that true?'

The cat was out of the bag. It seemed Phillip had learned something from Nue, and Nue had, in turn, learned something from Phillip. Now, they were simultaneously throwing verbal daggers at me. I guessed I deserved it. The damage was done. It was obvious my plan needed to be altered. I wondered briefly if there was any point in trying to get them together. They would both be on their guard now. But I had to try. I couldn't think of any other way to get what I wanted from them.

'That's correct,' I responded. 'Phillip's appointment is one of the reasons I wish to meet with you. I have made some decisions about my future. One of those decisions involves Phillip.'

'I see,' Nue responded.

'As long as you know, Phillip is here and why I have invited him, perhaps it would be good to have him join us at breakfast so the three of us can talk.'

I had to ask now. It would have seemed wrong for Phillip to simply show up at breakfast now without telling Nue. I knew I was taking a chance. Nue could turn me down, and if he did, my opportunity to force a confrontation involving the two of them was out.

'You can invite Phillip if you wish,' Nue replied.

'Thank you. Until then, have a pleasant evening.'

He hung up his phone.

Elated that our meeting had been rescheduled, I returned to the sitting room of the suite to tell Phillip. Ilana immediately stopped talking to him as soon as she saw me open the door, turning away with what appeared to be a frustrated look on her face. But I wasn't really concentrating on her at the time. My mind was focused on Phillip's question, which I had momentarily dodged when the phone rang. He had asked if I had informed anyone on the board about his appointment in advance.

But before I could offer him an answer, he said cheerily. 'I think I will run along now,'

That surprised me, but at the same time, I was relieved he had forgotten about his question.

'Phillip. That was Nue was on the phone,' I interjected. 'I'm meeting him for breakfast in the morning, nine o'clock, same place. I would like you to join us.'

'Yes, of course. See you in the morning.' Phillip promptly turned and headed for the door, making a quick exit.

7:25 P.M.
NUE

As the moon rose over the southern tip of Hilton Head

Island, light from its almost perfect orb cast a trail of flickering pale flashes over the placid dark waters of the Calibogue Sound.

To the west the sun was retreating behind the tall pines and live oaks that covered the island as the wind softened. Evenings on the island are normally a gentler, calmer time. The pressures of the day case away along with the intense light.

Nue sat alone outside in a chair on the big veranda of the Inn facing the water, pondering a day that had not proceeded anything like he had anticipated. A cup of hot coffee sat steaming on a table next to his chair. He looked content, but this was not true. His mind was busy, absorbed with a problem. He needed a new plan, and he needed it fast. Several alternative plans had been forming in the vast recesses of his nimble brain, but he was not yet ready to decide on which one should be used. Too many questions needed answers first. It would be foolish to make a plan without knowing all the facts.

Phillip was one question. It seemed all wrong for him to have joined forces with John. Although... Nue didn't blame Phillip. Nue had purposely left him behind when he didn't need Phillip anymore. But apparently, he had underestimated Phillip's resourcefulness. Or maybe it was John he had underestimated. They were both a mystery. Who had approached whom with whatever it was that they were planning? Was it John's idea or Phillip's suggestion? It didn't seem to make much sense from either point of view. Nue did not understand. He thought they hated each other. So, how could they have joined forces? This was the number one question on his mind. Why were they working together? What was the real reason for their alliance? Phillip seemed to think he knew the reason, but when Nue had probed his logic, Phillip began to lack confidence. Why? Was it because Phillip always suspected something wasn't right? Had Phillip ignored his suspicions because he so badly wanted what John offered him?

Nue admitted to himself that he had made a mistake leaving Phillip unattended. This much was obvious. Phillip was determined to be a player. The man was always showing up at inconvenient times.

As Nue sat buried in his problems, a gentle evening breeze

whispered through overhanging Spanish moss of a nearby tall oak, roaming over the large expanse of grass and trees fronting the Inn before flowing across the Sound to join the anxious winds over the ocean. Somewhere in the Sound a porpoise surfaced to breathe, its low snorting lost to the wind.

John was a complex man, far more complex than Nue originally considered. No new plan involving John would be simple. Gaining control of John's company was becoming far more difficult than Nue had first imagined. He began to wonder if it was worth it. Perhaps it would be better to abandon trying to take control of his company and simply destroy it instead. Once John's company was gone, a new company originating in Thailand could be established. The model John had successfully designed could be replicated, this time with Nue's family in control.

This thought pleased Nue. It was family after all which motivated him. Family was the reason for his existence. A day would come when his time as head of the family was over, but the family's legacy must continue to live in prosperity as it had for generations. Nue couldn't let it die during his time. Failure was unthinkable. He had to use all his resources to take back what rightfully belonged to him and his family.

He smiled.

Time was on his side. He would find a way. This night would be like all others: one more step towards achieving his goal.

As the moon rose in the east, casting tree shadows over the Inn's lawn, Nue viewed the moon as a sign of success. Its light would make the evening's activities easier to accomplish. It was almost time now.

Soon he would learn what he needed to know and then he would decide on a plan.

8:05 P.M.
PHILLIP

A TV screen filled with talking heads occupied Phillip's hotel room.

Flickering lights and animated lips spewing streams of

endless nonsense; babbling mouths employed by a twenty-four-hour news channel designed for the sole purpose of driving silence from its viewers churning minds with a constant barrage of noise.

On the outside, Phillip looked calm while preparing to go to his meeting. With practiced fingers, he tied his graying hair securely with a rubber band, viewing his lovely image in a bathroom mirror. A handsome man smiled back at him. But what Phillip failed to realize, as he gazed at himself in a worshipful fashion, was that the taut display of pulled hair tended to exaggerate the long protruding profile of his nose. But then, he never saw himself from the side, and therefore, Phillip seldom considered his most obvious physical deformity. However, even with a long nose, he was a handsome man who always dressed well and held his posture properly. He made a good first impression on people. His strongest quality was his voice. It was clear and penetrating. He could carry on a conversation across a crowded, noisy room, which was not an uncommon occurrence for him. He was one of those people who liked to be heard and seen. And it was hard not to notice him when he was talking and he was always talking.

Phillip had done his part in preparation for this evening's activities. He had met with the woman. She was far prettier than he imagined and very different from John's last girlfriend, the tall redhead who had died in a New York hotel room. The dead woman was a cosmopolitan city lady. In contrast, John's new girlfriend was considerably unsophisticated. This was immediately apparent from his brief conversation with her and it made it easier to manipulate her. In a way, Phillip felt sorry for her. He had not liked doing what he did, but it had worked.

It could have gone differently.

She could have complained to John, who was in the other room, but she had acted as Manuel assured him she would. She had simply listened quietly to Phillip as if he were the unfortunate bearer of bad news. She nodded and asked a few questions. She seemed resigned in a way. Like she knew what he would ask her to do.

She didn't want to go. This much was obvious to Phillip. Even in the short time he was with her, he knew she was loyal to

John, but she had no choice. The reason had been explained to Phillip. Her brother's life depended on it.

He wondered what she would tell them when they met. So much depended on the information. Phillip hoped she would say John had no plan other than the one which Phillip wanted to believe that he would soon become the COO of the company. But he still wondered if he was right. Had it been too easy? Had he been foolish? Had his desire to have the job blinded him? Had Nue opened his eyes?

He didn't know. But he did know Nue had asked some very pointed questions, questions which badly needed to be answered. But even though Phillip now harbored some doubts, he still hoped he was right about John. After all, John was not a deceitful man. John was not a liar. That's the reason Phillip accepted John's offer in the first place. Because it was straightforward, the kind of thing John would do, besides, Phillip knew he could handle the job. John was lucky. When John needed someone, Phillip was his man.

It was meant to be.

Phillip knew he was the man for the job and it would only be a matter of time before the board realized Phillip was more than capable of handling the position of CEO than John. John would then be pushed out, and Phillip would have his final revenge on both John and Nue.

It was all written in the stars.

Only one lingering doubt still remained before Phillip could be entirely certain of his future. And it had raised its ugly head in a remark Nue made about John's character, about John being an active man, always on the move. Nue questioned why John would want to slow down now. Now, in the prime of his life, why now?

Still, John had been close to death recently while visiting Thailand. Something like that can change a man. So, the real question was. Was John a changed man? Was he really ready to give up control of his company to Phillip? Phillip wondered. And even though he was still convinced it would really happen, that he, Phillip, would be running the company soon... a still small voice inside his head kept telling him it was never going to happen. And that made him nervous. As much as Nue wished to know what John was planning, Phillip needed the information even more.

He hoped John's girlfriend would supply the answer.

8:10 P.M.
CHARLIE

Charlie was bored.

Watching TV monitors for long hours could be boring, very boring when nothing was happening.

Sitting with a team of equally disinterested agents in a dark room with the shades drawn, he waited for something, anything, to happen. John had called to enthusiastically tell him about his breakfast meeting. However, Charlie knew the odds were long. He didn't think anything important could now be accomplished at this meeting. The element of surprise was gone. Everyone would come to the meeting with a guarded agenda. However, John was still optimistic, and this was the only reason Charlie decided to continue. Besides, everything was in place, so why not give it a try?

But Charlie had become increasingly pessimistic, convinced that nothing good was ever destined to come from this trip. The operation had been a long shot from the beginning. He should have known better. It was the plan of an amateur. Charlie had been slowly cursing himself all afternoon for having been talked into coming in the first place. He had considerable government resources and money tied up in this little venture. He would be obligated to make a report to his superiors when he returned to his office. And if he had nothing positive to report, it would not be pretty. He could imagine the grilling he was in for. He cringed at the thought.

In his mind's eye, he saw himself sitting around a long conference table surrounded by a group of straight-backed men dressed in white shirts and ties throwing questions at him like daggers. 'You expected to accomplish what?' they would ask. 'And at what cost to the agency?' 'Just how many agents went with you on this junket?' 'And I see in your report that a helicopter was employed?' 'Why was a helicopter needed?' 'What, because you were on an island?' 'Are you saying you couldn't get off the island without calling for a helicopter? Is that right? Were there no boats on this island?'

It would be a blood bath.

He knew it.

And he could never tell his superiors the real reason he had agreed. He couldn't say it because a woman he once loved had been killed by someone who was on this island. That wasn't logic, CIA-style logic. So, why had he done it? And if it was really because of Monica, then perhaps it was time to put her out of his mind and leave John to his own resources. John could take care of himself. He had enough money to hire security. He didn't need Charlie and Charlie could not afford to continue to justify using the CIA assets to shield John forever, especially after this latest debacle.

The video monitors continued to spread modulating light across the room as Charlie sat miserably musing to himself. This needed to end sometime someday, he concluded. He couldn't go on trying to revenge Monica's death forever. It was time to have a heart-to-heart talk with John. It didn't mean they couldn't be friends. And John could still call him if he really needed help. Charlie had grown to like John. This had not been the case in the beginning. Probably because he was jealous of John, not something he was willing to admit to himself, but he knew it was true. Fortunately, time and circumstance had changed him. He now saw John as a friend. Charlie would make sure John understood this.

And then it would be time to step back.

8:20 P.M. JOHN

'I think I will go to the lobby to look for some new magazines to read,' Ilana announced.

'Do you want me to go with you?' I asked, happy she was feeling well enough to step outside the room, even if it was only to the lobby. Hopefully, her depression had passed.

'I am fine, John. I don't need your help. I will be back in a few minutes. Do not worry about me.'

'Okay,' I lied.

She had been acting almost normal since dinner. Still, I

sensed something was bothering her. I hoped she would tell me when the time was right. As soon as the door to our room closed, I reached for my cell phone.

Brad answered. 'Yes,'

'Ilana just left our room to go to the lobby for some magazines. I don't think it's anything to be concerned about, but I would feel better if ...'

'Say no more,' Brad replied.

'Thanks. And Brad, don't let her see you. I don't want her to know I sent you.'

'I understand.'

I put down the phone while wondering if I was getting paranoid. I needed a diversion. It had been a frustrating, fruitless day. TV might be relaxing. I searched through the channels finally settling for one of the sports channels.

I must have been tired. A big meal and a few glasses of wine quickly took over, and I fell asleep almost immediately.

8:30 P.M. ILANA

The night air was cool.

Ilana had not considered the outside temperature. In her haste to get out of the room, she had forgotten to bring a sweater. Wearing only a thin, sleeveless, white cotton top and khaki shorts, she had not been outside since her run-in with that ugly man. It had been hot then. Now it was cool and getting colder.

An unwelcome shore breeze brushed through her hair and gently caressed some Spanish moss hanging from a nearby live oak tree as she quickly crossed the front lawn of the Inn, heading towards the beach. Rubbing her arms and holding them across her chest for warmth, fear, and anxiety ran rampant through her body. Dew covering the grass crept into her open-toed sandals, cooling her feet as she continued. She had dressed all wrong, but that did not matter. It was far more important to find Manuel fast, answer his questions quickly and return to John before she was missed.

On the shore, a great blue heron loudly squawked at an intrusion into his territory; his abrasive complaint breaking the silence of the night, sending a shiver of fear up Ilana's spine. The heron's obnoxious complaint was due to the arrival of a competitor landing too close at the water's edge. As Ilana watched, one of the angular black shadows standing on the beach rose on fluctuating wings and drifted off into the night to find a more solitary location along the shore.

Finding no one on the beach, Ilana stopped for a moment to get her bearings. She could still see the Inn, and she was convinced she had turned right after reaching the shore as the note instructed her.

During their brief time together in her hotel room, Phillip had given Ilana a note and made sure she read it. John was on his phone in the bedroom. Ilana was not stupid. She knew the phone call was meant to distract him long enough for Phillip to slip her the note.

It read:

Ilana,

Your brother is presently in his favorite bar near the marina, enjoying a beer. It would be best for him to continue to do so in peace. The choice is yours. I expect you to meet me outside the Inn at eight-thirty tonight. Simply turn right when you get to the beach and continue walking. I will find you. Come alone and do not tell anyone where you are going. Understand that if you do not follow these instructions, your brother will be forced to leave the bar and go for a very unpleasant boat ride.

The note was unsigned, but of course, she knew who wrote it: that ugly man from the jewelry shop. It was now in her pocket, evidence of why she was betraying John. If he ever wondered why she had gone, she could show him the note. It was the reason she had to obey. She had no other choice. Maybe, she thought as she walked alone on the beach maybe she would tell John about this man tonight. First, she needed to follow his instructions. To refuse surely meant death for her brother. She could not let that happen.

As she walked the hard sand of the beach, she got colder and more scared with each step. Her feet were chilled. Her sandals were soaked, and her arms were cold even though she wrapped them tightly around her body as the moon slid over the island. Fortunately, the moonlight made it easy to see. For this, Ilana was grateful. If it had been a dark night, she would have been even more afraid.

Waves washed slowly up on the shore, softly lapping in a quiet rhythm as she continued. The gray water looked strangely alive to her in the half-light of the moon, like a slowly rolling menace waiting for her, wanting to hold her small body in its cool, deathly embrace.

Ilana shivered involuntarily.

8:45 P.M.
JOHN

I would have slept longer, except my phone woke me.

I was out cold at the time, worn out by a tension filled day. Half asleep I picked up the noisy instrument and answered.

'Hello?'

'John.'

'Yes.'

'It's Charlie.'

'Yes.'

'You awake, John?'

'Not really.'

'I thought so. You sound half asleep. Take a moment to wake up because I need your complete attention.'

I glanced at my watch. It was quarter to nine. I wondered how long I had been out. 'Okay, I'm awake. Now, what do you want?'

'Brad tells me you asked him to follow Ilana to the lobby for some magazines. Is that right?'

'Yes, why?'

'Well, it seems she has wandered off somewhere on the beach. Is that something she normally does?'

'No.'

'Okay then. You are not going to like this, but I have to tell you. Apparently, she may have gone out there to meet a couple of Nue's bodyguards. Brad saw them approach her on the beach and she didn't seem surprised when they came up to her. And just to make things more interesting, Nue and Manuel are out of their room as well. It's possible she is going to meet with them.'

I was fully awake now.

None of what Charlie told me made any sense. Ilana had been afraid to go out of the room earlier in the day. Now Charlie was telling me she was outside wandering in the night, maybe to meet with my enemies. My body involuntarily tightened. A wave of adrenalin panic swept through my nerves.

'That can't be right,' I replied.

'Okay, John, take it easy,' he said calmly. 'We will deal with this.'

'What are you going to do?'

'I'm going to go find your girlfriend and see what she is doing.'

'I want to go with you, Charlie.'

'I don't think that's wise.'

'Charlie, you are not going to leave me behind. I will either go with you, or I will go find her by myself.'

'Okay, okay, calm down, John. Meet me at the back door of the Inn in five.'

8:50 P.M.
ILANA

Nue's two goons half pushed her down the beach.

Ilana was helpless to do anything except obey. Waves of anguish washed through her mind like storm driven seas as she was forced farther and farther away from the Inn. She needed a solution to her predicament and she needed it fast. She had tried protesting, but it didn't do any good. Nue's bodyguards simply ignored her and kept shoving her down the beach, farther from John and the warmth of their hotel room.

She knew she couldn't let this meeting take too long. If she was gone too long, John would begin to wonder where she was, and he might send one of Charlie's guys to find her. Or worse yet, he might come looking for her himself. This was not what Ilana wanted. What she wanted was to be able to explain all this to John when the time was right. Not having him find out like this, but she could do nothing to change her fate. Nue's two bodyguards were walking beside her, one on each side, pushing her with their big hands on her back whenever she slowed down. If she complained, they told her to be quiet.

They had appeared behind her out of the shadows. She had been alone at the time, walking in the semi-darkness on the shore in her damp sandals. Finally slowing because she did not want to get too far from the Inn, she had stood alone on the beach, cold and afraid, wondering what to do next, all the time fighting an urge to run back to the warmth and safety of John and their hotel room. But she knew she could not. She had to meet with the man as he requested. Her brother's life was once more in danger. She couldn't live with the thought she had caused his death.

Their big hands on her cold, bare shoulders had sent a wave of panic through her body. Come with us, they said. Gently but forcibly, they directed her down the beach away from the Inn.

Big blue herons, their nightly fishing vigil along the shore disturbed by the undesirable threesome entering their territorial fishing grounds, rose into the air like ominous black shadows, squawking their discontent and startling Ilana's already abused nerves. She badly wanted this to be over quickly so she could return to John. The two big goons had different plans. They were leading her to a place where they could talk, or so they said. She was already too far from the Inn for comfort. The manicured grass and comfortable lawn chairs were now behind her. A dark, forbidding old-growth forest ran parallel to the beach on one side, and the moving waters of the Calibogue Sound spread out on the other side. Cold and scared, she didn't want to take another step. And just when she thought she could go no farther, everything became worse.

A flash of light from the forest broke through the darkness, and the threesome abruptly turned away from the beach, and she was forced to walk into the forest towards the light. This only made her more afraid, but she was powerless to resist. They held her arms firmly, half carrying her and half pushing her. Sharp palmetto branches cut her bare legs as she was dragged roughly through the dense forest by the two silent bodyguards. Somewhere, one of her cold, wet sandals was lost among the damp, decaying leaves. Pain came with each barefoot step, from stepping on fallen branches and other sharp objects covering the damp forest ground. She wanted to scream for help, but it was too late. She was too far from the Inn.

No one would hear her now.

8:55 P.M.
JOHN

I followed along behind, last in line, as Charlie insisted.

He said I could come, but only if I stayed out of the way.

I agreed, even though it felt awkward. Kind of like I was the unwanted little kid tagging along behind a gang of cool, older boys. But I did as instructed because I had no other choice. Although, what I didn't tell Charlie was that I had slipped a silver-plated revolver under my belt before I left my hotel room. I could feel it as I walked, cool against my skin. It was Nue's gun, the one he had given me in Hong Kong. I don't remember exactly when or why I started carrying the gun in my suitcase. Probably took it with me because it made me feel safe when I was traveling. I was never sure that was true. And I don't know why I took it with me that night. I just remember having it.

After gathering on the curved cement driveway at the entrance to the Inn, our group of CIA agents and I proceeded around the building and across the grassy lawn towards the shoreline. Charlie's crew included two women and two men plus him, all trained CIA agents. I remembered seeing them carrying small black back bags. I really wasn't paying too much attention. I was anxious to get going. The thought of Ilana alone with Nue's goons in her state of mind concerned me. And I couldn't help but wondering why she left our room to join them in the first place. But the answer to that question would have to wait; wait until I knew she was safe.

A cool ocean breeze blew across the lawn as we walked towards shore. Lights from the Inn grew dimmer the farther we traveled. Fortunately, it was a clear night with a nearly full moon making it moderately easy to see once our eyes adjusted to the semi darkness. A ribbon of smooth pale beach sand separated the dark gray waters of the Calibogue Sound from the grassy lawn; leading us down the shoreline towards an undeveloped area of dense, primeval forest.

Charlie stopped after we had traveled for what seemed an excruciating long time down the beach. He wore a headset attached to a thin flexible plastic black microphone in front of his mouth. I assumed he had been quietly talking to Brad, who was giving him directions. I could not hear what was being said. Waves lapping up onto the shore drowned out most of their conversation.

He turned to us and whispered, 'Ilana is with Nue and Manuel,' confirming my worst fears. He then paused and looked at me. I assumed, waiting for some kind of reaction. When I didn't say anything, he continued. 'They are a short distance from here in a clearing in the forest. We are going to have to be very quiet now. If we can get close without being detected, we should be able to hear what they are saying.'

Charlie looked at me again. 'You sure you want to do this, John? It could get messy.'

'Yes,' I replied tersely with as much conviction as I could muster.

But the truth was I wasn't really sure I wanted to hear any of conversation between Ilana and Nue. I only wanted this nightmare to be over. However, as badly as I wanted to have nothing to do with any of this, I was equally curious to know what she was doing and why. Had she been working for Manuel and Nue all along? Was this why Ilana had been acting really strange? Was it all beginning to make sense in the worst possible way? Was it possible she had been betraying me? Was she capable of that?

I loved her and thought she loved me. She was, after all, the woman who lived with me in my house, slept in my bed and cooked my food. Could I be so wrong about her, such a fool I did not see the signs? Did I not understand a traitor lived in my house? Was I that dense? My gut told me no, but I had been wrong before about people. Mostly because I wanted them to be something they weren't. This had always been one of my greatest weaknesses. Even when the signs were clearly evident, I often dismissed them because I simply did not want them to be true. But in retrospect, I sometimes had to admit I was wrong.

I wondered if I had done this with her, wanted Ilana to be the woman I loved, loved too much to see the signs of her betrayal. I assumed this was what Charlie was thinking. Because why else would she sneak off and meet with these people in the middle of the night if she really loved me?

I was not ready to believe it. Not yet... But perhaps I was wrong. And that thought made me feel sick in my gut.

Charlie nodded to me as if to say, it's your funeral, John. If you want to hear what's being said, let's go.

Our little band of CIA agents and me, the unwanted tag-a-long kid last in line, headed into the old growth forest. Moonlight reflected off silky sheens of dew-covered spider webs hanging from the leaves of bushes as we proceeded. It was not easy going. Our progress was difficult after leaving the smooth beach sand behind. Plus, it was darker. Tall, majestic trees of the forest cast long moon shadows over a dense gray residue of decaying leaves and dead grass covering the rich, damp soil.

A real concern now was noise, making too much noise. Charlie cautioned us to slow down and be quiet. We did, but this didn't stop unseen twigs from snapping continuously under our feet, no matter how hard we tried to avoid them. Palmetto bushes, adorned with long rapier-like leaves, scratched at our arms and legs. Everything alive seemed to be reaching out to take a piece of us. Branches bent by agents ahead of me snapped back with whipping pain. I had to turn away more than once to avoid being hit in the face, but not often enough to avoid every branch intent on taking a healthy swipe at me.

Charlie slowed again, signaling me to come up front. I had been hanging back, trying to be cautious and quiet. I didn't want anyone to blame me for the mission going wrong.

'We are close now.' he whispered after I joined him. 'I suggest you stay here where it is safe. We are going a little closer to where Brad is hiding so we can understand what is being said.

He was right. I could hear people talking, but I couldn't understand what they were saying.

'No, I'm coming with you.' I said to Charlie.

He silently acknowledged my determination and again cautioned all of us to be as quiet as possible. I assumed his comments were directed mostly at me. I was the amateur in this group. I needed to stay out of the way. But I didn't want to be cautious, not now. Hearing Ilana's voice through the forest made me want to rush ahead and take her in my arms, protect her.

But if I did that, I would learn nothing. I needed to be patient and obey Charlie, no matter how hard it was for me.

We made progress, slow progress, cautious progress, me last in line again as Charlie insisted. It was frustrating. A growing dread began to occupy my gut as I crept through the forest. In the beginning, I was merely nervous, concentrating on trying to be quiet. Now, as our pace slowed and as we got closer, time seemed to stand still while my mind raced ahead, trying to understand how and why I had to come to be in this place in the middle of the night. Who was responsible? Even though I tried not to think bad things about her, thoughts of ugly betrayal continued to wash uninvited through my brain in images of stark clarity. I saw her laughing as she talked to Nue. They had promised her money, a lot of money. She had betrayed me again, just like the first time. Everything about her was a lie. She had continued to spy on me like before? It all seemed to be one long conspiracy.

I tried to analyze every scene I could remember, looking for signs I had missed. Like her crying, was it just an act? Was this why she could recover so easily? Was she only an actress in a charade?

My state of mind continued to deteriorate into an abyss of black doubt as we proceeded. The forest became, for me, a dense place filled with dark, forbidding images of distress. Fallen branches lying on the ground evolved into imagined snakes of fear wiggling through the tall grass in the shadowed half-light of the moon. Panic filled my brain with anxious thoughts. I felt lost and confused, ricocheting between worrying about finding her brutalized by Nue's thugs to being scared I would hear her conspiring to cause my death, laughing with my enemies, laughing at me. My heart raced as new fears like worms burrowed deep into my soul.

I knew I needed to stop this clatter of imagined fears from taking over my mind. I tried desperately to concentrate something else, anything else, like making as little noise as possible, carefully choosing places to step and avoiding fallen branches cracking under my feet. I searched for areas of grass in the gray night, places to take a step without making noise, soft earth still wet from spring rains. My tennis shoes slowly turned black as I sank into the mud as I followed behind Charlie's gang. Alternately, we would stop to allow Charlie time to listen to the voices in the air. Then, we would continue going forward again. Time became like a frozen flower, wilting slowly in the night as anxious, fearful thoughts dripped through my mind.

Brad heard us and came back. He said nothing, pointing at some bushes a few yards ahead. I assumed this was where he suggested we go, where we could clearly hear what was being said without being seen. Charlie motioned for me to join him, putting his finger in front of his lips, indicating complete silence as I followed him. He pointed at my feet; I assumed to make me look where I stepped and make no noise. I understood, carefully searching the ground, taking long, controlled steps, following Charlie's lead.

We could hear them better now. Their conversation was getting heated. Ilana's agitated female voice rose above the others, distinct from two lower male voices. Manuel spoke with a heavy Spanish accent, and Nue could be distinguished by his usual clipped Thai accent. It was easy to differentiate between the three voices, but still, I couldn't completely understand what they were saying.

Brad signaled from up ahead, his hand motioning down. We crawled the last few yards on our knees towards a place behind some palmetto bushes. The damp, cold earth under my hands seeped through the cloth of my pants as we proceeded.

Finally, we stopped and listened, my ears slowly adjusting to the agitated voices in the night.

9:10 P.M.
JOHN

Manuel spoke in excited Spanish.

Ilana replied with an equally animated Spanish expletive.

No one said another word for a couple of long seconds. I, of course, did not understand Spanish. I had no idea what they were saying, but it didn't sound agreeable.

Nue quickly assumed the role of referee. 'I think this lady understands you,' he said calmly. 'You do not need to yell at her.'

'But I need to speak loudly,' Manuel insisted, challenging Nue. 'How else can I force her to tell us what we need to know?' Disgust hung heavy in his voice. It was obvious he was becoming frustrated with both Ilana and Nue.

'Let your words speak for you,' Nue replied, his tone calm in contrast to an exasperated Manuel. 'Clearly explain to this lady what will happen if she does not answer our questions.'

'I have explained it to her,' Manuel spat.

Ilana remained silent even though it was her turn to speak.

They waited, but she said nothing.

'Do you understand what this man has told you?' Nue finally asked her.

'I told him I understand,' Ilana replied softly.

I couldn't see her, afraid to raise my head for fear of being seen, but I detected a shiver in her voice. Then I remembered she had left the room dressed only in a sleeveless top and shorts. It had not seemed strange at the time because I thought she was going to the lobby. Now I realized she must be getting cold as a cool breeze rustled through the leaves.

'Then why do you continue to refuse to tell us what we want to know?' Nue asked her calmly.

'But I have told you everything I know. Why don't you believe me?' she answered as forcefully as she could.

'Because you are a bitch,' Manuel's low malevolent voice

penetrated the forest like the growl of a hunting animal, followed by the sound of a hard slap echoing through the silent trees.

I involuntarily flinched from the imagined blow. Ilana cried out in surprise. I started to stand. Charlie grabbed my arm. Another loud slap was followed by her muffled cry.

'Hold her,' Manuel dictated.

Ilana cried out in pain.

'Talk,' Manuel demanded.

Another hard slap.

Ilana screamed

Slap.

Charlie grabbed my arm tightly, preventing me from rising.

'Talk bitch.'

The sound of Ilana softly crying wandered like the wind through the trees of the dark forest. No other sound was heard. It was as if the forest was listening breathlessly to the sounds of her pain, desperately waiting for her to stop crying before returning to its natural sounds.

'Stop him,' Nue demanded.

Someone acknowledged Nue's command with a grunt, and I assumed one of Nue's bodyguards got physical with Manuel because I heard the sounds of a scuffle.

'Si, si,' Manuel indicated he would cooperate.

Ilana's soft whimpering crept through the trees.

'It is time to place a call to your man in Belize,' Nue said to Manuel, hoping to appease his friend's anger. 'It is clear this girl is unwilling to help us.'

'But I have told you everything I know. Why would you now do this thing?' Ilana begged through her crying.

'Because you have not told us why John brought Phillip to this island.'

'Yes, why won't you tell us?' Phillip chimed in.

For the first time, I realized Phillip was also present. Nue must have convinced him to help in the short time they met in the afternoon. My breakfast meeting in the morning was instantly relegated to a useless exercise in futility.

'Because I don't know,' Ilana screamed at Phillip.

'I don't believe you, young lady,' Phillip replied rather haughtily. 'You are protecting your friend John. That much is obvious. It is also obvious you don't care about your brother. Manuel can have him killed with one phone call, little girl, don't you understand? You need to answer our questions.'

'Enough,' Nue spoke calmly. 'It is getting late... Manuel, make your call. I have heard enough. It is time for bed.'

'Please don't kill my brother,' Ilana screamed.

I began to stand again, but Charlie held me down.

'Then talk to us,' Nue said.

'I have talked to you.'

'You have told us nothing.'

'You asked me if I knew why Phillip was here.' Ilana replied. 'I told you I don't know. You asked me what John was planning for the board meeting. I told you I do not know anything more than what Phillip has told you. Why won't you believe me?'

Nue did not speak for a moment. I assumed he was judging the truth of her answers. Then he asked a question. 'Perhaps you can still save your brother. Maybe you can answer other questions.'

Ilana was silent.

'Well, what can you tell us to save your brother?' Nue persisted. 'Did anyone else come to the island with John we should know about?'

She had no choice. She had to tell Nue something. I relaxed for a moment. She would have to give up Charlie to save her brother. I no longer cared.

Nue instantly recognized from her silence that he had asked the question he should have asked before. 'Well, tell us. Has John brought people to this island you have not told us about?'

'Tell the man,' Manuel shouted.

'No need for that, Manuel. She will tell us,' Nue said.

I could barely hear what she said because she spoke very softly as if she didn't want anyone to hear her. I only recognized a few words including Charlie and CIA. After her statement, everyone was quiet. Nothing more needed to be said. Nue would understand immediately what this meant. As would Manuel. And if Phillip failed to get the significance of the information, Nue would explain it to him later.

Ilana waited, whimpering quietly.

'I think we have heard enough for tonight,' Nue finally said, signaling the meeting was over. 'Manuel, you will make your call now,' he spoke with a hint of anger in his voice. It was the first time I had ever heard Nue express real emotion.

'Why?' Ilana screamed. 'I have told you everything I know.'

'You are right. We can learn nothing more from you.'

'But then, why must you kill my brother?'

'It needs to be done,' Nue responded without explanation.

Manuel grunted approval.

Ilana yelled, 'You bastard.'

'Perhaps we can find another way to save your brother, little girl,' Manuel offered with a laugh. 'Perhaps you would like to visit my room tonight.'

Charlie's hand gripped my arm. My body trembled.

'I... I cannot...' Ilana cried as if torn apart.

'Enough,' Nue said. 'Manuel, you will do only as I have instructed, no more. Now leave us and make the call.'

'As you wish,' Manuel replied, disappointment escaping his lips.

'But you cannot do this,' Ilana's voice screamed into the empty forest.

'But I can,' Manuel spat back at her.

A high-pitched shriek of utter anguish escaped her open mouth, penetrating the vast crevasses of the dark forest, sounding more like the death scream of a wild beast being torn apart by devouring wolves than the cry of a woman. Her scream made the skin of my back sweat against the cold steel of Nue's gun under my belt. I stood, ripping my arm from Charlie's grip. I had heard enough. Ilana had endured enough. This had to stop.

Ilana charged Manuel before I could intervene.

Manuel saw her coming in the moonlight and waited. Pathetically, she swung at him, her small fists flying in a staccato rhythm. He held off her feeble attempts with one large hand while the rock-hard fist of his other hand delivered a powerful blow that hit her hard across the mouth, snapping her head back. Because everyone was watching her fall, they did not see me. Not until I reached down for her, helped her to her feet, and held her bleeding face against my chest.

Surprised at first, she looked up at me and then collapsed in my arms.

'Back off.' I held my hand up to Manuel who stood with his knees bent, his tight fist ready to deliver another blow.

'Ah, John, your timing is perfect as always,' Nue said calmly.

His two black suited bodyguards came to immediate attention, standing directly behind Nue, looking surreal, shadows in the half light of the moon. I could see them, but I could not see them clearly. Their faces were distorted, vague, almost unreal, their features partially visible in the moon's pale white light. It was as if everything existed in patterns of pale gray, devoid of color, perfect voices coming from ghostlike shadows of lifeless bodies.

'Not exactly,' I said, hearing my voice crack from emotion. 'It seems I should have arrived a few minutes earlier. Your manners toward women are appalling, Nue. You, of all people, I did not expect this from you.'

'It was necessary.'

'Your excuse for everything, Nue. And you, Manuel. I never really liked you. Now I know why.'

'I do not like you either, American.' He spit out the words.

'And Phillip, I see you have again joined forces with these criminals.'

'Was I ever going to be your COO, John?' Phillip asked.

Ilana moved closer under my arms, shivering, cold and afraid. Her warm body against me felt good. That's when I realized I was alone. Charlie had stayed behind.

'Tell me you aren't a liar,' Phillip continued. 'You never intended I would become the COO of the company. Did you? Wasn't that just a lie?'

'It was necessary,' I said, instantly regretting my words.

'So how are you any different from Nue?' Phillip asked, knowing he had me.

He did. I used the same words Nue used to justify his behavior.

'One difference, Phillip, I am not a murderer like Nue.' I replied. 'He ordered the murders of Arthur and Vidu.'

I turned to Nue. 'I know you had Arthur and Vidu murdered?' I said to him, hoping Charlie was listening.

'I have already admitted these things to you, John. How many times do I need to explain this to you? It was necessary because we have the same goals. I want to control the world market in sapphires just as you do. The lives of my family and thousands of Thai workers depend on me. You know that, John. Our game has always been understood by both of us.'

'This is more than a game, Nue. This is about murder. Rules apply to the game of business we play. Murder is not one of the rules of the game.'

'What rules, John? There are no rules. Take Manuel's Columbia, people from your country buy drugs from the people of his country. And then your government sends murdering soldiers to kill the people who make the drugs you buy. Is this not a game, John, just like the one we play?'

Manuel grunted in agreement.

'I don't play your game.' I said.

'But of course, you do, John. You lied to me. And you brought your CIA to help you play your game.'

'I had no choice.'

'Of course, you had a choice.'

'You started this war, Nue. Not me.'

'No, John, you started it when you formed a company. Do you still not understand? War is about money and jobs and food. Your company, the one that made you rich, your company is at war with my people. My country lost jobs, and my people lost their homes while you became rich. People in my country have gone hungry and died because of what you have done, John.'

'That's nonsense.'

'No, it is true.' Nue replied.

'Even if it is true, which I don't believe... it doesn't justify killing my friends.'

'People die in war.'

'My friend Arny and my girlfriend Monica, did they need to

die? Is that what you are saying?'

'I don't know who this Arny is,' Nue replied.

'Of course, you don't. He was gunned down in my apartment by a hail of bullets I suppose was meant for me.'

'It was a warning to you,' Nue responded. 'Nothing more.'

'A warning! So, my friend Arny wasn't supposed to die?' I yelled at Nue.

'Ah yes,' Nue responded. 'What does your government call this...collateral damage?'

'Well, understand this, Nue. Arny was more than collateral damage. He was a man. His death is a loss I feel every day. He was my friend, Nue. And you killed him.' The metal from Nue's gun suddenly felt very cold against the skin of my back.

'I did not know this man, Arny.'

'Does that make it okay to kill him?' I asked in anger.

Nue did not answer.

'And now Ilana's brother?' I said to him in disgust. 'Now you want to kill her brother.'

'The girl failed to answer our questions truthfully,' Nue replied, showing no outward emotion. 'It must be done.'

'No, it does not,' I fairly screamed at him.

He looked at me for a moment, trying to determine if I had lost my mind. 'John, we have stayed in this forest too long. It is late. We will have much to talk about in the morning.'

'We have nothing to discuss!'

'Oh, but we do, John.'

'What?'

'The changes you will make in your company.'

'What changes?'

'We will discuss these things in the morning.'

'What if I don't want to talk to you in the morning?'

'Oh, but you will.'

'And Ilana's brother?'

'You know the answer to your question.'

I took a moment to observe his pale face in the moonlight. He didn't look like a man in the colorless light, more like the ghost of a man.

'Do not kill her brother,' I demanded with all the strength I had in my body.

'This girl withheld information. And you John, you lied to me. It is time you understand who I am. Her brother must die,' he said with a hint of bitterness in his otherwise unemotional voice.

Manuel grunted his approval.

'Do not do this, Nue. You do not need to do this.' I said more forcefully.

He simply nodded to Manuel, who began to walk away with his cell phone in his hand.

Ilana involuntarily shivered in my arms.

Something deep inside me snapped in anguished pain. The hard metal of Nue's gun felt cold in my hand. I pointed the gun at him, staring straight into his cold black eyes as he backed against the trunk of an old tree in disbelief when he saw the gun. A heavy, painful ache filled with the memories of Monica and Arny moved rapidly in compressed time through my soul, each memory a millisecond of hot anger expanding like flashes of fireworks spreading across the dense black night sky. I didn't so much as pull the trigger. It was more as if the fingers of my hand involuntarily closed around the trigger of the gun in revulsion to seeing dead corpses running rampantly through the space of one horrific moment in my mind. As if all the blood and tears and anger from the past were now somehow released through my hand with one compressed reaction... the intense squeezing of the trigger several times, discharging anger into the cool night air.

The end of the gun barrel flashed bright. Hard lead flew with great velocity through the black night air, intent on destroying the man responsible for all my pain. His body jerked backward from the impact of the bullets, distorting his chest into an ugly red mess of torn flesh and cloth.

Nue fell against the tree, slowly sliding down to the ground in a sitting position.

I held Ilana tight against my body, suddenly afraid she was dead, lying limp against my body as Monica had been so many months before. But Ilana moved in my arms, her head down, her eyes closed to the horror I was witnessing, her face buried in my chest.

The gun fell from my hand with a thud, hitting the soft ground.

Blood seeped from multiple wounds in Nue's chest. He was badly hurt, dying.

I felt no sorrow for him, no guilt, no glee, only a passing feeling of having exhausted all the pent-up, old air in my lungs as if I had been unable to breathe for so long... until now. Now I could finally release the foul air from my lungs and suck in fresh air, new air.

In slow motion, I watched Nue's bodyguards go for their weapons. It was time to die, my time. I waited for what I knew would be my inevitable death, unafraid, almost content.

A hail of gunfire erupted behind me in the trees.

Invisible bullets guided by red tracer beams raced through the gray, misty night air, targeting the guards as I sheltered Ilana beneath me, folding my arms around her trembling body as Nue's goons fell on the rich, dark soil of the forest. Manuel reacted by running like a scared cat towards the beach, where he was tackled by Brad, falling and splashing into the ocean in a torrent of confused, thrashing water. Phillip immediately dropped to the ground on his knees to avoid being hit by a stray bullet.

Nue sat silently against the wide trunk of the old tree, which had kept him from falling flat on the ground, sitting upright, his bleeding upper torso resting against the tree.

He smiled at me one last time before closing his eyes forever.

MARCH 31, 10:15 A.M.
JOHN

Standing outside the main boardroom in the Conference Center of the Inn, I was afraid to go inside.

I didn't know why. I had no reason to fear. I could hear their voices. I knew who they were. They were my friends, partners in business, and members of my board of directors, all waiting for me, standing, talking, and drinking cups of coffee taken from a long table covered with a white cotton cloth. Eating rolls, coffeecake, or a bagel from a silver serving tray. Clear glass jugs filled with fresh fruit juices stood next to gleaming silver coffee dispensers offering regular or decaffeinated brew. The room's main feature was a large conference table in the center of the room surrounded by comfortable chairs. Everyone was waiting to sit, waiting for my entrance so the board meeting could begin. But I was reluctant to join them. I was a different person now. I was not the man they elected to be the chairman of the board only a short time ago. And I was surely not the man who formed a company seven years before which now controls most of the sapphire sales in the world.

I didn't know if I belonged anymore.

The board members had been on the island for a least a day, but I had seen only a few of them. Clarence came to my room yesterday. We had a long talk. And Tim stopped in with Sarah who wanted to see Ilana. The ladies embraced when they met. Ilana cried. The two of them spent the afternoon quietly talking together. A bond between them had been established in Australia which was deep and strong. I could hear them conversing softly together in the bedroom while Tim and I talked in the other room. I didn't tell Tim too much. I simply told him the truth as I told Clarence. I didn't feel like I needed to keep it from either of them. I knew they would understand, Tim especially. I remembered seeing him smile when I told him what happened.

But I couldn't smile with him. He wasn't there with me. He didn't see Nue die; Nue's chest badly disfigured, blood soiling his clothes. Tim didn't feel the weight of the gun in his hand as I did. Or the emptiness I finally felt when it was all over. Like a deep hole had been cut in my heart which could never be filled. For Tim, Nue's death was academic. A man who had tried to kill him was dead. Tim was happy Nue was dead. He didn't need to thank me. Tim said it silently with his eyes.

The members of the board were another matter. Charlie and I had argued about what to tell them. I said I didn't care if the world knew what happened in that forest. In a way I wanted it out in the open. I preferred to tell the board the whole story. Then let them decide what to do.

'And what will that accomplish?' Charlie asked.

'It's the truth. I don't care,' I responded.

At the time we were sitting in the room in the conference center where Charlie had his equipment. It was late on the night of the shooting. Ilana was sitting next to me. Two of Charlie's fellow agents were busy working with the electronic equipment. I think their names were Marisa and Tony. Brad and Steve and two other agents were still in the forest. A couple of helicopters had been ordered; a team of CIA agents were coming to clean the scene of the shooting. Phillip and Manuel were also still there. I assumed they were sitting on the beach in handcuffs where we left them. They were scheduled to be flown directly to Langley for interrogation.

Charlie said Manuel would subsequently be extradited to Columbia. His government would receive recorded evidence of his involvement in the planned murder of Ilana's brother in Belize. Charlie assumed the Columbians would lock up Manuel for a long time.

But the first order of business after the shooting was to have the CIA contact the police in Belize through the American Consulate. Charlie allowed Ilana to listen in on the conversation. The CIA wanted the local police to protect her brother. And they did because he called her later that night to tell her he was fine, unharmed.

Nue and his dead bodyguards were a completely different problem. Charlie had several phone calls with his superiors to discuss what to do with them. Problem was Nue's family was an old dynasty. They were very influential in the Thai government. Nue's death and the death of his bodyguards would not be easy to explain. Charlie's conversations with Langley sounded less than cordial. I remembered Charlie slamming down the phone after one particularly acrimonious conversation. We were all tired by this time; nerves shot.

'It may be the truth,' Charlie said to me when we were discussing what to tell the board members. 'But it accomplishes nothing, John. If you tell the truth, I will be forced to bring in the local police, and they will demand that it be treated like any other murder investigation. You will plead self-defense, but they will want to talk to Manuel and Phillip, who will, of course, tell a completely different version of the story from yours. The investigation will then become a huge nightmare for both of us. I will be required to turn over all my evidence. And if that is not bad enough, as soon as the FBI gets wind of what is going on, they will want to become involved. They will begin by asking why the CIA was in charge of this operation in the first place. Why not the FBI because it occurred on American soil. They will demand jurisdiction. I will try to explain to them that it was a CIA operation because of major international implications, but they will be in no mood to cooperate.'

He paused and looked at me. 'Are you beginning to understand?'

'I guess.'

'Well, if you still have any doubts,' he continued, becoming more and more frustrated that he had to explain any of this to me. 'You will probably end up in a jail cell and your friend here, Ilana, will be deported for participating in a felony. Now, have I said enough to convince you?'

'Okay, Charlie. I get it.'

It was almost morning by this time, a few hours before dawn. All the adrenalin in our bodies had been expended. Reserves of tolerance and civility had long ago been spent. We were operating on fumes. That's when we created the whitewashed version of what happened. I dictated it to Helen, who typed it. It stated Nue and Manuel had left the island by helicopter due to urgent business elsewhere. They sent their regrets to the board.

Their luggage was neatly packed by Charlie's guys and sent along with Nue's body and the dead bodyguards to Langley. By the morning after the shooting, their rooms were neat and empty, courtesy of the CIA agents who had arrived by helicopter. The Inn was informed of their urgent departure in the night. They were simply gone. Langley handled the rest.

Thankfully, we didn't have to explain why Phillip wasn't in attendance. None of the board members knew he had been invited to the board meeting. His departure in the wee hours of the morning was omitted from the release. Charlie said we could decide what to do about Phillip later. He would go with the others to Langley for an interrogation. And eventually he would most likely be released because what could he do? He wouldn't want to admit to being a member of an international gang intent on murdering an American CEO. Charlie doubted he would be a problem in the future.

Helen, for her part, had been a trooper. When we returned to the conference center after the shooting, she was in bed sleeping when I called to ask her to please come in the middle of the night without an explanation to the conference center. At first, she was reluctant, typical of her, always wanting a detailed explanation. But then, perhaps it was something she heard in my voice. I don't know why, but she came without an argument. That was not normal for her. When she arrived, she went right to work. She seemed to know instinctively what to do and why. Even Charlie was amazed at her efficiency.

Now, as I waited in the hall outside the board meeting room, I could hear her clear voice speaking to the board members, taking care of business as usual, serving coffee, and ordering more rolls from the kitchen.

I was already fifteen minutes late for the meeting by the time I arrived; something I never did. Usually, I am the first to arrive. I like to greet everyone when they come in. But today it took everything I had just to show up. I was mentally and physically exhausted.

All of us had worked through the night of the shootings. Our stories had to be coordinated. Charlie spent most of his night on the phone with Langley. Their helicopters arrived on the beach predawn. The area where the shooting occurred was isolated. Fortunately, it was low tide at the time the helicopters touched down. We hoped no one would be disturbed by the noise. Helicopters are not uncommon on the island. Some very wealthy people commute by helicopter. Charlie went to the site as soon as he heard the birds had landed. Ilana, I and Helen were ordered to stay with the other two agents in the conference center until Charlie returned.

The one thing I didn't realize at the time of the shooting was that it was recorded on audio and video tape, shot with special nighttime cameras. The recording equipment had been in the black bags Charlie's agents were carrying. I was too busy paying attention to what was going on in the forest at the time. I was not aware of what was happening behind me.

Back in the conference center, the tapes were transferred to computers to be sent to Langley for evaluation, all very neat and proper. The real truth was painfully clear to anyone who watched the tapes. But Charlie still felt the need to verbally finesse the situation. He told Langley I shot Nue to save Ilana's brother. It was a weak argument, and everyone in the room knew it, but Charlie said no one was going to care why Nue died, only that he was dead. He was a murderer. He had on several occasions been instrumental in the murder an American citizen and he had attempted takeover an American company by illegal means. This was not considered proper conduct by the US government. His death would not be an unwelcome event to the spooks at the CIA. Even so, he was a very important man in the political hierarchy of Thailand. The Agency was obligated to create a story to explain his demise. But this was what they did for a living. Charlie said to let it be. It was not our problem now.

In the morning, the sun appeared on the horizon over the ocean as it did every morning. Nothing in the sun's routine was unusual. But as Ilana and I walked to our rooms in the Inn, everything looked completely different to me. It was as if I had just entered a parallel world to the one, I inhabited the night before. I think I will remember that sunrise for the rest of my life. Ilana held my hand. We took a short walk to the beach to get some fresh air. She had spoken only a few words since the shooting, enough to thank Charlie for making the call to Belize about her brother. And then a short conversation with her bother. I was worried about her. Her lips were badly bruised where she had been hit by Manuel. A female agent had treated her cuts. Helen went to the Inn and returned with a sweater to keep her warm. She tried to talk to her and be a friend. But Ilana was acting sullen, quiet, buried in a world of her own.

When we finally returned to our hotel room, we took a few

minutes to say the words that needed to be expressed. I told her she didn't need to explain. It was all very clear to me. She had done what she did because she had no choice. Ilana showed me a crumpled piece of paper from her pocket, the instructions she had received from Phillip. I read it, but it only confirmed what I already knew. I held her and said I didn't blame her as she had cried bitter tears from long days of pain and worry. When she calmed down, we went to bed. We were both dead tired. We tried to sleep, but sleep didn't come easily. Every time I closed my eyes, I saw Nue's smiling face looking at me, blood and flesh distorting his chest. Ilana closed her eyes several times, but I wasn't sure she slept; she just rested in my arms.

Helen was unbelievable the next day. Despite the fact she had been awake most the night, she spent the day greeting the members of board when they arrived on the pier, arranging their hotel rooms, making sure they had everything they needed. Telling them I was under the weather, but the board meeting would go on the following day as scheduled.

I never came out of my room that day. Drapes were closed.

The night before the board meeting, I again tried to sleep with Ilana curled up in my arms. It was uncomfortable with her body buried against me, but she wasn't the problem. I was happy she was with me. She was like a ball of hope in my arms. I just couldn't sleep. Sometime early in the morning, I uncoiled from her embrace as the sky lightened and decided to take a walk on the beach to clear my head.

The golden sun rose in the east over the calm, steel-blue water of the Sound. It was another beautiful day on the island. I kept telling myself I should be happy. Nue was gone, out of my life forever. And Charlie was taking care of everything. He had come to my room the previous evening and told me not to worry. Said everything was going well in Washington. The shooting scene had been swept clean. There would be no long-term repercussions.

I thanked him.

Seems I had committed the perfect murder. My rival was gone. I didn't have to deal with him any longer. I could move forward with my plans for the company without fear of interference or instant death. In addition, my revenge was complete, revenge for all the pain this man had caused. I thought about how Nue had tried to convince me he wanted a truce when it was now clear that all really wanted was space and time to find a new way to steal my company.

My ordeal in the river came to mind, seeing all the dead bodies floating there, all the innocent lives lost. And Arny, his death in a hail of gunfire in the kitchen of my apartment; I could still see his blood seeping into the cracks between the tiles beneath his body. I thought about how Monica had died and how much I missed her. I wanted her with me now. I needed her to help me decide what to do. I tried talking to her under the sun's warming rays, but my only companion that morning was a solitary gray and white seagull strutting nervously on the beach sand until it gently cradled the wind under its raised wings and rose to fly off over the Sound.

I needed Monica for her understanding. I wanted her to tell me everything would be okay. But I didn't really know if she would agree. I wasn't sure she would approve of what I did that night in the forest.

As I continued to walk the beach in quiet exasperation, a porpoise raised its head out of the waters of the Sound and lazily flipped over, its shiny gray body slipping effortlessly into the water to feed. A flock of tiny sandpipers skimmed inches over the ocean, rising suddenly to land near me on the shore where shallow waves washed up over the sand before retreating back into the ocean, leaving behind a sparkling wet sheen over the gray beach. The sandpipers pecked nervously in the wet sand behind the retreating waves, scurrying along on pulsating stick legs, moving together as if they were one body, one mind.

Revenge is supposed to be sweet.

But my revenge tasted more like a bitter wine, not the sweet aroma I expected, more like the acrid stench of rotting fish, a sour taste in my mouth from an empty death. I tried to shake a dread funk that seemed to be invading my brain, but I could not. It was as if something inside me had died in the forest along with Nue. I wasn't the same person I had been before. Somewhere out in the forest, not far from where I now walked, I imagined my body lying dead, propped against a great old oak tree just like Nue.

More by instinct than anything rational, I decided I needed to find the place where it all happened. In my mind's eye, I could still see the tree where Nue had died. In fact, every time I had closed my eyes in the last two days, the image of him sitting against that tree appeared. I did not think I would have any trouble finding the place, but as I walked the shore looking for signs of a disturbance, I found nothing. High tides had wiped the beach smooth. Other than a clear core of a dead jellyfish and some horseshoe crab shells scattered across the grey sand; I discovered nothing. No deep imprints on the beach from heavy helicopters, nothing to indicate where they landed.

My problem was I had no idea how far from the Inn we had walked that night. My mind had been a mass of fearful emotions. Time had been badly distorted. Seconds of horror had lasted into infinity. Minutes turned into hours. The night belonged to the moon. Its glow created a surreal black-and-white world in the half-light. Everything looked completely different now, filled with distinctly defined plants and sharp, clear images of trees in perfect color. I was seeing a different world.

Charlie had told me his men swept the area, meaning that they had made the forest appear as if no one had ever been there. He was right. I had only my memories to help me find the place and they didn't seem to be enough.

Finally, I decided to enter the forest and walk parallel to the shoreline like before, hoping that would help me find the place. Each tree I passed was examined. None seemed right. I became increasingly pessimistic I would ever find the right one; the tree marking the place where Nue died.

A soft, warm breeze blew off the ocean through a nearby palmetto bush as I stood still for a moment, wondering why Nue had chosen an isolated place in the forest to meet with Ilana. Had he been intent on harming her from the beginning? Was this why he had retreated from the beach into the forest? So, his dastardly deeds would be unseen by anyone in the moonlight? But this didn't seem like Nue. He was a man capable of great violence, but not in this place and not under these circumstances. No, the violence he had contemplated that night was to occur a thousand miles away in Belize with the murder of Ilana's brother. I decided Manuel must have been responsible for choosing this place. It seemed more like a place that fit his temperament.

I continued aimlessly until I came to a couple of towering pines that appeared to open into a small clearing that looked vaguely familiar. However, approaching the place in daylight did not immediately make it recognizable. Still, there was an old tree bordering the clearing, which looked like the tree where Nue had died. But the ground around the tree appeared to be completely undisturbed and it was not until I bent down and brushed some new green leaves away from the base of the trunk that I began to see some evidence that this was the tree I was looking for. A faint red stain deep in the crevices of the bark appeared to spread down to the ground. It was like a shadow of pale crimson passing over the dark brown bark. You could not see it unless you were willing to stare at the tree for a minute. Only then did it become visible.

A momentary shudder passed through my body when it became perfectly evident this was the place. This was where Nue had bled to death. This was where he had smiled at me for the last time as he rested against the trunk of this old tree. For some reason, I did not understand; I rubbed my hand over the coarse bark where Nue had died as if I was trying to smear a residue of his blood on my hand; as if I wanted his blood to join with mine.

I had been wondering why he smiled at me. As I stared at the tree, it occurred to me that Nue was trying to tell me something, telling me I was just like him now. No difference, John. As if he was saying, 'Don't look down at me anymore from your moral high ground. You and I are no different, John. We are both of us murderers, combatants in a war... welcome John.'

She gently touched my shoulder.

I winced as if I had been cut.

'I thought I would find you here,' Ilana said softly.

I looked up at her as tears fell silently down my face. I couldn't help it. I was crying tears I never intended for anyone to see, private tears of anger and self-pity.

She extended her hand.
I took it, and she helped me stand.

BELIZE, MAY 17, 1:30 P.M.

Smoothly slipping through the pale blue waters of the Caribbean off the coast of Belize, driven by a gentle wind, we sailed for our favorite diving spot.

Fresh shrimp I had purchased earlier for an appetizer cooled in the refrigerator in the galley below, along with a six-pack of Belican beer. Ilana had volunteered to make our lunch. At least this is what she promised, said that it would be a surprise. I didn't doubt her.

When the jib sheet began to ripple in the breeze, I leaned over to turn a chrome winch handle a couple of clicks, watching with satisfaction as the big sail filled into a smooth curve of spreading white power. The knot meter increased to a healthy six to seven knots when the breeze freshened. Choppy seas ran with monotonous regularity against the sides of the boat, causing an almost unnoticed yet unsettling vibration to course through her resilient fiberglass hull. With this one exception, everything in my world was good at that moment. Ilana, especially, as she lay on a cushion in her bikini, her slim tan body soaking up the sun's warm glow in quiet contentment.

We had been in Belize for almost a week, and I was finally beginning to relax.

After the disaster on Daufuskie Island, we returned to Charlottesville, both of us intent on leaving for Belize as soon as possible. Ilana, perhaps more than I, was anxious to go. She badly wanted to see her brother, to hold him to be certain he was alive and well.

While still on Daufuskie island, Charlie had again assured her everything was fine. The CIA through the American Embassy had contacted the police in Belize City the night of the shooting and requested the arrest of a visitor who had previously assaulted a fisherman on the Island of Ambergris. They told the police Ricky could help them identify this man. It was explained to them that the offender was plotting to kill Ricky. Sometime later, Charlie received a call. With Ricky's help, the man had been identified and found. He was airlifted to a jail cell in Belize City, where he would be interrogated before being extradited to Columbia. Ilana had given Charlie an impromptu hug when she heard the news. Charlie looked embarrassed.

The man's friend, Manuel Ortega, would likely be his cellmate in his home country. The government of Columbia informed the CIA that they had for some time been looking for a reason to put Ortega away. Apparently, he was involved in more than just dealing with emeralds. Something about drugs was mentioned. They were thankful to the CIA. Complicity with assault, conspiracy to commit murder, and racketeering were the charges they would use to put him in jail. And if these were not reasons enough, they said they would find some other charges which would keep him locked up for years. Manuel was now in Columbia for what would likely be a long time behind bars.

Charlottesville had been a nightmare of work with no joy when we returned from South Carolina. All I really desired at the time was to leave, but I had a few items to attend to first.

Jason was first on my list, getting him settled in his new job. I had appointed him to be my new chief operating officer. I had given the speech to the board meeting on Daufuskie Island which I promised Phillip. I said I was tired of the grind, and although I was not ready to give up control of the company, I was anxious to turn over the day-to-day operations to someone else. I expressed confidence in Jason, said he had proved himself to everyone on the board by doing a great job in Hong Kong. He was ready to assume a more important role in the company. Therefore, I was promoting him to be the company's chief operating officer. He would be under my control, but I had no doubt he could handle the job without my interference.

He had looked stunned while sitting along the wall of the conference room, listening to my testimony of his skills. He was not yet a member of the board. He had no seat at the table. And I had not told him of my decision before the meeting. He had no idea a promotion was in his future.

In truth, I had nothing prepared for the board meeting. I had been too occupied with catching Nue in his lies. The meeting of the board had been neglected completely. But sometime during the sleepless nights before the meeting, it all became perfectly clear. I knew what I had to do.

The board meeting had gone well, nothing really out of the ordinary. With the exception of my appointment of Jason and my speech requesting a semi-retirement, the meeting was uneventful. No one really missed Nue or Manuel or even asked why they were not at the table. In a way it seemed perfectly natural for them to be absent, almost as if they had never been connected with the company.

We left for Charlottesville immediately after the board meeting. I told the members I was under the weather. Please accept my apologies. It would be better if I headed home early. The members were free to stay and enjoy as much time on the island as they liked. I thanked them all for coming and asked for a motion to adjourn. I heard later that several of them stayed with Jason and worked on company business while enjoying some recreational time. Helen took care of the details.

Charlie came back with me. A private chartered jet dropped him off at Dulles before heading for the Charlottesville airport. We had hugged long and hard at the airport. Both of us knew we had some unfinished business to discuss, but we tacitly decided it could wait.

I worked for almost three weeks once we were home, which wasn't difficult because in some respects, the work was therapy. I gave Jason a crash course in running the company when he returned to the office. But it was more for my benefit than his. He already knew what was required. He was a bright kid. His experience in Hong Kong had filled in deficiencies in his knowledge. He was prepared for his new assignment.

Helen had been my only problem. She had initially been reluctant to cooperate. She and Jason had been equals in the past. Now Jason was her boss. But in the end, she was extremely helpful. I elevated her to the position of office manager and suggested we hire a new secretary for Jason. Helen refused. She said she could handle both jobs. I knew her reasons. She wanted to have an intimate knowledge of what went on in Jason's office, and the best way to do that was to be his secretary. It was decided instead I would hire someone new to be my office secretary when I returned from Belize.

However, none of this was as important to Ilana as traveling to Belize, folding her arms around her brother, and giving him a long hug on the docks. Ricky, in turn, had smiled at her. A red, jagged scar on his jaw was hard to ignore. Ilana had touched it gently and lovingly. I stood to the side, observing their reunion. He eventually came over and gave me his hand. He did not say anything. He did not apologize, which was fine with me. It was enough for him to give me his hand.

I held it for a moment and smiled. 'It is good to see you, Ricky. I hope we can be friends.'

'We can be friends,' he replied and smiled at his sister who gave him another hug.

We ate dinner together that night. He and Ilana talked constantly. I listened, wondering at times if they knew I was at the table, which was okay with me because they needed to make up for lost time. I was content to sit quietly and enjoy their smiles.

Once a sailboat is fully rigged, almost nothing more is required except to point it in the right direction. In theory, you can adjust the sails for each shift in the wind or tides. But unless you are racing, it doesn't make much difference. A sailboat is not designed for fast transportation. Its purpose is steady progress. I set the automatic pilot and eased over to the cushion where Ilana lay with her eyes closed. A green emerald ring surrounded by small diamonds resided on her finger. I had given her the ring before we left for Belize. I wanted her to know I loved her. I didn't want her to ever question how I felt about her. When she saw the ring, she didn't say anything. She just put it on her finger and kissed me softly while tears formed in the corners of her eyes.

We no longer speak about the possibility of marriage. The ring was originally meant to be an engagement ring, but something has changed. Our relationship is not the same. We still love each other but with a different love. The killing night in the forest did not bring us closer together. Instead, it seems to have created a void between us, a place that words cannot erase. It is as if a shadow has been drawn separating us, a pale moon shadow exposing a sudden, bloody death. The memory of that awful night lingers over us. Our relationship lives now in a world where colors are no longer vivid. Still real, just not the bright, exciting colors that had painted our world before I killed Nue.

I ran my hand over her smooth brown body as she lay on the seat cushion of the boat, enjoying the warm sun. When she opened her eyes and smiled at me, I leaned over to kiss her sweet lips. She sat up to release the strap on her bra and let it fall from her body. Holding my head in her hands, she pulled me close so I could kiss her taut nipples. We made love that afternoon while our sailboat continued its inevitable journey on autopilot. The sea's warm, moist breeze floated over us as I rested in the passion of her glorious body.

When we arrived at our dive spot, the anchor was set. I retrieved our gear from below: swim fins, mask, and a spear Ilana used for fishing underwater. She dropped over the side quickly. I hesitated, looking into the clear blue water for a brief moment before diving in. The warm water flowed over my body as I glided down beside her, holding my breath.

I had once considered learning to scuba dive but decided I preferred swimming naturally underwater without the help of an air tank. Even though I am not a whale or a porpoise, and I can't hold my breath as long as they can, in my own human way, it is good to enjoy the sea as they do.

Ilana kicked ahead of me, her long tan legs working her swim fins, diving down near a coral outcropping surrounded by streaks of gold and purple, small colorful fish scurrying beside the reef's intricately patterned designs. Fish disappeared into the coral's sheltering crevices for protection before jutting out again in a game of catch me if you can. She was beautiful as she swam beneath me, her slim tan body at ease in the sea. I kicked enough to maintain my place underwater, watching her as she stalked a fish, which I assumed was meant to be our lunch. When the fish caught sight of her and darted away, Ilana stopped kicking to allow her body to glide naturally to the surface. Even though my lungs screamed for air, I was reluctant to rise. Releasing some air, I casually watched it bubble up through the clear blue waters above me, finally drifting to the surface as I watched Ilana turn over and dive back down. After rising to the surface, I lay on my back, kicking just enough to stay afloat as I rested on the surface, looking up at the dark blue sides of my boat. The sun warmed my body and I felt more content than I had for weeks.

Ilana eventually surfaced next to me, holding a wiggling fish on her spear. She smiled and headed for the boat, lunch in hand. I watched as she climbed the attached plastic ladder on the boat, water dripping off her smooth, tan body. I couldn't help but admire her. She was a beautiful woman.

Somewhere up on the deck of the boat, my satellite phone rang insistently, spoiling the sounds of waves slapping against the side of the boat in a gentle rhythm. It brought back the memory of a time which seemed to be decades ago, a time when I had climbed into the boat to answer the phone.

Not this time.

This time, I turned over and dove down into the warm blue waters, free to swim in God's paradise until I could hold my breath no longer.

THE END

See below for an excerpt from Book 5, 'Running from Regret.'

BANGKOK, THAILAND, DATE AND TIME UNKNOWN

A sudden, blinding desperation washed over the old patriarch as he slept.

An anger so dark and penetrating it felt as if his body had been hit with the driving force of a lethal weapon. Murky streams of intense rage and dark red liquid poured from his eyes. Involuntarily stumbling backward from the force of the blow, Luang landed hard on the ground, sitting upright against the rough bark of an old tree.

Slowly, through crying pain, his eyes adjusted to moonlight reflecting in silky sheens of dewy spider webs hanging in the bushes. Gray shadows from tall majestic pines and old oak trees fell over a dense residue of decaying leaves covering the ground where he sat. The pain in his chest seeped with warm blood soaking the front of his shirt. He was not dead, but he knew he had only a short time to live. Vague images of men illuminated by intermittent flashes of light burst all around him, accompanied by the sound of gunshots echoing through the tall trees. Shadowed figures ran and fell, screaming in fear and anger.

In the middle of all this anxious chaos stood a man, his face only sporadically visible in flashes of gunfire. Luang sensed he knew this man, but he could not say his name. A heavy metal gun fell from the man's hand, but the man didn't seem to notice the loss of his weapon. He simply stood in the middle of the mayhem and stared down at Luang with no pity in his eyes, no anger, nothing.

Luang smiled at the man. He didn't know why. Except it was as if they were brothers now. They shared something which gave them a common bond.

The old patriarch closed his eyes to his pain as the noise of gunfire slowly eased and dark shadows closed over the palely lit scene, obscuring the light of the moon. Lost in a world of vague gray images, the woodlands became a place where light could not see, could not penetrate. Luang knew he was dying in this dark forest, but he was not afraid. He felt only peace, a sad peace. The sound of waves breaking softly on a nearby shore, their rhythmic lapping, gave him comfort. His time was now done.

When Luang woke up from his nap, he was sitting in a chair in his flower garden, and the sun was shining. For a moment, he remembered nothing of his afternoon dream. Then it all came back to him in intense detail, causing him to sit upright, eyes wide, terror filling his heart. He had fallen asleep and had a vision. He instantly understood what the vision meant. It meant his nephew was dead.

And he had seen the face of the man who killed him.

AMBERGRIS ISLAND, BELIZE, FRIDAY, JULY 24, 1998, 8:10 AM

The awful experience we shared together was forcing us apart.

The fact that I was holding Ilana in my arms when I pulled the trigger to kill that man seemed to be the problem. Because every time I was with her, there appeared to be a shadow hanging over us. It was as if we were still together in those dark woods, staring at the face of the man I had killed.

The images of this terrible moment were ingrained so deep in my skull that I saw a murderer whenever I looked at my reflection in the mirror of her eyes.

I wondered how long it would be before I would stop seeing these images. I didn't know. But I did know everything had changed.

www.ingramcontent.com/pod-product-compliance
Lightning Source LLC
Chambersburg PA
CBHW070639310726

48982CB00001B/343

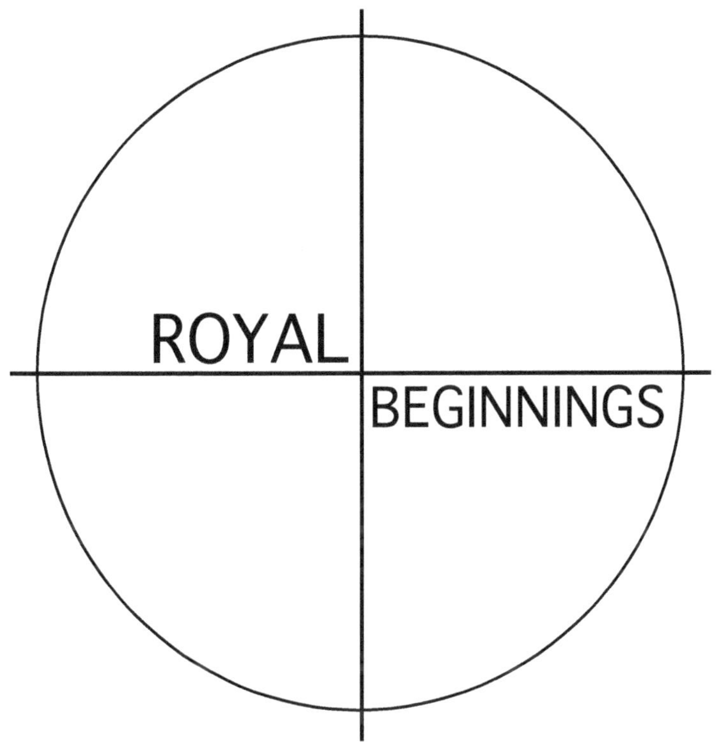
ROYAL
BEGINNINGS

Aly Kay Tibbitts

ROYAL BEGINNINGS

BATTALION PRESS

FARMINGTON, UTAH

Library of Congress Control Number: 2021906103
ISBN: 978-1-955192-01-9 (Hardcover Anniversary Edition)
ISBN: 978-1530094844 (Paperback)

Any references to historical events, real people, or real places are used fictitiously. Names, characters, and places are products of the author's imagination.

Front cover image by Aly Kay Tibbitts.
Book design by Aly Kay Tibbitts.

First printing edition 2016.
Anniversary edition, August 2021.

The text type was set in Garamond.
Book Design by Aly Kay Tibbitts.

For my readers:

Thank you for your support and feedback. I promise the sun is rising.
Consider this our Morningstar of more to come.

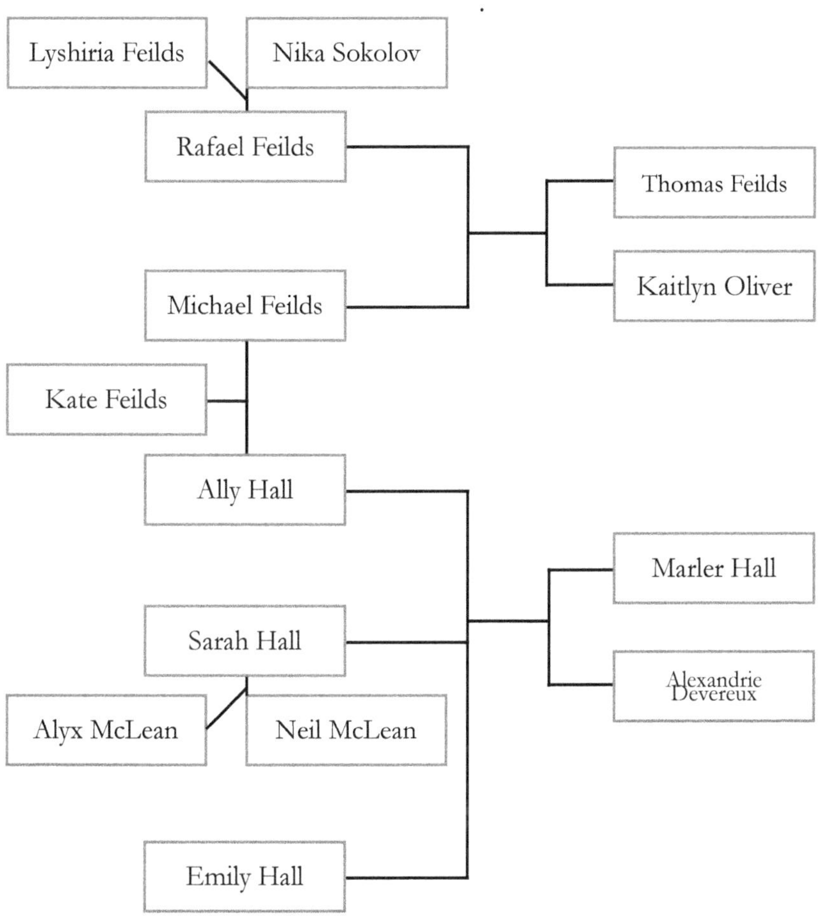
Lyshiria Feilds
Nika Sokolov
Rafael Feilds
Thomas Feilds
Kaitlyn Oliver
Michael Feilds
Kate Feilds
Ally Hall
Marler Hall
Sarah Hall
Alexandrie Devereux
Alyx McLean
Neil McLean
Emily Hall

June 2nd 2011

Dylan Hall finished his email and sent it off. He closed his laptop and scooted back away from the hotel table. As he closed his eyes and leaned his head back, his I-Phone began to ring. Without looking at his phone, he accepted the call and held it up to his ear. "Hall" he answered.

"My good friend, what have you been up to recently," a voice boomed through the phone. Hall sat up and opened his eyes.

"I beg your pardon, but I am not quite sure who I am talking to," Hall answered in an authentic British accent.

"You may not, but we do. You can lose the accent. We know who you really are. You know, it is quite hard to track you down, since rarely go home to visit your children. The new Director must be keeping you busy…"

"What do you want," Hall snapped. He took a deep breath and tried to piece together the pieces of the puzzle he was being given. The man had an American accent. He had CIA access to know that he was a top agent and had to have pretty high clearance, or a source with high clearance to know he worked directly for the new CIA director.

He had figured out exactly what the voice wanted before the voice answered, "We would like you to find Alyx McLean for us. We believe it would be quite beneficial to have you assist us with this assignment."

"I'm not open for hire." Hall stated. He racked his mind thinking of a reason they would call him. They knew he would say no. He had been the enemy of that group for years. His entire family had been. They had gotten desperate if they wanted his help.

"That's too bad. Unfortunately, this is a time sensitive assignment. My employer feels that Ms. McLean is already too old to be postponed any longer. I will have to call my second choice. I'm sorry we could not have the privilege of working together." The voice said before abruptly ending the call.

Hall took the phone away from his ear. The date on the screen read June 2nd 2011. His niece was turning 16 today. His sister had died a few years later, setting into motion a plan to protect their family against their enemies. He sighed heavily, already knowing what he had to do. Tomorrow he was flying home to see his family. He had been planning on staying the summer and doing all sorts of things with his kids. They were growing up too fast, but he knew that wasn't going to happen. Alyx McLean was flying to New York on the seventh. He needed to be on that plane.

Hall sent a text to his wife letting her know he was okay and that he was coming home. He then placed a call to one of his least favorite people. As much as he hated Rafael, he was the lesser of two evils. Besides, by helping him he could exploit him, while achieving what he needed to accomplish.

He had waited for years to get justice for his sister's death. The key to success, as it is with everything else, is patience.

Hopefully this was the chance to make sure Ally's death wasn't for nothing.

June 8th, 2011

14:29 BST (UTC +1)
London City Airport

There were many rewards to having a private plane. What it all boiled down to, essentially, was convenience. Having a private plane meant you traveled when it was convenient for you, and flew to the airport that was closest to your location. The biggest thing about private planes though was it was *private*. That meant very few people were on the plane. In some cases, only a single person was flown to their destination. This was the case for Alyx McLean.

Alyx knew *why* she took her Uncle's plane from New York to London, the biggest reason being security, but it annoyed her. Taking the private plane meant the long flight across the Atlantic was spent alone. The luxury of the plane had intrigued her the first time and the loneliness hadn't really bugged her. However, after five years, the appeal of the private plane was long since gone.

Alyx stared out the window as the plane touched down, and saw her Uncle's car pull up to the runway. As she sighed and leaned her head back, she realized that it wasn't just the appeal of the plane that was gone. The appeal of her summer trip was gone. While she heard her friends talk about different trips to Las Vegas, New York, and Washington, she always had the same story. Every summer she went to London, to stay with her Uncle. Sure, her uncle was Lord Michael Feilds, the Viscount Twickenham, and the place she stayed was Feilds Palace, but 16 years of the same vacation had become quite dreary.

Every fall after she returned to school, she was met by the same questions about London. Everyone wanted to know about the world-renowned sights that she had yet to see, or, when her classmates found out she had stayed a week *in* Buckingham Palace at the beginning of her eighth grade year, what it felt like to live like a Princess. (She had been very careful about not boasting about *that* trip since then). Yet the only thing she could tell them about London was that her wonderful cousin had made little improvement in her athletic capabilities, or that the balls were great. Most girls were jealous that Alyx had gone to London and been at state events that princes attended, brushing elbows with London's elite, but Alyx just found it all a bore. She and Kate were two of the youngest at the balls. She always played the dutiful niece and was polite and listened to all of the women who always had some problem to complain about. Sometimes there were handsome young men who would ask her and Kate to dance, but somehow even that felt wrong, like she didn't belong. She didn't like being in the spot light, and would have preferred to be in the shadows, gliding across the dance floor to do something that got her adrenalin pumping; something dangerous.

Alyx stood up, grabbed her iPhone 4 and Mac book, and put them in her large leather purse she used as a backpack for school. As she climbed down the stairs to the tarmac, Stephan Cross, the Chauffeur of her uncle's car, opened the door. Before she entered the car, Stephan greeted her in a very professional way, except for a mischievous smirk that he always seemed to have when Alyx was around. Despite his betrayal of knowing her quite well, the professionalism he displayed was something that Alyx had only ever witnessed while she was in London at the palace. Stephan closed the door behind Alyx leaving her in the roomy backseat of a 2011 Audi A6. The interior had nice black leather seats that were very luxurious. The car was still new and had that distinctive smell of new car and leather that Alyx loved.

"Did you have a good flight?" Michael asked. Alyx looked over at her uncle and cousin and smiled.

"Yes. Thank you." She answered. She observed the people in the car. Kate seemed different than she had a year ago and her uncle looked as if he could use a rise in spirits. Alyx tried to think of something she could say. "I like the new car. Audi's are nice. It's *much* better than that Jaguar that MI6 gave you last summer. I must admit though that I am partial to German cars. I just got a Volkswagen." Alyx finally said. She smiled and just looked out the window, for the first time she was actually seeing London. The buses and tourists, the age-old buildings with a priceless history, and Alyx just had to smile and whisper, "London's beautiful."

Michael saw the look in Alyx' eye as she stared out the window and decided to leave her to herself. He realized how little she had actually seen of London. London really was a place that many Americans loved to visit. The historical sights and the native accents drew many to this country every year. Alyx could probably brag that she lived here but she really didn't get to enjoy the sights. It would be better to let her see some of the sights than to pick a fight by admitting he liked the Jaguar XJ that MI6 had given him as part of their fleet.

Alyx stared out at the pedestrian traffic as they had stopped at the stop light. There were all sorts of people. She thought about how easy it would be to blend into that crowd, no matter who you were. It would be difficult to identify anyone in the crowd, yet there, in the crowd, was a female cyclist that Alyx recognized. She involuntarily looked back into the car, as if to verify a fact she already knew. Kate was in the car, but she had seen someone identical to her. Alyx looked back out the window as the light turned green and the car started moving. Alyx watched as the crowd spread out, hoping to get another look at the cyclist. Alyx looked all over, but she was gone.

Something about seeing the cyclist made Alyx feel uneasy, and the more she thought about it, the more details she recalled about the drive, how there had been someone behind them since they left the airport.

They had a tail.

She couldn't help feeling like something was wrong. It was a standard MI6 tail, in one of those Jaguar XJs that MI6 had filled their fleet with the previous summer. This was definitely MI6 with their standard 100 meters behind, as her uncle had explained to her years before when Rafael had been in town and they had been provided with a tail as part of the increased security against Rafael. The difference was Michael knew that time. If MI6 felt like her Uncle needed a tail, without him knowing, something was very wrong. The cyclist just proved it.

Her Uncle noticed her unease. "Is there something wrong Alyx?" Alyx didn't answer. "Is everything alright?" he asked again, only getting more concerned. "Alyx"

"Huh?" she said as she turned to her Uncle. "Sorry, I was just thinking." Alyx shook her head like she was trying to forget something, shaking off an evil thought.

"Is everything alright?" Michael asked again.

"Yeah, I just have a feeling that this summer will be more exciting than usual. That's all." Alyx smiled and looked back out the window.

Michael wasn't so sure. Something was wrong and he could see it in her eyes. She was so much like her namesake, his late wife Ally. She had the same hair, the same eyes, with the bright blue iris that was surrounded by a cadet blue ring. In some respects, she looked more like his wife Ally than Kate did.

Alyx had said she had a feeling. That was another thing that reminded him of his wife. Ally had had a very good instinct. If she had said she had a feeling about something, she was usually correct. The same was true of Alyx. Her instinct almost always proved correct. That is what scared Michael the most. Alyx had seen something that led her to believe there would be a change in their life this summer.

And she wouldn't tell him what it was.

14:53 BST (UTC +1)
Orleans Road, London

Lynn cursed herself for being made. She was a well-trained spy and couldn't believe she hadn't been more careful. All it took was a moment to kill a spy and for all she knew her little slip up could have just cost her dearly. She knew the importance of getting this mission *perfect* and she hoped she hadn't just messed it all up with her mistake.

Lynn was a good spy. That was the point of her training. She had been raised in a spy family to instill in her the most important lessons a spy needs to know. The result was a 14-year-old girl who was just as capable as James Bond, without the kills and the double-o-status. She could tail almost anyone, break into almost anywhere and hack almost anything. She had trained for one mission, and this was it. And she may have just blown it.

Lynn's assignment had been simple. It was a simple tail that any spy could do. It would take a real fool to mess it up and be detected. It consisted of several parts. The first was a black 2010 Jaguar XJ that tailed the Feilds' Black Audi from the London City Airport all the way to Feilds Palace, almost. The second was a rotating lead consisting of a silver Mercedes, a black Volvo, a white van, a blue Volkswagen Bora, a white Renault Clio, and a black Vauxhall Insignia. Then when Feilds' car turned on to Orleans Road, Lynn turned out and followed on her bike. She only had about a half of a mile to follow them and somehow *she* had been the one to be made.

All she had done was let her guard down for a second; she let her mind stray from her goals. Every spy knew how difficult their job was, they knew the concentration needed for the job, and the consequences for not keeping that concentration. For that reason, they eliminated distractions. All spies knew the unwritten rule; do not fall in love. If only it was that easy, to not love, not care. But it wasn't that easy, as Lynn had found out. It was really hard to turn your back on those who raised you, even if they told you to. She thought she had done a great job of controlling her feelings, until her adoptive parents disappeared, assumed dead. She had lost it, and even now, three years later, still struggled with the thought of it. They had taught her much of what she knew and she struggled to overcome the feeling that if they had been caught, then she would be too, that she wasn't a good spy.

Lynn watched the viscount's Audi drive through the gate of the palace as her thoughts strayed. Having feelings made you a great girl, but it was a recipe for a very bad *spy*. And the more she evaluated her life, the more she recognized the pattern.

Lynn continued past the gate where the Audi had turned in, to her meeting point where she met the black BMW that would take her into Feilds Palace. She ditched her bike at a park and climbed into the back seat. The car pulled away toward the Palace. Lynn looked over at her superior that sat on the other side of the car. "Are you ready Ms. McFeild?" he asked.

"Yes, quite" came Lynn's reply. She hated how formal it all sounded, but that was a spy's life. Always acting formal around other agents, acting as if you have no clue who they are even though you have known them for years.

"Everything that you should need is in the box." His hand moved slightly as a gesture that it was in the middle seat. Lynn picked it up and opened it to find the clothes she was to wear to the meeting with Feilds. She pulled the pencil skirt out of the box as her superior continued. Lynn did not look at him. She had seen him on several occasions and he was always the same. He had the same clipped voice now as when he sent her on her first mission. His dark hair was always kept in the same military length haircut and he always wore the same black suit with the tan rain over coat. He had always been stern towards Lynn. She thought it might have had something to do with who her mother was. Her mother's family was royalty in American espionage, so, naturally, Lynn was expected to measure up to their reputation, despite not being raised by them. If he felt any need to be more helpful and understanding as he prepped Lynn for her most important mission, he didn't show it.

As she pulled the pencil skirt on over her clothes, he continued. "You may read-in only the palace staff who will be most beneficial to helping establish your cover. Try to keep your exposure and existence to a minimum. We will try to keep MI6 presence scarce, as to not alert non-essential personnel of the threat. Unfortunately, that means you will be largely on your own. You will have no check ins. There are no reports to be written when you are done. We will also be informing your father of your existence, which means when you complete your assignment, you will not return to MI6 unless your father permits." He turned to look at her, and then broke character. "Unfortunately his habits tell us he won't." He faked a cough. "If you wish to return, you may when you can legally make the decision to return." Lynn pulled a briefcase out of the box and placed it in her lap.

"Threat analysis determined that Exchange Protocol is the best option, correct."

"Yes. It will be up to your discretion which protection protocol will best suit the situation once you are imbedded, but all of our intel suggests it is a mid-level threat best thwarted by the Exchange Protocol, that is, if you trust your mother's parameters." He answered.

Lynn didn't remember her birth mother, but she had read enough about her to know that she was rarely wrong. She had lived by her rules and protocols. The one time she'd broken them had eventuated her death. "We would be unwise not to trust them." Lynn agreed.

He nodded. "Well then. Unless you need clarification on anything I believe that's all." He finished.

"No sir." She answered. He nodded and opened his door. She did the same and followed him to the door of her new home.

14:55 BST (UTC +1)
Feilds Palace, London

The Audi pulled up to the massive front gates before slowly proceeding into the courtyard. As Stephan turned the car off, a couple of footmen opened the trunk and took Alyx' bags upstairs. The door attendant came and opened the car door for Michael, and he and Kate got out. They had long since given up on trying to open the door for Alyx; she was always much too fast to do it on her own. Many of the servants the family employed were strong young men, but they all knew Alyx could, and would take them down in a heartbeat.

There was often a look tourists got when they saw Fields Palace. Alyx no longer had that look. She looked bored, and she had just gotten here. She had the same look Kate had every time she came home: a look of familiarity. It was a look that Michael himself knew well. He had experienced the same feeling for years. As he saw the two girls together, he realized how stupid he had been to doubt that they could become fast friends.

If Kate and Alyx hadn't been two years apart and almost polar opposites, they might have passed as twins. They both looked so much like their mothers. It was purely personal preference that made them look so different. Kate had the same strawberry brunette hair as Alyx, but she had gotten the Feilds family straight hair. Alyx usually left her hair the naturally wavy she got from her dad. Kate's eyes were the same perfect color of blue that Alyx had, but darker. Kate was already quite tall, but still shorter than Alyx by two inches, it seemed.

They had different personalities to add to their physical differences. Michael would have liked to say it was due to being raised in two different countries, but he didn't think so. There was something deeper. Alyx had many of the personality traits of his late wife Ally. Kate did not. Given, Ally had died before Kate could form her own memories of her mother, and Alyx had been raised by her twin, who he who he knew to be identical to his wife in almost every way, personality among them. Kate was rebellious and ungrateful; she didn't have the qualities he had loved about her mother. Kate had a growing attitude of being disrespectful, ever evident the past year. Hopefully Alyx could influence her to change and mature into the young lady she was expected to be, taking on the title that would be passed down to her.

Michael looked at his watch. His appointment with MI6 was soon. They had some vital information that needed passed on to him. History suggested it was something to do with his older brother, who had forsaken his claim to their father's title and responsibility when he ran away to Russia to get married. Whether the meeting was about his brother, or something else, it was not something he needed Kate and Alyx involved in.

"Kate, why don't you follow Alyx upstairs and help her settle in?" he asked.

"Dad…"she whined.

"I'm sorry, it wasn't a question. Help Alyx settle in." He corrected.

Kate huffed off. Alyx looked at Michael in disbelief. He shrugged. This was normal for him now. Alyx followed her cousin, shaking her head.

With the girls gone up to their residence, he walked through the first floor to his office area. "Your three o'clock is waiting for you in your office sir," his secretary informed him as he walked in.

"Thank you. Hold my calls please." He said.

"Yes sir"

Michael walked into his office. He saw a man dressed in a very nondescript fashion standing by the window. "Can I offer you something to drink" Michael asked.

The agent by the window turned around, but did not answer, instead, a familiar voice answered from the couch by the door, "No thank you."

Michael turned to the couch. The agent that had been by the window walked up next to the girl sitting on the couch. "Kate, I thought I told you to go upstairs and help Alyx."

The girl quickly answered. "I'm sure you did, and Kate is probably doing just that. I'm Lynn, Lynn McFeild."

Michael went and sat down at his desk. "What is the meaning of this? Tyson, you may have been friends, colleagues, whatever you were with Ally, but this just is…"

"Michael, this is your daughter." The agent replied. Lynn catalogued what she heard. So he *had* known her mother and his first name was Tyson. Tyson Barnes didn't have a bad ring to it.

"I haven't seen you since just after Ally died, and all of a sudden, you show up with a girl who looks like my daughter, and you tell me she is my… how is that possible. If she's not Kate, she can't be my daughter. Maybe a niece, but not my daughter." Michael insisted.

Barnes pulled a paper out of his briefcase. "Her DNA test…" he handed the paper across the desk to Michael. Lynn subconsciously rubbed the inside of her left elbow as she remembered the needle that had been used to draw the blood for the test. "Of course if you don't trust our test, you can run one of your own."

"How old are you?" Michael asked Lynn.

"Fourteen, as of June 1st." She said.

"Why now? Tyson it has been 14 years. What games are you playing?" Michael asked.

"That's how long it took to train her." Tyson said.

"Train her? What made you think it would be ok to train my daughter as a spy?" Michael yelled.

"It's what Ally wanted, Michael."

"You don't bloody well know what she wanted. No one did. Not me. Not even her twin."

Barnes handed Michael another stack of papers out of his briefcase. "She did want Lynn to be trained. She wrote certain protocols, that should Kate fall into danger, Lynn could be activated to eliminate the threat. The reason we are bringing her to you now is because Chemist is planning something and she could better do her job from here than the outside."

"Her job? Tyson she's a child."

"Yes, her job, read the file would you. Ally really loved you. Even in death she did everything she could to protect you from her enemies, and your enemies."

Michael looked at Lynn. "She's a child! How can she possibly do her job? I couldn't even protect Ally from my enemies. She couldn't protect herself."

"Lynn is the one member of your family, of Ally's family, that your enemies and Ally's enemies don't know exist."

Lynn spoke up. "Mum knew what she was doing. She saw what was to come somehow. I'm ready for this. I only wish there were a way I could stop mum's enemies as easily as we will stop Chemist."

Michael looked at Lynn. She was even more like Ally than Alyx. She was selfless and brave. "I have no doubt." Michael said. "I just, I need time to process it I guess." He exhaled before continuing. "You said something about Chemist. I assume you mean my brother Rafael."

Barnes stepped forward. "Yes. Unfortunately, we were informed by one of our best assets that he is planning something: an attack on Kate this time."

"He has always been such a coward. He will never attack me directly, he won't ever call me like a normal brother, and he always finds a way to blame me everything that happened." Michael shook his head.

"That's why I thought using Lynn for this would be a good idea. You may not agree, but Lynn is well trained and she could easily swap places with Kate, and keep her safe. If we use Lynn this way, we could stop Rafael for good."

"I guess, it sounds like a risk Ally would take. You're willing to do this?" Michael asked.

"Yes." Lynn responded.

"I don't see why not then."

"Lynn remains with you afterwards. We will discuss specifics about that once we have Chemist. If everything is cleared up I will leave you to go about normal business." Tyson said.

"Yes. I'll have my secretary show you out." Michael offered.

"That's not necessary. I'll be in touch soon." Tyson walked out, closing the door behind him.

Michael sat in silence, looking at the daughter he had just been told existed. "You can have the room next to Kate." He finally said. "Alyx has the room on the east side of Kate's, but the room on the other side is open. I can have it made up for you. I'll call the girls down to take you up, show you around." Michael rambled, at a loss of what to say

"Thank you." Lynn answered.

"What did you say your surname was?" Michael asked as he dialed into the PA system.

"McFeild. Just like yours and Kate's but Irish. I couldn't have the same surname as you, so mum came up with it. It's my cover I guess you could say."

Michael nodded. It sounded just like something Ally would do. She designed Lynn's name to tell him that she was his daughter. She was speaking to him even now. How many times had she said she loved his mother's name? Kaitlyn. She had twins and their names were Kate and Lynn: Kate-lynn. Then McFeild was a combination of his last name, and Sarah's married name.

Apparently, he had never needed to protect Kate on his own. Ally had been doing it all along.

15:10 BST (UTC +1)
Feilds Palace, London

Kate sprawled herself across Alyx' bed, and watched as Alyx put the clothes she had brought in her suitcase into her closet. Kate gazed up at the ornate ceiling, and the simplicity of the bed Alyx had chosen a few years before.

"Alyx" Kate started.

"Yeah," Alyx called from the massive walk-in closet.

"Why did you choose this bed? You could have had anything you wanted." Kate asked

"I didn't want anything. I like practicality and affordability." Alyx said. She walked out of the closet. "That was practical, and something I would have bought if your dad had let me."

Kate sat up. "Oh." She said.

Alyx laughed. "What were you expecting me to say Kate?"

"Nothing, I guess." Kate shrugged.

"What's up Kate? Is something bugging you?" Alyx asked

Kate sat up straighter, back straight, feet touching the floor. "Why would you ask such a question?"

"Kate, I know you. You do not stay silent for so long, and you never ask a question with no meaning." Alyx asserted. "What's wrong?"

Kate paused and looked down at her feet. "What you said in the car, about the summer being more exciting, it… what did you mean?" Kate collected her thoughts enough to ask.

Alyx looked at Kate, contemplating how to tell her, or what to tell her. She had to decide if telling her she had seen someone who looked just like Kate was a good idea, how to tell her if it was, or what to tell her if it wasn't. Alyx didn't quite know what she had seen herself, just that she had had a feeling, and something had changed. Alyx looked at her cousin, the daughter of her mom's twin sister. Alyx was older than Kate was and had spent time with her Aunt Ally. Alyx had been raised in an American home with both a mom and a dad. She knew she couldn't have been more different from Kate. She didn't know what it was like to grow up without a mom. Sure Kate had told her about it, and in a way, Alyx was as much a friend, and sister figure to Kate as she was a mother figure, but it didn't mean Alyx felt what Kate did on a day-to-day basis.

Still Alyx was an only child. In that much, Alyx was just like Kate, and she knew that telling Kate she had seen someone who bore a remarkable resemblance to her, she might get hopes that she wasn't so alone, and hopes like that hurt when they were crushed.

"You know the feelings I get," Alyx started, her decision made, "I don't always know where they come from. Maybe it was my seeing London for the first time."

"You come here every summer." Kate said. "How can you have not seen London before? Why would you *want* to see London?"

Alyx laughed again. "That coming from *little city girl*. You try living in rural cities around the United States, where the tallest building is our City Hall, and that is because it has this little non-functional, purely decorative tower that makes it maybe five stories tall. Usually it's only three. I mean Kate, you live in a *palace*."

Kate looked down. "I may live in a palace, but I'm…, you're not alone. I think in a way, you live in a luxury I can only glimpse that when you come." Alyx nodded. She knew it was true. Alyx may have shared Kate's lack of siblings, but Kate didn't have the social life of school— she had no friends with whom she could discuss things. There was something about a security detail that drove people away.

"I'm sorry Kate, that's not what I meant, but I'm here now so what shall we do?"

Kate laughed. "*Shall* we do? Why did you say *shall*? Are you mimicking my accent because I rarely say *shall*."

Alyx started laughing with Kate. "I like this version of you *much* better." Alyx said in the middle of laughing. Kate smiled. "Seriously. What are we going to do?"

"Serious?" Kate asked, stomping her foot three times after.

The intercom came on, interrupting the girls laughter from the stomps, a ritual from when they were younger. "Girls, I need you in my office." Michael's voice boomed through the speakers, recently added. Kate threw herself back onto Alyx' bed.

"Well there goes all the fun…" Kate mumbled. Alyx got up and walked toward the door. "Where are you going!?" Kate shrieked.

"To your dad like he asked." Alyx said as she walked through the door. Kate jumped off the bed and chased after Alyx.

"Alyx!" she whined. "Why do you have to be so responsive?" she complained under her breath.

Alyx sensed that Kate didn't want to go. Honestly, she herself would prefer to stay up in her room and catch up with Kate, but Alyx had learned that no matter what, you respect authority, especially parents and family, like Michael was, and he had asked them to come to his office. Kate had changed over the last year, *drastically*. Alyx smiled to herself to think that she wouldn't let her bad attitude last beyond the summer.

Alyx spun around and walked in front of Kate backwards, a huge smile on her face, the dubious one she always had when she was about to propose something that she already knew Kate couldn't object to. Kate rolled her eyes. "What are you thinking now?"

"Oh nothing." Alyx smirked. "I was just thinking about the last time your dad called both of us to his office. Who had we met that day?" Alyx paused, pretending to think. "Oh yes, it was that really cute boy who was the teenage son of some diplomat in town. I believe I beat you into his office that day and, well, he followed me around that next week…" Alyx taunted.

Kate's eyes narrowed as she remembered that week a couple years before. She had been so jealous of Alyx that week, it wasn't funny. As she watched Alyx and realized what she was inferring, her eyes got wide. Alyx smirked as she saw that Kate had finally gotten what she was saying and turned around before starting to run. "Oh you!" Kate screamed as she took off, realizing that she now had to catch up to Alyx, the track star.

Alyx laughed as she ran, knowing that she had just convinced Kate to willingly *run* to obey her father. That and she knew there was no way Kate could stay even close to her, never mind pass her. It was almost too much fun, almost too easy to taunt Kate. It was almost not worth it. *Almost.*

Alyx listened to Kate's pounding feet, and heavy breathing behind her. Alyx looked over her shoulder while still running. "Come on Kate, you're making this too easy!" she taunted. Alyx turned her body around and started running backwards. "Someone obviously stopped working out after I left last summer." Alyx said, her breathing no heavier than normal, running backwards, still faster than Kate was. Alyx smirked before turning back around. "No more going easy on you," Alyx said, then picked up her pace to full speed.

Alyx slowed as she approached the door to her uncle's office then opened it and walked in. She came in and plopped down on the couch, "Kate will be here soon—" Alyx started, but stopped. "Who's this?" Alyx asked pointing at the girl on the couch next to her.

"Lynn McFeild. I'm Kate's twin." Lynn said.

"You— I saw you—"Alyx paused, at a loss of words. Her thoughts weren't coming as clearly as they usually did. Kate walked in and Lynn smiled at Alyx.

"You." Breath "Are." Breath "Evil." Kate said pointing at Alyx, not noticing the figure next to her until she noticed that Alyx wasn't smiling, she was confused, and it was evident on her face. Little did Kate know…

"Kate" Michael started, "Meet your twin sister Lynn. I would like you to show her to the room next to yours, the one on the West. That will be her room now." Kate stood stunned, panting. Alyx raised her hand. "Alyx, when have I ever made you raise your hand?" Michael said.

Alyx put her hand down. "Who's older?" she asked pointing from the girl next to her to the girl at the door.

"I…uh" Michael started. It dawned on him that he hadn't asked Tyson while he was still there.

"She is." Lynn said. "Lynn comes second in Katelynn, so I'm the second, or the younger one. Lynn leaned over to Alyx as they both looked at the panting Kate looking at her dad. "What did you do to her?"

Alyx laughed. "I reminded her about the last time that your dad called us to his office then took off running. Naturally, she followed."

"What happened last time?" Lynn laughed.

"We met a boy, and since I was the first one here, your dad had me accompany him everywhere while he was here. He was *cute*. Kate was jealous." Lynn nodded that she understood. Kate had been punished by not being able to talk to a boy she had a crush on.

"I'm not sure I understand how most girls think. I mean boys are competition right?" Lynn asked.

"That's how I see it…" Alyx agreed. Michael cleared his throat, before she could continue any further, giving her a look that she recognized from the time she spent translating in his office. He was about to make a phone call that was classified and needed the office cleared. Alyx gave a slight nod. "Shall I show you to where your new room is?" She asked Lynn.

"Should we drag her with us?" Lynn asked.

"Sure. You can carry her feet, I'll carry her head." Alyx said.

"I'll walk." Kate said. Alyx and Lynn got up off the couch and followed Kate out the door. Michael shook his head as he watched the three girls leave his office. He hoped Kate and Lynn could get along as well as Alyx had been able to get along with Lynn…

Only time could tell how this would all turn out.

15:18 BST (UTC +1)
Feilds Palace, London

The walk up the stairs was made in silence. Kate walked the three of them down the corridor. As she went, she pointed out Alyx' room, and then pointed out her own room. When they got to Lynn's room, Kate opened the door and held it for Lynn.

"Did you guys want to come in while I unpack?" Lynn asked.

"Yeah, sure." Kate said. She went in and showed Lynn to the closet. Alyx heard Kate talk about clothes and offer to let Lynn borrow some. Alyx smiled at the kinship that they shared. "You're not so alone," she whispered to herself.

Alyx walked away, and went into her room. She laid down on her bed and tried to think. Since running down stairs, she had been having a difficult time keeping her thoughts clear. She tried to recall information as she sat there, but not only could she not recall the information, but she spent so much effort looking for the next logical thought, she couldn't remember the previous one.

For the first couple of minutes, she tried to pass it off as oxygen deprivation. However, it went on for too long to be just that. She grabbed her swimsuit and towel then went downstairs to the indoor swimming pool the palace had. It was heated and Alyx knew it was her best bet for resolving her mental problems. Exercising brought a certain clarity she hadn't been able to find elsewhere. Her mind would go on autopilot, taking her where she wanted without too much thought. It cleared her mind. When she ran her track events, her mind cleared, and she heard nothing, or almost nothing. She didn't think about what she had to do to finish the race, her body just did it, and she was free from all the thoughts that hampered her conscious mind.

Swimming and cycling had a similar effect. Her arms and legs set a steady rhythm and she glided through the air or water, whatever it was she was in. That was what she needed now: clarity. She went into one of the stall like changing rooms and changed into her swimsuit. She left her clothes in the stall locker, grabbed her towel, and walked out to the pool.

Not everyone saw the joy that swimming laps could bring. It seems like the most boring part of swimming. Whenever there is a pool party, you never go and see a bunch of people swimming laps (that's swim practice), you see games. Yet that was Alyx' favorite part of swimming because it was relaxing. As she got in the pool and set herself into the rhythm of swimming laps, she expected her mind to clear, and it did. She focused on the problems she had seen, could not solve, and thought through them.

She thought about the parts of the story that bugged her, the parts that didn't make sense. Alyx understood the reasons behind her aunt's death. Rafael, her uncle's brother, and also his sworn enemy, had been the cause of her death, or at least that was what she, Kate and her uncle had been led to believe. Yet Lynn didn't say that. She said *this family's*, suggesting Rafael wasn't the alone, but there weren't any others to her knowledge.

Alyx tried to ignore what the implications of Lynn's statements had been, but Lynn's sudden appearance brought more doubts about being able to trust her parents than she liked. She enjoyed having relationships based on trust and Alyx thought that her parents had treated her in a very mature way, constantly discussing decisions that affected the family with her. Something about the situation brought all of those discussions back (not in as much clarity as at the time) and Alyx could almost find hidden double meanings in it all.

What else were her parents keeping from her?

Alyx glided to a stop and came up for air. As she held herself up on the side of the pool, her chin resting on the concrete, one of the twins walked in. Alyx gave a small laugh.

"You know if I didn't know better I might have made fun of Kate for acting like two people." She said jovially.

"What gave me away as Lynn?" she asked. She sat down on the edge of the pool next to where Alyx was resting, putting her feet in the water.

Alyx smiled. "I may not know you but I know Kate *very* well and she does not wear that shirt, *ever*. Trust me, I've tried." She said referring to the light blue athletic shirt.

Lynn smiled. "Now I know why she gave it to me."

Alyx nodded. "She's a sly one. Don't worry, we can take you two shopping and you can get identical clothes. I can't promise you won't hate it, but you know…"

Lynn laughed and Alyx joined in. Alyx dunked her head under the water quickly, pushing down the short hairs that had started to dry. As Alyx came back up, she zoned out, thinking about what she had been trying to work out, but everything was fuzzy again.

"Alyx are you ok?" Lynn asked.

Alyx snapped her attention back to Lynn. "Yeah, I…" Alyx drifted off trying to come up with an excuse "I think I'm just suffering with… le décollage horaire. As stupid as it sounds, I can only remember what it's called in French right now."

"Yeah, jet lag kills." Lynn agreed, "So what can I do?"

"Not much, I think. I think I'm just going to go to bed. I caught some sleep on the plane, but eight hours is a lot to lose." Lynn nodded and scooted over a bit to let Alyx climb out of the pool. She picked up her towel and went into the changing stall. When she came out dressed a couple minutes later, Lynn was still sitting on the edge of the pool, looking intently at the water. "It's been nice meeting you," She said as she walked out.

Lynn turned around to reply but she was already gone.

17:28 BST (UTC +1)
Feilds Palace, London

Lynn stared across the still water of the pool. It was great to finally be with family. She had made friends, sure, but family was different; it was natural. She had felt an instant kinship with Alyx and Kate. She understood Alyx because they had similar interests and Kate was fun and helpful. There was also that joking and loving teasing going on. She felt connected to them.

It was nice to finally meet the people she risked her life to protect.

Lynn looked up when she heard the bell that was used to indicate dinner. She looked at her dark blue diver's watch and thought to herself that she would either love or hate the punctuality of this place. When Kate said dinner was at 17:30, she meant on the dot.

Kate had given her the general idea, or basic itinerary of the place. Breakfast was ready anytime starting at seven and you could eat any time until 9:30 when they put it away and started on lunch. Lunch was served at noon, dinner at 17:30, and if you needed food at any other time, there was a smaller kitchen regularly stocked, and always open so you could make your own food. It was less formal than the rest of the house with a microwave, stove, oven and fridge, which made it feel like a normal house. There was a nice island with a sink in the middle of the room complete with tall chairs. There was also a nice table that Kate said was hardly used by anyone other than Alyx, and Michael had said Ally had too, long ago.

Kate had informed her that dinner was a formal meal. When Lynn had pressed her what that meant, she had said they liked to keep to the traditions of old: the several course meals, the fancy ball gowns, tuxedos, and the sort. When Lynn had expressed skepticism, she held her line. Kate *had* finally relented and told Lynn that her skirt suit would be fine, but for this occasion only.

Lynn pulled her feet out of the water. She hated the idea of wearing that awful thing again, but she had to do as her family asked. She headed down the corridor, turned, and walked down the corridor towards the closest lift. As she walked down the corridor, she ignored the french doors on her right that led to the courtyard, and the archways on her left that led into the library. She knew from studying the plans when she had first been told about her mother and who she was, that the library had tall two story vaulted ceilings, the south wall had huge floor to ceiling widows flooding the room with an enormous amount of natural light which added a special feeling to the room, and that Lord Fields owned an extensive collection of literature from all over the world. Unfortunately, she didn't think she would have much time to explore the collection that technically now belonged to her over the next few weeks, and she knew for sure she didn't have time to do so now. She walked straight to the end of the corridor and pressed the button to go up. The lift immediately dinged open. Lynn pressed the button for the fifth floor.

This house was excessively big. The spy in her thought of all the places to hide, how easy it would be to disappear, do this or that. She briefly thought that she should enjoy this place, before she remembered that she had to keep it secure. As the doors opened and she was sprinting down the corridor to her room, she decided it was too big.

She was in and out of her room in no time. Her training had made her faster at changing in and out of clothes. It made it harder for someone to recognize you if you weren't wearing the same thing as a minute before. She sprinted down the corridor again, or as close to a sprint she could do in the awful skirt and tight-toed shoes. She wanted to see if Alyx was coming down and tried to, but when she went to open the door to Alyx' room on her way, it was locked and she thought she heard a shower running. She didn't have enough time so she continued down to dinner.

By the time she had gotten back down to the formal dining hall, dinner had been served. She peeked through the archway that led into the dining hall and froze. She waited and watched, unsure as to whether she could go in, and if she could, if she should. She watched her family as someone on the outside looking in, something she had been trained to do. She stepped back and observed with detached interest.

She watched as her family, her father, her twin, laughed at some joke that they had shared. Kate pointed her fork at her dad and made some remark in the gasps of air between laughing fits. Her father, *the* Michael Fields, who had visited with the Queen on a number of occasions, laughed hard enough that he was red. At that moment, she was no longer the girl, but the agent, trying to gather the information needed to fit in when she decided it was time to infiltrate. That was when she moved, a calculated movement, maybe, or an accident, but she reached over and stroked the ornate trimming around the arch, and the laughing stopped. Michael turned towards the door and saw Lynn. "You're late" Michael said with a tone so serious it was like a flipped switch from the tone he had heard him using with Kate.

She looked down at her feet. She didn't belong here. She was an outsider. This had always been the cover she had the greatest difficulty with successfully pulling off. She would say she was wrong to push herself into worlds she didn't belong to, to try to live lives that weren't hers, but that was her job. She did, however, feel that it was wrong to push herself into this world. This was her family, but she felt as if it were another mission. She didn't know how to be a daughter, a sister, a cousin. She knew how to be the spy, and she was good at that.

She belonged to her mom's world, not her father's. Not to a world with formal dinners, with family. She sacrificed that so her family could enjoy that. Not her.

Lynn took a deep breath in, closed her eyes, breathed out, and then opened her eyes. "Sorry." She began humbly, not at all sounding like the experienced agent she was. "I was... Alyx and I were... We went..."Lynn tried to explain, but nothing seemed right. Lynn didn't really have an exact activity she was doing, she didn't do anything with Alyx, she had simply talked to her and it had been a while since that conversation had ended. Lynn could have come up with any plausible lie she could to explain why she hadn't been to dinner on time. She was good at creating covers. She could have said she was checking security measures, or finding the blind spots. But it all sounded wrong. They were all lies.

"I lost track of time and had to hurry to get changed when I heard the dinner bell." She finally admitted. It was as good as any explanation she could have come up with and was rooted in truth. The dinner bell had thrown her off guard, but not because she didn't know what time it was. It was the spy's curse, to have that sound of the monotonous tick of the seconds of the clock passing by. She could wake up and automatically she knew the time. There were other variables involved. As an afterthought she added, "I hope this is formal enough?"

Michael turned to Kate. Lynn watched as they exchanged a knowing look. Of all the things she had been trained for, reading expressions was the hardest. A spy needed to know if her company believed her, if they were suspicious, hiding something, etcetera, etcetera. She had picked it up. She was good at it. At least she had thought she was. She watched the exchange and turned to leave. There was something there that seemed to say she didn't belong, and Lynn agreed. She stopped at the sound of sudden laughter. It was as full and pleasant as it had been when she walked in, natural. It wasn't forced, but completely natural and comfortable.

"Come back Lynn." Michael managed between laughs. She turned around and walked back to the archway. Her father sat there, his right hand out beckoning for her to sit next to him. Lynn walked around and sat on her father's right, with Kate on her right. "We saved you a seat between us." Michael beckoned the butler, signaling for him to bring out Lynn's food.

Kate kept looking over at Lynn and laughing, Michael letting out a chuckle here and there. Lynn looked between them. "What?" Lynn asked at a loss to why they were laughing.

"Dinner's… not… formal." Kate giggled. Lynn looked to her father and saw his smile grow. She looked between her sister and her father, for the first time noticing their clothes. Michael was wearing the same thing he had been when she had met him in his office, dress slacks and a polo shirt. Kate wore a nice blouse and jeans. Lynn was still glad she had changed, but suddenly felt ridiculous wearing a skirt. For some reason she felt like the athletic shirt was a little underdressed, no matter what they said.

Lynn's plate was brought out, along with the rest of the food. She chuckled to herself to think her new family had gone all out to play a prank on her. They weren't so different from other families. Lynn may not have belonged to the formal dinners, or the family life even, but she sure could make an effort to fit into her family. She paused to think that she may have belonged to her mom's world, but this was part of it. Her mom was big on family, and even if Lynn wasn't, that didn't mean she couldn't try to be.

18:17 BST (UTC +1)
Feilds Palace, London

Alyx flopped face down onto her bed, hair still dripping wet, already in waves. She had put on a pair of light blue running shorts and a white V-neck short-sleeved shirt. Technically it was a men's undershirt, but it was cheap and easy to personalize, and comfortable. She had used light blue puff paint to write her last name on the back of the shirt. Her first name was written on the sleeve, and she and her friends had written a cute saying on the front in the same color as her name.

She closed her eyes, trying to evade the pounding headache, the dry mouth, and to succumb to her desire to sleep. She had never experienced jet lag, but she knew that this was *not* jet lag. It was a good excuse to use on Lynn, and Alyx had hoped to use it to explain her own worry off, but it didn't make sense, and, unfortunately, she couldn't convince herself it did. That just meant she was left with no explanation for her maladies.

She flipped over onto her back and stared up at the ceiling. She had also ruled out dehydration. It sounded just like the symptoms of dehydration, but she knew that she had made sure to drink plenty of water, and she had made sure to have much more to drink since she had first started to notice the headache and dry mouth. It hadn't gotten any better, if anything it had gotten worse.

She picked up her I-phone off the bed next to her and ignored the notification on her lock screen, boasting "Bernard S Jackson kicks off 2012 Presidential Campaign," as she looked at her phone to confirm the fact she already knew. It was about six in the evening. It didn't take much effort to do the quick calculations to tell her it was only ten in the morning in the small Californian town of Tracy where she lived, eight hours behind London. Maybe her exhaustion had a plausible explanation and it wasn't connected to the other symptoms. She had been up for 26 hours with only fitful naps on planes since then.

She grudgingly stood up and started walking to the door. She may have been up for 26 hours but she needed food and more water before she went to sleep. That and she needed to let her uncle know she was going to bed so he wasn't expecting her at any later time.

She padded out of her room and went to the elevator. She took it all the way down to the ground floor and exited into the corridor. As she walked into the Dining Hall, Lynn looked up at her. Alyx studied Lynn for a second and could only crack a smile. They had played the newbie joke on her. Alyx could only imagine what Lynn must be thinking looking at the ultra-casual clothes she was wearing.

Alyx walked through the dining hall to a corridor that led back to the self-serve kitchen. She grabbed a paper plate from the cupboard and walked back out. She went to the empty side of the table, closest to the archway. She served up some food and set it down, then went back to the kitchen to get a water bottle. She grabbed one from the fridge and walked out again. She came to stand behind the chair meant for her and waited for a pause in the conversation.

"Hey Alyx" Kate acknowledged.

Alyx smiled. "Hi." She replied. "Hey, Uncle Michael, I wanted to let you know I was going to go to bed. I think I'm a bit tired from the flight."

"Okay that's fine." He replied, a sort of sad smile on his face. It was a smile of understanding, meant for comfort. It would have helped, but Alyx knew that this was not just fatigue, but it wasn't something to worry her uncle about.

"Thank you" Alyx said. She picked up her plate and her water bottle and walked out of the room, heading back up to her room.

June 12th, 2011

09:40 MSK (UTC +4)
Feilds Estate, Moscow Russia

Lyshiria ran through the gates of her parents' estate, and slowed down to a walk. As she walked around the statue towards the front door, she paused her music and took the earbuds out of her ears. As she walked up the two steps that took her to the elegant mahogany doors with beautiful frosted glass insert, she removed her I-pod strap from her right shoulder and pulled the cleverly hidden key from behind the I-pod.

She opened the door and went in, dropping the key and the I-pod in a basket set on a beautiful hallway table as she entered, and retrieved her I-phone from the same basket. She unlocked it checking for the time and any new messages. She scrolled through her messages disinterested, then dutifully replied before relocking it.

She stretched her legs out a little bit before walking through the tiled entry. It was narrow, but stretched upward, opening onto the second story balcony at the top of the staircase. She walked past the staircase entrance and through to the main rooms of the house towards the kitchen. She entered the elegant kitchen to find her father sitting at the head of the table. The place in front of him looked newly cleared, and her father sat reading his English newspaper of choice. The front page boasted an article about the results of a London election. Their housekeeper was at the sink washing some dishes, which Lyshiria assumed were her fathers from his breakfast.

Lyshiria walked past the island where the housekeeper was to the fridge. She opened the door and grabbed the water pitcher from the center shelf. It was one of the pitchers commonly found in America that had a filter that the water ran through, removing particulate matter, before storing it. She set it down on the counter of the island and turned around toward the cupboard that had the cups in it. She grabbed one of them, a beautiful glass cup that her mother had had since as long as she could remember, but that she had only been able to use for the past few years, and poured herself a cup of water.

"Where have you been?" Her dad asked as she put the pitcher back.

"Я пошел для пробега," she answered in her native tongue. She took a drink from her cup of water, enjoying the refreshing cool after her run.

"Lyshiria Anastasiya" he scolded, "When I ask you a question in English, you answer in English. That goes for any language, and you know that. Try again."

Lyshiria rolled her eyes. "I went for a run. I go for a run every morning." She answered, her English flawless, very slightly marred by her Russian accent, more sounding like a natural British citizen, sounding perfectly like the Russian Brit she was.

"Better," he said, returning to his paper. "I need you to come see me in my office later, I have something to discuss with you."

"Why can't we discuss it now?" Lyshiria asked. "I have to pack for the trip to London with mother tomorrow."

"It is a discussion requiring privacy." He answered.

Lyshiria looked at the housekeeper, not showing interest in their conversation, but her work. "She doesn't speak English, only Russian."

"It is a more serious discussion." Her father snapped. Lyshiria nodded. "I have a meeting in a few minutes; it should run until about noon. If you will stop in after lunch, I would greatly appreciate it."

Lyshiria nodded in understanding. "I'll be there."

"Thank you." Her father said. "You have turned out very well Lysh, very well."

11:59 MSK (UTC +4)
Feilds Estate, Moscow Russia

Lyshiria stood in the middle of her room by her semi-packed suitcase. There were clothes strewn out on her bed and there was a pile behind her of clothing she had decided not to take, now practically blocking off the entrance to her closet. Lyshiria was stressed. Her mom held a key position in Russian Intelligence and because of her position had been asked to attend the conference held in London. Lyshiria may not have had the clearance, nor the permission to attend the actual conference, but her mom had secured the extra plane ticket for Lyshiria to go with her, as she was an only child and thought that she could use the bonding time. Lyshiria knew her father would like to go as well, but he wasn't allowed in London, especially not during the Intelligence Conference, unless he wanted to be arrested by British officials, and that wasn't something anyone wanted, especially not him. That meant that it was just Lyshiria accompanying her mother, and thus she felt extra pressure to represent her family, especially her family name, well. She was, after all, half-British.

Lyshiria looked at the clothes on her bed. She didn't have all that much that she thought would make her look presentable in London. That made it so the choice she had to make wasn't so much what to take but what not to take. She had been staring at the clothes on her bed trying to make a decision for hours, and yet the decision remained unmade, and her bed remained covered, her suitcase unpacked.

The clock in the hall struck noon, making all twelve incessant dings. Lyshiria half expected the day when that noise would turn her into a Cruella DeVille. Every time she heard it she wanted to, and usually did, throw herself onto her bed and cover her head with a pillow or two. On this unfortunate occasion, she couldn't, but dutifully, grudgingly, stood up and looked for the best possible way to the door, the easiest way to escape the madness that surrounded her. It took her awhile, but she eventually found a way to the door. Lyshiria silently wished she could escape her life just as easily…

Lyshiria got down stairs just in time to be served with her mother. They had three full time staff members that ran the house. They had the housekeeper, a cook, and a driver, not counting the grounds keeper, and other various maintenance staff who were paid weekly but only came on an as needed basis. It was the cook who brought their meal out to them, having finished it moments before. "Thank you" her mother, Nika, said in Russian. The cook dutifully nodded and pattered back to the kitchen. "Are you ready for tomorrow?" She asked Lyshiria.

"Not quite. I'm having a hard time choosing what to take to wear." She admitted, using the same Russian that she always used with her mother.

Her mother nodded. "I remember my first trip to London with your father. I was so concerned about my English being hard to understand or my clothing making me look out of place. At that point I was also concerned the English would not be the kindest to me, the tensions being what they were between our two nations during the Cold War."

"I thought you met father in the UK?" Lyshiria asked, taking a bite.

"Oh no. I met your father when he accompanied his father here for diplomatic business. I made many trips to London after that. Your father's family threw an annual Field's ball. I wasn't allowed to attend it with my father until a few years after my first trip to London. I met many friends at those balls, and I try to maintain those friendships. Ally was one of my best friends in London. I never understood your father's dislike of her. She was so kind to everyone. When your uncle Michael inherited the Feilds estate, to your father's chagrin, Ally became the mistress of the house, and she was a great hostess. She was a great person overall…" Her mother lamented.

"Do you ever regret that you didn't get to be mistress of the Fields estate?" Lyshiria inquired.

Her mom laughed. "Your father does. I much prefer Moscow to London. Sure, I like to visit, but Moscow is my home. Your grandfather recognized that. That's why he insisted that your father renounce his British citizenship. No, Ally was much better than I could have ever been at it. She fit in everywhere, even London, in a way I never could have."

Lyshiria finished her food and placed her napkin on the table. "Father requested that I to meet him after lunch. Can I be dismissed to go to his office?" She asked.

"Yes. Would you please tell him that I missed him at lunch?" Her mother replied. "And remind him we are leaving tomorrow so it is extremely important that he make it to dinner."

"Yes mother." Lyshiria stood up and left the room, heading for her father's office. As Lyshiria approached, the door opened and an American she had seen with her father on a few occasions walked out, followed by her father. "Ah Lyshiria, your timing is impeccable. Dylan, have I ever introduced you to my daughter?"

"Not formally, I'm afraid." The American replied in his native accent.

"How unfortunate. I'll take the liberties now, if you don't mind. Lyshiria Anastasiya, this is Dylan Hall. Dylan Hall, this is my daughter Lyshiria Anastasiya Feilds."

"I am pleased to meet you Mr. Hall." Lyshiria said, trying to keep the annoyance of her father using her full name to introduce her out of her voice.

"The honor is mine. Your father speaks very highly of you and your skills. I look forward to working with you." He complemented.

"Thank you." She acknowledged, not showing her utter confusion.

"Would you mind finding your own way out Dylan?" Rafael asked. "I am afraid I have business with my daughter I need to attend to."

"Of course" Hall cooed. He shook hands with Rafael, then Lyshiria, and then turned down the hall to the front door. Rafael motioned to Lyshiria to enter his office. Lyshiria entered and turned around, to see her father close the door, then walked back around behind his desk.

"I asked to talk to you because I need you to do something for me while you are in London. I trust that you will be able to get it done. It should be fairly easy, and it will give you some great experience." He started.

"Okay. What is it?" Lyshiria questioned hesitatingly.

"Dylan has agreed to help me with something, to kidnap Kate for me, but he needs help. He needs someone on the inside for him, someone who knows her well enough to coerce her outside during the annual Feilds ball, which happens to be occurring while you and your mother are in town."

"I can do him no good since I won't be *at* the ball. I can't be the inside man when I haven't been invited." Lyshiria reasoned.

"But you and your mother have been invited. Everyone from the Intelligence conference has been invited."

Lyshiria conceded, "What do I have to do?"

Rafael smiled "Convince Kate you are her friend and convince her to go outside with you at just before 20:30. Dylan is leading everything. He will give you specifics once you get to London."

"Okay" Lyshiria agreed, silently cursing herself for allowing herself to be her father's pawn.

June 13th, 2011

11:01 BST (UTC +1)
London Heathrow Airport

Flight 163, from Moscow touched down at Heathrow airport at just after 10:30 AM local time. By 11, Lyshiria was standing in front of the airport with her mother. Nika looked down at her watch. "Well, the conference doesn't start until tomorrow morning, and we will need to get up fairly early. That means we have 9 hours to spend before we need to think about sleeping. Obviously we need to check into the hotel, and drop off our luggage, but what else do you want to do?"

Lyshiria looked around. "I have no clue."

Her mom smiled. "There is a lot to do, but you have plenty of time to think about it. Ah, the car is here." The driver got out and took their baggage to load it in the trunk. Lyshiria and her mom waited patiently as the driver loaded their bags into the trunk, then were helped into the car. The driver closed the door behind them then walked around to his door. He merged back into traffic. Entering London, Lyshiria's mom sighed. "London is gorgeous. I am so glad you came with me; see where it was your father grew up. Maybe we could go sight-seeing."

"That sounds nice." Lyshiria agreed.

"Oh, but there is so much to see, I don't know where to start. There's Buckingham palace, and the Tower of London. There is so much along the river, and there is so much history that revolves around the river. You know, Feilds Palace is along the river Thames. Did you know that Feilds Ball is Friday? We were invited to it. I would love to take you so you can see the palace your father grew up in."

"I didn't know." Lyshiria lied.

"Oh no," her mother began with a growing grin. "That means that you didn't pack anything formal for the event. We just must go shopping. I cannot have you going improperly dressed and I must have you go to your father's family's ball."

"Mother," Lyshiria sighed exasperated. "Father said *no* shopping." A smile began to grow on Lyshiria's face as she realized what her mom had done.

"Your father cannot tell me that I cannot go and buy his daughter formal wear for a ball that he of all people should know is very important. The alternative to us buying new clothing is that we will simply not go, and your father will not let any opportunity to make his brother's daughter look inferior to his own pass him by. He will let us go shopping. He has no choice."

Lyshiria almost wondered at how evil her mom could be. She was more manipulative than most people were and that was putting it mildly. She fit very well into the politics of Russian Intelligence.

"The only question that remains is what to do first. Should we sight-see or shop?" Lyshiria smiled at her mom's question, the answer already evident on both of their faces.

11:35 BST (UTC +1)
Selfridges, London

"I look ridiculous." Lynn complained as she saw her reflection as she walked in the door.

"You look ridiculous?" Kate mocked. "I'm the one wearing the wig and these ugly sunglasses that do nothing to flatter my face, but just hide it. Why do I have to wear this again?"

"Because it would create quite a stir if there were suddenly two of you shopping and my cover would be blown." Lynn explained.

"And you get to look like me *why*?" Kate whined.

"Because she is protecting you dummy." Alyx said over her shoulder. "Now both of you, zip it. We are here to get Lynn new clothes to match Kate's and to look at dresses for the ball on Friday. If anyone asks, Kate, you are a friend of the family, and please don't say anything other than that." Both twins sighed exasperated. "The faster we do this, the faster we go home and you can put your own clothes back on." Alyx bribed. The twins seemed to perk up a bit at that and continued to walk. Alyx led them to a store associate.

"Ah Miss Feilds, Miss McLean, what can I do for you?" The associate asked.

"We are here to get some clothes for Kate and her friend, and we were hoping to be able to look at formal dresses for the Field's ball on Friday as well." Alyx said, following the script they had discussed before leaving.

"I am assuming it is going on your father's account" he asked Lynn dressed as Kate.

"Yes" she answered.

The associate nodded and led them back into the store. Alyx watched as each of them chose outfits and asked the other what they thought. Alyx was more than pleased to stand back and watch the two girls act like the sisters they were; half-hoping she had been blessed with one herself.

Her reverie was interrupted by a voice from behind. "Miss McLean, you don't mind if I stand here by you do you?" it asked. Alyx turned to see Stephan, the staff member her uncle had chosen to send with them for the trip.

She smiled sweetly. "Of course not, now that there are two of them arguing over clothing, there is no telling how long we'll be." She joked.

"Why aren't you looking at clothes?" he asked.

"They are a bit too expensive for my taste. I buy most of my clothes at home, and I can't stand the price tags on these clothes. It makes me cringe, knowing that it is hard work to earn that money and to throw it away so easily." she commented.

"I see" he replied simply. "That's refreshing to hear." Alyx nodded but remained silent. She quickly got lost in thought once more, until Stephan spoke up. "Miss McLean, it appears that Lyshiria and her mother intend to enter the store." Alyx turned around and looked. "Should we tell the twins we need to leave?"

"I don't see why." Alyx reflected. "They could have had no knowledge of us being here, and Kate is disguised. Lynn's cover is safe, and if she tries something, the cameras will only help us catch her red handed. If you would be so kind though to watch the door so they can't leave with either of the twins, that would be greatly appreciated."

Stephan nodded and after Lyshiria and her mom entered the store, slowly made his way back to the door to hover around it. Nika caught sight of Alyx and almost stopped dead in her tracks. "Ally?" she asked confused.

"No, sorry, I'm Alyx McLean. I'm the cousin of the Feilds." Alyx introduced herself.

"Of course" Nika exclaimed. "I saw you just last year at the Feilds ball. You have grown quite a bit this last year. You are looking even more like you aunt than ever." Her English was heavily accented by her

Russian, but her smile was bright enough to light a room. "I do not believe you have met my daughter Lyshiria. This is her first trip to London."

"Очень приятно." Alyx greeted in Russian. Lyshiria and her mother both looked surprised.

"You speak Russian?" Nika asked.

"Yes. I love the language and begged my parents to let me learn it. I think they tried to learn it at one point in time because we have a Russian Literature book in our home, and have for about as long as I can remember."

"Your aunt spoke Russian." Nika stated. "Did you know that?"

"I'm afraid not. I didn't get to know her before she died. I was much too young." Alyx repined.

"You are almost the embodiment of her." Nika commented.

"I'm sure her daughter would be disappointed to hear that." Alyx laughed, graciously accepting the complement.

Nika smiled. "What brings you here? Don't you live in the United States?"

"Yes. I come to London every summer. I'm in town today with Kate and her friend. They wanted some new clothes and dragged me along. If you want I can help you and Lyshiria though."

"That would be great. If you wouldn't mind helping Lyshiria, I need to call my husband. We aren't supposed to be shopping, so I need to tell him why we are." Nika excused herself.

"Well, what are you looking for?" Alyx asked Lyshiria. "Just some of the London Fashion or…"

"I didn't realize I would be attending the Feilds Ball on Friday." Lyshiria admitted.

"Oh, so formal gowns. That's funny because I need to choose gowns for Kate and her friend for the ball as well. Probably myself included. Let me get a store attendant to help us." Alyx smiled. She found an attendant and brought them over. He showed them to formal wear, and Alyx fetched Kate and Lynn. They tried on an assortment of dresses. Kate and Lynn laughed, joked, and acted like the friends they were supposed to be. Lyshiria looked and felt left out somehow. She silently questioned how she could ever do what her father asked her to if she couldn't even have fun with Kate trying on dresses.

Alyx noticed Lyshiria staring in the mirror and went over to her. "It's a very nice dress," Alyx complemented. "I think it is perfect for you to go to the ball in."

"You think so?" She asked, startled by the girl next to her.

"Yes. Simple is often the best way to go. No one realizes that." Lyshiria looked over at Kate and Lynn. "Kate will come around." Alyx said noticing where Lyshiria was looking. "I know she hasn't really acted like it today, but she is usually very nice. She was just reunited with her friend though and she has kind of stuck like glue to her recently." Alyx explained.

Lyshiria looked down. "I'm not sure if that would be such a good thing, her becoming my friend." She paused for a second. "You have been very nice and honest with me." Lyshiria started again. "Is Kate a nice person?"

"For the most part, Kate is wonderful. She has her moments, but we all do, so I would say yes. She is a very nice person." Alyx answered.

"My father seems to have something against her. I would like to talk to you again. Can you meet with me?" Lyshiria asked.

"I don't think that should be a problem. I'm sure I could bribe one of the palace staff to drive me into town later. Or if you like, I can meet you on the Feilds grounds." Alyx said. "Do you want to exchange phone numbers?" Lyshiria nodded. "Why don't you change and then we can." Lyshiria headed back into the changing room and Alyx got her phone. She and Lyshiria exchanged phone numbers, and then Alyx went and got Nika. Nika came in and payed for Lyshiria's dress, and after saying good-bye to Alyx, left.

Soon after, Kate and Lynn were ready. They laid their clothes out on the counters, waited to be rung up, and then left carrying their bags. Alyx then brought three dresses up. "You got their measurements, correct?" She asked.

"Of course." The attendant answered. "And Lord Feilds would like them altered to fit perfectly?" he asked.

"Yes. When can he have them picked up?"

"They should be ready Wednesday afternoon."

"Thank you for all your help." Alyx said as she was getting ready to leave.

"No thank you. Lord Feilds is truly lucky to have you around during the summer. You have a positive influence on Kate." Alyx gave a small smile of gratitude, then left.

15:27 BST (UTC +1)
Feilds Palace, London

Lynn looked at Alyx in disbelief. "You told Lyshiria that you would *what?*"

"Meet with her. It's not a big deal, she and I seemed to connect and it will very possibly help us figure out what she is planning to do. Whatever her father has asked her to do, she's not happy with it, and if she doesn't want to do it, she might help us." Alyx reasoned.

"You think that Rafael's egotistical daughter will turn on her *dear daddy* and help us instead. You were sick last week. Are you sure you are feeling better?" Lynn criticized.

"I'm fine" Alyx lied. "I feel much better." Not a lie. She really did feel better, just not quite fine. The nausea she had felt the day after she got to London had passed, fortunately. That was all the house knew about. She hadn't told them about the headaches that hadn't stopped. They made thinking for any period of time impossible. Noises were excruciating—but she was better. She had a handle on it.

"*Really?* That's why you think it's a good idea to meet Lyshiria. Who is the spy here again? Because I'm pretty sure you aren't. What makes you qualified to decide that meeting with Lyshiria is how we fulfill *my* mission. It's not even your mission. Why do you care?"

"I may not be the spy. I may not be her sister. At least I was here for her, and I *am* her cousin. Just because I'm not her sister doesn't mean I don't care about her. Just because I'm not a spy doesn't mean I can't read people, or I can't read situations and make good judgment calls. I'm good at that sort of thing. You don't have to be a spy to be good at reading people. I could read Lyshiria. I'm going to meet with her. End of discussion. If you want the intel she gives me, fine you can have it, but I won't make you take it." Alyx argued. She stormed out of the room, leaving Lynn fuming.

Kate walked into the Library. She looked towards the door where she had just come in and the pacing, muttering Lynn in front of her. "So this is why Alyx was storming out of here. What happened?"

"Alyx is being stupid." Lynn complained.

"I've known Alyx for 14 years, and she may be a lot of things, but stupid is not one of them. Stubborn, sure, maybe even calculated, or annoyingly right, but she is never stupid." Kate listed. "What did she do?"

Lynn sighed. "It's not what she has done; it's what she is going to do. She told Lyshiria she would meet her, and apparently, she plans on keeping that promise."

Kate smiled. "So like I said, not stupid, but stubborn."

Lynn made a frustrated noise. "Aren't they the same thing? Stubbornness causes you to make stupid decisions."

"This is Alyx we're talking about. She always has a reason for her decisions, something usually pretty well thought out. If she is being stubborn about something, it's because she has decided that she has made the best choice. She has a reason. So let's hear it. Why did she say she was going?" Kate prodded.

"She *thinks* that *Lyshiria*, Rafael's *daughter*, will help us take down Rafael."

"There it is!" Kate exclaimed. "You know, it may sound crazy, but she probably has a much grounded reason for that. I mean, did you *see* how they got along. I think Lyshiria and Alyx bonded faster than you and I did. Despite the fact that you and I had that kinship, sharing blood, which made it really easy for us to become friends. Alyx just has the natural ability to make friends. People trust her. So we should too."

"Spies are taught *not* to trust; *anyone*, not even family. Doing that can get you killed."

Kate huffed. "You don't *trust me*? How could you not trust *me*? How could you not trust *Alyx*? She has kept me safe longer than you have, and you don't seem to be trying as hard as she is. So thank you, but I think it would be smart to trust Alyx. And if you aren't smart enough to trust Alyx, I don't trust you."

"You think Alyx has kept you safe? She's put you in more danger. Her just being here in the summer makes you a bigger target." Lynn argued.

"*What?* Why does Alyx being here make me a target? She's not a target."

"Just forget about it." Lynn said weakly. "You were right; I was just being stupid in not letting you win the argument."

"No. You definitely *thought* something was going on, if you don't *know*. What does your *security clearance* give you that we don't already know?" Kate asked, not letting Lynn drop the subject so easily.

"Forget it. I was just talking nonsense. I was jealous, that's all. I'm a spy; I do well at making things up on the spot." Lynn lied. Kate looked her skeptically, not wanting to let it go. "Do you want to come with me to let Father know we might have a lead?"

Kate shrugged. Lynn left the library, heading for the elevator. Kate shook her head, frowning at her sister who didn't seem to want to let anyone know what she knew.

16:47 BST (UTC +1)
Richmond Park, London

Alyx sat on a bench on the West side of the Sidmouth Wood of the Richmond Park. She gazed at the trees, thinking about the times she had seen the park. She was surprised how big it actually was. Alyx made good use of her time, reading a book she needed to read for her summer assignment. The book was slow and boring, but Alyx trudged through it, resolving that she did not want the little free time she had in Tracy with her friends before school started spent doing her summer assignments.

Alyx looked up to the sound of crunching gravel. "Oh good you found it." She commented as Lyshiria walked up. Lyshiria smiled.

"Tourists guides help more than you could imagine. Is that a good book?" Lyshiria asked, pointing to the book open on Alyx' lap as she sat down next to her.

"Not particularly. I have to read it for school, and I prefer to make the most of any time I have." Alyx book-marked the page then closed the book and set it to the side. "How can I be of help?"

"I'm sure you know who my dad is, Michael's brother Rafael." Lyshiria started hesitantly. Alyx nodded encouraging her to continue. "You probably also know that he doesn't like Michael very much. My mom feels he is responsible for your aunt's death. I fear that she may soon see me as responsible for Kate's." Lyshiria paused.

"You don't want to be a part of your father's plan to kidnap Kate," Alyx guessed "but you couldn't tell him no when he asked."

"How did you know that my father was planning on kidnapping Kate?" Lyshiria stuttered.

Alyx sighed. "Well, MI6 informed Michael the day I arrived that they suspected that Rafael had plans that involved Kate. I believe it was the eighth. They suspected that you were somehow involved, and with you being in town this week, they told us so we could increase security. Michael can't keep much from me I'm afraid."

Lyshiria shook her head. "I didn't even know what my father was planning until he asked me to help him yesterday. How did MI6 know?"

Alyx looked surprised and rubbed her forehead. "I don't know. They must have some source. Your father is viewed as quite a threat in this country." Alyx put her hand in her lap and looked back at Lyshiria. "I wouldn't let it ruin your first time in London though. I've heard there are some great sites to see."

Lyshiria gave a brief smile, and then frowned, realizing what she had said, but hadn't explained. "I'm afraid it already has. Father asked me to help someone he knows, someone he's paying. He asked me to befriend Kate so Friday night she would trust me enough that she will go outside with me, to get her away from the security, so the person he is employing can kidnap her. Then who knows what will happen to her. Why does he want to harm Kate?"

"He's dragging the new generation into the feud that courses between the brothers. It sounds like he is trying to pitch cousin against cousin to me. He wants the feud to continue into our generation, and it sounds like it won't take much. Kate is already afraid of you." Alyx assumed.

Lyshiria looked horrified. "But I have nothing against her. I only just met her today. I want to get to know her…" She trailed off.

"Don't worry" Alyx comforted, "This is exactly what your dad wants, but who said that we have to fall into his plan." Alyx gave a dubious smile.

Lyshiria returned the smile. "You have an idea, don't you?"

Alyx' smile disappeared as she remembered the conversation she'd had with Lynn right before she left. Lynn was right. She wasn't the spy. She had no clue what she was doing. She had probably only endangered herself in coming here. She shook her head, feeling stupid to have believed she could have convinced Lyshiria to turn on her father. "It's nothing. It's stupid, it won't work." Alyx finally said.

Lyshiria looked down at the ground disappointed. "My mom said if anyone could help me it would be you. She always speaks so highly of Ally, and she told me that Ally thought you would grow up to be better than her, at least as far as she told my mom." Lyshiria looked back up. "Maybe I was just desperate, but I thought she was right, that you could help me stop my dad."

Alyx felt overwhelmed. "You *want* to turn on your dad?" Alyx exclaimed. Lyshiria nodded, a half smile growing on her face. "And you want *me* to help you. I'm not a spy. Heck, I'm not even *British*. I shouldn't care about what happens to the fortune of the one of the richest people in Britain. Well, besides, of course, the fact that they're my family. They're yours too, but, I mean, we're not related. Shouldn't you be approaching Kate, not me?"

Lyshiria laughed. "I thought you came here to get me to help you stop my dad."

"I did." Alyx admitted. "I just thought I would have to convince you to turn on him…"

"You didn't, obviously. Honestly, I'm tired of him treating me as if I'm his employee. I'm his *daughter*, I'm not supposed to do his dirty work." Lyshiria complained. "So…, do you have a plan? Will you help me?"

Alyx smiled. "Of course I will." Lyshiria stood up, and Alyx followed. Lyshiria held out her hand, and Alyx took it. They shook hands. "This will be a fun week won't it?" Alyx asked.

Lyshiria returned the smile. "Of course it will be." She laughed. "You know, my dad told me when he asked me to help him yesterday afternoon that this trip would give me some great experience. Don't you think it's funny that when he told me that he had given me a menial role in some stupid plan of his, now I'm going to play a key role, in a much better plan?"

Alyx shook her head and looked down. "You haven't even heard my plan yet."

"I don't need to. *Anything* you can come up with is much better than what my dad can. Trust me." Lyshiria began to walk away. "Thank you"

Alyx shook her head, picked up her stuff and walked off in the opposite direction.

17:34 BST (UTC +1)
Feilds Palace, London

Alyx walked in the door, returning from Richmond Park to hear yelling. The words were inaudible, but the message was clear; Michael was not happy about something. Alyx strolled down the corridor towards a lift. As she entered the rather large sitting room, turning towards the elevators, she nearly bumped into Stephan, who was coming out of the sitting room, from the direction of Michael's office.

"Where have you been?" He hissed. "Michael is pissed that you disappeared. He thinks that it's my fault for letting you slip away."

Alyx laughed. "He thinks you could stop me from leaving when I want to? Lynn couldn't stop me. How does he think anyone else can stop me when Lynn couldn't?"

Stephan gave Alyx a hard stare. "I like my job here."

"You wouldn't lose it because of me." Alyx chided.

"You didn't see how mad he was when Lynn told him where you were going."

"It wasn't your fault, and he would have seen that."

"You're right. Now that you're back, I guarantee that he is going to be ten times more upset at you."

"For what? Going to the park? He can't get mad at me because I have been London 16 times now, and this was my first time seeing anything of London besides this Palace, the church building I go to every Sunday, and the airport."

"Well good luck, because he wants to see you."

"He'll see me at dinner." Alyx pushed the button for the elevator and it opened.

"As long as I'm not the one who has to tell him, I don't care. By the way, he called your parents."

"That's nice" Alyx commented, as the doors closed. She took the elevator up to the fifth floor, exited the elevator and walked over to her room. She went through her closet to the back servants corridor, where there was a supply closet (one on every floor for easy access), and a set of stairs so the servants could go through the house unnoticed. Alyx walked from her room to the supply closet and grabbed out a few large poster-sized pieces of paper, some markers, and tape, closed the closet, and then walked back into her room.

Alyx went into her closet and taped one of the poster-sized papers on a wall in her massive closet, on one of the walls that she didn't have clothes. She took the marker and labeled it *what we know*, and began writing things down, drawing a sort of spider map, with Rafael in the center. After about 10 minutes, Alyx took a step back and looked at the work she had completed. There were still quite a few gaps missing, but she had a couple of days to figure it all out, so she didn't worry about it when she heard the bell for dinner. She made sure everything was in her closet, turned off the light, closed the door, locked it, and left her room like she had been doing that sort of thing her entire life.

Alyx was the first one in the dining room and took the seat that she had adopted as hers over the past few days. Lynn entered next, the joke that had been played on her a few days before long forgotten. She wore one of the new pairs of jeans they had just gotten, and a nice, but very nondescript, shirt. Lynn saw Alyx and freaked out. "Alyx!" She nearly screamed. "You had me scared to death, and I thought it was my fault. I am so sorry for not being more understanding… We may not agree on certain things, but that doesn't mean I can't listen." She apologized.

Kate walked in almost disinterested. "I told you she'd be back" Kate walked over to Alyx and made a huge gesture that made it clear she was going to tell Alyx a secret to make Lynn jealous. "You called me a histrionic drama queen yesterday. You were wrong." Kate whispered. Michael walked into the dining room as Kate continued. "You should have seen how these two acted when we couldn't find you. My episode wasn't half as bad as either of theirs."

A mischievous grin grew on Alyx' face. "At least now you know where you got it." Kate pretended to be hurt and Alyx laughed. Michael was not amused.

"You were gone for three hours," he stated. "Where were you?" Dinner was brought out and served to each of the four individuals sitting around the table. Alyx began eating disinterested in her uncle's concern. "You had a good many of us gravely concerned. I called your parents."

"So I've been told, not that it matters, because what I did today was no different from what I do almost every day in Tracy." Alyx mumbled.

Michael glowed red with anger, but kept from yelling. "What you do in Tracy and what you do here are two very different things. You are not as safe here, not with Rafael and the target you become being associated with me." Lynn choked on the water she was drinking. Everyone looked at her, and then Michael continued. "Do you have something to comment, Lynn?" She shook her head no. Kate looked at her sister skeptically, once again suspecting she was hiding something.

"I guess you don't want to stop Rafael then," Alyx blurted.

"Don't you get smart—"

"Because I went to Richmond Park to talk with Lyshiria, and guess what, *she* asked *me* to help her thwart her father's plan to kidnap Kate, to stop him from changing the war between brothers into a war between cousins. You don't want to stop him, that's fine. I'll tell her I can't meet her anymore." Alyx snapped. She got up from the table and left, and no one could stop her.

19:42 BST (UTC +1)
The Safford, London

Lyshiria sat watching TV in the hotel room. The suite that they were staying in was quite nice, and was fairly large too. Her mom was in her bedroom talking on the phone, with whom she assumed to be her father. She was using hushed tones and the conversation almost sounded heated. Lyshiria stretched out on the couch and played on her phone as the TV played some British comedy show, where half of the jokes flew over her head.

Lyshiria grew board of the game on her phone and she set it on her lap, turning her attention to the TV. As a foreigner, she couldn't help but finding the comedy a bit stupid, but then again, most comedy was stupid. The point of comedy was so you could laugh at other people's stupidity; at least that is what it seemed like to Lyshiria.

Lyshiria tore her eyes away from the TV when her phone began to ring. She turned down the volume on the TV, then picked up the phone. She didn't recognize the number, but she remembered her dad's indication that Hall would contact her once she got to London. She dutifully answered the phone. "Lyshiria."

An American voice replied. "This is Hall. We need to meet to discuss the particulars for Friday's events."

"I understand. What is my duty?" Lyshiria coaxed.

"Not over the phone. Tomorrow, while your mother is attending the conference, I want you to meet me at Buckingham Palace, at noon exactly, by the gates with the guards. If you are a minute late, I'm leaving and I call your dad." Hall threatened.

Lyshiria nodded then spoke. "I understa—"

She couldn't even finish the word before the phone disconnected. Lyshiria sent a quick text to Alyx asking for help. She waited for a reply, and received a reassuring text from Alyx, saying she was on it and that she would meet her at her hotel in the morning to discuss it. Lyshiria caught eye of her mom coming out of the room and locked her phone. Her mom gave her the phone and told her that her dad wanted to talk to her. Lyshiria smiled and carried the phone into the bedroom. Talking to the American was hard. Talking to her father would be harder.

Fortunately, for her, her father trained her well in the art of espionage and deception. She put on the best-pleased daughter face she could then started. "Hi dad, how was your day?"

June 14th, 2011

11:30 BST (UTC +1)
QEII Conference Centre, London

Alyx walked out of the conference center and looked around. She had half an hour until the conference went into a recess for Lunch. She had about that long to find and talk to Lyshiria. She was supposed to meet her father's man in half an hour and Alyx had agreed to come before that meeting was supposed to take place. She and Lyshiria had arranged all the details that morning when Alyx went by Lyshiria's hotel. Lyshiria would have preferred that Alyx wait with her all day, but Alyx translated at the conference.

Alyx had been translating for her uncle since she was 13. She had learned yet another language the year before and her uncle decided to put her talent to good use. He had pulled strings at MI6 and gotten her the clearance necessary to translate for him. Usually it was no problem. Alyx found it easy and a fun practice of her linguistic skills, but this time, her concentrating to translate from the many languages she knew into English magnified her headache beyond the point she could cope. She probably could have lasted until the Lunch recess, but she appreciated the break that meeting Lyshiria gave her. Her uncle approved it and he was just fine without her. He just had to use the same translators that everyone else did.

Alyx found Lyshiria fairly easily. She looked anxious and was pacing back and forth. She very obviously looked out of place. "I might be new to this" Alyx started, stopping Lyshiria's pace mid stride, "but I'm fairly certain that when waiting for a covert meeting, you want to don't attract a lot of attention to yourself."

Lyshiria turned. Alyx sat down on a bench and patted the space next to her. Lyshiria sat down and sighed. "Am I really *that* noticeable?" She shook her head. "I'm nervous. What if I give it away that I'm going to turn him in?"

Alyx smiled. "If you can fool your dad, who knows you really well, then you can fool any stranger you feel like. You probably could have fooled me if you wanted to. Heck, for all I know, my uncle could be right and you could be fooling me right now." Lyshiria frowned.

"I'm not" She blurted, almost too quickly. It was almost fast enough to scream guilt. Almost, but not quite, so what it was actually conveying was nervous innocence. Lyshiria was trying to prove herself to Alyx, trying to earn her trust.

"I know, but for some reason, you choose me. I'm just saying, you could have fooled me, because until yesterday, I had never met you. I didn't know you or your habits. Neither does your father's man. You said your father was trying to train you to be a spy when we talked this morning. If he did a good job, and I think he did, then you can do this. That and you won't be alone. I'll watch you from over here."

Lyshiria nodded and stood up. "Thank you Alyx."

"No problem," Alyx smiled. "Now, go get him."

12:00 BST (UTC +1)
Buckingham Palace, London

Hall caught sight of Lyshiria by the gate and gave a small sigh of relief. He was annoyed that Rafael had assigned his daughter to help him. He was trying to set Rafael up so he could avenge his sister's death, but he pawned the job off to his daughter. It didn't matter because he would get Rafael if it killed him. He had a meeting with Tyson Barnes in 15 minutes, during the recess for the conference that Barnes was attending. Barnes had assured him that everything was under control, that he would put an agent on the Rafael case right away. Hall was just hoping that it was the one he suspected it was. Lynn had quite the trove of information when it concerned her cousin. If his enemies wanted Alyx, he needed to find out why.

Hall approached Lyshiria, completely missing the girl that was watching him from across the street: none other than the same Alyx McLean he was working to protect. "We have a lot to talk about and no time." Hall hurried. "First thing, we need to discuss names. Your father may know me by Dylan Hall but that is not my name." Hall lied. "In London, I am known as Nicholas Radford. The name might be compromised, but as long as you don't tell anyone with MI6 the name, we should be good. And you should probably find a more English code name. Lyshiria Feilds has already been flagged by MI6."

Lyshiria shrugged. "I'm open to suggestions, Nick. It is ok if I call you Nick isn't it Nicholas."

Hall smiled. "I was thinking Ana. It doesn't matter the last name."

"I've already met the target, and she met me as Lyshiria. Alyx was more than kind. She may be my in into the family." Lyshiria shrugged.

"I can't help it. I'm with my mother and she likes to introduce me to almost everyone."

Hall turned grim. "Fine. I will still call you Ana." Hall's blue green eyes sparkled with a look of annoyance. "When do you plan on heading to Feilds palace and what is your plan for getting Lll-" Hall shook his head, "Kate outside Friday night?"

Lyshiria casually glanced towards the bench Alyx was sitting on. Alyx gave a brief reassuring nod and Lyshiria turned back. "I've got that covered. I will probably work out the kinks, but don't worry about it. What door do I bring her out of, where do I bring her, what do I say. I need more details if this is going to work."

Hall cursed under his breath. "I have a van that I will use. It will be disguised as a catering van. Your father loaned me a team. They will be standing by the open door. Take her out the doors by the servant's staircase. It is through the banquet hall, down the cor-ridor to the large servant run kitchen, through a huge opening in the wall, you will see the staircase. Turn right through that door, and you should see the door. The van will be out there. There is no code, nothing to say. Take her out there after the dinner, during the ball. I'm going to say probably about 20:30. Then return back inside as if nothing happened. Does that work?"

Lyshiria shrugged. "If it doesn't work, I'm telling my dad it was your fault." Hall checked his watch. "Do you have something better to do? My father is *paying* you to help me, and for someone who earns their money taking odd jobs, I think he is paying you pretty well, so if you have something better to do than help me, I can tell my dad, and you can kiss your money good bye." Lyshiria taunted.

Hall rolled his eyes and turned his head, casually checking their surroundings. As he did, the sun caught his dark hair just right that it looked blonde, and Lyshiria wondered how many colors his hair had been for the jobs he had taken, or if the current color of his hair was his actual hair color. "We've been here for too long. Any longer and people will start to get curious. I already have the feeling that we are being watched." That last part wasn't a lie, and Hall couldn't figure out who was watching them. It was driving him nuts. "So unless you have anything else you want to discuss, we need to leave."

Lyshiria shook her head, and glanced over at Alyx. "No, I think we're good." Hall smiled and left without saying anything else. Lyshiria returned to the bench where Alyx was sitting. "I got some great intel."

"I told you that you could do it." Alyx said. She checked her watch then looked up at Lyshiria. "Now we have 15 minutes before I have to leave for the conference. Let's start working on a plan."

12:20 BST (UTC +1)
QEII Conference Centre, London

Hall walked briskly toward the conference center. He was running five minutes late for his meeting with Barnes, and Barnes was not known to wait for anyone, even a Hall, any member of the family of CIA legends. He had even been known to leave if his sister was late, and she was his favorite Hall. He gave her almost everything.

Hall peeked through the crowd and found Barnes. Hall sliced through the crowd and found himself in front of Barnes, next to Michael Feilds. "Barnes, sorry I'm late." Hall said as he approached, using his British accent.

Barnes looked at him with a removed interest. "Nicholas Radford, meet Michael Feilds, our Director of Information at MI6." Michael turned to see who was standing next to him. "Michael Feilds, meet Nicholas Radford, one of our informants on Chemist."

Michael smiled. "So, Dylan, you are the one to thank for the warning of this week's threat."

Barnes jumped in quickly. "His name is Nicholas."

Hall waved him off. "Nicholas is my UK alias. I was born Dylan Hall." Hall had resumed his native accent.

"Any relation to Ally Hall?" Barnes asked suddenly interested in the conversation.

"She was my sister, thus my interest with Rafael and his downfall." Hall admitted.

Barnes cocked his head with interest. "Why not come to me with your real name. I always clear my schedule for a Hall."

Hall smiled an almost evil glint in his eye. "I prefer to get in on my own merit, not my family's. Now if I may, about Rafael, I wanted to ask what agent you put on the case."

Barnes looked at Michael. "Lynn McFeild, Michael's daughter."

"Good." Hall commented.

Barnes and Michael exchanged a concerned look. "Is there something that you know that we don't?" Michael asked.

Hall shrugged. "She seems to be a bit of an expert on Alyx, so I have a plan."

"I still don't get it." Michael said. He looked at Barnes and Hall as he waited for an explanation. "How did you know about Lynn? Why do you need to an expert on Alyx?"

Hall looked down at the ground. "You need to know that I am reading you guys in on this because you will have a direct say in the repercussions following Friday's events. I received a call from someone in the Circle of Fifths about a week ago, asking me to find Alyx McLean. I then volunteered to help Rafael, because I have been in contact with him, trying to prove myself so I could turn him in later. I knew about Lynn, because your wife told me and I've met her on an occasion or two."

"I don't understand" Michael said.

"Kate isn't in any danger because I am the one who is supposed to kidnap her. I must beg you two though, that when I kidnap Kate, and help you nail Rafael, ignore me. I need to talk to Lynn."

Michael looked at Hall. "Kate isn't in any danger because Lyshiria has reached out to Alyx. She is working with Alyx to create a plan to arrest her father."

Barnes shook his head. "If Rafael somehow ends up with Kate, it sounds like it will be a very big mistake. Hall has infiltrated, Lyshiria has defected, and Lynn is undercover."

Hall looked between his companions. "If we have such a great safety net, I think we should step back and let the girls do what they like. Let them form the plan."

Barnes shrugged. "That will be easy for me. I already told Lynn that she has no MI6 help, no reports."

"That leaves you Michael." Hall gestured toward Feilds.

"Alyx isn't really listening to me anyway. She disappeared on me for three hours last night."

"Do you have a reason for wanting the girls to do it Hall? You think their inexperience will help you achieve your goal?"

Hall looked at the ground and shrugged. "I don't really view them as inexperienced, they are great minds, and I'm sure working together, they can become much more, I mean look at their parentage. No, I think we let them succeed at their mission, but all three of us know that Rafael won't go down unless we can link him to the crime. I have to carry out a separate mission; Lynn will have to go missing, and show up with Rafael on the English border."

Barnes face lit up. "And then you have your time to get the information about why your enemies want Alyx." Hall smiled. They looked at Michael, waiting for an answer.

"I guess I can live with that."

Barnes looked at the other two. "None of the girls can know about this, not your real name," Barnes commenting pointing to Hall, "she knows you, not who we are really going to target, not when. Neither Lynn nor Alyx with their clearance can find out about it, so as far as the three of us are concerned, this meeting didn't happen. Nothing mentioned is to go on MI6 servers. Understand?"

Hall looked confused. "I understand Lynn, but how does Alyx have MI6 clearance?"

Michael smiled, finally in a loop someone else wasn't. "She's my translator. MI6 wouldn't hear of it without giving her clearance." Hall nodded in understanding. "Actually, here she comes now from her meeting with Lyshiria, so I better go. See you two in a few days."

Barnes gave a stern look to Feilds. "Remember, not a word."

"Not a word about what, Tyson?" Michael winked and walked toward Alyx. Hall and Barnes parted just as professionally into the crowd, and no one in the crowd could have told you if there really had been three men there, or if it was their imagination.

17:35 BST (UTC +1)
Feilds Palace, London

"Are you sure she said Nicholas Radford?" Lynn asked Alyx.

Alyx sighed, trying not to get exasperated, but it was hard because Lynn kept questioning her about everything she said. "Yes and apparently he told her not to tell anyone with MI6. That means that he *must* be on their servers. I checked but was told that my clearance wasn't high enough, which is weird because my clearance is just as high as your dad's is."

Lynn huffed. "I found him." She turned to Alyx and squinted her eyes. "You have what type of clearance? The Information Clearance is the one dad has. If that is what you have, then of course you couldn't access it. The Information Clearance, no matter how high it is, cannot access personnel files, especially not of informants."

"Good to know" Alyx mumbled, looking over Lynn's shoulder at the information MI6 had on Nicholas Radford. There wasn't a picture like they were hoping, but the file had some interesting facts. "Wait, Radford is the Rafael informant."

"I guess that means the danger Kate is in just plummeted." Lynn commented. A smile grew on Alyx' face. "What?" Lynn questioned. "I don't like that smile."

"I was just thinking," as Alyx said those words, Lynn groaned. "If there is little danger here, then there is no harm in using both of you Friday night."

"No. I'm going to stop you right there. No. It's a *terrible* idea." Lynn interrupted.

"Hear me out a second. I'm convinced, looking at this file, that MI6 would have told you if they knew, and Radford would have told MI6, unless there was an angle, and he was trying to play both Rafael and MI6. I want to throw off his angle by putting both of you out there. I know it is a risk, but I'm thinking, if he has been in contact with MI6, he has some knowledge, even if it is only an inkling, of your existence. I bet *that* is his angle. He is expecting that MI6 would put you on the case to protect your twin and that you will protect her by taking her place. So by putting both of you out there, the pressure to get the right twin increases, and the chances that he messes up increases."

"Do you realize you sound crazy?" Lynn asked.

"Lynn, think about it for a minute. It makes sense." Alyx prompted.

Lynn pondered it for a second, reading the MI6 file. "Zut." Lynn whispered. "I think you're right."

"I usually am…" Alyx muttered to herself. Lynn ignored her and began nervously biting her right thumbnail.

Lynn suddenly looked up at Alyx. She pointed at her. "*You* already have a plan. *Don't you.*" Alyx nodded. "*Fine,*" Lynn relented. "We do it your way. Let me hear your plan."

Alyx gave Lynn another dubious smile. "You're going to have to come with me." She stood up and walked out of the office Lynn had taken to be hers. Lynn followed Alyx to the elevator and took it up to the fourth floor. Alyx then led Lynn to her room, and took her into the closet.

Lynn gasped when she saw the collection of poster papers taped on Alyx' walls. There were already five and there were lines drawn from poster to poster connecting the various parts of the equation. "When did you do this?"

"I started the night I first met with Lyshiria." Alyx admitted.

"*Last night.* You did this *last night.*" Lynn shook her head as she traced the lines that connected pieces of the puzzle. "Wait, you already have a line connecting MI6 and Radford. How did you know? I only just now told you he's working with MI6."

Alyx shrugged. "I was there watching as he talked to Lyshiria. That meant that when I saw him near the conference center a little bit later, I recognized him. I then assumed that he didn't want Lyshiria to tell anyone with MI6 because then she would discover that he *is* MI6, and that he was setting her up."

Lynn threw her hands up in a sort of surrender. "Fine, you were right. Your plan exists as *the* plan for Friday, but after Friday, no more. It's too dangerous." Lynn walked out of Alyx' closet then out of her room.

Alyx stared at the posters boasting her talent. "I'm done when I want to be." Alyx muttered to herself.

June 17th, 2011

13:56 BST (UTC +1)
QEII Conference Centre, London

The palace was in chaos, all of the staff preparing for the ball. The closing ceremonies for the conference were taking place, and by the time Alyx and Michael got home, there would be a mere three hours to prepare for the five o'clock dinner. Lynn was nervous. Alyx had assured her that everything would be taken care of. Lynn had yet to see her dress, the same as Kate. That was why Kate was freaking out. Lynn was freaking out because she had yet to see a detailed action plan for the night's affairs.

Alyx translated the last few words from the German delegation for Michael. As Michael stood to close the conference, Alyx leaned back, knowing her job was done, hoping her headache could now go away. She was so relieved about being done, she didn't pay attention to her uncle's remarks. She caught snippets like, "Please remember what we discussed here," or "Keep your promises." However, it wasn't until Michael reminded, "You have all been invited to Feilds Palace for a formal dinner, followed by the annual Feilds Ball. It begins at five. I look forward to seeing you there," that Alyx actually perked up. Friday had snuck up on her so easily, and she wasn't quite ready.

Michael sat back down, having closed the conference and dismissed its members, to gather his things. "Uncle, I'm afraid there are a couple of things we must do before we return home." Alyx urgently whispered.

"Hmm?" Michael vocalized disinterested. "And what might that be?"

Alyx breathed out slowly to calm herself. "We must go by the Jewelers and Selfridges."

Michael looked up startled. "I completely forgot." Alyx nodded, saying she had as well. "I guess that is why I keep you around." He joked. He became more serious looking at the concern Alyx showed. "Sorry." He apologized. "Of course we must go before we head home. Please let Stephan know and have him inform palace staff."

Alyx stood up and left to do as she was told as Michael picked up the rest of his stuff. She was long gone and too far away to see him pass an envelope off to Nicholas Radford.

15:12 BST (UTC +1)
Feilds Palace, London

Alyx walked in the door with huge garment bags. When they heard the door open, Kate and Lynn ran toward Alyx. Kate tried to take the garment bags, Alyx held back, and continued toward the elevators. She froze at the sound of Lynn's venomous voice. "You're Late," it said.

Alyx turned around. She looked at Lynn. She looked so sweet and innocent, and maybe that is why MI6 had used her so effectively. Alyx knew better after living with her over the past week. Lynn was a very dedicated spy, and didn't react well when things didn't go her way. She hadn't been happy that Alyx had kept her plan from her. Lynn loved being in the loop, and it bugged her beyond belief when she was left out. Alyx had heard her share of nasty curse word over the last day or so. Lynn thought she was getting away with it, because after all, it was in bizarre languages, but Alyx knew more languages than Lynn did. Nothing could slip past her.

Alyx studied her cousin. She liked Lynn, but she could tell that something was bugging her, more than Alyx just keeping her plan from her. No, as Alyx had gotten to know Lynn better, there were things that annoyed her, like there was more to the story than Lynn was telling her, and she herself was proof of that. Lynn was evasive when anyone asked her about her training or previous missions, more than was necessary. Then there was how she seemed to favor her left shoulder, how she seemed to have the tale-tale sign of an American accent, one from the West coast, and she definitely had spent quite a lot of time on a beach somewhere. Those observations let Alyx know three things:

Lynn had been injured, it had happened fairly recently, and Lynn had been in California.

Alyx wanted to ask her why she had gone to California, but that would only make Lynn more upset at her than she already was, and Alyx knew that Lynn had to be calm for her plan to work. Alyx shrugged, partly to show disinterest in Lynn's wrath, and to make herself forget the questions that had started to cloud her mind the moment she saw Lynn in the street for the first time. "Stephan called to let you know we had things to do before we came home. It's your fault you didn't answer." Alyx turned back around and headed for the elevator again. "Now we need to get ready, so if you could put your anger behind you and come to my room in thirty minutes to get your dress, that would be great. In the meantime, I am going to shower. We have a plan to discuss."

Lynn folded her arms as she watched the door close behind Alyx. It always seemed as if Alyx could see right through her, and Alyx knew as much to know Lynn didn't like it, Alyx knew more about her than everyone else did, everyone, that is, except her boyfriend.

Now that Alyx had dangled that stupid dress in front of Kate, Kate was delusional, and Lynn was afraid that she couldn't get her twin to concentrate again that night. Kate was blabbering something about dark bags and how it was so unfair and that Alyx did this to her every year. Lynn desperately wanted to punch something and make it stop, but that something would be her sister, and that would do her no good.

Lynn turned toward Kate and thought of a solution to stop the annoying chattering of a silly teenage girl. Lynn smiled. "What do you say that we go look at those dresses of ours?" Lynn started.

"She locks the door Lynn, we can't."

Lynn cocked her hip. "You know, it has been two entire weeks since I picked a lock. My lock picking kit needs some good use, and I would *love* the practice. What do you say? Do you want to learn?" Lynn taunted. She could see the realization of what she was saying dawn on Kate's face. Lynn turned to go upstairs and Kate ran after her.

15:42 BST (UTC +1)
Feilds Palace, London

Alyx walked out of her bathroom dressed in the same shirt and shorts she had worn to bed her first night in London. She squinted her eyes at the two garment bags that she had laid on her bed before her shower. "She didn't," she mumbled. "She wouldn't." She walked over to her door, unlocked it and opened it. She saw Kate and Lynn waiting, patiently, too patiently for Kate. "You didn't," she said to Lynn. Lynn visibly fell.

"How did you know?" Lynn whined, giving herself away.

"I just have a sense when it comes to that sort of thing." Alyx said. "Besides that, Kate is waiting *patiently*. She *never* does that. You do realize I make her wait to bribe her right?"

Lynn's eyes widened. "Bribe her to do what?"

Alyx rolled her eyes. "Bribe her to behave tonight."

"I'm right here," Kate complained.

Alyx and Lynn both looked at Kate. "We know."

Lynn sighed. "She was being annoying, and I could either do this, or punch her. I chose this. Besides, I finally got to do something with my twin that I enjoy doing, and *Kate enjoyed it too.*"

Alyx crossed her arms. "For your sake, I hope she behaves tonight. Now, who wants me to do their hair?"

Kate didn't wait for another invitation to enter the room.

16:00 BST (UTC +1)
Feilds Palace, London

Lyshiria and her mother sat in the backseat of the chauffeured car Russian Intelligence had provided for them on this trip, as their driver pulled through the gates of Feilds Palace. Lyshiria looked down the road and saw the river Thames. Her mother was right to say that the palace was on the River, like all the other great sites in London.

They were an hour early, and if they had been anyone else, they wouldn't have been let in the gates, but Alyx had cleared it with the staff. She needed Lyshiria there to read her in on the plan. She needed to meet the team.

Their driver pulled up in front of the grand double door entrance. Stephan approached from his waiting place next to the stairs and opened the door. He put out his hand and escorted Nika out of the car first, followed by Lyshiria. In a very professional way, he then stuck out his hand and escorted Nika up the front stairs to the door. He opened it, then stuck out his arm, the way so many do to indicate *after you*. He followed Lyshiria through the door and closed it behind them, patiently waiting as Lyshiria gave Alyx a hug. "Thank you for all your help," Lyshiria commented. She backed out of the hug and looked Alyx up and down. "Shouldn't you be wearing your dress?"

Alyx gave a dubious smile, not answering the question. Instead, she commented "You look amazing," referring to the lavender dress with a wrapped left shoulder. Stephan walked around them. "We are upstairs." Stephan opened the first set of the french doors and Alyx led them through the door and into the sitting room. Stephan walked past them and opened the hidden door that hid the elevator from the sitting room.

"I've never seen that door." Nika marveled.

Alyx smiled. "We don't use it for formal occasions, and as the story goes, Michael didn't know it existed until Ally started exploring the house."

Nika nodded as they walked through the door. "It's very convenient."

Alyx walked through the door last, Lyshiria and Nika already in the waiting elevator. Stephan discreetly stopped Alyx as she walked by, leaning into her ear, his face away from the others to whisper, "Are you sure about this? Are you sure you can trust them?"

"Of course I am." She answered, turning to face him. To the others it appeared they were discussing palace business. Lyshiria watched the exchange out of boredom.

Stephan let go of her arm. "I hope so. I like my job."

Alyx rolled her eyes and gave a dubious smile, raising Lyshiria's suspicions about their conversation. "I love you too." Alyx joked. Lyshiria read her lips and slyly looked away. "You won't lose your job if I mess up. You aren't responsible for my decisions and actions." Alyx walked into the elevator and it closed. Lyshiria kept her eyes down, ashamed that she had just spied on Alyx. Stephan stood, looking at the closed elevator doors, and let out a deep breath. Someone had to tell her. Someone had to tell her, or she would figure it out, and he had no clue what how angry she might be to discover they had all been lying to her for years. She had too much talent it wasn't a matter of if, but when.

Alyx was slightly agitated by Stephan's concern. She rode up to the third floor with Lyshiria and Nika. Suddenly she was suspicious of them. She knew it was just nerves from talking to Stephan, but it was hard to shake. Stephan was like family, but something about him made her second guess herself, and that was on a good day. He had been on edge since she had gotten here. For some reason, it made the regular nerves worse. She didn't like second guessing herself.

The elevator dinged as it opened, allowing Alyx to show Lyshiria and her mother to Lynn's office, where Alyx' posters now hung. Lyshiria and Nika walked in and had to make sure they weren't seeing things; that there were really two of Kate. "There are two of her." Lyshiria said, stating the obvious. "Why are there two of her?"

Alyx nodded as Kate and Lynn stood in their matching burgundy dresses, with a two inch strap that crossed the left shoulder and a ruffle on the front. "Lyshiria, Nika, meet my cousin Kate, and her *twin* sister Lynn. She surprised us all when she showed up a week and a half ago bearing news."

Lyshiria's face slowly showed realization. She smiled as she slightly nodded her head. "Your MI6 contact."

Alyx smiled. "Of course."

"And what is your plan for tonight?" Nika asked.

Alyx gestured for Lyshiria and Nika to take seats then stepped to the side, allowing Lynn to take the lead. "Well, when MI6 first sent me last week, the plan was for me to come in and take Kate's place, keep her safe, but then the situation changed a bit." Lynn started.

"I came forward." Lyshiria filled in.

"Exactly." Alyx said. "The plan was still supposed to be that Lynn take Kate's place, thus the reason why you guys didn't meet her until tonight. If we were going to go with that plan, we had to minimize the exposure we gave to Lynn so as to not compromise Kate's safety, and our plan, but Tuesday's information changed things a bit."

"When you told Alyx about Nicholas Radford, she asked me to use my MI6 clearance to check him out. That was when Alyx officially took over and changed the plan."

Kate mumbled from her seat on Lynn's left. "In other words we still have no clue what we are doing and I'm bored."

Lyshiria looked at Kate. "Well I trust her."

"Is everyone ready for the plan?" Alyx asked

Michael walked into the office. "I believe we are now." He said. Alyx smiled.

Alyx turned to her posters that she had been working on, most of the blanks filled in. She explained the connections, her reasoning behind why Kate was safe, the back up protocols that had been put in place, such as the staff members duties during the dinner and ball, the mechanisms that were being used to secure doors and windows, besides the one they knew Radford admitted he wanted to use, and what the alternative security was for that door. Alyx looked up at her audience, getting ready to close. "We know Radford is working with MI6. That leaves one question unanswered, one problem unsolved. If he is not working for *your* father, then we have no clue who or what he is really after. That is why I'm putting *both* twins out there. We need confusion; we need to control the odds. I am betting that whatever his plan is, it hinges on Lynn being the only one out there. If we have both twins, no one knows which one is which—it's the only way we can throw him off.

"That makes your job harder, Lyshiria. It would work better if you could find Lynn to take her outside, but you will just have to do your best and choose one. It doesn't matter which one, because they will be safe either way."

Alyx paused looking at Lyshiria for feed back. Lyshiria nodded. "I like it."

"I do have one more thing." Alyx admitted. "Michael helped me, but I felt they were essential." Alyx pulled out four boxes and handed each of the three girls a box, keeping the fourth box for herself. Kate opened her's first and was so stunned she was completely still and silent for once. Alyx continued. "Since we don't know who or what Radford is after, I decided that it was necessary that we each have our own GPS tracker, in case something goes wrong. Each of these necklaces have a GPS beacon in the silver. It can be turned off after tonight if need be, but for tonight, we need the GPS.

"As far as I know, we could all be a target. Your father is after Kate." Alyx said gesturing to Lyshiria. "If Radford is working for your father, then Kate is in danger, but I doubt that is the case. My money is on Radford being after the secrets that Lynn has access to. Thus, Lynn could be a target. Radford could be after revenge on your father. If he is, he could be looking to fulfill that revenge by taking you." Alyx said, once again looking at Lyshiria. "That leaves me." Alyx shrugged, and Michael started rubbing his forehead, not liking how close to the truth Alyx was getting with her guesses. "As far as I can figure, my father is FBI. He has enemies, thus the reason for the annual move, until I begged to stay in Tracy. I can be used as leverage."

The room was silent as Alyx finished. "We don't know what he is after, so we need to cover all the things that count. The four of us are important, and tonight we will make a difference. We need to be safe." The three girls put on their necklaces. "I need to go get dressed, the guests can be arriving any time." Alyx finished, dismissing herself from the room. Kate and Lyshiria followed, the two cousins finally getting some bonding time. Lynn stayed with her father and Nika. "She has talent." Nika commented. "She's like her mother."

Lynn and Michael just nodded. Alyx may have figured out quite a bit, but each of them still had different puzzle pieces—pieces that only they had, and that Alyx hadn't found. Each of them sat there relieved that their secret had not been uncovered by Alyx' genius. *Yet.*

But the puzzle was unfinished, each of their secrets clutched close to their chests, which meant Alyx didn't have the entire picture; no one had the complete picture. And that was more dangerous than anything else.

19:21 BST (UTC +1)
Feilds Palace, London

The Grand Hall was full of music, dancing and conversation. Kate and Lynn were split up, according to the plan. They talked to different people, no one knowing which twin they were talking to. Occasionally, Kate and Lynn would dance with someone who would ask them, but as Alyx had planned, the attention wasn't focused on them. If it was, it would be easier to discover which twin was which; their every move, every mistake, would be evident, and scrutinized thus making it more likely for their adversaries to figure out the difference between the twins. And, of course, it would be more likely that someone would notice when Lyshiria took one of them outside, their hope for the evenings extra curricu-lar events to remain covert, vanishing.

Instead, the attention shown on Alyx. Lynn knew she didn't like it, but she seemed completely comfortable with it. There was not one dance she wasn't dancing with one of the diplomat's sons. Alyx was laughing and smiling through all of it. She was the perfect spy. First, she had been sneaky. She hadn't put on her dress until right before dinner. It was a flattering dress. The strapless dress showed off her flawless shoulders, when they weren't covered by the crème pashmina. The skirt was long, hanging from her waist straight to her ankles. She wore heels that a model would wear, and honestly, it only added to the effect. She looked like a model in that misty rose colored dress. It showed her figure and she had a beautiful one.

Hall stared at Alyx, her plan working well. Michael came up behind him and laid a hand on his shoulder. "I'm glad to see you made it. I'm afraid we might have a problem though."

Hall nodded, his eyes still on Alyx McLean. "Alyx is drawing quite a bit of attention tonight. People will be talking about it for weeks."

Michael grabbed Hall's arm and turned towards him, blocking his view of Alyx. "That's the problem. Alyx put both twins out here and is drawing the attention towards her to distract you. She is dangerously close to figuring out what you're up to."

Hall froze. "*This is Alyx' plan*? Why would you let *Alyx* make the plan?"

Michael stared at Hall in disbelief. "You told me to let the girls make the plan."

"Yeah, but I expected Lynn to remain in charge." Hall cursed. "Do you know which twin is Lynn?"

"No clue. Alyx put them in the same *bloody* dress." Hall sighed at the news. "What are you going to do?" Michael asked.

Hall stared at Alyx. She was a worthy opponent, just not quite good enough to beat him—he hoped. "I can handle it." He said. He walked off. Michael sighed, hoping Hall was right.

20:30 BST (UTC +1)
Feilds Palace, London

Lyshiria looked at the clock hanging in the grand hall. She made a small gesture to Alyx, indicating it was time. She looked at one twin then the other, trying to figure out which one was Lynn. She chose one and grabbed her arm. "It's time." She whispered. The twin nodded and followed Lyshiria through the banquet hall to the door Radford had told her about. Lyshiria found her father's men and pushed the twin toward them. She walked away, around the front of the vans like planned.

Suddenly, *she* was pulled into a van.

Lyshiria came face to face with Alyx. "Is everything going okay?" She asked. Alyx turned to watch the computer screens. She was not in the dress she had been wearing minutes before. Now she was wearing all black, and no indication how she changed so quickly. She had a black short sleeved shirt tucked into a pair of black running tights finished off by a pair of black running shoes, with white soles. Looking at Alyx, Lyshiria was slightly scared. Alyx had a black drop holster, that she had gotten from who knows where. On the right side there was what looked like a gun, and on the left, a pocket knife and two magazines. "Alyx?" Lyshiria asked again. "Is everything okay?"

"Peachy," Alyx said. She was biting her thumb nail as she stood there watching the surveillance.

"What's wrong?" Lyshiria asked.

"You grabbed Kate, and our men can't move in, not without loosing Kate." Alyx said. She turned her head and Lyshiria could barely see an earpiece in her ear. She definitely looked like a soldier.

Lyshiria looked at the computers. "How do you know it's Kate? How can you tell them apart?" Lyshiria asked, frightened beyond belief that she had messed up Alyx' plan, that her father *would* get Kate. Alyx shrugged, suggesting she just *knew*. Lyshiria studied the computer. Kate had to be terrified. She was surrounded by Rafael's men. Lyshiria would have been terrified and they were working for her own father.

Lyshiria jumped at the noise of the van door opening. She turned and saw Alyx leaving. "Alyx, where are you going?" Lyshiria whispered.

"To get my cousin." Alyx shrugged. "Can you close the door after me?" Alyx reached up and pulled herself up using the top of the door frame. Lyshiria watched Alyx climb up onto the top of the van, almost as if there was no effort in it. Lyshiria closed the door as she was asked. Alyx heard the door close and stood up. She silently ran from the top of one van to another, balancing weight so to not make too much noise, to not give herself away. She jumped off the second to last van, into the crack between the vans. She rolled her landing, pulling the tranq gun from her holster as she did. She pressed her back to the side of the van, listening to the Russians around her cousin. "Shouldn't you be fighting back?" One of the guards asked Kate in English. He turned to one of his compatriots and started speaking in Russian. "This isn't the girl we are supposed to kidnap."

Alyx was right, Radford *was* after Lynn. *Not* Kate. While she may have been the one to argue the point, she was stunned that she had actually been right, when almost everyone else told her she was wrong, but she couldn't let her shock prevent her from saving her cousin. She peeked around the corner of the van and started shooting tranquilizer darts. She dropped four of the five guards in a matter of seconds. The fifth one charged her just as her gun jammed. Alyx tossed the gun, using her martial arts skills to deflect the blow the fifth guard tried to deliver. The fight didn't last long. The slow Russian was no match for her speed and accuracy.

Alyx enjoyed taunting him. She threw several jabs at him, then stopped, letting him take a few punches. She deflected all of them, making it clear that he could never land a punch on her. She fake yawned as she deflected yet another one of his punches. He saw the game she was playing, and turned to run away. Alyx ran after him, quickly catching up to him. As she got close to him, she jumped into the air, as if she was hurdling, pulling the toes of her lead foot up and planting it in his back, her toes barely between his shoulder blades. The force of her momentum threw off his balance, causing him to face-plant into the gravel. Alyx fell too, as she knew she would from hurdle practice, but her anticipation helped her land on top of the Russian, pulling out her knife as she did. She held it to the side of his neck, and moved her mouth close to his upturned ear. "Don't move, or I *will* kill you. *No one* touches my family."

Kate stood frozen, stunned from what her cousin had just done to the five Russians that were trying to kidnap her, frightened at the darkness that Alyx was exhibiting. "Um, Alyx? Where are the guards?"

Alyx didn't answer. She kept her eyes deeply focused on the guard she was holding down. "All clear. Area secured." She said, her earpiece transmitting it. "Move in."

The Russian on the ground started muttering in Russian. "Rafael will be mad. I am not safe." He changed back into broken English. "You are not safe. He will know your part, and he will hunt you." Kate gasped.

The guards came running out, starting to collect the unconscious guards. "Rafael means nothing. He is going down with you. So in a way, you are right. You aren't safe. How do you think he will act towards you in prison?" Alyx replied. Two guards came over and took the Russian. Another one wrapped a blanket around Kate. Together, Kate, Alyx, Stephan, and the guard that had given Kate the blanket walked back to the van. Stephan opened the back door. Kate climbed in first, Lyshiria giving her a big hug. "Thank goodness you are alive and safe."

Kate turned to Alyx, still standing outside the van. "Thanks to Alyx. I'm still trying to process what you did out there." She gasped as she looked at Alyx' hands. "Alyx, you're bleeding!"

Alyx looked down at her hands. She hadn't noticed before the red coming from her hands, but now that Kate had pointed it out, she could suddenly feel the throbbing. She just balled them up into fists, trying to continue to ignore the throbbing. "They're just minor cuts, from the gravel. I've had worse from Track. Besides, we don't have time to worry about it. We have other problems."

Stephan pulled her up into the van. "Fine, you can tell us all about it as we clean your cuts."

20:38 BST (UTC +1)
Feilds Palace, London

"I was right." Alyx said. She winced as Stephan dabbed the cuts on her hands with Hydrogen Peroxide.

Kate looked at Alyx. "What do you mean?"

Alyx looked at her hands while Stephan cleaned them. "One of the Russians said that you weren't the girl they were supposed to kidnap because you weren't fighting back."

"What does that mean?" Kate asked growing frustrated.

"It means that as far as those men were concerned, you were never the target. Lynn was. I was right."

Everyone was silent for a little bit. "My father said Kate." Lyshiria argued.

"Your father wanted Kate, but Radford was after Lynn, and Radford was in charge of your father's operation."

"Thank goodness we stopped them. If it weren't for your plan, he may have gotten Lynn." The guard complemented.

Alyx pulled her hand back from Stephan and jumped up. "Sit back down. I'm not done yet." Stephan scolded.

"No. We can't waste any more time. Radford wasn't out there. We didn't capture him. He is still out there. The question is where is he? He is our real problem, so if we can't answer that question, then Lynn is still in danger." Alyx argued.

Stephan stared at Alyx. "I personally oversaw security. I may not be able to tell you where he is, but I can tell you where he's not. There is no way he got into Feilds Palace. Everyone who came in either had their name on a list or an invitation signed by your uncle. Lynn is safe."

Alyx felt like she had been punched in the gut. "Everyone from the conference got in." Alyx muttered.

"That's what I *just* said. Did that Russian hit your head?" Stephan reached for Alyx' arm to get her to sit down again. She pulled her arm away quite violently.

She looked at Stephan, a wild panic in her eyes. "Radford was at the conference. Radford *is here.*" Alyx jumped out of the van. No one could stop her as she ran from the van, back into the palace. Stephan tried to catch her, running after her, but he wasn't any more successful than Lyshiria or Kate, both of which ran, or fast walked, after him. By the time they found her, she was back in her gorgeous pink dress and pashmina, slicing across the ballroom toward Michael. It almost made Lyshiria wonder if maybe Alyx had a twin as well.

Alyx stopped next to her uncle and interrupted his conversation. "Uncle, where is Lynn?" Michael turned toward his niece.

"Alyx, where are your manners?" He asked. He turned back to his conversation. "I'm very sorry, Alyx usually has much better manners. She just hasn't quite been herself the past couple of days."

Alyx let out a deep breath and put on her best smile. "I'm sorry. I'm Alyx, Lord Feilds niece. It is very nice to meet you Mister…"

"Jackson." The man answered with a real American accent.

Alyx smiled and tilted her head down and to the left very slightly, a form of greeting. "I'm so sorry, but I'm going to have to steal my *wonderful* uncle of mine for a second or two. It's a matter of urgent family business."

Jackson nodded, acknowledging that it was fine for Alyx to take her Uncle. He watched the tall beauty walk off with her uncle. "So this is the Alyx McLean everyone talks about," he pined, "Quite the girl."

20:51 BST (UTC +1)
Feilds Palace, London

"Alyx what is this about? You're being ridiculous. That man was a very important man in the United States Government and said he had very important information for me about Ally's death."

"Don't listen to him." Alyx said out of reflex, almost subconsciously. "We have a problem. Radford is here, he is after Lynn, and I can't find her."

"What?" Michael said.

"Radford is here."

"No, I heard that, but I think you just told me to *not* listen to the *one* man who is willing to tell me why my wife died."

"You are loosing sight of what is important. Lynn isn't here. We need to find her."

"I need to know what happened to my wife."

"You can't trust him okay. He isn't here to help you. I doubt he knows anything, he is just trying to get your trust, but he doesn't deserve it."

"You don't know him."

"No, but I know American behaviors, and customs. I also know my feelings. Do you know what his first name is?"

"No."

"He doesn't want you to know what his first name is. That means that he either has something to hide or it's not his real name. Don't give your full name because then you can google them, or in our case, run it through government databases. I have a feeling about it. We can't trust him. Can you please help me find Lynn and Radford?"

"There." Lyshiria said pointing through the crowd. "I just saw Radford over there. I think he is heading for the door."

Alyx slid into the crowd, quickly slicing across the Grand Hall toward the door. Alyx just barely caught sight of Lynn's Burgundy dress going out the open door. Alyx hurried through the rest of the crowd, but Radford and Lynn were too far ahead of her and the crowd was too thick. Alyx reached the door and ran out. She got outside just in time to see Radford get into a car, giving her a small wave, a sign of victory. They had played this game of plans, and he had won this stage. He had Lynn. Alyx ran after the car as it drove down the gravel driveway, but she had changed back into her heels and even her sprint was no match for the car's power. All she could do was watch as the tail lights faded into the darkness, taking her cousin with them.

23:49 BST (UTC +1)
Feilds Palace, London

Alyx sat on the Grand staircase, back in the blue shorts and white shirt she had been wearing after her shower. It was almost midnight, but she sat, chin in hands, elbows on knees, watching Stephan sweep the grand hall, without having any trouble staying awake. "Are you sure I can't help you?"

"I like my job too much," was Stephan's answer.

"I swear you have a hidden meaning behind that phrase. You use it all the time and no one can like a job so much that you won't accept help, especially since Michael doesn't care." Alyx complained.

"You should be in bed."

"I'm not tired." Alyx said, her voice low and monotone, muffled by her hand that she rested her cheeks on. Stephan knew what that tone meant. She was disappointed. Radford had beaten her, and she wasn't taking it well. She was not passing any of the responsibility of Lynn's disappearance onto anyone else. She was carrying the entire burden.

"It's not your fault." Stephan tried to reassure. Alyx rolled her eyes. Stephan went back to sweeping.

Alyx shot up at the sound of someone knocking on the door. She bounded down the stairs and sprinted across the foyer. Stephan dropped the broom and started to chase after Alyx, not about to let her do his job, *again*. Alyx pulled up on to her toes and pumped her arms faster, sprinting even faster. She slowed to a stop as she came to the door and opened it. Stephan hadn't planned his stop and came slamming to a stop behind Alyx, startling Lyshiria standing on the other side of the door.

"You two are friendly." Lyshiria commented, unwillingly remembering the moment she had witnessed a few hours before alongside the moment unfolding before her now.

Alyx shrugged. "We've known each other for, what is it, twelve years."

"Something like that." He answered in a non-committal way. Alyx let Lyshiria in, and Stephan jumped in to take her overnight bag. "I'll take this up to Alyx' room for you. Are you sure you didn't want your own room, we have four open guest rooms on the same floor I could make ready for you."

"It looks like you have enough to do, we will be fine. Thank you." Lyshiria thanked. Stephan took off with her stuff for the sleepover Alyx had arranged. Lyshiria waited until Stephan was gone before turning to Alyx. "Are you two dating?"

"What?!" Alyx coughed. "He is *five* years older than me."

"I won't tell anyone."

"We are *not* dating. He's like an older brother." Alyx corrected. "One very annoying older brother, I'll give you, but like an older brother." Alyx did an sort of shiver. "Ew, you though we were dating?"

Lyshiria laughed at Alyx. "You kind of were acting like it. I saw you tell him 'I love you too' earlier."

Alyx shook her head. "Again, he was being annoying. I was stopping him. He does this thing, where he tries to control what I'm doing by implying he will lose his job because of me, and it drives me nuts so my only recourse is to be annoying back. You would not believe how well it works." Alyx smiled a conspiratorial smile. "You on the other hand, are completely his type."

"His type?" Lyshiria asked confused.

Alyx nodded. "Blonde, foreign, and *completely* out of his league." She answered. "Come on, we need to start working on our plan to get Lynn back."

Lyshiria nodded, and they headed off.

June 18th, 2011

08:57 BST (UTC +1)
Feilds Palace, London

Lyshiria walked into the office where she and Alyx had been planning the night before. She was surprised to see Alyx staring at a computer screen. The idea had been that they were going to plan for a little bit, then go to bed. Lyshiria had dismissed herself around three in the morning, too tired to continue. Alyx had told her that she would be in her room shortly. It was now approaching nine, and Lyshiria had seen no sign that Alyx had ever been up to her room.

"Alyx, what are you still doing up?" Lyshiria asked.

"After you went to bed, I realized we were going about this the wrong way. We were trying to find Radford, putting together everything we know, but then what were we going to do? Michael nor MI6 will let us go on hunches, we need proof, and I need convincing evidence that only we can find them. Then I realized, in all the confusion last night, I forgot that Lynn was wearing her necklace. Only *I* have access to that feed. We have our evidence. Now all we have to do is talk to Michael." Alyx said, practically bouncing off the walls with excitement.

Lyshiria looked at Alyx. "After you get some sleep."

"I don't need sleep." Alyx argued. She left the room and went straight for Michael's office. Alyx knocked and peeked her head in. "Uncle, I need to talk to you."

Michael sighed. "Come in." Alyx opened the door and walked in, finding herself in a room with two well trained MI6 officers. "Alyx meet Tyson Barnes. Barnes is leading the team that is going in to arrest Rafael."

Barnes rolled his eyes, seemingly annoyed by the intrusion. "As I was saying, intel indicates that Rafael will be meeting for the exchange in Romney Marsh at a Lydd Airport. We know that he has access to a private plane, which is probably why he chose that location. We will have maybe 5 minutes to grab Lynn and arrest Rafael. If we mess up, he can be back in Russia before we can say 'I guess we mucked that up'."

"Lynn won't be there." Alyx blurted, she wasn't sure where it had come from, but she knew it was true.

"Alyx, these are the professionals, they know what they are doing."

"And I know my instincts. Radford is playing an angle. He won't take Lynn with him."

"So what are we supposed to do?" Michael asked.

"Wait a minute here, are we really going to let a teenager, the same teenager that mucked up this mission in the first place, create the plan to fix the mess?" Barnes argued. "I'm not going to stand for this."

Michael sighed, knowing that Barnes had a point. "Alyx, can you please let them worry about it?"

"I know I have no credibility, but please, I know I'm right. I don't care about your plan for Rafael, I just want to help Lynn. Let me go after her, and if she ends up in Romney Marsh, then I will back off and let your *professional* team take care of it." Alyx promised. "That was why I came in. I was up all night thinking about it, making my plan to rescue Lynn."

"At least she has dedication." Barnes mumbled.

Michael stared at Alyx. "Dedication comparable to Ally's." Michael let out a deep sigh. "Fine, but you are not going alone. I want Stephan with you. He will make all of your travel arrangements." Michael pressed a button on his phone and spoke. "Stephan, I need you in my office."

"There is another thing." Alyx started. "I would like it if Lyshiria could come with me. She has been helpful so far."

Stephan peeked his head in the door. "You wanted me sir."

Michael continued looking at his niece, studying her. "Yes, I need you to take Alyx and Lyshiria looking for Lynn. You will make all travel arrangements for them." Stephan nodded in understanding.

"Thank you Uncle," Alyx smiled.

"I am only giving you until next Saturday, the 25th."

"I understand." Alyx turned to leave. "I will go get ready."

"Alyx" Michael said. Alyx turned around in the doorway. "Be smart. Be safe. I can't lose you too."

"I will." Alyx turned again and walked off with Stephan.

"I can't believe you told her yes." Barnes criticized.

Michael stared at the door that Alyx had just left. "I had a choice, I could tell her yes and make her take Stephan, or she was going to go off on her own. She's stubborn that way. At least this way, Stephan can keep her in line."

Barnes shook his head. "I hope you know what you are doing."

"Alyx is good. If we hadn't set her up to fail, she would have succeeded. She almost did anyway."

10:42 BST (UTC +1)
White Rock Hotel, Hasting, UK

Lynn sat in the passenger seat of the black Jaguar. "So when are we meeting Rafael? That *is* what you are doing isn't it?" Lynn said annoyed.

"You talk too much." Hall turned the car right into the parking lot of a hotel in Hastings.

"And you don't talk enough, especially since you are Dylan Hall, not Nicholas Radford, and you just happen to be my—"

"You need to stop talking. You think you are such a good spy, yet I beat you at your own game."

"I left of my own accord." Lynn argued. "You didn't even knock me out."

"I'm regretting my choice right about now." Hall muttered.

"I can help you stop him you know." Lynn looked over at Hall. "Mum meant me for this."

"Yes, but she meant you for more than just this. I have this one covered." Hall parked the car and turned it off. "Right now, I have questions about Alyx."

Lynn crossed her arms and rolled her eyes. "She doesn't realize it but we all live in her shadow, don't we. I mean it was mum and Sarah first, but now it's Alyx. Their handpicked replacement. Even my own mother choose her over me."

"That's not what I'm talking about and it never happened. Your *mum* didn't choose Alyx as her replacement, *they* did. The enemy did, and your mother died trying to protect her, because, honestly, she is our only hope of defeating them."

"I've heard it all before, there is no need for me to hear it again. I'm just tired of being her shadow. Do you have any idea how hard it is to be her shadow?"

"Have you forgotten I've *tried?* At least you've been able to stay there."

Lynn grinned. "I play smarter, not harder."

"Get out of the car already."

  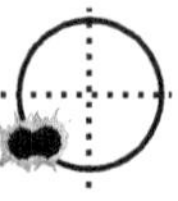

"Your enemy tells you to find Alyx McLean, and you say *hey, let me kidnap her cousin who's job it is to protect her?*" Lynn yelled. She stood across the bed in the hotel room that Hall had paid cash for an hour before.

Hall put his hands together in front of his body. "I haven't put her in any danger."

"Sure you haven't." Lynn rolled her eyes, and began walking away from Hall.

"Where are you going?" Hall asked her.

"I'm going back to Feilds Palace where I can do my job, and you better let me, otherwise I will begin to think that you did this intentionally, and I'll call you a traitor." Lynn went to storm out of the hotel room.

Hall pulled a tranq gun out of the bag he had next to him. He aimed it at Lynn and took three shots. She crumpled to the ground. "And here I was hoping I wouldn't have to use force. It doesn't matter because I *will* do what I need to."

June 19th, 2011

04:33 BST (UTC +1)
Go Sing Chinese Take Away, Lydd, UK

Hall walked out into the open. "Hall. There you are, I was afraid that something had gone wrong." Rafael stood up. "Where's that girl?"

It was still dark out, the breeze that blew out of the early morning was chilly. The parking lot of the small restaurant in the small town of Lydd was deserted, perfect for their early morning rendezvous. "Not here." Hall said.

Rafael smiled. "When will she be here."

Hall stepped forward his face lighting up under the pool of light he had stepped into, the light created by a small streetlight. "You really don't get it do you. She's not coming. She never was going to come. You were played, by everyone."

"Lyshiria will be bringing her soon. You backstabbing American."

"No she won't. She gave you up the minute she touched down in London."

"And you? When did you turn against me?"

"The moment you killed my sister."

Rafael stared at Hall. Suddenly his eyes glistened with recognition. "Hall. That was her last name before she married."

"Yes it was. You drove away everyone you loved. There is no escape for you." Hall pulled the gun from his waistband, the black metal glinting in the early morning light that had recently appeared. "Give it up Feilds."

Rafael frowned. "This all revolves around Ally Feilds death, doesn't it? That is when everyone turned against me."

"Michael would have tried to mend the relationship before that. Your irreparable mistake was killing someone everyone loved, killing the family member."

"What about Alyx? Didn't she—"

"How do you know about that?"

"A mutual friend sent me a video. Why are you protecting her? Isn't it a bit hypocritical?"

"*STOP* talking."

Rafael smiled. "I don't think I will. It's distracting you from taking me into your MI6 contact." Rafael took a step forward. "What would Michael think of her if I showed him the video?"

"WE AREN'T TALKING ABOUT ALYX" Hall yelled.

"I wonder if she even knows. That would be interesting if she found—"

Hall gripped the gun he was holding tighter, struggling to keep his finger from tightening on the trigger. "We removed her from that life to keep her safe. Don't you dare drag her back into it." He muttered, his anger still simmering. He took a deep breath, followed by another one.

Rafael put his hands up, a sadistic grin growing on his face. "Go ahead, arrest me. I will go to trial. It will be a very public trial, considering I killed Ally Feilds and conspired to kidnap Kate Feilds."

Hall squeezed a button on the grip of his gun, sending a signal to his phone in his pocket. "So you admit you did it?" Hall questioned, the anger constricting his voice.

Rafael laughed. "Of course I do. I hated Ally and the happiness that she shared with my younger brother in *my* house, *my* estate. So I killed her. I slipped poison into her water and then she died, but I couldn't do it soon enough. She gave birth to that *wretched* girl, so I asked my daughter to befriend her so we could kidnap her. I admit it all." Hall squeezed the button again. "None of it matters though, because you won't arrest me."

Hall let his grip on his gun slacken. "And why might that be?"

Rafael turned up one eyebrow. "Public trial means lots of witnesses. I will have quite an audience to tell all about Alyx." Hall let the muzzle of his gun drop, pointing it at the ground. Rafael got into his car, waving as he passed Hall.

Hall waited until Rafael was out of sight then pulled out his phone. He sent a quick message to accompany the audio clip. He got back into his car, putting his gun on the passenger seat. It was time to head back to Hastings. He had an uncooperative Lynn to deal with.

04:56 BST (UTC +1)
Lydd Airport, Lydd UK

That was number 20. He had gone 2 blocks, and it was the 20th Jaguar he had seen. He knew that the British loved their homemade cars, but this wasn't America. It *was not* normal to see that many Jags, like it was to see that many Fords in America. If he would have been in London, he wouldn't have thought anything about it. But he was in Lydd. There was no purpose for 20 MI6 issued Jaguars to be in Lydd. No purpose unless they were after him.

Rafael cursed under his breath. He had grown up in MI6. He knew all their small operating procedures, including the fact that Jaguar was the official car used by MI6, because his dad had implemented them. It didn't matter that his dad had kept them secret, because, after all, they were classified. He had grown up in a Palace with the MI6 director. You picked things up. And just because your dad was powerful, didn't mean you were perfectly behaved, you just learned how to get away with it. Like when he had learned how to break into his father's office while he was away to steal a passport and go see his girlfriend without getting caught.

Of course it would take his perfect little brother to figure out how he slipped in and out of the country after all these years. All he could hope was he could make it to his plane before MI6 could find him.

Rafael pulled into the airport parking lot and returned the car to the rental place, paying cash for the few hours he had used it. As he merged into the crowd of British travelers, he looked just like them. His blue jeans and tan sweater over a white dress shirt made him look like every other man in the airport, because as far as the people he was walking with knew, he was. He was raised in England. He *looked* like them. He *talked* like them. If he hadn't chosen to follow his heart to Russia, he *would have been them.*

He was still British at his core. No one saw it that way, but he was.

Suddenly his father's voice whispered through his memory. *"MI6 can have agents anywhere, do you know how you know if the person in front of you is one of them Rafael?"*

"No father? How do you?"

"If they are a good agent, you won't be able to, but if you are a good agent, you will just know."

The agents he was up against were good agents, but so was he. Rafael started picking the agents out of the crowd. The man with the tweed jacket. The woman with the red scarf. The young couple with the small luggage. They had no tells. He just *knew* they were spies.

And they were everywhere. There was no way he was going to be able to get on that plane. It made sense. Hall wouldn't have let him walk other wise. Hall would have shot him where he stood.

"Where's your boss?"Rafael yelled. All of a sudden, it was like the world stopped moving. "Is everyone in here MI6? Because that is the feeling I'm getting here, and I want to see your boss."

05:02 BST (UTC +1)
Lydd Airport, Lydd UK

"Is everyone in here MI6?" Barnes straightened from his perch behind his tech guys in their back office of the airport. "Because that is the feeling I'm getting here," Their live audio crackled from the computer speakers. "and I want to see your boss." Barnes stood frozen, carefully studying Rafael through the computer screen.

"Sir" one of his tech crew said, breaking his concentration. "What are your orders?"

Barnes looked at the agent. "Give me a status update."

"All of are agents are in place and ready to move on your order."

"And the audio clip that Hall sent us?"

Another agent removed his headset. "Full confession, for both crimes."

"Arrest him." Barnes ordered. The surveillance feed erupted in chaos as the agents surrounded Rafael. Barnes picked up his gun and put it in the holster he wore on his side, the gray t-shirt and jeans doing little to conceal it. He turned away from the computer screens, and walked for the door.

"Where are you going?" A panicked techie asked.

"He asked to see me."

When Barnes walked into the terminal, Rafael was already kneeling on the floor in handcuffs. "Ah, so it's Tyson Barnes running this operation. You always were hiding in my brother's shadow. Makes sense that he would have you on this."

Barnes laughed. "Your brother isn't my boss."

"That's right, it was my sister in law that had you wrapped around her little finger. Oh wait, she's dead and she still does."

Barnes face turned crimson in anger. "She was one hell of an agent."

Rafael put his hands forward gesturing to his cuffs. "You don't want to do this. McLean, Alyx McLean, she's not who you think she is. You arrest me and I will expose her."

Barnes folded his arms, looking right in Rafael's eyes. "And who might she be? Is she not the niece of Ally Feilds, the woman you killed? Because you can try to tell me that McLean isn't her niece but I wouldn't believe you. McLean looks *just like* Ally. And that's not the only thing that she has in common with her aunt. So please, tell me—what might I not know about her?"

"McLean is dangerous. She's not *any* teenage girl. She's not a force I would want to reckon with, but she's a force that must be stopped, before she stops the world."

"I think I would rather let her run wild." Barnes looked up and out the window into the morning. "Maybe she will catch more guys like you. I mean she's the one that got your daughter to turn on you." Barnes turned back to Rafael, observing the anger and disbelief his comments had elicited from Rafael. "You know, I learned my lesson with Ally. She too was described as a dangerous force to be reckoned with, and she was. I learned that it was better to work with her, because other wise, she would do the job anyway and make me look bad. You work with people like Ally and Alyx, and it makes you look good."

"McLean is more dangerous, more unpredictable than my brother's wife. You can't control her. There is no telling what disaster will follow in her wake. Ask Hall what disaster she has already caused. I don't think he wants anyone to know, he was spooked when I mentioned it to him." Barnes' face went white. "You don't know where Hall is do you? I'm not entirely sure, but for some reason, I think this entire thing was for Alyx. That American was pretty interested in her, and Alyx played an essential role in taking me down. It's a lure to draw her out, to expose her."

"Expose her as what?"

"A killer."

Barnes laughed. "She's a 16 year old girl. You expect me to believe that she would be capable of killing someone."

Rafael shrugged. "I guess we will see when my trial brings it to light and she's questioned about it."

Barnes looked Rafael in the eyes. "You're not going to expose anything in your trial. We have a recording of you confessing to your crimes." Rafael's face fell. "Oh yeah, I forgot, you can't bluff your way out when the other player has the winning hand."

"Tyson, think of the implications this could have if she really does have skeletons in her closet. McLean could bring Hell's fury down on your head." Rafael begged.

Barnes turned his back on Rafael, signaling his men to move Rafael. "I'm not connected to her. If she falls, she falls alone."

20:40 BST (UTC +1)
The Lansdown, Hastings

"I'll find her." Alyx said walking into the room. She had her phone to her ear as she looked over at Stephan and rolled her eyes. "Yes I understand Uncle." She paused and the others could barely hear the voice talking on the other end. "Thank you." Alyx made a gabbing gesture with her hand. Lyshiria saw it and choked back on a set of giggles. Stephan tried not to smile. "Did I not tell you. I know I shouldn't say I told you so, but…." Alyx bobbed her head from side to side. "I'm not cocky, just pleased that I was right and I desperately want to rub it in that obnoxious agent's face." Alyx rolled her eyes again. "Okay…. Yes…. I understand…. Bye."

Lyshiria looked at Alyx expectantly. "So" She drew the word out. "What did Michael say?"

Alyx smiled. "We have until the tenth of July, which is when they have scheduled your debriefing. Until then, we have free reign, as long as we are trying to find Lynn."

Stephan stood up and walked over to the door way. "So in other words, MI6 has no clue where Radford or Lynn are, and now it's up to us to find her." He turned and muttered into his hand. "I *hate* babysitting you McLean."

Alyx cocked her hip and folded her arms across her chest. "I am sixteen years old, I *do not* need you to babysit me. Make yourself useful, and maybe I won't ditch you the first chance I get."

"Definitely a brother-sister relationship." Lyshiria joked. "I was very wrong in my assumption"

Stephan narrowed his eyes, his body language screaming *what are you talking about*. He looked away from Lyshiria, back at Alyx. "Fine, I'll be useful, but how can I be useful when *we don't even know where we are going?*"

Alyx smiled again, looking at Lyshiria. "I think I like it when he doesn't know everything. I don't know, should I tell him? It would ruin what I have going for me."

"Might as well." Lyshiria shrugged, laying back on the couch of the hotel that Stephan had reserved for them. "I mean, he did pick out a great hotel to let us spy in luxury. He deserves just a tiny little treat." Lyshiria made a motion with her fingers, holding them maybe a centimeter apart in front of her right eye.

"Children, I am babysitting children. Please act your *bloody* age." Stephan complained.

"Lynn is in the hotel down the street." Alyx shrugged "Or at least she was the last time I checked and asked you to book this hotel."

"You know this how?"

Alyx pulled out her phone and opened an app. "GPS." She showed Stephan her screen, with a big red dot down the street from the green arrow that pointed at their current location. "Now all we have to do is go down the street and pull Lynn out."

Stephan stared at Alyx. "No. No way. There is no *bloody* way I am letting you walk down the street to knock on that maniac's door."

"Not your choice." Alyx sassed. "I'm in charge of this operation."

Stephan looked at Lyshiria. "Why is the youngest in charge? Who on earth would put the youngest in charge? I mean I'm twenty-one, and you're what? Eighteen? Nineteen?" Why is the sixteen-year-old telling us what to do."

"Michael put her in charge, something about being a genius." Lyshiria cocked her head to the side to say she didn't care. She herself *had* asked the same sixteen year old for help a week before. "And I'm eighteen *and a half.*"

Stephan rolled his eyes. "You are not going down there by yourself, you are not going down there with us, *we* are going to call MI6 and ask for an assault team." Stephan picked up his phone and dialed a number.

He looked Alyx right in the eyes as the other side answered his phone call. "Yes, my name is Stephan Cross, I work for Michael Fields." Stephan continued his call as he left the room.

"Aargh" Alyx threw her hands up in the air. "Always undermining me." Alyx stormed out of the room in the other direction.

Lyshiria shook her head with a crooked smile. "An American genius, a British servant, and a Russian spy in training. I would have thought that I was going to be the one to walk out on the other two. I think the friends have more problem than the foes." Lyshiria commented to herself. "This is going to be a fun three weeks."

June 20th, 2011

08:34 BST (UTC +1)
The Lansdown, Hastings

Lyshiria sat on the couch, flipping through a magazine she had bought from the Hotel lobby. Alyx and Stephan hadn't been in a room together since their fight the night before. Alyx was furious, Stephan was stubborn. Lyshiria had tried for hours to find some common ground between the two. She had gone between the two of them for hours to no avail. She had finally given up and went to reading this *pathetic* magazine.

Lyshiria looked up as she heard someone walk in the door. "I'm not playing the go between game anymore. If you have something to say to Alyx, tell her yourself." Lyshiria looked back down at the magazine.

"I would if I could find her." Lyshiria dropped the magazine and leaned forward. "Have you seen her? Do you know where she is?"

"The last time I saw her, she was in her room, but that was a few hours ago."

"Well, she's not there now."

"You don't think she would have—"

"I do. It's not the first time she's run off, not even the second or third. She does this sometimes, and I should have expected it. It would have been better for me to just listen to her, for us to go together." Stephan ran his hand through his hair. "Damn it Alyx."

"When is the MI6 moving in?"

Stephan let out a deep breath. "Not soon enough. For all we know, he could have already captured her, that is if he didn't kill her on sight."

"You like her, don't you?"

Stephan turned on Lyshiria. "What do you mean?"

"Your concern, it's not normal. It's the kind of concern people show for the people they love."

Stephan stared at Lyshiria. "Maybe I do love her, but if I do it's because she's my—" Stephan stopped suddenly. "She's *like* my sister. I have to be an older brother to *someone*."

Lyshiria rolled her eyes. "You know, us girls don't always need a brother or boyfriend to look out for us. Sometimes, the thing we really need is the friend, and from what I saw last night, Alyx was reaching out for the friend, and instead you acted as the brother."

"Fine, I admit it, I messed up last night, but right now, we need to do something. We need to stop Alyx so she won't get killed, if she hasn't already been."

Lyshiria laughed. "While I admire your chivalry, that isn't what she wants. Trust me, she has a plan, and when she needs us, she will let us know." Lyshiria stood up. "One thing you forgot, was that I choose to go to her, and that was because I could tell she already had a plan. She had a plan before we left London, before she even got permission to find Lynn. If you didn't notice that, you are either blind, or stupid, or both."

Stephan put his arms up, as if he was surrendering, turned around and left the room. Lyshiria picked the magazine up and continued reading. Lyshiria brushed her hair back behind her ear, where a small earpiece was hiding.

"Your plan better work McLean, because other wise, Cross might just kill me."

The earpiece crackled in her ear as Alyx' voice came through. "Trust me, it will." Lyshiria looked up at the door Stephan had just exited. "MI6 already messed this up once. They weren't even close. We may only have one lead, but it is one more than MI6, and I was the one to find it."

08:38 BST (UTC +1)
White Rock Hotel, Hastings

Alyx checked her phone, for probably the millionth time in the past few minutes. The green arrow was on top of the red dot. She looked at the door in front of her. This was it, this was the hotel room that Lynn was in. Now all she had to do was go in and fight Radford to free Lynn. Alyx half hoped that Stephan hadn't been so stubborn. It was going to be hard to beat Radford. She could have used his help, but he hadn't given her much of a choice.

Alyx slid her phone into the waistband of her running tights and then let the keycard she had stolen from the house keeping cart fall out of her long sleeve into her hand. She slid it into the card slot and pulled it out. The light on the door flashed green and Alyx quickly opened the door, silently sliding into the room. She bounced on the balls of her feet, ready to counter any attack that was made on her, or make one of her own if she saw him first, but the room was empty. There was not a sign in sight that Lynn had been there, but she knew that she had, because the red dot was almost right where she was standing.

Alyx looked down at the floor, and then she saw it. The beautiful silver loop with the six diamonds and the large amethyst at the bottom of the loop, with a smaller one below it. Alyx leaned over and picked it up. It was Lynn's necklace. She had been there. Alyx was just too late. Radford had found the necklace, moved Lynn, and left it behind. He was taunting her. He was playing a game. "I will find you." Alyx whispered. She activated the earpiece in her ear. "Hey Lyshiria, I need you and Stephan over here now. Its room 314. They're gone. We need to scour for any clues as to where they may have gone."

"Got it" Lyshiria responded. "We'll be there in a few minutes."

Alyx deactivated the transmitter and sat down on the nearest bed, the bed Lynn had sat on just a day before. She looked around the room, looking for places Lynn would have hidden clues. She checked behind pictures, the trash, under the mattresses, between furniture and the wall underneath drawers, the bottom of chairs and tables, all with out luck.

When she finished, she was standing by the door. Alyx looked at the room, realizing she had gone about it the wrong way. If Lynn was going to hide clues, then that meant she wanted to be found. If she wanted to be found, she was a captive, not a spy, and she was looking for the more subtle things. Everything needed to be checked again, scrutinized. It was going to take hours, if not days.

Or minutes if a person knew where to look.

By the time Stephan and Lyshiria knocked on the hotel door, Alyx had a devious smile. "Hey Stephan, how fast can you get us to France?"

12:58 BST (UTC +1)
The Lansdown, Hastings

"What were you thinking? What if he had still been there? Were you going to attack him by your self? You're acting like a *bloody* idiot, and I know you're not." Stephan scolded.

Alyx smiled, somehow liking the chastisement. Lyshiria watched from across their room dumbfounded that Alyx could be so flippant when being yelled at. "That's why you're going to take me to France, isn't it?"

Stephan shook his head. "Why would I? After the stunt you just pulled, I have half a mind to take you back to your uncle right now."

Alyx bubbled. "The other half of you says I'm a genius and Lynn's best bet of rescue."

Stephan stared at Alyx. He hated it when she did that. It was like she could read his mind. She always knew what he was thinking. Sometimes she seemed to know it before he knew it himself. He narrowed his eyes. "I have yet to see why we should go to France."

"Because that is where Lynn is."

"You were in that hotel room for what? Ten minutes? Lynn's necklace was in the hotel room, so I know you can't still be tracking her, so how do you know that Lynn is in France?"

"She told me."

"Lynn told you she was in France! What? Do you have a psychic connection with her now?"

"Yeah. I'm in your head too, you just don't ever let me talk to you." Alyx quipped. Stephan jerked back a little. "No, Stephan, I used hard detective work, and found a clue." Alyx pulled the piece of paper out of her waist band. "Lynn must have scribbled it on a piece of paper when Radford left for a potty break or something."

Lyshiria got up and came across the room to inspect the paper. It had three boxes with the letters *B*, *W*, and *R* in them. "How does that tell you that we need to go to France?" Lyshiria asked.

Alyx grabbed her laptop and typed a few words. "It's the french flag." Alyx spun her laptop around to show the other two a picture of a French flag. It had three rectangles running top to bottom, and the colors were blue, white, and red. "Blue White Red, B W R."

Stephan put his hand up. "Okay, so they were heading for France. Before we go to France, we need to know where in France they are going. It may not be as big as America, but it is still plenty big, and we need to narrow down the search radius."

"I think I can figure it out, but I'm going to need your help." Alyx looked between Stephan and Lyshiria. "Oh, and Stephan, I want to move our base of operations to Paris until we can narrow it down farther."

"Ooh. Paris sound nice. I've always wanted to go to Paris." Lyshiria agreed.

Stephan looked between the two girls. "Unbelievable."

Alyx shrugged. "I couldn't pass up an opportunity to go to Paris, besides, that is the most likely city he would go to. He is an American. It is probably one of the only cities in France he has ever heard about, besides Normandy, and I don't think Normandy is exactly the city a kidnapper would take his victim."

"Normandy is a region, not a city." Stephan corrected.

"And we don't really learn that as Americans. The only thing we are really taught is that on D-Day, the allies raided the beaches of Normandy."

Lyshiria laughed. "The allies. Maybe we should go to Normandy. As much as I want to go to Paris, it seems more fitting we go to Normandy."

Stephan shook his head. "I think we should stay here until we have a better idea of where they could be."

Alyx looked at Lyshiria. "No, I think Lyshiria is right. The last time an American, an Englishman, and a Russian were working together, it was World War Two, since then we've been in a cold war with the Russians, and relations right now are still icy at best. It seems almost scripted, the three of us going to one of the last places our ancestors fought side by side."

"So what? You want to start calling us 'the allies'? It's not as if we are going after a German." Stephan scoffed.

"We don't know *who* we are going after. I mean I met him as one person, he told me his name was something different. For all we know, *Nick* could be a German whose name is Dachs."

Alyx sighed. "I need to find out more about this guy, but my MI6 clearance doesn't let me."

Stephan smiled. "I can help you with that." He reached out for Alyx' laptop. "May I?"

16:39 BST (UTC +1)
The Lansdown, Hastings

Alyx stared dumbfounded at the computer screen. "This is the MI6 file. You have MI6 clearance? But not the informational clearance that Michael and I have, you have an agent's clearance like Lynn did."

"Don't act so surprised. I know you have suspected me for a few years." Stephan said. He stood behind Alyx, marveling his own handiwork as Alyx sat inspecting the MI6 file. "Besides, you know who your uncle is. A fair share of the staff are MI6."

"I may have suspected it, but that doesn't mean that I thought I was right. I like to create weird stories or explanations for certain people, but that doesn't mean that they are right." Stephan leaned down and put his hands on the back of the chair Alyx was sitting in to get a closer look at the computer screen. "For instance, there is this cute football player that was in my Algebra two class Freshman year that was *super* smart. He was the only one that had a higher grade than me in the class, and the French teacher said that he was like a different level than all the other kids, so I said that he must be a spy, and I have this whole story worked out for him, but he is probably just some brilliant kid, maybe like me."

"Yeah, he's a spy." Stephan said, distracted.

"What is it?" Lyshiria asked.

"It's probably nothing." Stephan mumbled, standing up. "I was just looking at the known aliases he has listed with MI6. I mean, Zachary Durham? That seems like a bit of a stretch doesn't it?"

"He has a pattern." Alyx blurted. "His Aliases follow a pattern." Alyx grabbed a pen and paper and started scribbling initials. *AE, BF,*

CG, DH, EI, FJ, GK, HL, IM, JN, KO, LP, MQ, NR, OS, PT, QU, RV, SW, TX, UY, VZ, WA, XB, YC, ZD. She circled the NR. "Nathan Radford." She circled the ZD. "Zachary Durham." She circled the PT. "Paul Tibbet." She circled the GK. "George Kidd." She looked up at Stephan. "He picks his names because they are 4 letters apart."

"That's crazy. How did you crack that?"

"I see patterns. Now, can you use your *wonderful* clearance and look for names fitting these initials going to France in the past 24 hours?"

Stephan sat down next to Alyx and moved her laptop over in front of him. "I guess I can try. After your hard work to create this comprehensive list, it would be a bloody shame to waste it." Alyx smiled. "It will take a while to write the search parameters and then to do the search, so why don't I go get us some food? When I get back we can eat, then you can go get some sleep while I work on it."

Alyx stood up and walked off to her room. Stephan looked at her list of initials, then grabbed his keys and got up.

22:35 BST (UTC +1)
Feilds Palace, London

Rafael sat in a dark room, tied to a chair. His eyes were closed, his instinct for using the dark room and the down time to his advantage, kicking in. They can't get in your head if you have your senses about you, and the best way to do that, is to rest every opportunity you get.

The door opened and Rafael's eyes shot open. He looked up to see his brother slide in the door. "So now they sent my brother in, to see if he could break me. Sorry to break it to you, but it won't work."

Michael nodded. "Our father taught us well." Rafael clenched his jaw. "But I don't think this is what he had in mind when he trained us. He didn't want us attacking each other. He wanted us working together."

"Well, that backfired when he gave you my half of his estate."

"You knew that was the deal when you left for Russia. You got your wife's estate in Moscow, I got the estate here in London."

"Yeah, well, I felt that deal was broken when agents started tailing my wife and my newborn baby."

"Dad never sent agents after you."

"Your wife said different."

"Is that why you killed her?"

"No, I killed her for other reasons. Reasons that you don't want to know." Rafael settled back in his chair. "I liked your wife, you know, she brought and odd sort of balance between our families."

"You mean until you killed her?"

Rafael rocked forward. "Ok, fine, I killed her, I already con-fessed, but it doesn't change the fact that she was an amazing person." Rafael bowed his head. "I really messed this up. Not to mention I drove away my daughter. Maybe it's better this way."

"Maybe you should look at it as you drove her towards a good friend. She went with Alyx to find my daughter."

Rafael looked up, a sincere pleading in his eyes. "Please, bring her back. Get her away from that girl. She's not safe if she's with McLean."

"I sent my best employee with them. There is no way that any harm will befall them."

"You don't get it, trouble does nothing but follow that McLean girl. People around her *die.*"

"That's funny coming from you."

"What can I say to convince you? Even if danger doesn't follow McLean, don't you think that sending an American, an Englishman and a Russian across international borders will raise flags."

"They're teenagers."

"Really, your employee is a teenager."

"No, but the girls are. And the girls are the ones that came up with the plan that kept you from getting Kate."

"I thought they were looking for Kate."

Michael smiled and knocked on the door. As the door opened Kate walked in. Rafael looked at the girl in front of him. "Michael, I don't understand. You said Lyshiria was with Alyx looking for Kate."

"I never said that they were looking for Kate. Kate never left the palace. I said they were looking for my daughter. You see, Ally was more stubborn than any of us thought. She wasn't going to go down with out a fight, and apparently that fight involved not telling anyone she was carrying twins. You see, I was recently reunited with Kate's younger sister, Lynn. Lynn has MI6 training. She was Ally's protection that you didn't come after us after she was dead."

"Well, apparently it worked." Rafael sighed, then looked down at the ground.

"Yeah, I'm just hoping that I didn't lose a daughter in the process."

"Hall never brought her to me. Talk to him."

Michael studied his brother. "I'm not done here. I will be back with more questions." Michael opened the door and escorted Kate out of the room.

"I know you will, and I think it's time you had some answers concerning your wife's death."

The door closed behind Michael, but he didn't move on. He was supposed to feel better seeing his brother locked up for what he did to his wife, but he didn't. All he could see were the games that he used to play with his brother in this basement.

"Dad are you ok?" Kate asked.

Michael looked up at the daughter that was becoming more and more like his late wife. He gave a sad smile. "Yeah. Let's go eat some thing."

"Ok." She said. Her eyes said that she didn't believe him, but just like her mother, she didn't push it. She took her father's arm and walked with him up the stairs into the secret room off the sitting room.

June 21st, 2011

06:20 BST (UTC +1)
The Lansdowne, Hastings

"It's probably nothing, Kate. It has to be hard on him, interrogating his own brother. He is probably just thinking about the time they were still friends and asking what went wrong." Alyx consoled. She had the phone sandwiched between her ear and her shoulder as she washed her hands. She rubbed her eyes trying to wake herself up. "No, I don't have anything new to report. Stephan was checking up on a lead we had last night when I went to bed, I haven't had a chance to check in with him yet. What about you? Did you hear anything interesting yesterday?" Alyx dried her hands then grabbed the phone with her hand. "I know you don't like to listen in on your dad, but ever since Lynn showed up, I get the feeling that there is something our parents never told us, and maybe your dad will mention it when talking to his brother. Even if I'm just being paranoid, whatever Rafael tells your father could help me find Lynn." Alyx leaned against the sink. "That *is* interesting." Alyx crossed one arm over her chest, wedging it under the elbow of the arm holding the phone up to her ear. "I promise I'll be careful, and I'll let you know what we find." Alyx stood up as someone knocked on the door. "Yeah. I've gotta go. Talk to you later." Alyx disconnected the call and stuck the phone in her pocket.

Alyx opened the door, finding Stephan leaning on the frame. "You're up early."

"Not really. Not early *enough* considering that every moment we waste, Lynn could be closer to death."

"So then I take it you would like to see what I found out looking at the passenger lists of all the forms of transportation heading to France."

Alyx nearly mowed Stephan down. "Of course I do!"

Stephan stuck his hand out, putting it on Alyx' shoulder to keep her at bay. "What were you talking to Kate about?"

"Are you really going to blackmail me?"

"Yes."

"She's concerned about her dad, and I wanted to ask her if there was anything they learned yesterday from Rafael that could help us."

"And."

"Rafael seems to think that someone is after us. He wanted Lyshiria back in London because it wasn't safe."

"I guess we need to watch our backs, and that means no more of you running off by yourself."

"I guess that means that you need to stop undermining me. And let me see what you found."

"Make me."

"July 3rd, 2008."

"You wouldn't dare."

"I would, now show me what you found."

Lyshiria walked up, studying the scene before her. "What happened on July 3rd three years ago?"

"Nothing" Stephan said too fast. "I was just going to show Alyx what I found when I searched the records. Care to join us?"

"It would be suspicious if you didn't let me."

Stephan turned away from Alyx, walking over to the table where her laptop sat. "So I ran those initials, and there were a few hits, but only one fit what we were looking for. We needed those initials paired with a female traveling companion.

"June 20th, an Adler Eckstein boarded a boat in Hastings. He bought two tickets, the second for his female daughter, who was listed as Lovisa Eckstein. I ran the name through the MI6 database, and guess what, it was a name that Lynn used for a mission to Germany. On the mission, her out was going to visit her father in France. Get this, her father for that mission was a cover with the name of Adler Eckstein, and MI6 bought a house in that name to fulfill her cover in France. Guess where that house is."

"Normandy?" Lyshiria asked.

"Yes. In the city of Évreux to be specific." Stephan held up a small piece of paper. Alyx snatched the paper from Stephan.

"Is this the address?"

"Yes, and I booked our hotel already. We leave this afternoon."

"The allies are ambushing the German in Normandy."

"Lynn must have known that Radford was taking her there using the German aliases and suspected that with the people involved in the original plan, I would make the connection and know where to look. Honestly, it was Lyshiria that made the connection. You really do make a good spy." Alyx complemented.

"I made it as a joke, you are the one that made the connection, and discovered the initials." Lyshiria folded her arms. "I'm just glad that I can be of any help, just being with you makes me feel like the ten minutes I was actually considering kidnapping Kate can be forgotten."

"It is."

Stephan looked between the girls. "We will only be able to save Lynn if we all work together. Last night was an example of that work." Stephan stared Alyx down. "No more doing things by yourself. You have people you can trust. Use them."

Alyx stared down at the ground. "I will." Alyx looked back up, meeting Stephan's eyes. "I promise."

12:25 CEST (UTC +2)
Rue Millet, Évreux Normandy France

Lynn pulled at the ropes restraining her wrists, the rope biting and tearing at her wrists in the process. "I won't tell you anything Hall." She called across the room.

Hall didn't even glance up from his laptop. "You will."

Lynn looked around the room. She knew the house. MI6 had bought it for a mission, and she had lived in it for 3 months in preparation for the mission. It had been hard to perfect her German accent, but eventually she did, and she was sent to Germany. When the mission was over, she came back here. She had stayed for 4 months that time, recovering from the shoulder injury she had sustained, and getting used to speaking in her British accent again. Undercover work was hard that way. Sometimes you are in a cover so long, you forget who you really are.

Lynn wondered what cover Hall was currently living, hoping that he would be the sensitive uncle, not the harsh father, or the hardened soldier. In reality, he could be any of those, or any selection of millions of others. It was a gamble she had to take.

"Would you mind loosening the ropes a little." She asked breaking the silence. "My wrists are raw and they hurt."

Hall smiled, still working on his laptop. "You should have thought about that before you started pulling at the ropes." Hall paused for a minute, stopping his work and twisting his face to say he knew exactly what she was doing. "Oh, wait. You did think about that. You were trying to fool me like you did the guy in Spa." He looked back down and went back to work.

Hall wasn't any of his covers. He was himself, the one and only Dylan Hall, one of the CIA's best agents. Unfortunately, he was always smarter than anyone gave him credit for.

"I suppose you won't let me go to the bathroom." Lynn tried.

"I'm not the idiot in Turkey."

"I need some water."

"Singapore."

"UNTIE ME YOU MONSTER!" She finally yelled. Hall looked back up.

"What comes next?"

"I don't know. Those four have always worked before."

"I will tell you what will work this time." Hall said. He closed his laptop and folded his hands on the table. "You tell me what I need to know about Alyx, and I will untie you, and let you leave."

"I'm not going to, *traitor.*"

Hall opened his laptop back up. "Have it your way."

Lynn rolled her eyes, but gave up. There wasn't going to be any tricking Hall into untying her. She was going to have to work on another plan.

June 23rd, 2011

17:16 CEST (UTC +2)
ibis budget Évreux Centre, Evreux France

Alyx paced in front of the array of computers they had set up on their hotel table in Evreux. "I don't understand why we can't just move in and stop that bas—"

"Alyx" Stephan warned.

"What? He kidnapped my cousin, *and* he's *taunting* me." Alyx huffed. She plopped herself down in a chair farther away from the computers than the others. "He thinks he's better than me just because he has 20 years on me."

"We have eyes and ears on him. You know that the smart thing to do is run surveillance on him for a while. We need to learn his patterns. Once we do that, we can move in when his pattern tells us we have the best chance of success. We want a plan that offers us low risk, and high success. That comes with preparation."

"That comes with time that we don't have. Besides, I may not be a spy, but I know that those two don't go together. It's an oxymoron. Now high risk, high success isn't." Stephan turned around, rolling his eyes at Alyx' stubbornness. Alyx picked up a tranq gun she had kept from the supplies they had for the Ball and cocked it. Stephan spun around. "Then again, maybe I need to just go in by myself again."

"*Seriously?* I thought we were past this *child*-like *foolishness*."

"That was before you came up with this *stupidity*."

"This isn't stupidity, this is what a *good spy* would do. You need to stop being such a *bloody* fool and use your brain. Stop following your hormones. You're smarter than that."

"You should stop being such a stuck up *pénible*—"

"I *know* you did *not* just use a french word so you wouldn't have to swear in English. What would your parents think?"

"Pénible is *not* a swear word."

"No, but if you would have said the equivalent in the English language you would have used one."

"BOTH OF YOU, *STOP. STOP NOW.*" Lyshiria yelled. Stephan and Alyx slipped into silence, turning to Lyshiria. "Stephan has a good plan, so we stick to it and Alyx, you *will* abide by it, or so help me, I will tie you up myself. Stephan, when Alyx thinks we need to move in, there will be no arguing with her. Any objections?"

"No." Alyx and Stephan mumbled.

"Good." Lyshiria turned back to the computer screens. "We should probably watch the feeds 24/7. We could set up shifts overnight to be fair, maybe 3 hour shifts?"

"That sounds good." Alyx conceded. "I'll take the first shift."

June 26th, 2011

12:37 CEST (UTC +2)
ibis budget Évreux Centre, Évreux France

The hotel Stephan had booked for them had been a nice one, but you couldn't tell looking at it now. Alyx had huge papers up all over the place. To Stephan and Lyshiria it looked like madness. There seemed to be no order to the chaos. Alyx was sitting in the middle of it when Stephan walked back into the hotel with food.

Her eyes had the same mix of desperation and calculation they displayed before he had left for food. He walked over to where Lyshiria sat in front of the computers. "Please tell me she took a break while I was gone."

"Nope." Lyshiria said, she glanced up from the computer to look Stephan in the eyes. "You know, with hind sight, maybe we should have just raided the house. At least maybe then she would have slept."

"It's been three days, how has she *not* passed out yet?"

"Do you see her?" Lyshiria asked, picking up one of the sandwiches that Stephan had gone out to get. "She is literally bouncing off walls." Lyshiria turned in her chair so she was facing Alyx. "She is more alert now than she was three days ago." Lyshiria illustrated her point by throwing the sandwich at Alyx, who was turned to the side. Her left hand shot up and caught the sandwich mid-flight, while her eyes remained trained on the posters. She didn't even blink. Her attention was completely on the posters as she unwrapped the sandwich and took a bite. Stephan shook his head and Lyshiria turned back to him. "She seems to gain energy the longer she's awake"

"That, it might seem, but psychology tells us that sleep is essential to our physical and mental well being. Everyone has their breaking point. I'm afraid of what hers will look like."

"You won't see it." Alyx said, her eyes still focused. "I'm studying psychology in my free time, and I happen to know that meditation can often provide the relaxation needed to maintain the homeostasis of the human mind and body, but it also lets me work through the problem at hand."

"Alyx, you are going to need some proper sleep. Meditation *is not* enough."

"Yeah, later." Alyx said. Her voice had taken an odd tone to it. She turned to the other two. "I think I found something." Alyx turned back to the posters. "I mean, it's a complex pattern and I may be wrong, and it doesn't tell us much about Radford, but I think that Lynn is trying to send us a message. I mean, we know from the audio we have, that Radford has a computer he has been using, but our visual is coming from outside the house, so we don't know what he's been doing. I've tried analyzing the pattern of his typing, but it's too hard to tell what he's been typing. I think that Lynn can see, and she is trying to tell us. Her handcuffed arm clinks aren't random. They come in groups. I think she is using morse code."

Stephan looked at the pattern Alyx was highlighting. "I know morse code, I think I would have noticed it."

"And so would Radford, that's why she spilt it up. Some words she completed over the course of an hour and a half, because then, until further analysis, the clicks would just seem random. The morse code started six hours ago. That must mean that starting six hours ago, Radford was making some preparation that Lynn thought we should know about."

"Do you know for sure that it is morse code?"

"Yes. So far, I've gotten *f-i-n-d-e-j-u-i-n*, but I'm not very good at morse code."

"Let me see." Stephan stepped in front of the posters. "Alyx, this is gibberish. I mean, the part that you already figured out is *find ejuin. Ejuin* isn't a word, at least not in any language I know."

"It's not English."

"You don't say."

"It's French."

"Sure it is. I think you need some sleep."

"No, seriously. It's not *find ejuin*, it's *fin de juin*. End of June. I thought you knew French."

Stephan rolled his eyes. "I didn't study it as extensively as you did." He stepped closer to Alyx. "I know a total of about 50 words, half of them numbers."

"Well, can you read out the letters the morse code translates into?"

"a-p-r-o-p-o-s-d-e-t-r-e-f-u-s-i-l-l-e"

"Lyshiria, did you turn off the feed on one of the bugs?"

"I see *d'être*, but that is the only french word I am recognizing."

"No, I haven't touched anything."

"*Apropos d'être fusille*. What does that even mean?."

A crazy look entered Alyx' eyes. "*Fusillé*. She was saying *À propos d'être fusillé*. About to be *shot*." Alyx turned to the computers. "And now Radford is killing our bugs. We don't have time to wait. We need to go *now*."

A sense of urgency entered Stephan and Lyshiria. Stephan picked up the keys he had dumped on the table with the food. "Let's go."

Alyx picked up a tranq gun and tucked it in the back of her pants and headed for the door.

13:27 CEST (UTC +2)
Rue Millet, Evereux France

Stephan pulled the car up in front of the house on Rue Millet. "All the bugs and cameras have been disabled." Lyshiria reported from the backseat.

"What is the plan?" Stephan asked Alyx. Alyx sat in the car staring out the window at the house.

"Save Lynn."

Stephan rolled his eyes. "Besides the obvious."

"You two should go in the back. I'll wait a minute to let you get around to the back, then I'll enter the front door."

Lyshiria leaned forward. "Do I have to go in?"

"We don't have eyes or ears, so yes. We don't know what we will be dealing with."

Stephan looked at Alyx. "We are there to back you up. Don't forget. You don't have to do this alone."

"Is anyone else concerned that we are about to perform an unsanctioned operation. If we are caught by the French police, we *will* be thrown in prison."

"Lynn is worth the risk." Alyx argued.

"We won't get caught." Stephan looked at the house. "The average police response time is ten minutes. So we have five."

"Understood" Alyx nodded. The comment was directed at her, and even though she had agreed, she was already trying to figure out ways she could push her limits.

13:29 CEST (UTC +2)
Rue Millet, Évreux France

Alyx pulled the pocket-knife-looking lock-pick-kit she carried with her out of her back pocket and evaluated the lock as she pulled the tension wrench out of its storage place in the housing of the picks, before unfolding the pick she decided she would need, and set to work on the front door. She heard the lock click long before her promised minute mark was up, but she opened the door anyway. She found the alarm system and disabled it. It wasn't even challenging. When she walked into the kitchen, she knew why.

Lynn was gone. So was Radford. She had known that was why Radford was killing the bugs. She had just allowed herself to hope that they could get there before he disappeared again.

Her hope evaporated at the sight of the empty house, taking her ability to breathe with it.

She barely heard the back door open. The room was a spinning blur. She saw everything, but it didn't mean anything. *She had failed. Again. Another point for team Radford.* "I have to beat him." She mumbled to her self.

The sound of feet creeping into the kitchen filled her ears with a ringing silence backing it up. She spun around and aimed her tranq gun at the body that had been creeping up behind her, but never got the chance to fire, because a strong hand pulled it away gently. "Alyx, they aren't here. We need to go before the cops show up."

"The cops aren't coming, I turned off the alarm." Her thoughts blurred. "MI6, 0646" She rambled. Stephan put a hand under arm. "MI6 safe house. We'll be safe here, and that way if he comes back, we can ambush him." Alyx' legs began to give out on her, but Stephan kept her standing up.

"I need to get her back to the hotel. Her sleep depravation is catching up to her."

"If we carry her into the hotel, questions will be raised. We should stay here, even if for just a little bit. That way we can see what we can find. Radford must have left *something* behind."

Stephan buckled a little bit as more of Alyx' weight fell on his arm. "Fine. I will check the security system, then I will go grab our stuff from the hotel and check out. We'll need it, I'm sure."

Alyx nearly fell to the floor as she finally fell into a deep sleep. As Stephan caught her, Lyshiria giggled. "May I suggest maybe finding a place to lay her down first." Stephan glared at Lyshiria, then picked Alyx up and carried her into one of the bedrooms.

As he left to get their stuff from the hotel, he gave Lyshiria a stern look. "If anything happens to her, I will make sure that you go down with your father."

"Oh, because it's *always* the Russian's fault?"

"No, because you are Rafael's daughter, and I never trusted you. I don't have the luxury Alyx thinks she does in choosing who to trust."

Lyshiria shrugged. Stephan closed the door, and Lyshiria sunk into a chair. She hated her father.

June 27th, 2011

09:42 CEST (UTC +2)
Rue Millet, Évreux France

Alyx rubbed her eyes as she walked into the Kitchen. She looked at Lyshiria and Stephan sitting at the table. She could feel the tension in the room before she even spoke. "How long was I out?"

"Well that depends on whether or not Lyshiria changed the clocks while I was asleep." Stephan mumbled. Lyshiria shot Stephan a dirty look. Alyx couldn't help thinking *if looks could kill.*

"You still don't trust her?" Alyx asked incredulously.

"He told me that if anything happened to you when he left to get the stuff from the hotel, he would hold me personally responsible."

Alyx looked at both of them. *Really?* "Can you two kiss already so I can go back to finding my cousin?" Lyshiria turned bright red.

Stephan looked indignant. "I don't trust her. Like father like daughter."

"Fine, but I am finding my cousin, and if you don't want me running off again, I would suggest that you work together to make that happen." Alyx walked closer to the table. Did you guys find anything in the spare moments where you weren't trying to kill each other with dirty looks?"

Stephan slid a paper off the table and handed it to Alyx. "Just this, the written version of Lynn's morse code message." Alyx quickly glanced at it, then set it down.

She walked out of the room back to her room, and returned a few minutes later in what a regular teenager wore everyday, what Alyx usually wore everyday. She walked right past the other two and towards the front door.

"Where are you going?" Stephan called. He jumped up and was on her heels in no time, grabbing her arm when she didn't answer."

"I need to go talk to the neighbor, and I am assuming that neither of you two did, because it seems that your French *sucks.*"

Stephan narrowed his eyes. "Not all of us can be *linguists*. I'm lucky I know Russian."

Alyx made a sad, almost pouty face. "Je suis vraiment désolé, mais ça m'est égal. Et il est neccessaire que je parle avec le voisin." Lyshiria grinned. "Et il ne comprend pas." Alyx turned to Lyshiria. "Will you please translate for him."

"You are assuming that I understood what you said, which I didn't. Not a word." Lyshiria raised her hands in surrender.

"Then you two can bond over your lack of French knowledge, and google it. I'll see you when you figure it out." Alyx turned toward the door and started walking out.

"Where are you going?" Stephan called after her.

"You'll figure it out once you figure out how to speak French."

10:13 CEST (UTC +2)
Rue Millet, Évreux France

Stephan looked up from the computer screen. "'But I don't care.' Why on earth did you not let me chase after her? She was just insulting me using her French."

"I thought you knew French. I mean, you knew what, oh what was the word she used?"

"Pénible?"

"Yeah, that was it. You understood that when Alyx used it."

"That's because Alyx uses it all the time on Kate, to her face, no less, because calling some one a pain in the arse in another language is less insulting. Only an American would think so."

"Well I didn't know that it was insulting."

"Alyx doesn't switch to a language that you don't know unless she is insulting you under her breath, or doesn't want you to know something."

"I see your point." Lyshiria looked down at the scribbles that Stephan had made just after Alyx left. "I don't think she was just insulting you the entire time. It sounded like she told us where she was going."

"I wouldn't have needed to translate this had you let me just follow her, *like I should have.*"

"She has a plan, I could see it, and it involves us arriving where ever she is going after she does. Just finish typing it into the translator." Lyshiria watched as Stephan finished typing the scribbles into the translator. Lyshiria read over Stephan's shoulder.

I'm very sorry, but I don't care. And I need to go talk to the neighbor. And he doesn't understand.

She looked down at Stephan. "Ok, I'm sorry. She really was just insulting you. She had already told us she was going to talk to the neighbor." Stephan rolled his eyes and stood up, walking toward the door, while Lyshiria stared at the words on the computer screen. "I thought she was better than that." She mumbled, clearly disappointed.

Stephan stopped by the door. "Are you coming?" He observed Lyshiria's dejected form and walked back over to her. He pointed to the words on the screen. "I know Alyx too, and this was not her usual put down. You were right, she has a plan. That plan involves us going out there right now."

Lyshiria got up and walked over to the door. Stephan smirked. Maybe she wasn't completely like her father.

Stephan followed, quickly reaching the door and opening it for Lyshiria. "Shall we see what Alyx is up to?"

10:10 CEST (UTC +2)
Rue Millet, Évreux France

"Excuse-moi" Alyx said to catch the attention of the neighbor that was out in the yard. "Je m'appelle Alyx. Je suis une touriste américaine. Cette maison est la propriété de mon oncle. Je lui ai parlé mardi et il m'a dit que je peux utiliser sa maison, mais j'ai pensé qu'il a vécu ici et j'ai pu visiter avec lui. Alors, je me demandais, savez-vous où allait mon oncle?"

"Your French is impeccable." The neighbor said in English, heavily accented by her French. "I am afraid you just missed your oncle. He and his daughter left yesterday. I think he left to take Lovisa back to school. She is not here often but he is all the time. He should be back in just a couple days."

"So he didn't tell you where he was going?"

"I'm afraid not. I don't think he spoke French. Lovisa does but I didn't get a chance to talk to her."

"Thank you for your help any way." Alyx turned as she heard the front door of the MI6 safe house open. "Well, it looks like my friends need me back. We are planning the next leg of our journey."

"Are you touring France or Europe as a whole?"

"Europe" Alyx answered. Stephan and Lyshiria stopped next to Alyx. "Thank you so much for your help, but we really need to figure out where to go next. It was nice talking to you."

"De rien." The neighbor smiled. Alyx turned and walked back towards the house closely followed by Stephan and Lyshiria.

"What the hell was that about?" Stephan cursed once they were back in the house. "We were supposed to be laying low. In case you didn't notice, we kind of broke into an MI6 safe house."

"He's been living here." Alyx blurted.

"What do you mean he's been living here?"

"The neighbor said he was here all the time. We need to search the house to see if we can find anything that can tell us about him. Maybe that can lead us to where he went."

Stephan sighed. He hated it when Alyx was right. She always made him look stupid.

11:26 CEST (UTC +1)
Rue Millet, Évreux France

Stephan, Alyx and Lyshiria met in the kitchen, as agreed, when they were done searching their parts of the house. Alyx came in last, and plopped down in a chair. "Nothing, I found *nothing*."

Lyshiria mumbled. "All I found was a movie we could watch." She slid a DVD onto the table.

Alyx gasped and started muttering in French. Stephan looked over at Lyshiria. "I forgot how much I hate French." Lyshiria gave him an odd look. "You try living in a house where the language is screamed at the top of your little sis—" Stephan stopped himself short. "I hate the language, ok." Stephan spun on Alyx. "What are you mumbling about?"

"Bring me the note, you know the written version of Lynn's message." Stephan rolled his eyes, but left to get the note. Alyx took the DVD out of the case and put it in the computer's disk drive.

"Are you really going to watch a movie? I thought we needed to find Lynn." Lyshiria criticized.

Alyx smiled, not answering the question. She fast forwarded though the movie as Stephan laid the scrap of paper on the table. Alyx paused the movie and grabbed the piece of paper, smiling again. "Just what I thought. Lynn, you clever spy."

"Will you please explain what is going on? I have lost my patience with your cryptic mumblings." Stephan crossed his arms, giving Alyx his best, get-on-with-it-slash-older-brother stare, which was pretty convincing. Lyshiria couldn't help but think that Stephan really had been an older brother to someone at one point in time. If she was reading him right, he had failed at protecting his little sister, and when he met Alyx, he had transferred his responsibility onto her, his redemption for the little sister he failed to protect.

Alyx gave him a devious smile. Lyshiria got the feeling that Alyx was exponentially more difficult to protect than the little sister he had failed to protect. Maybe that was why he had joined MI6.

"*Fin de Juin, à propos d'être fusillé.*" Alyx read.

"We know, we have seen that. End of June, about to be shot."

"Lynn wasn't saying that it was the end of the month, she was saying it was the end of a person. June is a name."

"You don't know that." Stephan criticized.

"But I do. In the French language, months and days of the week aren't capitalized like they are in English. Things like places, or *names of people* are. Lynn would know that, which means she intentionally capitalized June. Why else would she leave us a written copy of her message." Understanding dawned on Lyshiria's face, skepticism clouded Stephan's.

"Say you are right, who is this June that is about to be shot, and why is it important?"

A devious smile spread across Alyx' face. Lyshiria looked between the paused movie and the note Alyx was holding. "No way." Alyx nodded answering Lyshiria's disbelief. "Lynn used *Knight and Day* as the code for her message."

"Yep, and that means that Radford was taking Lynn to Austria."

"Are you telling me that you think that we need to go to Austria because this movie was in this house and it took place in Austria." Stephan pointed to the computer.

Alyx rolled her eyes. "Do you *ever* watch movies? *Knight and Day* did not take place in Austria. Well, maybe part of it did, but that's not why I say we need to go to Austria." Alyx un-paused the movie, letting it play from maybe 55 minutes in. "The name of the character who is played by Cameron Diaz is June." Alyx explained briefly.

Stephan watched the movie, shaking his head at the obliviousness of the character. "This is stupid, she had an army moving in, and she doesn't notice a thing. Why do you watch this stupidity?"

Alyx frowned, wanting to criticize Stephan, and tell him that it was a comedy, but instead she let it go. Afterall, he hadn't seen all of the movie, so he wouldn't know that. She waited until Diaz said *made in Austria*, then paused it again. "Make more sense now? June is about to be shot, by the afore mentioned army moving in on her, which we can assume would have been the end of her life, the *end of June*, and she says *made in Austria*. I know Lynn saw this movie, because I made Kate and Lynn watch it with me."

Stephan looked less skeptical, but needed more convincing. "Austria is a big country. We need a city, at least, before I can narrow it down to reasonable search area."

"Salzburg." Lyshiria blurted.

"Why *Salzburg?*" Stephan sounded exasperated. Inwardly, he couldn't believe how well Alyx and Lyshiria were working together. They were piecing together pieces of a puzzle that he didn't even know existed.

"When they do go to Austria in the movie, it's to Salzburg." Alyx shrugged. "Besides, from a spy's perspective, it would be perfect, he could make a quick escape into almost any of the countries around it. It is really close to the German border, and it wouldn't take long to go to Switzerland or Italy. I'm sure he could even escape into the Czech Republic or Slovenia. It's a spy's city."

Stephan hardened his stare as he contemplated what Alyx had said. She really was a precocious young woman, especially when it came to thinking like a spy. "Fine." He finally started. "We leave for Salzburg tomorrow." Lyshiria and Alyx started jumping up and down with excitement. "*But.*" That one word got them to stop. "I want both of you to do extensive research on Lynn and any history she may have with Salzburg, then see if you can find anything on Radford. I'm going to make our travel arrangements."

Alyx gave a devious smile. "I can do that. Why don't you challenge me?" She took the DVD out of the computer and left the room with it, Lyshiria closely following.

Stephan shook his head. How could anyone believe that Alyx was just a *normal* girl?

July 8th, 2011

18:28 CEST (UTC +2)
Salzburg, Austria

Lynn was hungry, cold and thirsty. Her head pounded with a headache from dehydration, and her tongue was scratchy. It was a deadly combination.

"May I please have some water?" She croaked.

Hall gestured to a large cup of water sitting in front of him. "This is yours." Lynn reached out to grab it and Hall pulled it back. "First, you need to tell me everything you know about Alyx."

Lynn flopped back and crossed her arms. She would have just run for it, but Hall had been smart and kept her tied up until she was weak. Now that she was, she knew she had two options: she could run for it and die from dehydration, or she could answer Hall's question and receive the water she desperately needed. She eyed the door as a hopelessness overcame her. "I'm not sure how what I tell you can help you. You already know almost everything I do. I caught you up just two months ago."

"Give me anything" the desperation in his eyes surpassed even *her* desperation for water, and she was massively dehydrated.

Lynn studied Hall. For the past few days she had been treating him like the enemy but the small emotions he let slip through told her he really was trying to help. "I haven't noticed anything but I know that the Promising Generation is stationed near her. She is friends with your children at school, and she seems to trust your son."

Hall pushed the glass of water towards Lynn. Lynn grabbed it and took a big gulp. "We leave for London tomorrow. I promised your dad I would have you back in time to help him get any last minute confessions out of your uncle before he is turned over to the judicial system." Lynn set the empty cup back on the table and Hall got up to refill it. He came back and set a full glass on the table. "After next Saturday, you can live the life you were born into." Lynn nodded.

A knock came at the door, interrupting their conversation. As Hall left to get the door, his hand resting on the gun in the holster in his waistband, Lynn picked up the glass of water. Hall opened the door, and was met by a well placed blow to his head. He crumpled to the ground before he even had the chance to pull his gun.

20:00 BST (UTC +1)
MI6 Headquarters, London

Barnes paced his office and glanced at his watch again. Hall was two hours late for his call in. Something was wrong. Halls *did not* miss call ins. They were always perfectly on time, and Dylan was no different.

Barnes picked up the phone, unable to wait any longer. He was supposed to wait until an operative missed two call ins to take action, but this was a Hall, and this Hall happened to have the daughter of Feilds. Michael needed to know, and maybe if he called Michael, Michael would be able to calm his nerves. Maybe Alyx had caught him, which meant she was much better than he had given her credit for, and that was the reason that he had missed the call in.

Either way, he needed to make the call. It was just one part of the many unfavorable tasks his position gave him. He wanted to be in the field making the call ins, not be the one receiving, or in this case, not receiving call ins. He hadn't had much choice in the promotion. He had made a promise to Ally that he would be the one to train and watch her daughter and the only way he could keep that promise was to take the awful desk job.

Barnes entered the last number of Michael's phone number and hit the green call button. In a few minutes, his job could be gone though, if he had messed up and let Lynn disappear. Michael may not have been his boss, since technically they were equals, but Michael held more power in the MI6. After all, he was his father's son. Michael could make sure that Barnes was cleared out of his office by the end of the day.

"Feilds estate." A female voice answered the phone. "How may I help you."

"I need to talk to Michael Feilds. Will you please connect him to me?"

"I am afraid Lord Feilds is busy and requested that all calls for him to be held," the woman informed him. "I can take a message for you"

Barnes closed his eyes. "No, this takes precedence. Find Michael and tell him that Tyson Barnes is on the phone and needs to talk to him. Tell him it's about Hall and his daughter Lynn."

"Hold a minute please." The phone clicked and music began to play. Barnes sighed. He hoped it wasn't as bad as he thought. Then again, the last time a Hall had missed a call in, they had been seriously injured, and ended up dying.

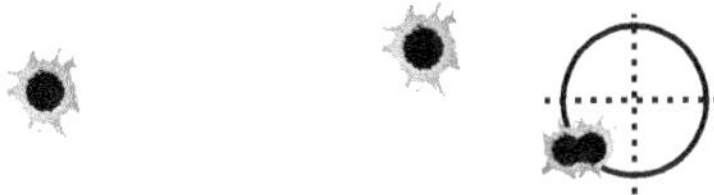

Michael sat across the table from Rafael. The two of them stared daggers at each other. "You obviously want to know *something* Michael. Why don't you just come out and ask it? Stop playing this silly game." Rafael was getting tired of the silence, he could feel his brother judging him. He would have preferred it if Michael just came out and said what he was thinking. "You always did act like you were better than me, you acted like you were perfectly obedient, but in truth you have done all the same things did. You figured out how I snuck into and out of the country because you did the same thing to go visit Ally in California. You are just as much of trouble maker as I am, but you always got away with it. I dare you, say you're better than me."

Michael fumed. "You killed my wife. My *wife*, Rafael."

Rafael studied his younger brother. He had no clue what kind of life his wife had been living before she died. "Did you know that your wife never gave up spying?"

Michael narrowed his eyes, not appreciating the change of subject, a counter interrogation technique that their father had taught them, but he played along. "She was a spy, that's not something you can change, so yes, I knew. She was working closely with Barnes. He got a promotion out of it."

"If you think that your wife was working *for* MI6, you are sadly mistaken. Something I know from leaving and going to Russia, when you live in a country like America or Britain, you *never* really abandon it."

"Then what do you think my wife was doing? Spying on Britain for America? We are allies, Rafael, not enemies, not like Britain and Russia were, and arguably, still are."

"She was using her position to protect her family. Think about it. You told me that Lynn was sent to MI6 to protect you from me, but we weren't fighting until *after* Ally died. Lynn has another purpose. Whether she knows it or not." Rafael paused, trying to read his brother. "You know where Ally came from. She was a spy. She thrived on secrecy. The twin. MI6. CIA. There were probably so many layers to her secrets, we haven't even scratched the surface."

"Why did you kill her? For her secrets?"

A deep sorrow entered Rafael's eyes. "I didn't want to—" Rafael cut off abruptly as the door to the interrogation room was opened.

Kate poked her head in the door. "Father, can I talk to you for a minute?"

"I'm afraid I am in the middle of something." Michael said, staring at his brother who had just almost told him why he had killed Ally.

"Michael," Rafael started, "I lost my daughter by putting her off when she asked to talk to me. I will still be here when you come back. What good will answers do if you don't have the daughter that your wife loved enough to sacrifice her life."

Michael clenched his jaw, but stood up and walked out the door with his daughter. "What is it?"

Kate was pale as she clenched a piece of paper. She unfolded it. "Tyson Barnes called, he wants to talk to you. He said that it was about Hall and Lynn, whatever that means."

All color left Michael's face. "Bloody hell."

His brother could wait.

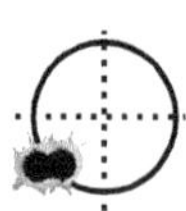

"I know that we aren't supposed to do anything about it until he misses a second call in but—"

"Dylan doesn't miss call ins." Michael finished. He sat in his office using the secure line to talk to Barnes.

"Exactly. That's why I called. There is something seriously wrong."

"And you haven't heard anything from Lynn either."

"No. I was hopeful that you had heard from Alyx though."

"I haven't talked to her since just after you captured Rafael. You don't think she *actually* found him do you?"

"I hope it's her and not someone else." Barnes paused. "Rafael sounded crazy babbling about the American that told him Alyx was a threat to our way of life, but maybe there really was an American and he caught up to Hall."

"Who are we dealing with?"

"The Hall family has a good network of enemies."

"Circle of Fifths?" Michael asked.

"It is a possibility."

"Rafael was just insinuating that my wife's family had enemies. Maybe the enemies my brother knows about are the same ones after Dylan now."

"It might be worth a shot. Do you think he will tell you about them?"

"Maybe, he was starting to open up to me about Ally when you called."

"Good. Ask him. See what he tells you. Meanwhile, I will try to track down Hall by checking his last known location. Can you also check in with Alyx, see if she has anything? If you can do it in a discreet way so she doesn't know anything is wrong that would be ideal."

"I'll have Kate do it. Check back in a few hours, and I'll tell you what I found."

"I will call in four hours."

Michael checked his watch, making a mental note of the time. "Okay. I'll be expecting it." Michael got off the phone and paged Kate. The real search began now.

July 9th, 2011

00:14 CEST (UTC +2)
Salzburg, Austria

Hall woke up with a pounding head ache. He moved to grab his gun but felt the bite of ropes on his wrists instead. "Lynn this really isn't funny. Untie me now."

A cold laugh sent shivers down Hall's spine. Not Lynn, that was not Lynn. It was the same voice who had called him, asking him to look for Alyx. "Oh, I'm sure Lynn would love to help you, but you see, she is a bit tied up at the moment, oh and that pun was entirely intentional." A man walked around so he was facing Hall. "The great Dylan Hall, so easily defeated. You know I'm disappointed, I was hoping for more of a challenge. Then again, I set a glorious trap and baited it with something so precious. You never really stood a chance against me."

Hall let his murderous rage slip through into his eyes. "Trap?"

The man in front of him laughed again and Hall's blood froze in his veins. "Ah yes. You throw the name Alyx McLean out there and you are bound to have a Hall come out of hiding to protect her." The man shrugged his shoulders. "If my predictions are correct, McLean will be the end of the Hall dynasty and its power." He stopped laughing. "Well, that is as long as she is a tool in our arsenal. If she's not, then I'm afraid she is a tool no one else can have."

"So you already told me what you were after, are you going to further your mistake and tell me who you are and who you work for, so when I escape I can ruin your dastardly plans and then come after you to obtain justice?" Hall deflected the utter despair of failing into sarcasm.

The man laughed again, making Hall's hairs stand on edge. "You *know* who I work for, but sure, I'll tell you my name, but not because I don't think you will escape, but because I want you to know that whatever happens after this, happens in my name, and you can do nothing about it." The man smiled. "Phil Jackson, and I will be kidnapping Lynn from you. Kidnapping the kidnapped from the kidnapper. Untraceable."

Jackson turned and left the room. Hall cursed.

He heard Lynn grunt behind him. "What was the claim you made about not putting Alyx in any danger?"

"The better question is how Jackson found us in the first place. You don't have another tracker on you, do you?"

"No, you took the necklace off in Hastings, so basically, we're dead." Lynn criticized.

"I've been leaving hints behind for Alyx. That's where the bugs in France came from. It was Alyx." Hall admitted.

"So not only are we doomed, but you are leading Alyx right to the man who wants her dead." Lynn hissed. "Bloody brilliant plan Hall."

Jackson reentered the room and the two of them stopped talking. Jackson pulled Lynn up and dragged her out of the room. "Thanks for the present." He called.

Hall began working on a plan as he tried to slip his bonds. If Alyx had figured out his last clue, and he suspected she had based on the call he'd gotten from the neighbor at the house in Évreux, he predicted she would be here within the hour.

Why did he always have to achieve the impossible?

Hall still didn't know what he could do to find Lynn when he escaped. He was out of the ropes in 5 minutes, and he could have slipped them sooner had Jackson not taken the knife he had hidden in the back of his jacket. *How Jackson had found that particular knife he had no clue.* Hall was getting ready to slip out the door in the kitchen when something bright orange caught his eye. He turned and saw a post-it on the fridge. *That was not there earlier.*

Hall walked over and plucked it off the fridge.

CALL ME CONFIDENT
AND BOASTFUL,
BUT I'M STAYING IN
AUSTRIA.
-P. JACKSON
P.S. THE BUNDESPOLIZEI
RECIEVED A TIP THAT
DYLAN HALL WAS
RESPONSIBLE FOR
OCTOBER 2005.

"Damn." Hall cursed. He looked at the time. He had half an hour before he estimated Alyx would arrive, and he could only hope the police didn't catch Alyx when they showed up. He needed to get out of this country, *fast*.

That meant he had to leave it to Alyx to find her cousin. She could do it, he just didn't know if he wanted her to. He stuck the post-it in his pocket and found the pad the note had been written on. He scribbled a quick note, then disappeared out the door. He was in Germany before a half an hour had passed.

01:17 CEST (UTC +2)
Salzburg, Austria

Stephan watched over Alyx' shoulder as she picked the lock. "Where did you learn how to do that? And don't tell me Lynn taught you, because I'm not an idiot, and happen to know that the skill you are showing is that of an expert."

The locked clicked as it opened and Alyx smiled. "Sometimes I lock myself out of my room, or the house." She opened the door and made a gesture for Stephan to enter. "It kind of just came naturally. Oh and I practice a lot. One time my dad caught me practicing on the garage door, so he bought me a lock kit that you can change the key on so I could practice in my room, probably so the neighbors wouldn't see me."

Stephan rolled his eyes. "Your parents didn't care?"

"They tried to tell me to stop, but gave up. It came in handy the time we all got locked out of the house, so I think they decided as long as I wasn't breaking into houses, I was ok."

Stephan walked into the house with his gun in his hands and began methodically checking the house. He decided not to mention the fact that technically she *was* in fact breaking into houses now. At least she wasn't climbing through the window of an enemy safe-house unarmed. "It looks like he has cleared out already."

"Well, we know he was just here because there is residual heat left in the house." Lyshiria informed them over coms. "And why I got stuck in the van with the computers I will never know."

"One of us had to, and you wanted to stay in the car in France." Alyx rationalized. Stephan rolled his eyes. "And I needed to pick the lock."

"You *wanted* to pick the lock. I'm MI6. I could have picked the lock."

Alyx brushed the comment off. "Well, if he just left, he must have left in a hurry, which means he could have made a mistake." Stephan stuck his gun in the back of his pants. "Let's fan out and see what we find."

Stephan walked back to the bedrooms while Alyx checked the living room. She tore the cushions off the couch and checked in the cracks, under the couch and anywhere something could have slipped through a crack, literally. As she was getting ready to move onto the kitchen, Stephan came through the coms. "Alyx, you may want to see this."

Alyx slipped through the hall and entered the bedroom. "What's up."

"Two chairs, two sets of ropes." Stephan turned to Alyx. "Lynn wasn't the only hostage here."

"But she was everywhere else." Alyx mumbled. Stephan watched as she fell into one of her trances. She kneeled down as she inspected the ropes. She puttered around as she mumbled things to herself. Stephan knew she was silently memorizing every detail of the situation, her photographic memory making it effortless. "Who was the second hostage? Was it someone else Radford kidnapped, or…"

"I don't know, but maybe it has something to do with him leaving in a hurry." Stephan answered, even though he was pretty sure that her question was rhetorical.

Alyx continued to stare at the scene in silence, and Stephan didn't try to get her to talk.

The silence broke when Lyshiria came on coms. "I hear sirens. Did you set off a silent alarm?"

Alyx looked up at Stephan. "No, I hacked all of that before we even walked up to the front door." Stephan looked embarrassed. "Are you sure that they are headed here?"

"The translation showing up on my screen from the police scanner you two hacked says that they are headed to your current location." Alyx watched as Stephan silently cursed. "You two might want to start getting out of there. I give them two minutes tops before they break that door down."

"Do you have everything you need?" Stephan asked Alyx. She nodded. "Good let's go."

Alyx left first, walking towards the front door, Stephan on her heels. Suddenly she stopped and spun around. Stephan had to cut his stride short to keep from running into her. Her eyes took on a wide, concerned look. "I never checked the kitchen." She went to walk past him, but he stuck his hand up and stopped her.

"Forget it. We don't have time. Police will be here anytime."

"I *have* to check the kitchen." She pushed her way past.

Stephan silently considered which was worse, enemy spies, or the police. He didn't like the sound of either. "Lyshiria, pull around to the street behind the house. We are going to be taking the back way." Stephan followed Alyx into the kitchen. "We don't have much time, so search quickly." He turned to the opposite side of the kitchen and began opening cupboard doors and drawers.

"Look, there is a note on this pad of sticky notes." Alyx said. "If only I could figure it out—"

Stephan raced over and grabbed the pad of sticky notes and shoved it in his pocket. "You can figure it out later, now let's go."

Alyx stuck her tongue out at Stephan but headed for the back door. She and Stephan raced across the back yard and scaled the fence. Luckily they found the back yard of the house behind empty and they made their escape through the yard unnoticed.

Stephan pulled the door closed on the van and Lyshiria drove off mere seconds before the Austrian police raided the house.

09:37 CEST (UTC +2)
Salzburg, Austria

I'm a spy, but on your side. What the hell was that supposed to mean?

Alyx had been staring at the note for hours now. Stephan and Lyshiria had gone out to see what they could find out about the raid they had almost been caught in earlier, and had left Alyx behind at the hotel. Alyx had no doubt that part of it had to do with Stephan trying to keep her where she was more easily controlled. There was no hiding his contempt for her decision to check the kitchen.

Sure, he *had* claimed that someone needed to keep an eye on things at the hotel, *and* that she could use the time to figure out the note, but she could see the underlying message. *If I take you out with me, then I can't control you, and if I can't control you, I can't protect you.*

She didn't need to be protected, but try explaining that one to Stephan. It was impossible.

"I give up. It's gibberish." She said to herself, throwing the note pad down on the table and folding her arms. She could speak multiple languages, and she couldn't figure out what one note, written in her 1st language, meant.

I'm a spy, but on your side — D Hall

That was it. Just a short cryptic note. Alyx stared at the pad on the table. It was like it was mocking her. Radford was mocking her. It was a stupid lyric from a stupid song. Ok so it wasn't stupid, but she was annoyed that all she had found in the house was a sticky note with one line from the song *Private Eyes*. She had figured out that was what it was early on. Radford had even given the name of one of the members of the band. Hall and Oats. Daryl Hall and John Oats. D Hall.

Alyx cocked her head as she looked at the *D Hall*. The movement caused the light bouncing off the paper to throw a shadow across something she hadn't seen before. She picked the pad back up and ran her finger over the paper. There were impressions left in the paper from whatever note had been written on top of it. Alyx ran the paper through the copy machine quickly to preserve the notes he had been studying then gently colored over the sticky note to read the impression.

"*Bingo*" Alyx whispered.

Alyx looked at the new note. Well, *that* answered a few questions. There was a third player in this game. He probably kidnapped Lynn from Radford. Alyx stopped as she read the bottom of the note.

Dylan Hall. D Hall. DH.

Alyx rummaged around a stack of papers they had in a folder by the computer. She found the paper she was looking for and quickly scanned the page. *DH.* Just like she thought. The same pattern she had discovered when she had cracked the Radford alias.

He hadn't been telling her who the song was by, he was telling her his real name. For some reason, he wanted her to know he was on her side, *although that was yet to be seen*, and the impression was the answer Stephan was currently trying to find.

She was still mad that Stephan had left her at the hotel, but this almost made it worth it. *Almost.*

09:49 CEST (UTC +2)
Salzburg, Austria

Lyshiria looked over at Stephan as he was driving. "Was it really necessary to leave Alyx. She would probably be of more use to you than I will."

Stephan gave a small half smile. "You aren't as useless as you would like us all to believe." He quickly caught himself and suppressed his smile. "And her time is better spent trying to figure out that message."

"You realize she is pissed right?"

"Don't care." Stephan parked the car and looked down the street at where the police cars were still parked in front of the house. "I don't know what happened, but this is more police than they would send to a regular break in."

"Do you think that they figured out that there was a kidnapper using the house?"

"I hate to say it, but I'm afraid that there is even more here than they would typically use for that."

Lyshiria looked down the street. "*What* did we get ourselves into?"

"I don't know." Stephan admitted. He looked down as his phone rang. He hit a button on the steering wheel. "This is Cross." Stephan answered.

"Stephan, thank heaven. Please tell me you are with Alyx." Kate's voice sounded tinny as it came through the car speakers.

"No, I left her at the hotel while Lyshiria and I went out to check something. Why?"

"She's not answering her phone. Hopefully you can answer my question though. You guys haven't found Lynn yet have you?"

"No." Stephan admitted. "He keeps getting away right before we get there."

"Oh." Kate's disappointment echoed through the car. "Well, my dad told me to call and remind you that he wants you guys back in London tomorrow."

"Thanks for the reminder." Stephan replied. He picked his phone up out of the center console as he received a text message. "I will make arrangements to come home tonight. Alyx won't be happy." He finished distracted.

"It sounds like MI6 is already taking on the search. Lynn should be home shortly after you guys. I hope." Kate tried to sound optimistic but failed. Stephan looked over at Lyshiria and saw the same skepticism he had. As much as he hated to admit it, Alyx had gotten them much closer to finding Lynn than MI6 could have.

"Kate, I don't mean to crush your hopes, but it has been three weeks—" Stephan stopped as he saw Lyshiria frantically trying to get his attention. *What?* He mouthed to her. She pointed out his window, down the street at where two policemen stood looking at them.

"Bloody Hell." Stephan blurted.

"What?" Kate's concern caused her voice to raise an octave.

"Nothing." Stephan lied. He started the car back up and started to drive away. "Hey Kate, I have to go, but I will have Alyx call you."

"Okay?"

Stephan disconnected the line. "Call Alyx." He told the car. He turned to Lyshiria as he dug a card out of his pocket. "Use your phone and book us tickets to London, within the hour. We need to leave the country."

Lyshiria started typing stuff into her phone as Stephan stuck his foot to the floor. Lyshiria squealed as she was thrown back into her seat. Stephan accelerated again as Alyx' phone went through to voicemail. He knew she wasn't asleep because he had left her with the note to figure out, and it wasn't like her to not answer her phone. Something wasn't right.

10:03 CEST (UTC +2)
Salzburg, Austria

Stephan barged through the door of the hotel and saw Alyx sitting on the couch staring at the TV. "Hey Stephan." She greeted.

Stephan fumed. "You sent me to voicemail ten times, making me think something was seriously wrong, and all you can say is *Hey Stephan*? Why the hell did you not answer your bloody phone?"

"I was mad at you. I decided if you wanted to protect me so bad, I would let you worry. Call it pay back for leaving me behind." Alyx sassed. Lyshiria raised her eyebrows. There was no denying that not answering her phone could be described as nothing less than petty, but there was something oddly effective in the decision to not answer her phone—she'd made Stephan worry, and pissed him off at the same time. Alyx was *quite* vindictive.

If this is what Alyx did for something as small as Stephan leaving her at home, Lyshiria would hate to see what Alyx would do when she finally found Radford.

"Then why did Kate call me concerned because you hadn't answered her phone when she had called you?"

"Michael is using her to keep track of what we are doing. Oh, and if I would have answered the phone, she would have reminded me that we are supposed to be back in London tomorrow, and I couldn't keep looking for Lynn." Lyshiria coughed. "You didn't" Alyx gasped.

"We need to leave the country before the police figure out that we were in the house that is currently swarming with law enforcement." Stephan said.

"Lynn is still in Austria." Alyx argued.

"You don't know that."

"I figured out the note, so yeah, I do."

"We couldn't figure out what the police know, and they seemed very interested in us when we went back. We aren't safe." Stephan insisted.

"Yes we are. They are after a man named Dylan Hall for something he did in October of 2005. Dylan Hall, or D Hall, DH, is the man we have been chasing, but his note tells us he is on our side, and whoever told the police that Dylan Hall is the one responsible for the October 2005 events, has Lynn and is staying in Austria because he knows that Hall can't go after him. We are the only ones who can find Lynn, and it seems it is more important than ever."

"The police were looking for a terrorist, that was what got that response out of them." Stephan mumbled.

Lyshiria looked horrified. "Dylan Hall. So you mean that the name my father knew him by was his *real* name?"

"I know Dylan Hall, at least the name. Hall is the last name of a family of legendary American Spies. Then again, it is called a legend for a reason. Anyway, Michael knows him. I've seen the name on the guest list for Feilds Ball."

"Lynn was never in danger. We've been chasing tails, probably so they could keep us out of the palace while they interrogated Rafael." Lyshiria concluded. It was weird to hear her call her own father by his first name, but no one said anything about it.

"But now she is, because Hall doesn't have her anymore, his enemy does, and this time, an enemy of an enemy *is not* a friend."

"Because Hall isn't our enemy. He is on our side."

Lyshiria and Alyx both turned to Stephan, silently begging him to let them stay and look for Lynn. "You better pack. Our flight leaves soon."

July 10th, 2011

13:43 BST (UTC +1)
Feilds Palace

Alyx ignored the other two the entire flight back, and her wrath didn't end there. As soon as they landed, Lyshiria was whisked off for debriefing, leaving Alyx and Stephan in the car alone. He had hoped to talk to her, explain why he had made them leave, but as soon as she got in the car, her headphones went in and her music was cranked way up. He wanted to grab her arm and tell her it was for her own safety, or to tell her he liked his job, but their relationship had evolved since then. This trip had shown each of them what they and the others were truly capable of.

Alyx was capable of much more than Stephan had initially thought. In reality, she had carried the rest of them. She was good enough to find her cousin. He had no doubt that if they had stayed in Austria, Lynn would be home within the week, but Stephan knew Dylan Hall, and if Lynn had been kidnapped from him, then the people they would have to go against to rescue Lynn were good, and dangerous. It would be suicide for Alyx to go up against them.

What scared him the most was that she didn't care.

As soon as the car came to a stop, Alyx was running into the house. That had to be a new record for how fast she had opened a car door. He wasn't sure if the car had even come to a complete stop before she'd jumped out. Worse, Stephan knew that as soon as she was inside the house, she would disappear, and he wouldn't get a chance to talk to her.

Sure enough, Alyx disappeared. She was good at that, especially in the palace. Stephan was pretty sure that was one of the reasons she liked the palace, and why she still tolerated coming here every summer.

Ally may have died when she was quite young, but somehow, she remembered her. It was easier for her than it was for Kate, because Ally was her mom's twin, but there were some memories she was certain were Ally, not her mom. They were just brief flashes, like a door here, a laugh here, but they were there, and it made her feel closer to the person she was named after.

Then there was the secret room.

The story had been that while Ally was living at the Palace, she was rarely seen during the day. She was exploring the huge house that she now called home. She had found many rooms that had been forgotten over the years, but once Ally found them, they had been reopened and were quite frequently used. There were still murmurs amongst the staff, however, that Ally had found one last room, that she didn't tell anyone about, and kept secret for herself. The secret room. Ally had taken Alyx there, she knew she had, and every summer, at least once, Alyx would visit it, disappear like her aunt had all those years ago.

Occasionally Alyx felt bad for keeping it a secret, as it was Ally's secret room, and Kate would probably love to catch glimpses of her mother that the room gave off, but Alyx felt that Ally had more secret rooms, and that Kate and Lynn would both have their own secret place to disappear, but Alyx didn't know if they really did, and didn't dare to ask.

Alyx silently sliced through the palace toward the secret room. She walked up the east staircase and entered the second story of the library. She walked into the section containing French Literature and found *Les Liaisons Dangereuses*. Straight up two shelves and over to the right three books. Alyx easily found the book that served as the trigger to open the door to the secret room. Alyx smirked, sure that somehow Ally had chosen the book for the trigger. Alyx may have vaguely remembered the secret room from when she was young, but she had found the secret room by herself a few years ago. It was in the French literature section, a language that Alyx had always had an interest in. The trigger itself was a book by Gérard de Villiers, a spy novelist, whose books seemed almost prophetic, or so Alyx had heard. His books were a bit too racy for her to read, as in *ever*, never mind, the ten year old version of herself that had found it.

In other words, the trigger was definitely meant for her to find it. French spy novel: it was the best of both worlds to a 10-year-old Alyx. She had been very lucky that what she found was a secret room, not a new novel.

Alyx pulled on the spine and watched as a hole opened up in the floor next to her. She grabbed the flashlight she had stashed behind the trigger and turned it on. She climbed down a few stairs and turned around, pushed the button and continued walking as the door slid shut behind her.

She had officially disappeared.

14:22 BST (UTC +1)
Feilds Palace

Alyx ran her hand over the wood table in the middle of the room. She spun, taking in the room. No matter how many times she came here, it always took her breath away. *Ally's secret room.* Hers now.

Alyx gently placed a photo of Kate and Lynn next to the other pictures that Alyx had been bringing down here since she found the room. "We met Lynn this summer." Alyx said. "I lost her, and I don't know where to go to find her." Alyx sighed and sat down in a chair at the table looking towards the line of picture frames on the bookshelf. "Michael of course is being impossible and won't let me go continue searching for her. I think if I knew where I could start looking I would just go, but I don't, so I can't." Alyx looked around the room. "And now I'm talking to dead people."

Alyx suddenly sat up straighter, looking at one of the framed pictures. *It couldn't be that simple.* Could it? Alyx stood up and looked at the picture closer. It was a picture of Ally, Alyx' mom Sarah, Dylan Hall, and Emily, the aunt that was more like an older sister to Alyx, but that wasn't what had caught her eye. It was the the words on the frame. *I'm a spy but on your side.* Alyx walked over and picked up the picture, carefully studying it, trying to figure out what hints it gave. She studied the snow capped peaks. If Lynn was in Austria, then she knew where Lynn was.

Lynn was in the Alps, in Austria maybe, but in the Alps none the less.

Alyx picked up her flashlight and flipped off the lights. As she started to climb the stairs to go back into the house she turned around. "Thank you Ally," she whispered. "I won't let you down."

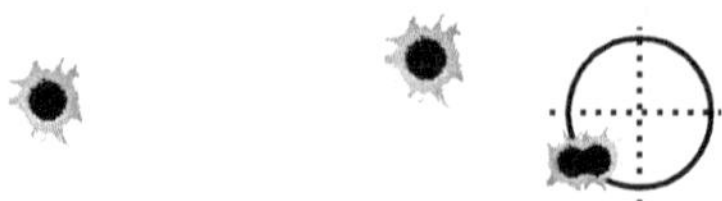

Alyx sat on her bed looking at satellite images of the Alps on her laptop, trying to find any indication of where Lynn might be. So far she had marked ten possible locations and hadn't even looked over half of the Austrian alps. She knew she needed to hurry because she was planning on leaving as soon as everyone else was asleep. She hadn't decided yet if she was going to steal one of her uncle's cars and drive (that was her most plausible option, but the worst one for the sake of time) or bribe the pilots of her uncle's air plane.

As Alyx was the thinking about how to get to Austria, her mouse fell over a spot on the map that was like it didn't exist. There was just a huge blurry spotted hole in the map. She sat up, curiously looking at her computer screen. The image looked like something she had heard described a few weeks earlier at the Intelligence Conference. The speaker had been saying that terrorists with deep pockets had started to use technology to hide the specifics of their compounds, making it harder for the world's intelligence agencies to use satellite images to plan attacks. The distortion on the satellite image could definitely hide a small cabin, where Alyx suspected Lynn was being held.

She now knew where, all she needed was a plan.

July 11th, 2011

00:17 BST (UTC +1)
Feilds Palace

Alyx waited until she knew the entire house was a sleep, before slipping out of her room. She slid her camping backpack onto her shoulder as she crept down the corridor. She was almost to the stairs when a voice stopped her. "You know, I told Michael that I didn't think you would be any trouble, that you wouldn't run off."

"If this is where you tell me you like your job too much, you can skip it. I'm just going out to the courtyard to get some fresh air." Alyx lied. Her voice was laced with venom that stung Stephan to the core and he visibly cringed. He had used that phrase too often.

Alyx saw him cringe and almost felt sorry, but she reminded herself that the more guilt she put on him, the more likely he would be to let her slip out that door, and then she could be gone. She decided to lay into him.

"You know, this job seems like it is too important to you. It's more important than your friendships. Tell me, if you want to be my friend, why do you continue to do the dirty housework? Shouldn't you be trying to move up in the world to prove yourself?" Alyx paused, steadying herself, trying to get the taste of her words out of her mouth. "But if being my uncle's servant really means that much to you, fine. I won't do anything to jeopardize that, but I also won't stay here to watch you waste your talents."

Stephan took the words, pushing down the desire to argue back. She had no clue what he was really doing here, and if he got his way, hopefully she would never have to, but he was afraid it was already too late. "What's in the courtyard that you need a backpack?" Alyx crossed her arms. "You know where Lynn is don't you."

Alyx cocked a hip, tilting her entire body so her shoulders were slanted, her right one higher than the left, but kept her head straight. She gave a devious half smile, her eyes saying *wouldn't you like to know.*

Stephan took that as enough of an answer. "How do you plan on getting there?"

"It's a toss up between stealing a car or bribing the pilot to fly me."

Stephan smiled on the inside. He should be horrified that Alyx was so good this, but then again, he couldn't help but feel like she was ready for whatever might get thrown her way, and that gave him a tremendous amount of relief. "Ooh, the jet pilot is hard to convince to do anything off the schedule, he likes his sleep." Stephan teased.

Alyx picked up on the lightness of his tone. "Oh yeah? That's good to know."

"The helicopter pilot though, now he would be easy to convince. He owes you for being a jerk to you." Stephan smiled. "I'll go get him. You can go wait by the helicopter."

00:39 BST (UTC +1)
Feilds Palace

Alyx leaned against the helicopter, her patience almost gone. She hadn't even known that the helicopter pilot was different from the jet pilot. Yet here she stood waiting for the supposed pilot. Alyx half suspected that Stephan had made it up so he had time to get Michael, and get her in trouble. She was not going to let anyone keep her from finding Lynn, even if that meant she had to fight her uncle to let her go. Michael would probably send Stephan anyway, and he deserved a good punch. She wouldn't even feel bad about it.

Alyx clenched her fists when she saw Stephan walking toward her. As Stephan neared, Alyx called out. "I thought you could convince the helicopter pilot to fly me." She pulled her back off the helicopter so her back was straight and spread her feet shoulder width apart. She was getting ready for a fight. "So tell me, is Michael coming or are you doing his dirty work for him like you always do?" *She didn't trust him.* The thought hit Stephan harder than any punch could. If he was going to protect her, he needed her to trust him, but he had ruined any trust she had by bringing her back.

"If Michael knew I was here right now, he would probably find some way to revoke my helicopter license." Stephan gave Alyx a smile as he held up the keys, hoping it would make her relax. She didn't, but clenched her fists even tighter. "I don't just drive the car and collect laundry you know."

"I know, you also *spy* on me for Michael."

"That's not fair Alyx."

"It's true *isn't it?* You are always there to catch me sneaking out or back in. You are always there to tell me no, and list all the things that could go wrong when I already know. So please, tell me why it's not fair."

Stephan sighed. She was going to make him tell her. "I don't do any of those things for Michael. I do it because I want to protect you." Stephan stepped close to Alyx and looked down at her. "That's why it's not fair."

Before Stephan knew what was happening, he was lying on his back on the ground. "I don't need to be protected." Alyx insisted. She climbed up into the helicopter. "Now, I need to go to Austria."

Stephan groaned as he got up off the ground. Protecting Alyx meant more pain than he'd ever agreed to, and most of that pain was afflicted by Alyx herself. He kept hoping that sooner or later she would learn to accept the help. Otherwise she might not live as long as she needed to.

03:26 CEST (UTC +2)
20,000 feet over Germany

Alyx looked at Stephan as he flew the helicopter. "Do you have any family?" She finally asked.

Stephan kept his eyes on the controls, he clenched his jaw. "No, I'm part of the MI6 orphans program, or I guess I should say, I *was* part of the MI6 orphans program. I'm a bit too old now."

Alyx nodded. "Sorry for asking." The headsets made Alyx feel like they were even farther apart than they were. Stephan sounded thousands of miles away. "Lyshiria just mentioned to me that she thought that you had a sister, at least at some point."

"I did." Stephan glanced down at the controls his hands were on. "Can we wait until another time to talk about it though? You shouldn't distract the pilot." Stephan hoped Alyx wouldn't push it. He didn't like the complications talking about his past would bring.

Alyx smiled dubiously. "I wouldn't be distracting the pilot. You're not flying."

"What are you talking about?"

Alyx twitched her hand that was resting on the controls in front of her the helicopter mimicking the movement she made with her hand. "I've had the controls for the past five minutes."

"Are you insane? You don't know how to fly. You could kill us both."

"You are probably right. I have been watching you and have a pretty good sense of how to fly this thing, but anything changes and I would crash, and we would die, unless I turn the controls back over to you and I am the one who has to since the main seat of a helicopter is the right seat. I know you were hoping I wouldn't know that, but I do. So here's what is going to happen. You are going to tell me about your sister, and why you are so protective of me, and I will give you the controls back." Alyx threatened.

Stephan hated how manipulative Alyx was. He didn't know where she had learned it, but it was something he would never learn to like. "I failed her." Stephan said after a long silence. "That's why I joined the MI6 orphans program. I wasn't strong enough to save my sister, I wasn't going to fail again. Then, a couple years into training I was assigned to Feilds Palace, and I met you. You are the age my sister would be if I hadn't failed her. I guess I saw you as a way to show I was stronger, you were a way to compensate for my initial failure. I wasn't going to fail my sister twice."

"I'm not your sister. I don't need protection."

"My sister didn't think so either. And I still lost her." Stephan swallowed. "But you're right. You don't need protection, but you do need help. Let me help you so I don't lose you like I lost my sister. You don't have to do this alone you know."

"Do you have the controls?" Alyx asked.

Stephan sighed, realizing he wasn't going to get an answer out of her. "Yes, I have the controls."

"Good, because I never took them from you in the first place." Alyx let go of the controls in front of her.

  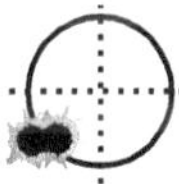

"There. That cabin has to be what the cloaking was hiding. The coordinates match." Alyx said. "Set it down right there, then we can lead an assault and get Lynn."

"No"

"What do you mean no? You just got through giving me a nice speech telling me that you wanted to help me. Where is the help now?"

Stephan clenched his jaw. She had a way of turning his words against him. "I said no because I *can't* land there. As much as I want to, it's not possible. We are going to have to find another way to get there."

"Thanks for flying me." Stephan heard her words but didn't quite register what they meant. Suddenly a warning popped up on the screens in front of him.

"Hey Alyx, this is saying that the back door is open, can you check it out for me. We may have a malfunction." Stephan waited for a reply, but none came. "Alyx, did you hear me?" Still nothing came. "Alyx?" Stephan glanced to his right where Alyx had been. She was gone and in her place was her headset. He risked a quick glance back and his heart sank. The door *was* open and there was a parachute missing. Alyx had jumped. He just hoped she knew what she was doing.

04:08 CEST (UTC +2)
The middle of the Austrian Alps

Alyx landed softly and she ran forward a little bit, just like she had when she had gone skydiving. She smiled as her phone vibrated in her pocket. She pulled it out, ready to decline the call, fully expecting it was from Michael. Instead she saw it was from Stephan. She swiped her thumb across the screen and put the phone up to her ear.

"I really hope you're not texting and flying. You'll lose your license for sure." Alyx answered.

"I found a clearing to land in, but what the hell do you think you were doing. You could have killed yourself."

"But I didn't." Alyx argued.

"What did you jumping out of the helicopter accomplish? I bet you are probably miles away from your target and have no clue how to get to the cabin where they are keeping Lynn."

"Are you *so* sure that you are willing to put money on it?" Alyx almost sang the taunt. "Because you would lose."

"Where are you then? A quarter of a mile away?"

"Nope, try the roof."

"You landed on *the roof?*" Stephan's voice rose at least an octave. "I don't believe it. You have never parachuted before and somehow you jump out of a helicopter, don't die on your way down, open your parachute and land *on the roof* of the target."

"It's not my first time. I've been skydiving."

"For some reason, I find it hard to believe that your parents let you go skydiving."

"They didn't." Alyx stated. "Now, if you don't mind, there are some bad guys I need to teach not to mess with my family."

Alyx hung up before Stephan could protest. She made sure the vibration on her phone was turned off, then started texting Stephan.

We need a plan.

16:42 CEST (UTC +2)
COF Safe house in the Austrian Alps

Lynn hung her head. She could feel her entire body trembling. She was weak. She hadn't eaten anything in days. Now she was stressed to add on to it. This Jackson guy was wearing her so thin that she would have no choice but to tell him all her secrets. She was beginning to think that coming out of hiding was a huge mistake.

Jackson waltzed into the room, a huge bounce in his step. He was enjoying this. He was a psychopath. Although Lynn had already guessed as much, now it was all the more apparent. "I am in quite the dilemma." Jackson started. "You see, I need the information you have about your cousin, Alyx McLean, but I happen to know that you would rather sacrifice your life than give her up to me, as that is what your mother did too. Pain won't work, fear of death won't work."

"How would *you* know what my mother would do?" Lynn asked, her voice full of venom.

"Simple." Jackson came close to Lynn, lifting her chin. "I'm the one who killed her."

"No, you're lying. Rafael did. My dad's brother did."

Jackson smiled. "Go get the tape. She doesn't believe me." Jackson paused looking Lynn right in her eyes. "How would you like to join your mother? I will make sure Alyx joins you soon."

Lynn used all of her strength to fight against her bonds. "Don't you dare touch one hair on her head. She isn't involved in any of this."

Jackson laughed. "Now I know your weakness." The guard that had left to get the tape returned. "Play the tape for her until I get back. That might be enough to get her to talk." Jackson left the room and the guard put the tape into the TV and hit play.

19:00 BST (UTC +1)
Feilds Palace, London

Kate tip-toed through the palace, Lyshiria close on her heels. "Where are we going Kate?"

"I need to talk to your dad about something, and I thought it might help if I have you with me." Kate replied. She opened the secret entrance to the basement. "Here we are, step down carefully."

"Kate, please tell me you are joking. Talking to my dad is probably the worst idea ever. He lies through his teeth about everything, even to me."

"He doesn't have reason to lie about what I need to ask him." Kate argued. "I found proof that he didn't kill my mom like he said he did."

"Why would he lie about that?" Lyshiria asked. "If you are trying to free my dad for me, don't. He's guilty and I know it."

"What if he's not? If he's not, my mother's killer is still out there, and someone needs to find him."

Lyshiria sighed, unable to argue with her. She didn't believe her father was innocent, but she could tell she wasn't going to get anywhere arguing with Kate either. Kate paused by a door and turned back to look at Lyshiria. This was where they were keeping her father. Lyshiria knew that Kate was asking her if she was ready. The question didn't need words, neither did her answer. She nodded.

Kate punched the code into the key pad by the door and the door clicked open. Rafael looked up as the door opened, expecting it to be his brother, who had yet to return. The surprise was evident as Kate and Lyshiria entered the room instead. Lyshiria saw the cuffs that held her father in place. She knew as his daughter she should feel sorrow, it should have pained her that her father was locked up, that he had been torn from her life, but she felt the opposite. She was slightly happy, he was finally receiving the consequences for his actions.

"What can I do for you ladies?" Rafael asked. Kate couldn't help but realize how much he looked and sounded like her own father. "I sincerely hope that it's not to break me out. That would not go over well, because, quite simply, I'm not sure I want to leave."

Now it was Lyshiria's turn to be shocked. "You *want* to be here?" She turned away from her father and looked at Kate. "I told you we shouldn't come down here. He's a *psychopath*, and we should get out of here *right now*."

Rafael looked between his daughter and the twin in front of him, intrigued. Kate threw Lyshiria a look that was so much like Alyx it threw Lyshiria off guard, then turned to Rafael and crossed her arms. "I'm here because I need a question answered. Why did you tell my father you killed my mother, because you know you didn't."

Rafael leaned back, his body language telling Lyshiria that he was going to try to avoid the question. "You know, my daughter is right. You don't want to be down here. Why don't you go back upstairs?"

Now it was Lyshiria's turn to cross her arms. She squinted her eyes. "You are avoiding her question." She took a step forward. "That means that Kate is *actually* onto something here." Lyshiria nodded her head in Kate's direction. "Why don't you answer her question?"

Rafael sighed. Kate was smarter than everyone gave her credit for. There was a calculation to everything she was doing that proved it. She had brought Lyshiria because she knew him better than most, and she could read him, as much as he tried to block her out. "How did you figure it out?" He asked after a pause.

Kate smiled. "Since Lynn showed up, I got a feeling that she knew something no one else did about Alyx, and you confirmed it, so I started fact checking. Medical records showed that Ally was poisoned in Russia one day before you returned to Russia from a secret trip to London. Really, I wouldn't have figured it out, except you mentioned to my dad that grandpa had agents watching you, which means there were witnesses that placed you here in London while my mum was being poisoned *in Russia.*"

"Ally asked me to lie, say I poisoned her." Rafael said. "I never much liked the plan, but I liked your mother, I respected her strength, and I couldn't tell her no. Especially since she was doing it for her family, for you, your twin, and Alyx, not to mention my brother."

"Why did she not want us to know who really killed her? Who poisoned her?"

"Some American tortured, and poisoned her, leading to her death. When she showed up on my door step, she was battered and bruised. She was barely three months pregnant, and she cared more about the safety of the child she was carrying than her own life. When she asked me to lie for her, she told me it was to protect Alyx, and that if things became worse, I was to distract her. Alyx can't find out the truth because she would never cease until she caught Ally's killer, and Ally's killer is looking to kill Alyx' too."

"That's why you wanted Lyshiria back here. You think that my mum's killer is the one who has Lynn, and Alyx chasing after her will end in her death."

"I don't think, I *know.* Your mother was smarter than *anybody* ever knew. By asking me to take credit for her death, she was also making me an enemy and putting me in a unique position to help. I have been in contact with the people who killed Ally. I know what they want. That's why I contacted Hall, and sent you here to kidnap Kate. Ideally, Michael would have kept Alyx away from Feilds Ball, knowing the danger. Then again, it doesn't sound like anyone told my brother how much danger his niece was in."

Lyshiria shook her head. "And why should we believe any of that? You can't seriously expect you can play the villain for years, and suddenly twist everything you've done to look like the hero."

"Answer one question for me. Where is Alyx McLean? She was supposed to come back with Lyshiria, am I right, yet she's not here."

"She's in bed sleeping." Lyshiria stated. "She didn't feel well when we got back."

"Alyx is a very curious girl. If she were here in the palace, she would have followed the two of you down here. If I were you, I would figure out where Alyx McLean *went* before she ends up *dead.*"

20:16 BST (UTC +1)
Feilds Palace, London

Kate barged into her father's office despite the protests of his secretary. "Dad, Alyx is gone, so is Stephan. I think she left to find Lynn."

Kate realized too late that there were three sets of eyes on her, but she realized by looking at them, they were all as concerned as she was about Alyx being gone. "Do you have any idea as to where she might have gone?" Michael asked her, ignoring the fact that there were two strangers in the room with him.

Lyshiria came running into the office, ready to pull Kate out, but froze. Hall was here. In Feild's Palace. "Why don't you ask *Dylan Hall*, or should I say, Nicholas Radford, the man Stephan, Alyx and I have been chasing across Europe?"

"Didn't you say you texted Cross and let him know the training mission was over?" Barnes asked Hall.

Hall stared Lyshiria in the eyes as he nodded in response to Barnes' question. "She's in Austria. That's where Lynn is, that is where Alyx would have tracked her."

Kate crossed her arms. "Well, you morons should probably get a team to Austria because according to Rafael, this is an elaborate trap to get Alyx."

"*My brother* killed *your mother*. Why would you listen to *anything* he has to say?"

"Because he didn't kill mum. Mum asked him to say he did so Alyx would stay away from the man who killed her, away from the man who wants to kill Alyx." Kate yelled.

Lyshiria looked at the men in the room. "Did you guys know Alyx was in danger?"

Michael and Barnes remained eerily silent. Hall nodded. "She was the reason I took the job from your father. I suspected the most likely place for them to find her would be at the Intelligence Conference, so I gave her food poisoning on her flight to New York. I was hoping it would be enough to keep her away from the conference."

"Now her picture from Feilds Ball is in every tabloid here in the UK, asking where *Alex Feilds* came from." Barnes added.

"And Stephan. You said he was involved in this?" Lyshiria prodded.

"I asked Michael to let Alyx come after me, preferably with a trusted agent. He chose Stephan. We needed to get her away from the cameras and the paparazzi that have been watching the palace all summer," Hall explained. "I believed Feilds Palace was the most dangerous place for her to be this summer."

"Well, you messed up, and now if we don't move, she is going to die like mum." Kate insulted.

"I guess we need to move then." Barnes said.

21:54 CEST (UTC +2)

COF Safe house

The cabin was shrouded in shadows, easily concealing the teenage girl picking the lock at the front door. Alyx was glad she had brought her dark gray hoodie with her, as it helped conceal her as well as protect her from the chill of the night. Alyx held her breath as she moved the last pin into place and the lock clicked open. She quickly placed the lock pick tools in their case and slipped it into the backpack on her back. She slipped in the door and quietly closed it behind her. As she sliced through the cabin, her black Nikes didn't make a noise.

Alyx had taken down three guards before anyone even knew what was happening. Alyx found Lynn easily by following the light whimpering. Alyx hung by the door, observing the situation. There were five guards in the room with Lynn. If she was going to get all of them, she had to move quickly. She pulled up onto her toes and did a couple of quick bounces.

Alyx sprinted at the nearest guard, using her element of surprise to take him down with a hurdle kick, as she decided she would call it. The rest of the guards quickly caught onto what was going on, and all decided to charge her at the same time. Alyx kicked herself up into a back flip, putting herself over next to Lynn. She quickly checked her pulse as she flung her backpack off, setting it next to Lynn. Alyx dropped to the ground and pulled her pocket knife out of her sock, flicking it open as she did. She rolled into a tumble and stuck the nearest guard's foot with it. She pulled herself into a hand stand, then fell forward knocking the guard out. With the skill that would do any gymnastics coach proud, she used her momentum to cartwheel herself into position, where she could fight the remaining three guards. As the guard on her right threw a punch, Alyx ducked, grabbing his hand and using his momentum to throw him into the guard on her left. The guard right in front of her, looked at his comrades, then turned to run. Alyx cartwheeled back to her knife, pulled it out of the guard's foot and threw it. The knife spun through the air, plunging itself perfectly into the last guard's shoulder. Alyx ran at him. As she neared, she reached out, ripped her knife out and threw an elbow to his temple. He crumpled to the ground before he could groan.

Alyx ran over to her cousin, taking the hood off her head. "Lynn, I need you to wake up. We need to get out of here." Alyx clipped her knife back in her sock and zipped open the backpack. She pulled out a bottle of water and pressed it to Lynn's lips.

Lynn's eyes fluttered open. When she saw Alyx her eyes went wide. "Alyx, you can't be here." Lynn's voice was hoarse from screaming and dehydration.

Alyx pulled her knife back out, then cut the ropes that were binding Lynn to the chair. "Lynn, I'm going to need you to stand up, can you do that for me?"

Lynn looked her cousin up and down. She looked like a teenager, but she sounded like a well trained operative. How she could wear a hoodie and blue jeans and think she could rescue her, she had no clue. Lynn nodded weakly and went to stand up. As soon as she let go of the chair, she began to topple to the ground. Alyx caught her, then looped her arm around her left shoulder to stabilize her. As Alyx flung the back pack onto her right shoulder, Lynn noticed the guards lying immobile on the ground. "You did all of *this*?"

Alyx coughed a little. "Yeah, I guess they didn't have much of a chance." Lynn though she was going crazy, because she could have sworn Alyx then giggled, "Don't touch my family."

"How are we getting out of here? I don't think I can hike out." Lynn moaned as they walked out the front door.

"I may have convinced your dad's helicopter pilot to hover over the clearing with a ladder dangling down. Do you think you can climb?" Alyx asked, as the blades of a chopper became audible.

"I can barely walk." Lynn retorted.

Alyx silently cursed. Stephan had been adamant that he could not land in the clearing by the cabin. Alyx took the flashlight out of the backpack and turned it on and off, short short long long long. Lynn recognized it as morse code for two. Alyx shoved the flashlight back in the backpack. "We will have to hike about half a mile north to meet our ride. Do you think you can make it?"

"I will try." Lynn groaned. Alyx handed Lynn the water bottle she had used to pour water down her throat just minutes before and Lynn gulped it.

"Let's go."

23:04 CEST (UTC +2)
COF Safe house

"What do you mean she got away?" Jackson growled. "There is no way that *McFeild* was capable of doing all of this. She was dehydrated and tied up. *Who helped her?*"

The guard held a bandage on the back of his right shoulder where he was bleeding from the knife burying itself into his skin. "I didn't see. It was over too fast. It had to be a well trained agent." He lied.

Jackson came up behind the guard and dug his finger into the knife wound. "I don't like liars. It is clear to me that you are a coward, that you were the last man standing, but that you decided to run, only you didn't get very far. Now. Who. Did. You. See?" Jackson dug his finger in a little bit more with every word of his question, causing the guard to struggle away. Jackson didn't let go, though.

"Ok, ok, it was a girl, but what she could do wasn't *human.*"

Jackson pulled his bloody finger out of the guard's knife wound, walking around to face the guard. "We aren't living in a universe where there are superheroes with superpowers. This isn't a Marvel or DC comic book. So obviously what this *girl* did *was* human, but you weren't strong enough to defeat her. You were weak. Do you know what happens to the weak?" The guard shook his head answering that he didn't. Jackson wiped the blood on his finger off on the front of the guard's shirt. "Darwin had the theory of Natural Selection, that the weak will die, and the strong will live, eventually creating a superior species. I believe that sometimes natural selection needs to be helped." Jackson drew his gun and fired a quick succession of three shots and the guard in front of him fell.

"Kalen, Lynn is out there somewhere, and my guess is that Alyx is the one that helped her escape. Find them, and bring her to me. You know what to do with Lynn."

Kalen smiled. "Yes sir."

23:35 CEST (UTC +2)
Forested Alps surrounding COF safe house

Alyx helped Lynn sit down on a fallen tree, then pulled another two bottles of water out of her backpack. She opened one and handed it to Lynn, who quickly gulped it down. Alyx opened her own and sipped the water. "You haven't had water in while have you?"

"Not much." Lynn whispered. Alyx nodded then checked her phone.

"We still have about half way to go, and I don't know when those guards will wake up, but guaranteed, when they do, they will start hunting us. We really need to keep moving."

"I know, but I'm not sure how much farther I can go, and you trying to help me is wearing you thin. If we did run up against trouble, you wouldn't be able to fight to protect yourself, and you are really the one that they want. You are the one that needs to be kept safe."

"*What are you talking about?*" Alyx asked.

"Mum was a spy, a pretty good one too, and she had enemies. Those enemies believe that *you* are her replacement, her heir, if you will, and now that I've seen what you are capable of, without training, I believe it too. They are after you. They killed mum to protect their empire, and I am convinced that they will kill you too."

"I'm not leaving you."

"Alyx, please, protect yourself." Lynn begged.

Alyx pulled out her phone and dialed Stephan then put her phone up to her ear. He picked up after the third ring. "Stephan, I'm going to need your help getting Lynn back to helicopter. Do you have our GPS coordinates."

"Yeah, I'll be right there."

The line went dead as he hung up. Alyx locked her phone and stuck it back into the backpack, then looked over at Lynn. *"I'm not leaving you."*

23:40 CEST (UTC +2)
Forested Alps surrounding COF safe house

Kalen combed through the woods carefully, his sniper rifle tucked up next to his shoulder, prepared to fire as soon as he he found a target. Kalen carefully looked for recently disturbed grass and branches, and so far, he had been able to follow the path that they had taken, but other than that, had found no sign that he was on the right path.

Kalen was becoming frustrated at the lack of evidence, almost frustrated enough that he missed what he was looking for. As he began to carefully place his foot down along the path he was following, he heard a plastic crunch. Kalen froze, slowly removing his foot from the plastic he had stepped on. Kalen quickly kneeled down to the ground and began examining the source of the noise. He smiled. *Perfect.* Water bottled by a British company. He was following *exactly* who he wanted to be.

Kalen stood up then looked around for the trail he had been following. With a stabbing pain in his gut, he realized that the trail was gone. The hairs on the back of his neck prickled. They were here, hiding somewhere. He looked through his scope, fully prepared to shoot at the first thing he saw that moved. He narrowed his concentration to find any human noise. He listened intently for the squeak of shoes, for the sound of breathing. He spun to his right when he heard a gasp. "Alyx" sounded like yell coming from Lynn's mouth in Kalen's intense concentration.

Kalen slowly moved forward to find where the noise had come from. As he neared the bushes at the edge of the clearing he caught a glimpse of the girl Jackson had been certain held answers concerning their target. She should have been terrified. She wasn't even near strong enough to escape, and he had his rifle aimed for her head. Yet for some reason she smiled.

Too late, he realized he had fallen into a trap. One second he was looking through his scope at Lynn and the next, he was staring at a face shadowed by the hood of a hoodie. Some of the girl's strawberry brunette hair fell out of the hood, giving her an *all-the-more* sinister look. Kalen looked up above him. She had been hiding in the tree. He laughed. "I'm impressed, you really are as good as they thought you were."

She smiled. "You haven't even seen half of what I can do."

Kalen threw a punch meant to get Alyx into a position where he could take her down and capture her. Instead, Alyx jumped up, catching a low hanging branch, and spun herself up onto it, then dropped down behind Kalen. As she landed, she crouched down to the ground, once again pulling her knife from her sock. Kalen spun around when he heard the distinct noise of a spring assisted knife locking open.

"Stephan, now." Alyx yelled. Kalen turned in time to see a man of about 20 grab Lynn, picking her up and running. Kalen went to go after Lynn but stopped when he felt the bite of the knife tearing into his tricep. Alyx was the distraction, but in his defense, she was a *damn good* distraction. She was well capable, *and* had a knife. Jackson might forgive him for letting Lynn escape if he captured Alyx.

Let the games begin. Kalen turned back to where he thought Alyx was, but she was gone. He looked up as he heard the bristle of leaves. He ducked out of the way just in time, as Alyx came crashing down right where Kalen had been. In her disoriented state from the jump down, Kalen moved in, putting her in a choke hold. Kalen smiled as he pulled her head into his chest, his arm cutting off her breath. A few more seconds and she would pass out and he could take her into Jackson. He thought the fight was over.

That was his first mistake.

Alyx ignored Kalen's grip around her neck, and rolled herself into a ball. As he pulled her close to his chest, she flung her body up. The force of her 125 pound frame knocked Kalen over, and she rolled herself out of his grip. Her feet landed on either side of his head. Alyx delivered a very calculated punch to his temple, strong enough to knock him out, but not strong enough to kill him. Alyx picked up the backpack she had stashed in the brush then sprinted off toward the helicopter.

Epilogue

July 24th, 2011
London, England

"The office is exactly the way I remember it being." Rafael said when he heard his brother enter. He turned around to see Tyson Barnes and Dylan Hall with his brother. "So where is Alyx now?"

"Home." Michael replied. "She left as soon as she got back with Lynn. I assume some of it was to avoid a rather ugly conversation with me."

"And Stephan Cross?" Hall asked.

"He will face disciplinary actions, but he will remain an agent here. We cannot ignore the fact that his choice to help Alyx brought Lynn home." Barnes answered.

The four men were quiet for a second. "So what is next for us? Now that we know that Alyx is in danger?" Michael asked.

"I'm headed back to Tracy. I might drop in and see my family for a couple days, but then I need to talk to some CIA operatives stationed there. They should have information about Alyx, I hope."

"I have some CIA contacts that I am going to reach out to, try and figure out who the men in the video of Alyx' one sided fight are." Tyson shrugged. "Then implement the fighting techniques she used into our agent training."

The four of them stifled laughter. "If you two will keep us in the loop, I believe Rafael and I will catch up on some lost time." Michael looked over at his brother, who seemed to wholeheartedly agree. "I still can't believe that was *our* Alyx in the video. I mean we were all trained in this room, and I don't think any of us could have done what she did."

"We've all met her parents." Hall replied. "There should be no wonder."

August 1st, 2011
Washington, DC

Kalen Mckenzie stared at the screen of his computer as he listened to the annoying hold music playing through the speaker of the phone he was holding to his ear. His desk may have faced the wall in the apartment that Jackson had been using as an office, but Kalen could feel Jackson's gaze on him. Jackson was not happy with him, and if this phone call paid off, he would only *begin* to atone for letting McLean get away.

Kalen subconsciously rubbed the bandage on his arm where McLean's knife had sliced his skin. It was going to leave a scar. Jackson wanted to recruit McLean, and was fairly confident in his ability to do so, but Kalen was hoping she would resist enough that he could repay the favor.

The hold music stopped, the person he was talking to coming back on the line. Knowing his uncle was watching helped him conceal his excitement he felt at the news the associate gave him, but he was on the way to restoring his uncle's faith in him.

Kalen hung up the phone turning to Jackson. "McLean flew on her uncle's private jet back to the states, so the records of that flight are hard to access. However, she *did* fly commercial for the final leg of her journey. There are records that Alyx McLean was aboard flight 324, non-stop direct from New York to San Francisco," Kalen reported. "I found her."

"San Francisco is an International airport, is it not?"

"Yes." Kalen answered.

"And how many cities does the San Francisco airport service?" Jackson asked, looking up at his nephew.

"I don't know." Kalen admitted. "Its a major airport, so I'm assuming quite a few."

Jackson nodded. "You didn't *find her*. You simply narrowed down our search area from the entire country to a portion of one of the country's largest states." Jackson pulled out his phone, selecting a number and dialing. As the phone began to ring, he held the phone up to his ear. "San Francisco is the home of the Bay Area Rapid Transit, or as the locals call it, Bart. McLean could have boarded one of their trains at the airport and traveled to any city in the four counties that it services."

Jackson paused his lecture as the person on the other side of the phone answered. "I need you to enter a BOLO for me. There is a training program in the San Francisco Bay Area, correct?"

Kalen waited, measuring his breaths as he waited for Jackson to finish his call. Fortunately, it didn't take him long to convey the information to the person on the other end. When Jackson hung up, he was ready to give Kalen his next task.

"Find her. Monitor CIA chatter about McLean. See if there are records showing she boarded a BART train, and where she got off if she did. Get me a city we can search. Until then, I don't want to see you." Jackson ordered.

Kalen nodded, standing up and walking out the door.

August 5th, 2011
Tracy, California

Peter Carlyle drifted off as he sat in the room that should have been his dining room, listening to Nathan Levy, the Director of the Promising Generation Training Program discuss various mundane topics. For a group that was meant to be training to be the CIA's next generation of highly qualified field agents, they spent too much time sitting in this room discussing topics that had nothing to do with espionage.

Peter was drawn back as he heard the group's CIA liaison, psychologist Dr. Ignatius Wraith begin speaking. "The training division has given you a training mission of sorts. A BOLO has been issued for this young woman." Wraith used a remote to put an image of the young woman on the TV in the room.

Peter stared at the picture that was frozen on the screen. The image was clearly taken from a video, and may have been low-quality, black-and-white security camera footage, but he knew that the girl's eyes were a piercing blue. He knew, because he'd caught himself looking at them more than he'd ever admit.

"Don't let her appearance deceive you. She attacked one of our guarded safe-houses in the Austrian Alps on the evening of July 11th. She put nine of our own in the hospital. She killed the tenth." Wraith paused, making eye contact with everyone at the table to ensure that what he'd said had sunk in. "Intelligence suggests that she is heading to somewhere here in the Bay Area next."

"And the training portion is what, exactly?" Cameron McKay asked. He was one of the oldest members of the group at 19, and was one of the few members who had actually completed training at the Farm.

Technically he, as well as the director Nathan, and a handful of others, were graduated from the training program, but stuck around for reasons Peter couldn't even guess.

"It's a training in identification and observation. Once you find her, they want you to figure out who she is, what she wants, and keep an eye on her until the CIA can decide how to proceed." Wraith reported.

Nathan finished the briefing. "You guys know the drill. If you see her, report it to Peter or I. We will decide where to go from there." He turned to Peter. "Is there anything you would like to add?"

Peter looked away from the frozen image, expending more effort than should have been necessary to pull his attention away from the girl. Her name was on the tip of his tongue. *Alyx McLean, age 16. She attends John C. Kimball High School. She's brilliant, if her grades in Algebra II are any indication.* But instead of rattling off what he knew about the girl, he decided to lie. "Nope." He said.

Nathan nodded. "Ok. Meeting adjourned."

All of the members of the Promising Generation stood up, dispersing towards the door. Peter stayed seated, leaning across the table toward Wraith. "Can you by chance get me a copy of the video that picture was captured from? I'd like to analyze it to see if it can tell us anything else." Peter asked.

"The CIA already has their full time analysts on it." Wraith said dismissively, not looking up from the file he was pushing papers into. "Your time would be better focused on making sure you pass all the required exams so you can begin your mission immediately after graduation."

"School doesn't start for another week." Peter argued.

Wraith looked up at him. "Your French and Italian are flawless?"

"My French could admittedly use a little bit of work, but I've already been emailing with the French teacher at Kimball, and he has agreed to help me…" Peter replied, "Once school starts, which means I need something to do until then."

"I've given the Generation a task. Why don't you help with that." Wraith ordered, then he too got up, and left.

Peter went back to staring at the still image on his TV of Alyx McLean, the girl he'd sat behind two years before in Algebra II. She was intelligent, considering she'd been placed in a class for Sophomores and Juniors as a Freshman, and if that wasn't enough for her, she wasn't just in the top percentage of the class, but she was challenging Peter for *the* top spot. She was quiet, and observant, and used those traits to help her blend into crowds to the point where she almost disappeared. That was what had made him notice her finally. Her observation seemed to make her eyes this beautiful piercing blue that always portrayed constant thought.

He hadn't been able to stop noticing her since.

He'd chosen not to speak up during the briefing, because he felt like something was being held back, and the fact that Wraith wouldn't let him see the footage only added to his suspicion. Fortunately he knew her cousin.

There was only one question he wanted to know the answer to: What did Alyx McLean do this summer?

He had just over a week before school started, and she would be rubbing shoulders with most of the Generation. All he could do was hope no one saw her around town before he figured out what to do.

Acknowledgements

I first got the idea for the book that became *Royal Beginnings* the summer of 2009. The only reason this book exists, and I didn't stop writing it after two months, as was the fate of every other book I tried to write before, is the result of the support and instruction given to me by several people. I owe many thanks to them. Thank you to all the teachers who helped me improve my craft. Thank you to Mr. Carlo, who introduced me to the series that hooked me on spy novels. Thank you to Ms. Chamberlain who taught me creative writing, and made me a better writer (I walked into that class with a very shaky plot for this book, and the skills you taught me helped me improve it). Thank you to Mrs. Maslyar and Mr. Lee who both agreed to read this book and give me feedback. And while this book was already written and published when I took your class, thank you Professor Jeff Metcalf. I learned so much about Young Adult Literature in the classes I've taken from you. Most of all, to all of you, thank you for your kind words of encouragement.

Thank you to my family. Thank you Devan for spending late nights with me planning both my series and yours. I can't wait to see what stories we tell. Thank you Mikayli for putting up with my rambling about my books, and always being the first person to read my books as they come off the printer. Thank you Mom for reading my book, and sending me emails and suggestions of people who might be able to help me with my book. Thank you Dad, for always being supportive of me, and making sure to tell everyone that I'm a great writer. Thank you Lon for calling me your favorite author, and making me smile every time you see me. Thank you Patrice and Jackie for buying my books, even though I would be more than willing to give you copies.

I also owe many thanks to my many friends for putting up with me talking about my books *constantly*. Thank you to Torri Christensen for reading the chapters I give you and giving me your honest feedback, even when you have no idea of context. Thank you Crystal Molina, for putting up with Devan and I as we talked about our books. Thank you David Molina for using your Graphic Arts degree to look at the first version of this book and point out everything I did wrong. I think I fixed everything…finally. Thank you Maddyx Byrd for reading these books right after Mikayli, and helping me make the book trailer for this book.

Most of all, Thank you to all of the various writing partners and groups I've been blessed to be part of. Thank you to Sydney Cruz and Dominic Salemi who helped me during the writing of this book. And Thank you to all the members of the CGB (Creators's Guild of Bountiful) for letting me talk about my books, and in return, letting me hear and read the stories you are writing. I'm glad that I can call myself a founding member, and that we came up with such a perfect name.

And Thank you to all my co-workers who hounded me for signed copies of my book. To my Smiths 444 family, I'm pretty sure you guys are the reason I sold so many books. I *will* become famous, if only so the books you guys bought will be worth something someday. To my fellow writing tutors, thank you for putting up with my craziness when I made appointments with you, and for sending other creative writers my way. I loved helping the students you sent me in their creative endeavors.

Many, many thanks are also due to the readers. Thank you for reading this book. I promise I have many more stories to tell, and I promise they get better.

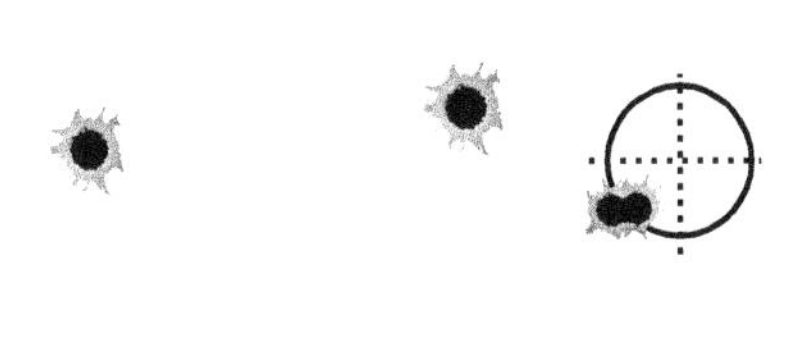

Bonus Scene

July 3rd 2008

Alyx sat up, elbowing Kate in the side to drag her attention away from the tabloid she was reading. "What?" She whined, dropping the magazine onto the bed in front of her, not bothering to get off her stomach.

"It's official. I'm bored." Alyx complained. "Let's do something."

Kate dropped her head into the bed. "What's with you. You always have to *do* something. Why can't you be the stereotypical lazy American?"

"Children aren't supposed to sit around doing nothing all day." Alyx argued.

"You finished reading all the books you brought, didn't you." Kate asked, finally flipping herself around and sitting up facing Alyx.

"Yes." She admitted.

Kate smiled. "By the way, you're a teenager now. I'm pretty sure teenagers are supposed to sleep in way too late, and do absolutely nothing all day." Kate jumped up, off the bed. "Ooh, I know. We could go watch a movie."

Alyx shook her head. "We've already watched all the movies in your theatre." She laid back down. "I think I'm just bored, imagining all the fun things my friends back home are doing."

Kate sat back down on the bed, frowning down at her cousin. "Like what?" She asked.

"The 4th of July is tomorrow." Alyx started.

"I know." Kate interrupted.

Alyx sighed. "It's a holiday back home. There are going to be parades, and fireworks, and parties. There are movies about it, and it always makes its way into songs, and I don't know what it's like, because I'm always here in the UK, and the last thing you guys want to do is celebrate a day that marks the anniversary of your defeat."

"It's Independence Day, isn't it?" Kate asked.

"Yeah." Alyx said. "It's the day the US declared its independence from Britain."

Kate went over to a shelf in her room, picking up a book with a worn binding. Alyx watched her out of curiosity. Alyx always assumed that the shelf that sat in Kate's room was there more out of decoration than to provide usefulness, as the only thing Alyx ever saw her cousin reading was the tabloid magazines their aunt Emily sent her from California.

"Mum kept a journal when she moved here to marry dad. She mentioned a few times that she mostly missed her family, who couldn't come to visit all the time, but she also mentioned missing celebrating Independence Day." Kate explained, opening the journal to show Alyx her mother's perfect penmanship explaining everything about the American holiday she missed. "Dad is gone tomorrow. What if we use mum's journal to recreate an American Independence Day party?" Kate suggested.

"And who would we invite to this party?" Alyx asked, running her hand over the impressions her aunt's pen had made on the paper.

Kate smiled. "There is an American High School nearby. I'm sure if we offered them a party at a Palace, they couldn't refuse." Kate pointed to the page. "My biggest concern is how to get all of the American flags and such to decorate."

It was Alyx' turn to smile. "Leave that to me. I can annoy Stephan into helping me retrieve the supplies we need."

Alyx ran down the hall way to catch up with Stephan Cross, one of her uncle's youngest employees, and the young man who had basically grown up along side Alyx and Kate. He was five years older than Alyx, but she didn't view that as a problem. His being older meant he could buy things for Alyx and Kate that they couldn't buy for themselves. It also meant he could drive them places, as they couldn't legally drive themselves.

"Stephan, I need a favor." Alyx started. "I need you to get me strawberries, blueberries, white cake mix, and whipped cream—you know, the stuff in the can. I also need sheets of red, white, and blue construction paper, I have scissors, but I will need small wooden dowels, and some tooth picks and tape. Oh, I might need some chocolate cake too. And cream cheese, heavy cream… wait what do you guys call it…double cream I think, and powdered sugar.”

“What are you up to?” Stephan asked, suspiciously watching Alyx as she walked beside him.

“Nothing.” She lied.

“Red, white, and blue. I believe there is an important US holiday tomorrow that is often celebrated with those colors.” Stephan posited. “So try again. What are you up to?”

Alyx shrugged, annoyed that Stephan knew her so well. “Kate was reading her mom’s journal, and Ally mentioned something about the parties she would attend to celebrate the holiday. Since neither of us has ever celebrated the 4th of July, we thought it might be fun to recreate the parties Ally wrote about.”

“You got bored again, didn’t you.” Stephan forced.

Alyx huffed. “Maybe I did, but you wouldn’t deny the motherless girl an opportunity to feel closer to her mother, would you?”

“I hate it when you and Kate play the dead mother card.” Stephan breathed.

“I don’t play the dead mother card—I play the dead aunt card.” Alyx corrected.

Stephan glared at Alyx. “It’s not fair, and you know it. Especially since you know *I* am an orphan.”

“Which means you understand why Kate wants to do this, and you will get me anything to make it happen.” Alyx finished, her smile a little too wide.

“I will get you the food and the paper.” Stephan conceded.

“Oh, and some sparklers, and what ever other fireworks you can get your hands on.” Alyx added.

“Absolutely not.” Stephan insisted.

“But Ally wrote that the fireworks were her favorite part. You don’t want to deprive Kate and I of the best part of the holiday, do you?”

“I could lose my job.” Stephan argued. “And I like my job.”

"You won't lose your job. Michael isn't here. He won't know." Alyx countered.

"Fireworks are large explosions shot up into the sky." Stephan corrected. "Someone *will* see, and Michael *will* find out."

"But he doesn't have to know it was you. You have Friday night off. If you get us the fireworks, you can honestly say it wasn't you setting them off. Kate and I will be the ones getting in trouble, not you." Alyx suggested.

"Yes, because I'm going to give explosives to a 13-year-old girl, and leave her without supervision to set them off. I think not." Stephan insisted.

"I promise, no one will know you were involved. But Kate *needs* to have fireworks, so she can feel close to her mom." Alyx appealed.

Stephan sighed, looking at Alyx "I will get you the food, paper, and sparklers, and I will *think* about getting you some fireworks." Stephan put up his hand as Alyx started to skip away in excitement. "I won't make any promises."

Alyx continued skipping back down the hall. "If you think about it, you're going to say yes to us."

Stephan watched as she turned the corner and disappeared. He hated that Alyx knew him so well. Now he had to figure out where to get fireworks.

Kate and Alyx sat next to each other in the family kitchen that was rarely used by anyone other than Alyx. Since the Feilds Estate provided for a full time kitchen staff that cooked all of their meals in the commercial size kitchen just next door, Michael and Kate saw little point in using the small kitchen to cook their own food. Alyx, on the other hand, spent nine months of the year helping her parents contribute to family meals, and as a growing teen-aged athlete, she needed more than the very structured three-meals-a-day that the palace kitchen staff provided.

The two girls sat at the countertop in the barstools that reminded Alyx of home, or at least one of her homes, as her parents seemed to move every year. The house she'd lived in for the previous school year had been in Utah, and she may have hated the snow, but there was an island in the kitchen with barstools, and she'd really enjoyed that island. She'd never asked for much when her parents were moving, but this year, she asked that when she got back from London, she found an island in the new house in California. With the white sheet cake baking in one of the kitchen ovens, and the chocolate cake mix she'd asked Stephan to get being baked into cupcakes in another, Alyx and Kate used the spare time to cut out and glue together American flags of all sizes. They already had a stack of small ones glued to toothpicks to put in the cupcakes once they were ready, and they were working on the larger ones that they planned on using to decorate the public areas of the first floor where they would have their party. Stephan had even gone so far as to get them streamers that they could use to decorate the courtyard, so they felt their party would come along quite nicely.

But still, Alyx was concerned about guests.

"Are you sure they will come?" Alyx asked Kate.

Kate shrugged. "I may not be very popular at my school, but there are some benefits to my claim to a title after all. Americans are enamored with father's title, and I was right. They seem to love the idea of throwing a 4th of July party at a real English Palace. And when I promised them fireworks, I think I sealed the deal. Apparently they don't typically have fireworks. Not even the embassy lights fireworks."

Alyx smirked. "Imagine that. No fireworks at the London embassy."

"Did you know that dad gets invited to the embassy celebration every year? That's what's he's attending on Saturday." Kate admitted. "I keep hoping he will invite me, but he hasn't yet."

Alyx bit the inside of her lip as she glanced over at her cousin. "I'm sorry Kate. I'm sure he's just waiting until you're older."

Kate shrugged. "Probably. Until then, we'll just have to throw our own."

"Yes, we will." Alyx agreed. "Yes, we will."

Kate walked up next to Alyx, who was watching the party from one of the balconies above the courtyard where they had music playing, admiring their handiwork. The scene was similar to the ball Michael had hosted the month before, but also much different. Instead of having a live quartet play classical music for guests to waltz to, Alyx had found the sound system, and had plugged her laptop into it, which was playing a shuffled list of the current top hits in America, with a few patriotic songs mixed in here and there. Instead of the grand hall being filled with a bunch of the world's diplomats and spies wearing their fanciest clothes, the courtyard was a mingling of American teenagers, the sons and daughters of American ex-pats and diplomats wearing their most patriotic clothes, creating a sea of red, white, and blue.

Kate smiled. "I told you they would come."

Alyx nodded. "What can I say? You were right, once again." Alyx pointed across the courtyard to the figure at the barbecue. "My only question is where did Stephan find that barbecue? Because we both completely overlooked that detail, yet there he is, flipping burgers."

"Where did he find those clothes?" Kate asked.

"I bet he bought them when he bought our supplies. I don't think he trusts us very much." Alyx hypothesized. "It's his night off. He could be doing anything, yet here he is, feeding our guests."

Kate nodded, but remained silent for a moment, taking in the sight of the party they had created. It was much as she had imagined it should be after reading her mother's journal. They had even opened up the courtyard to the indoor pool, and the splashing sounds of teenagers enjoying various pool games could be heard despite the music. She could see why her mum had spoken with such longing for the parties they would host in California, and silently wondered why she hadn't ever thought of hosting one of her own before. While she could imagine all the trouble they could get into if her father found out, she couldn't help but thank Alyx for getting bored. "Thank you." Kate said quietly.

"It was your idea." Alyx insisted. "Thank you for giving me the opportunity to host a real American 4th of July party." Alyx paused, smirking. "I think next year, I will smuggle some real American flags into my luggage."

Kate turned to look at her cousin. "Next year?"

Alyx nodded, turning to face her cousin. "As long as that's ok with you. By my count, I've missed twelve years of 4th of July parties, and you have missed ten. I would like to make up for the missed opportunities."

Kate nodded, looking back down at the party. "I think that sounds like a very good idea."

They waited until it was dark before they cleared all of the teenagers to the sides of the courtyard and pulled out the fireworks that Stephan had found for them. Some of the guests were content with just holding one of the sparklers, others climbed up onto the balconies of the courtyard, and watched as they lit off the aerial ones. They didn't have very many, but they were able to do a nice ten minute show before they ran out.

Stephan sat off to the side, letting Alyx and Kate have all of the fun of lighting the fireworks, figuring he would step in if something started to go wrong. He did like the idea of having plausible deniability, should Michael find out. He could honestly say he hadn't set off a single firework.

While he had given Alyx plenty of grief about the 4th of July party, he could honestly say he enjoyed it. After all, he wasn't much older than some of the people Kate had invited to this party. He forgot that sometimes. He may have been forced to grow up faster than most people, and he had quite a bit of responsibility in his job, but he was still a teenager. Every once in a while, it was ok for him to act like it, and have fun.

The fun disappeared, however, when his phone buzzed. With the fireworks gone, he felt safe to run inside, and get as far away from the noise of the party as he could before he answered his phone. "Yes, sir?" He answered.

"I'm hearing reports of fireworks at the palace. I know it's your night off, but can you go check on the girls. Oh, and break up what ever party they seem to be throwing." Lord Feilds asked.

"I'll be there as soon as I can." Stephan promised.

"Good. I'll be home tomorrow morning. I will deal with them then." Lord Feilds promised.

As soon as Stephan entered the courtyard, Alyx' eyes found his. Her smile faded. She knew. She whispered something to Kate, and the two of them began walking around the courtyard, letting their guests know it was time to go home.

Kate and Alyx sat patiently on the couch in Michael's office as he finished up the call he was on. He had been on the phone all morning trying to put out the figurative fires that their party had started, so when he finally hung up and turned to the girls, he didn't seem all too happy.

"Do you two have any idea of the problems your little party has caused?" He asked finally. "Not only is it on the front page of every newspaper and tabloid this morning, but it embarrasses everyone attached to the Feilds name." He looked at each girl individually. "What exactly were you two thinking?"

Alyx shrugged. As the older of the two girls, and the visitor, she had already decided she would take all of the blame. She and Kate may have fought about it the night before, but Kate sat with her mouth closed. "I was bored. I spend every summer here, so I don't get to celebrate my national holiday, so when Kate showed me the journal, I couldn't help myself. I had to throw myself a 4th of July party. I take full responsibility."

"What journal?" Michael asked.

Kate clasped the journal that had been her only connection to her mother. The last thing she wanted was for her father to take it away, and sever any tie she had to her mum, but she couldn't let Alyx take all of the blame. "I suggested the party. Mum's journal mentioned the parties she went to in America for the holiday, and I wanted to see what it was like." Kate took a deep breath, handing the journal to her father, open to the entry about the party.

Michael looked down at the journal reverently. He recognized the journal as the same book his wife had carried around after she married him. He'd given the journal to Kate for her tenth birthday, hoping to give her something from her mother as well as himself. He'd never read the journal himself, and now, looking at his late wife's perfect penmanship, he wondered what else those pages may have held that he would rather Kate not read.

How could he punish his daughter for wanting to feel closer to her mother?

Michael set the journal down on his desk, deciding to read it himself before returning it to his daughter. The last thing he needed was another incident that the party the night before had led to. "There are many reasons why setting off fireworks last night was a horrible idea, including complicated politics, and various fire threats. As I can't expect you two to have much knowledge of the reasons it was a bad idea, and I believe I can put out the figurative fires, especially given Kate's motives, I will simply tell you that it was in *very* poor taste, and tell you not to do it again." Michael informed the two girls.

"The fireworks or the party? Because it seems to me that the party was very good for foreign relations." Alyx quipped.

Michael glared at Alyx. Maybe she knew better than she was letting on. It also concerned him that the girls had admitted Kate came up with the idea, it was Alyx' boredom that made them actually execute it. "And where might you have gotten said fireworks?" Michael pushed. "Because I suspect that person who bought them for you *did* have some knowledge of it being a bad idea. And yet they bought them for you anyway."

Stephan froze in his spot in the corner. This was it. He glanced over at Alyx. She was smiling about it.

"And who says I had anyone buy them?" Alyx asked.

"You had to get the fireworks from somewhere." Michael insisted. "Where did you get them?"

Alyx shook her head. "You know, I'm not sure I remember." Stephan shook his head in disbelief. Alyx knew that Michael was ready to go easy on her, yet she sat there blatantly avoiding Michael's question despite the repercussions that might have on her.

He couldn't help but feel indebted to her loyalty.

"Very well." Michael sighed. "If anything, this just shows you can keep a secret when needed. How would you feel about using your talents to translate for me?"

Alyx shrugged. "Might as well."

Michale nodded, expecting she would agree. "You two are dismissed." Michael watched quietly as the two girls left the room. As soon as the door closed, Michael addressed Stephan. "Thank you for coming to check on the girls last night."

"No problem, sir." Stephan replied.

"You know Alyx quite well. What do you think of her translating for me?" Michael asked.

Stephan tried to keep the surprise of being asked off his face. "I think she is well equipped for the task. I'm less sure of the timing. It might be perceived as a reward for her misbehavior."

Michael nodded. "I thought so. I'm afraid that if I don't give her something to do, she will get bored again. She has a nasty habit of creating international incidents when she's bored."

Stephan nodded. "Then I think it would be a marvelous idea to keep her busy."

"That's what I thought." Michael agreed.

Follow Alyx McLean and the fight against the terrorist organization known as the Circle of Fifths in

the PROMGEN files

A
L
I
G
N

C
O
Y
S
T

P
E
R
D
U

Keep reading for an exclusive sneak peak from the next novel.

Friday
August 5th, 2011

11:54 PDT
Tracy, California
Promising Generation Training Program Headquarters

Peter Carlyle drifted off as he sat in the room that should have been his dining room, listening to Nathan Levy, the director of the Promising Generation Training Program discuss various mundane topics. For a group that was meant to be training to be the CIA's next generation of highly qualified field agents, they spent too much time sitting in this room discussing topics that had nothing to do with espionage.

Peter was drawn back as he heard the group's CIA liaison, psychologist Dr. Ignatius Wraith begin speaking. "The training division has given you a training mission of sorts. A BOLO has been issued for this young woman." Wraith used a remote to put an image of the young woman on the TV in the room.

Peter stared at the picture that was frozen on the screen. The image was clearly taken from a video, and may have been low- quality, black-and-white security camera footage, but he knew that the girl's eyes were a piercing blue. He knew, because he'd caught himself looking at them more than he'd ever admit.

"Don't let her appearance deceive you. She attacked one of our guarded safe-houses in the Austrian Alps on the evening of July 11th. She put nine of our own in the hospital. She killed the tenth." Wraith paused, making eye contact with everyone at the table to ensure they understood what he was telling them. "Intelligence suggests that she is heading to somewhere here in the Bay Area next."

"And the training portion is what, exactly?" Cameron McKay asked. He was one of the oldest members of the group at 19, and was one of the few members who had actually completed training at the Farm. Technically he, as well as the director Nathan, and a handful of others, were graduated from the training program, but stuck around for reasons Peter couldn't even guess.

"It's a training in identification and observation. Once we find her, they want us to figure out who she is, what she wants, and keep an eye on her until the CIA can decide how to proceed." Wraith reported.

Nathan finished the briefing. "You guys know the drill. If you see her, report it to Peter or I. We will decide where to go from there." He turned to Peter. "Is there anything you would like to add?"

Peter looked away from the frozen image, expending more effort than should have been necessary to pull his attention away from the girl. Her name was on the tip of his tongue. *Alyx McLean, age 16. She attends John C. Kimball High School. She's brilliant, if her grades in Algebra II are any indication.* But instead of rattling off what he knew about the girl, he decided to lie. "Nope." He said.

Nathan nodded. "Ok. Meeting adjourned."

All of the members of the Promising Generation, who had been sitting around the table stood up, dispersing towards the door. Peter stayed seated, leaning across the table toward Wraith. "Can you by chance get me a copy of the video that picture was captured from? I'd like to analyze it to see if it can tell us anything else." Peter asked.

"The CIA already has their full time analysts on it." Wraith said dismissively, not looking up from the file he was pushing papers into. "Your time would be better focused on making sure you pass all the required exams so you can begin your mission immediately after graduation."

"School doesn't start for another week." Peter argued.

Wraith looked up at him. "Your French and Italian are flawless?"

"My French could admittedly use a little bit of work, but I've already been emailing with the French teacher at Kimball, and he has agreed to help me once school starts..." Peter replied, "which means I need something to do until then."

"I've given the Generation a task. Why don't you help with that." Wraith ordered, then he too got up, and left.

Peter went back to staring at the still image on his TV of Alyx McLean, the girl he'd sat behind two years before in Algebra II. She was intelligent, considering she'd been placed in a class for Sophomores and

Juniors as a Freshman, and if that wasn't enough for her, she wasn't just in the top percentage of the class, but she was challenging Peter for *the* top spot. She was quiet, and observant, and used those traits to help her blend into crowds to the point where she almost disappeared. That was what had made him notice her finally. Her observation seemed to make her eyes this beautiful piercing blue that always portrayed constant thought.

He hadn't been able to stop noticing her since.

He'd chosen not to speak up during the briefing, because he felt like something was being held back, and the fact that Wraith wouldn't let him see the footage only added to his suspicion. Fortunately he knew her cousin.

There was only one question he wanted to know the answer to: What did Alyx McLean do this summer?

He had just over a week before school started, and she would be rubbing shoulders with most of the Generation. All he could do was hope no one saw her around town before he figured out what to do.

Monday
August 15th, 2011

10:57 PDT
Tracy, California
John C. Kimball High School

The sprawling, single story, outdoor campus of John C. Kimball High School in Tracy California was buzzing with energy. The courtyard of concrete sidewalks and grass hills was dotted with students displaying their exuberant school spirit, wearing their various pieces of orange and blue clothing.

School spirit was always on brilliant display the first day of school, and this year was no different. Besides the students who decided to wear the too-bright school color of orange, no one had lost their lanyards yet, so the bright icons were still visible around everyone's necks, and every Fall Sport was wearing their uniforms, especially the cheer and dance teams, who could be seen next to the orange polo shirts that represented the football team.

Having just opened three years before, this was the first time the school had seniors, and somehow that made everything about the first day of school better, and brighter. Maybe, with Seniors, Kimball would finally have a formidable football team.

Alyx McLean walked through the crowds, feeling the energy buzzing. She felt like if she were to scream "Let's go Jag-uars" everyone in the courtyard would respond to her call. The thought brought a smile to her face, but she let the thought come and go. Instead, she brushed past one of the Leadership kids, covered with school spirit from head to toe, and whispered the cheer in his ear. As she slipped into the cafeteria, she heard the fruits of her whisper sweep the students eating lunch outside, their voices rising above the sound of the music.

She may have taken a step into the spotlight at Fields Ball the summer before, but it was time to return to the shadows.

As she walked into the lunchroom, no one noticed that her backpack was already weighed down with textbooks. No one looked her way as she pulled her long wavy, strawberry brunette hair out from under the strap. She was invisible, and she liked it that way. She was good at this. She was good at blending into the crowds, slipping through the shadows, but still leaving her mark, even if no one but her knew.

She arrived at a booth towards the back of the cafeteria, slipping her heavy bag off her shoulder, and sliding it under the bench of the booth. As upperclassmen, it didn't matter that it was the first day of school, because the habits of the previous two years returned, and they sat in the same spot they had everyday for the past two years. Despite there being two different lunch periods, with the classroom of each students' 4th period class determining whether they had first or second lunch, all 4 of Alyx's friends had managed to have the same lunch all three years they'd attended the school. As she slipped into her place next to her friend Savannah, she couldn't help but smile, and think about how the only reason she survived the shadows, was by having a strong group of people to tell her when she was going too far.

"What's wrong with applying to Delta College?" Thane asked. He was one of only two guys in their friends group. She had met him when she had first moved to California, and lived next door to his family. As an only child, she had been drawn to the brother-sister dynamic between him and his younger sister, Chelsi. Fortunately, he didn't mind her joining his friend group, where she had met Kaden, the other guy in their group, and Savannah, both of whom were attending Wicklund, the K–8 school she had attended when she first moved to California four years before.

"Nothing, if you're a normal person." Carlie said. "I think Savannah was just hoping you would be applying for one of the CSUs she is applying for." Her reply caused not one, but two red faces to appear, but that wasn't good enough for her. "If you're Alyx, the only thing wrong with Delta is that it's not Oxford."

Alyx held her hands up in surrender. "Hey, I think there is nothing wrong with Thane applying to Delta, so don't drag me and my choices into this."

"It's not that it has to be Oxford, it's the fact that it's not in London. If you haven't noticed, Alyx happens to be our resident Brit." Savannah corrected.

Alyx rolled her eyes. "That's what happens when I spent my entire childhood moving. I've spent more time in London than I have in any one city here in the US. London feels like home, and I think I have a descent shot at getting into Oxford, so why not?"

Savannah smiled, warning Alyx, too late, that she had just fallen into one of Savannah's traps. "And how was London this summer?" She asked Alyx.

While it didn't seem like it from the outside, that was a dangerous question coming from Savannah. She was one of the more popular members of their friend group, with a propensity to participate in the school rumor mill, meaning she had either heard something from someone else, or she was hoping for something to add to the rather dull first-day talk.

The *last* thing Alyx needed was to be the subject of Kimball's juicy gossip. She was already being talked about in half of London's tabloids, albeit under the wrong name. She was enjoying the quiet of Tracy, and if one of her classmates decided to cash out on her after connecting the rumors to the tabloids, she could kiss any chance of a future in espionage goodbye.

Alyx shrugged. "You know, same old same old." She lied. "Actually, Kate has a twin, so that was new."

"Is Alyx telling you about her new boyfriend?" A boy asked as he slid into the booth, squeezing Savannah and Alyx into the wall. Unlike the rest of his friends sitting in the booth, Kaden was wearing his class of 2012 shirt, with khaki shorts, and knee-high orange and blue socks. He, like Savannah, was quite popular, and heard most of the school's rumors, as was to be expected from someone in leadership.

"Boyfriend?" Alyx asked skeptically.

Both Savannah and Kaden nodded. "*The Daily Star* had quite an interesting article about Prince James new girlfriend, Alex Feilds." Kaden told her.

"I read about it in the *Enquirer.*" Savannah added. "I recognized you in the pictures. Nice dress, by the way."

Alyx knew she had made quite an entrance at Feilds' Ball. That had been the goal. She needed eyes on her for their plan to confuse Radford to work. And it almost had. What she hadn't accounted for was that she would draw the attention of the tabloids. If she was being honest, she didn't know anyone from the press attended. She knew Feilds' Ball for what it was: a celebration for the end of the Intelligence Conference. But Feilds' Ball? That was one of London's hottest events, attended by almost everyone with a title, so the world's intelligence officers could hide in the crowds.

Four sets of eyes settled on Alyx, waiting to hear what she had to say about the prince. But she had nothing to say.

"If I had known that all it took to get you to move on from your ridiculous crush on Peter Carlyle was a prince, I would have tried that two years ago." Carlie complained.

Alyx looked at her uncharacteristically quiet friends. "I'm not dating Prince James." She finally said.

With her denial, their booth erupted into a cacophony of arguments, the loudest of which being *prove it*.

She could prove it. She could tell them exactly what she had been doing that night, and by extension, what she had done the rest of the summer. The question was what rumor would she rather have circulating school: she was dating a prince, or she had saved her cousin.

Alyx glanced over at the table of football players in the center of the cafeteria, surrounded by cheerleaders, members of the dance team, and leadership kids.

"Exactly how much of the school has heard the rumor?" She asked distracted.

Carlie and Savannah shared a knowing look, recognizing the look on Alyx' face. Savannah reached across Alyx towards Kaden. "Pay up." She demanded.

Kaden sighed, pulling a 5 dollar bill out of his pocket. "How did you know?" He complained.

Savannah shrugged, handing the 5 back to Kaden. "But if you could go get me some pizza, that would be great."

Kaden rolled his eyes, but got up and walked toward the lunch counter.

Alyx just glared at Savannah. "You never answered my question. Who. Has heard. The rumor?"

"No one. Kaden and I like to borrow Emily's British tabloids from time to time, so we saw the pictures. I told Kaden you were still hung up on Peter."

It was Alyx' turn to roll her eyes. Her aunt, Emily Hall, was a bit obsessed with reading the British tabloids, a habit she'd picked up when they were her only source of information on Ally, Alyx' mom's twin sister. Alyx should have know that introducing Kaden and Savannah to her Aunt would be a bad idea, but these were the first friends she had gotten close enough to that they felt like family, so she did. Now she was paying for it.

"So…" Carlie dragged out the word. Alyx could guess what was coming next, and Carlie's audible delay in asking it was filling Alyx with more dread than was fair, or necessary. "Are you going to explain why you were dancing with a prince, but you aren't dating him?"

"I dance with James every year." Alyx answered. "This year, someone simply caught it on camera."

Savannah shrieked. Carlie rolled her eyes. Kaden looked back and forth as he approached with Savannah's pizza.

"Alyx just calls him James." Carlie told Kaden.

"And she dances with him every year." Savannah added, her mouth full of the pizza she had grabbed off the plate before Kaden had a chance to sit down.

Kaden looked at Savannah suspiciously. "But she's not dating him. She still likes the football player she refuses to talk to, like a crazy person."

Kaden's question was answered by a chorus of nods.

"Why?" Kaden asked.

"We're friends, but we both like someone else." Alyx admitted.

"And he told you? Do you know who?" Savannah asked, too excited to wait until she was done chewing to ask her questions.

Alyx just drew her thumb and pointer across her lips in a zipping motion.

Thane raised an eyebrow interrupting before Kaden and Savannah started their loud pleas for Alyx to tell them. "I believe she is trying to distract us from the more important question." Thane observed. "If you dance with *James* every year, why is this year the first year the tabloids published the photo?"

Alyx shrugged. "Maybe they liked my dress." She suggested. "Oh, by the way, I may not be able to eat lunch with you guys this year. I'm supposed to study French with Mr. Martin durning lunch. I'll find out today after school."

Carlie narrowed her eyes at Alyx. "Thane's right," Carlie said, "You're trying to distract us."

Alyx stared at her friend, neither of them breaking eye contact. Carlie was the one who finally broke, which was to be expected. She turned to Savannah. "What did Alyx' nice dress look like?"

"It was this gorgeous rose pink ball gown, paired with a cream pashmina. She had her hair in this elegant updo—I *almost* didn't recognize her." Savannah gushed.

"It was a sleeveless dress designed by Victoria Beckham." Kaden added. "How did you get her to design a dress? Since she launched her line, she's been a hot commodity."

"I used my uncle's name." Alyx said, shoving food in her mouth. She knew where Thane and Carlie were going with their line of questioning, and she wanted every excuse she could find for not answering them.

"If it was a custom dress, why was it sleeveless?" Carlie asked.

Alyx hated how perceptive her friends could be. She should have known Carlie would be the one to think the sleeveless dress was suspicious. While Thane had introduced her to Savannah and Kaden at school, she had met Carlie at church. Since she went to church with Thane and Carlie, they would be the ones to know her standards of modesty. If she didn't translate for her uncle, who was the master of evasion and obfuscation, she might be concerned about her friends breaking her.

"I was the distraction." Alyx said.

"Distraction from what?" Thane asked.

Alyx glanced at her watch, doing math to figure out how long they had left at lunch. Fortunately, it wasn't long.

"Well, you know, there was Kate, and Lynn. And Lynn is Kate's twin, but she just showed up and it was her introduction to the public, and they can be a bit intense. Plus there was Lyshiria, and—" She cut off as the bell rang. "Gotta get to class." She snapped the lid onto her container of food, shoving it into her backpack. "Finish this later?" She asked with a smile, tossing her backpack back over her shoulder as she started walking away. As her head turned back toward the door, she caught sight of Peter Carlyle in his bright orange polo shirt, as he stood up from the table he'd shared with his friends. Peter was laughing at something one of his teammates had said, but he turned and seemed to glance at the table Alyx had been sitting at. She could have sworn a frown crossed his face, but it was small, and disappeared.

Alyx turned away before he noticed her staring. Sometimes she wished she wasn't so invisible to certain people.

14:10 PDT
Tracy, California
John C. Kimball High School

Peter Carlyle was grateful that Alyx McLean was as invisible as she was. Despite being in classes with half of the spies in Tracy looking for her, Peter had made it through the day without any positive reports of seeing the girl in the photo. The longer it took the other members to realize that the girl they were looking for had been right in front of them, the longer he had to figure out how to use the files Lynn had sent him. Unfortunately, he doubted her invisibility would last. After all, he had noticed her for the first time when he was in the same Algebra II class sophomore year, and hadn't been able to stop noticing her since. It wouldn't take long for her intelligence to catch the attention of one of the seniors who were part of the Promising Generation, especially since she was a junior taking the classes a year early.

He knew the best way to help her was to do everything he could to behave as normal as possible. That meant he needed to prepare for the AP French test just like Wraith wanted him to.

With his football gear on for practice, and his duffle over his shoulder, he walked into Mr. Martin's room, causing the teacher to look up from his computer. "Bonjour monsieur Martin." Peter greeted.

"Bonjour Pierre," Mr. Martin replied, using the French version of Peter that he had chosen to go by the first year he'd taken French from the teacher. He reached up to the control panel just next to him on the wall, with buttons for the projector and speakers in the room, using the nob to turn down the volume of the French music he was playing. "Comment ça va?"

"Ça va bien." Peter replied. The classroom had the desks arranged the same way all of the language classrooms had them. The desks were in rows of four facing the center aisle, which allowed the teacher to walk up and down the aisle in front of the students as he taught. At the back by the door, Mr. Martin had a bookshelf with the classroom set of textbooks he kept available for students to use during class. At the front, the whiteboard spanned nearly from wall to wall, stopping just over Mr. Martin's desk in the opposite corner from the door. Peter made his way through the center aisle to the row of desks closest to Mr. Martin's desk, slipping into the third desk back so he was sitting right next to Mr. Martin.

"Bien." Martin replied. "You are not the only one who contacted me about preparing for the AP French test. The other student is also fluent, so I can imagine no reason why the two of you can't study together and do very well on the test."

Peter nodded. "That sounds great to me. The only problem with that is I have football practice after school."

"I believe she has tennis. She should be on her way, so the two of you can work something out."

Alyx shrugged her bag of tennis rackets up onto her shoulder as she opened the door to the French classroom. Mr. Martin looked at the door with a smile. "Ah, elle est ici." He told the student sitting next to him. When Peter turned to look at the student he would be studying with for the next year, Alyx had a hard time forcing herself to keep moving. "Peter, meet Alyx."

Peter couldn't help but smile as he watched Alyx walk toward him, wearing her workout top and tennis scort. The only thing that gave her away as a tennis player instead of a cheerleader was the odd shaped padded bag that held her rackets. In her hand, she carried a bike bottle which at the right angle, Peter could tell was full of water.

Alyx stopped at the end of the row of desks Peter was sitting in, giving an awkward wave in response to Mr. Martin's introduction.

"Both of you have expressed interest in taking the AP French test in May. You are both fluent enough, I don't think there is much more for me to teach you. What you most need is preparation for the test, such as practicing the written, verbal, and listening sections. That can best be accomplished by having you two study and practice together. I can give you assignments to keep you on track, and I'll meet with you once a month, maybe more often depending on how much help you need. How does that sound?"

Alyx tried to control a blush that threatened to color her cheeks. She had this curse when it came to talking to the boys she liked—it never went well—so she chose not to, unless it was completely necessary. She had been in Peter's Algebra II class for an entire year—all 180 school days—and she had said maybe 10 words to him over the course of that school year. Now she *had* to talk to him, in French, if she was going to get into Oxford.

"That sounds good to me," Peter answered. "We probably need to figure out when we can meet. I get done with football about 5:30pm, so I'm free anytime after 6:30."

Alyx shrugged trying to look and sound nonchalant. "I could do 6:30. Your house?"

"I mean my parents are never home…" Peter said.

"Probably not the best idea." Alyx admitted, mortified she'd just invited herself over to his house. The curse continued.

"What about the same time at your house?" Peter asked.

"My mom is in the trauma center until 7:00 tonight, so as long as my dad doesn't get called on a case, he won't be home until 7:00 at the earliest. I'll have to check to make sure." Alyx explained.

"Of course." Peter nodded his head saying he understood. "Mr. Martin, can I use a sticky note?" Mr. Martin handed him one. Peter took it and stuck it on the desk he was sitting at, pulled out a pen, and scribbled something on it. He peeled it off the desk as he picked up his duffle from under the desk and stood to leave. He handed the note to Alyx as he walked by. "Text me when you get an answer."

Alyx stared at the number in her hand, realizing as the door banged close that she hadn't said goodbye. How was she supposed to study anything with him if she was already distracted?

The problem wasn't him. It wasn't his well-trimmed blonde hair, or his piercing blue eyes. No, the problem was that she had imagined Peter give her his phone number on occasions. It was a fantasy she sometimes indulged when the boredom of life got to her, but she had never let herself hope it might really happen.

Now she just had to pray that she was good enough to get into Oxford.

"Thank you Mr. Martin." Alyx said as she turned to leave. "I better get to practice."

Mr. Martin nodded. "Let me know if there is anything else I can do to help."

"I will." Alyx told him, then left the door.

Oxford. Alyx thought as she walked to practice. *Oxford is the goal. And I can't let a cute football player distract me from that.*